I0823321

A Beast Slinks Towards Beijing

A Beast Slinks Towards Beijing

A Novel

ALICE EVELYN YANG

wm

WILLIAM MORROW

An Imprint of HarperCollins*Publishers*

 For information, address HarperCollins Publishers, 195 Broadway, New York, NY 10007. In Europe, HarperCollins Publishers, Macken House, 39/40 Mayor Street Upper, Dublin 1, D01 C9W8, Ireland.

HarperCollins books may be purchased for educational, business, or sales promotional use. For information, please email the Special Markets Department at SPsales@harpercollins.com.

hc.com

FIRST EDITION

Designed by Michele Cameron

Interior art: @Varts/Shutterstock

Library of Congress Cataloging-in-Publication Data

Names: Yang, Alice Evelyn author
Title: A beast slinks towards Beijing : a novel / Alice Evelyn Yang.
Description: First edition. | New York : William Morrow, an imprint of HarperCollins Publishers, 2026.
Identifiers: LCCN 2025003969 (print) | LCCN 2025003970 (ebook) | ISBN 9780063419292 hardcover | ISBN 9780063419308 trade paperback | ISBN 9780063419315 ebook
Subjects: LCGFT: Historical fiction | Novels
Classification: LCC PS3625.A6773 B43 (print) | LCC PS3625.A6773 (ebook) | DDC 813/.6—dc23/eng/20250401
LC record available at https://lccn.loc.gov/2025003969
LC ebook record available at https://lccn.loc.gov/202

ISBN 978-0-06-341929-2

Printed in the United States of America

25 26 27 28 29 LBC 5 4 3 2 1

To Baba and Mama,
All the words I have are for you.

A Beast Slinks Towards Beijing

PART I

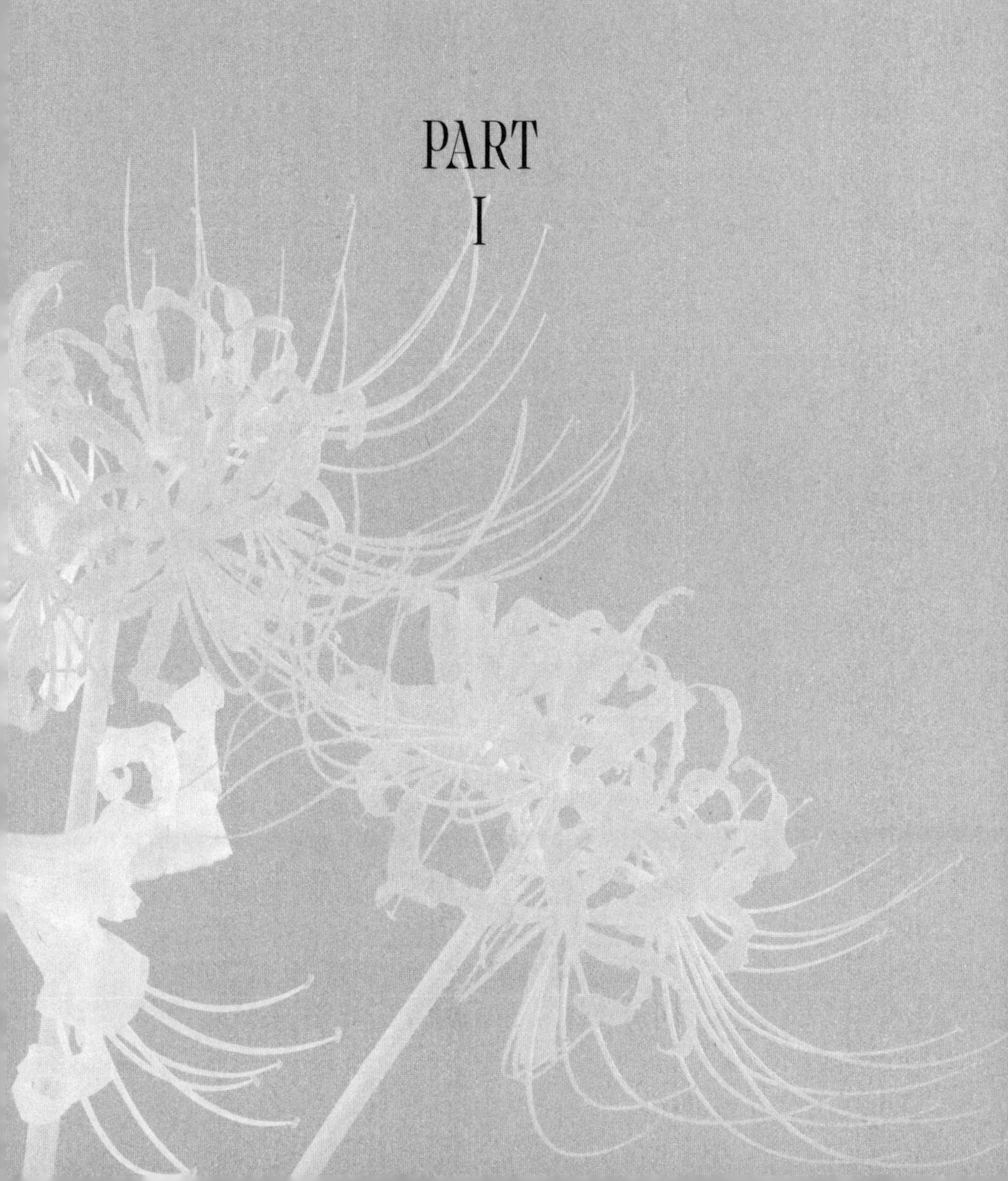

One

Qianze
2017
Manhattan, New York

IN AUGUST, QIANZE'S CHILDHOOD NIGHTMARE returned with a vengeance.

In the dream, Qianze was chasing a hare through a forest, but the forest was foreign to her. Absent were the streamerlike Spanish mosses of Virginia, the sweet bay magnolias, the dogwoods and crepe myrtle trees she'd grown up with. This landscape was unkempt and wild, in the browning of an Indian summer.

Qianze was so sure-footed, so light on her soles, that she felt like she was floating. Branches and burrs splintered underfoot, but she barely registered the pain with how fast her legs moved. She was always knocked back by the tangibility of the dream: the slap of dry wind against her cheeks, the woody smell of damp boughs, the searing brightness of the afternoon coaxing out a strange saturation.

It did not feel like a fair chase. She could not explain it, but she felt like she was playing a rigged game where the hare always wins. She knew intrinsically that the hare was something unearthly. It went through the motions of being hunted, but its eyes flitted back to her with a bored expression. Not like a real hare, but a trickster god in animal skin.

The hare was albino: bone-white fur, red eyes. Not dark enough to resemble blood, but bright and surreal: poppy red, red-vinegar red. The hare paused, and she skidded to a stop.

Closer now, she could see its pupils were a pale pink, and they surveyed her, dilating and contracting. The two squared off a few feet from each other, Qianze crouched low to the ground, preparing to pounce and snap the tiny bones of its neck. Her tongue sang the taste of rabbit stew. Then, the hare rose on its back legs and underwent a strange transformation, growing taller and larger until their eyes were level. A small crown of shuddering, staglike horns emerged from the animal's skull. The jackalope seemed smug. It gave her a rictus grin.

Inside its mouth were two rows of rotten teeth—yellow, blackened, serrated, missing. And before she had time to react, it lowered its head and charged. She instinctively put out her right palm to stop it and felt the stunning pain of an antler slicing through the thick flesh—

She jolted. It was the visceral feeling of horn breaking through skin that always woke her. She felt cold sweat soaking her night clothes. She sat at the edge of her bed and let her breathing even out. The air conditioning had shuddered off at some point in the night, and the inside of the apartment was thick with mid-August heat. Qianze absently rubbed circles on her fleshy palm where the false wound radiated pain like there was still deer velvet inside, infecting her from within.

In a state of half sleep, she peeled her damp clothes off, changed into a new pair of pajamas, and blearily made her way to the living room. Her father's loud snoring flooded the space with noise. The sound was as foreign to her as her father, who had walked back into her life just as abruptly as he had walked out of it eleven years prior. She pounded the air-conditioning unit once, twice—Ba's breathing stuttering in tune with her left fist—until it reluctantly gasped to life. She went back to bed, sliding her right hand beneath the cool underbelly of her pillow to soothe the phantom pain.

IT HAD BEEN A WEEK since Qianze had dragged Ba from the porch of her childhood home to her apartment in New York—a week and two days since she received the call summoning her back to Virginia.

It had been a Saturday. August 5. Qianze spent it removing her broken AC unit and retrieving a new one that she'd bought from an online marketplace. After lugging the heavy thing ten blocks, she discovered it was only semifunctional and seemed to turn on and off with no rhyme or reason. She was filled with an overwhelming urge to push it out the window onto a passerby so that someone else's day could also be ruined by it—the intrusive image of their insides and the AC parts painting the sidewalk in red and silver viscera looping in her mind. Qianze got the call close to midnight. She was in the bath, which she'd filled with cool water and melting ice, and was pointing a handheld fan at her face. The phone screen flashed "Myrtle Avenue Renters." She considered letting it go to voicemail. She would later regret that she had not.

The Myrtle Avenue renters were four sophomore sorority girls living in Qianze's childhood home back in Virginia. Myrtle Avenue lay on the border between a nice suburban neighborhood and a college campus. Over the years, it had become the site of off-campus housing and then a makeshift fraternity row, known for its parties. Renting the property annually had been easier than selling it.

"There's a man hanging around the porch," one of the girls said. No greetings or niceties. Kendra, Qianze thought. Or was it Sandra? She could never tell. They all sounded the same.

"Hi, Kendra, how are you doing?" Qianze asked pointedly. She could hear the background din of a party.

"Sandra," the caller corrected. "Did you hear what I said? There's a man hanging around the porch."

Qianze sighed. Somehow, she'd become the pseudo-landlord for the Myrtle property. Most of the college renters were too impatient to decipher Ma's accented English. Never mind that Qianze was several states away, the tenants still treated her as their catch-all handyman.

"Okay. And you're calling me and not the police why?" Qianze asked, though she suspected the ongoing party had something to do with it.

"He says he knows the past residents."

This piqued Qianze's interest, and she sat up, sending cold water splashing over the sides of the tub and onto the tiled floor. "Well, what does he look like?"

A pause and then rustling of plastic blinds. "Tall, Asian, old. Maybe sixty?"

"Glasses?"

"Yeah."

"Fuck." Qianze sucked in a breath. Then: "Did he give you a name?"

"Something I can't pronounce." Sandra paused. "I think he's a little off in the head. But he looks like you."

Qianze tried to decipher whether this was the casual racism underlying most of her interactions in southern Virginia or if the man on the porch was the resurrected ghost of her Ba, who had left them eleven years and one month ago almost to the day.

"His name, was it Weihong?"

"Mmm, something like that."

"Can you send a picture?"

An exasperated sigh from the sorority girl, as if Qianze had just asked her to perform a Herculean task. "One sec." There was a pause, and Qianze felt her phone vibrate. "There, just sent."

Qianze pulled the phone away from her ear to see the incoming picture. It was taken through the window, and the quality was grainy, lit only by the single porch bulb. But sitting there on a patio chair was a man who was unmistakably Ba. His eyes cut through the lens, the screens, the near-four-hundred miles that separated them until she could envision herself in Sandra's place, standing in the entrance room of the house, peering out the dirty windows to find him there as she had naïvely hoped she would in the years since he had disappeared. Suddenly, she was fourteen again and filled with longing.

Over the past decade, she'd worn through the image of her father so many times that the memory of his face had become corrupted. She played a cruel game with herself, imagining what he looked like each year since he had left. Was his hair now streaked with silver? Had he grown out the stubble that had once prickled the top of her head whenever he embraced her?

He looked nothing like how she imagined. In place of the tall, thin frame from her memories was a bulging beer belly. His face had gotten ruddy, remnants of rosacea on his cheeks visible even in the darkness. The whites of his eyes looked yellow and jaundiced.

"Hello? Are you still there?" Sandra asked, breaking Qianze out of her reverie.

"I'm here."

"He says he's going to come back every day until he talks to the past residents. Can you get rid of him?"

"Do you know where he's staying?"

"I didn't ask. Are you going to come fix it? He's creeping everyone out."

THE NEXT AVAILABLE FLIGHT WAS the following day on Sunday, August 6, and Qianze had to work the entire way there. The summer had been a busy season, and her team was on a brutal schedule as they neared the end of an investment-fund audit. Qianze spent every hour in the airport and on the plane with her laptop on her knees.

When she touched down in Virginia, she felt the unbearable, swamplike heat, as familiar to her as a scar. Qianze's Uber deposited her unceremoniously at the bottom of the driveway of the Myrtle house. The azalea bushes were in full bloom for the summer, their color a Lunar New Year red. There was a shaded figure sitting on the porch and a blond head in the window behind him, peering out at Qianze through the curtains. Sandra's annoyed expression seemed to say, *Finally*. The curtains snapped shut.

There was no fence around the wide lawn. Instead, it sloped upward in an expanse of green, littered with beer bottles and red Solo cups: a garden of debauchery. She picked her way through it to the porch.

"Ba?" she asked, and he stirred, looking at her inquisitively. There was a blankness in his face. Up close, she saw that his skin had grown transparent, and she could map the dark veins swimming below the surface of age-spotted cheeks. The tail of the clear wire of a hearing aid dangled from his right ear.

"Hái'ér?" *Child?*

Her stomach bottomed out and rationale fled her head. All she wanted to do was embrace him, to have his presence enfold her like it had so many years ago. She was suddenly aware that all this time there had been a wound in her, growing and goring, and that one phrase pulled at the edges of it, trying to stitch them together. She wanted to sob, and she wanted to shout, and she wanted to hurl plates and fists and mean words, but all she did was purse her lips.

"Yes," she said at last, "it's me. You need to come with me, Ba. You can't stay here."

He looked at her, confused. "Oh. Okay."

He followed her in the docile manner of a hurt stray. They went back to New York on a bus so hot, the interior seemed to melt and wilt like a Dalí painting. At least it had Wi-Fi, so Qianze's manager could message her multiple times on Teams to follow up on her weekend work. This was a welcome distraction from the close, heavy-breathed presence of the man beside her, who was essentially a stranger.

In her mind, Ba's new, bloated skin thawed and came off in waxy drips under the bus's heat, revealing the father she knew and resented.

QIANZE HADN'T HAD A ROOMMATE since her first apartment in the city, and she remembered why. The discomfort of living with another person, with *Ba*—the awkward silences, the dances around the bathroom threshold, the negotiation for the communal space—was multiplied tenfold by their history.

Qianze had always liked making a room her own. In childhood games of play-pretend, she'd settle into nooks and decorate with a few select belongings, turning small spaces into refuges. Her little homes included a blanket fort behind the couch; a box for their washer she'd rescued from its fate on trash day; and the shade under a particularly tall branch of the magnolia tree at the end of Myrtle Avenue. It was a quaint game, one for an only child who hadn't known true smallness.

Her apartment in New York was small, but she reveled in it being hers and hers alone. There was a narrow, fluorescent-lit entry hallway that led into a kitchenette and living room. The bedroom was small and fit only a set of drawers and a full bed frame. There were many things that bothered her about the apartment—the walk up four floors, the lack of in-unit air conditioning, the occasional mouse—but the smallness was not one of them. Not until Ba arrived.

He'd brought a duffel bag, which had clinked and clanged all four flights up. It contained two handles of liquor and three packs of cigarettes among some clothes and a handful of other possessions.

After she made up the couch with spare sheets, she watched, dumbfounded, as Ba sat down, unzipped his bag, and took a swig from a bottle. Then he lit a cigarette. The father she knew did not drink more than a glass of wine at holidays. He definitely did not smoke. For a moment, she worried she'd brought home an impostor, some unrelated man prowling around her old home.

She cleared her throat. He peered at her through the smoke that had gathered in front of him.

"The bathroom is there." She pointed at the door. "There are towels and soap and all that. Do you want something to eat?"

"No," he said with a cough. He adjusted his hearing aid.

"Okay." She nodded. "I'm going to be in there if you need anything." She retreated into her bedroom.

Ba's new chain-smoking habit, combined with the nonfunctional air conditioning, created a choking fog that seeped in under her door. Once it was late and she heard her father snoring, Qianze darted through the darkened living room like a cockroach to use the bathroom. For the rest of the night, she drifted in and out of sweat-soaked sleep. Sensing her regression, the jackalope, the subject of her childhood night terrors, nuzzled itself once more against her subconscious, flitting in and out of her dreams.

The events surrounding Ba's return had happened faster than Qianze's brain could process them, creating a time paradox where she existed in both the past and the present. She was simultaneously Qianze Before Ba and Qianze After Ba.

The Monday morning after his arrival she awoke as Qianze Before Ba, forgetting that he'd returned. The only sign that something was amiss was the return of her nightmare, which left her irritable and on edge. Feeling out of sorts, she rolled out of bed to begin her morning: washing her face, brushing her teeth, getting dressed. Only, once she left the sanctuary of her bedroom, she found Ba hunched over the toilet, spewing the sick of yesterday's liquor. She got dressed while waiting for him to vacate the bathroom and ended up dribbling toothpaste on her work clothes. For the rest of the day she could smell the faint odor of her father's vomit perfuming her clothes.

In the office, she could return to being Qianze Before Ba. Better, she could be Kenzie—her Americanized name—another accountant cog. Just one of the many University of Virginia graduates at a Big Four consulting firm. She let the drudgery of emails and financial statements consume her, blocking out any thought of Ba's return. If she dwelled on that, she would lose herself in all the questions and emotions it dredged up. Her manager let her off early at eight in the evening. He reminded her that this was a "special allowance" and that she'd have to "sort out her personal life by the end of the work week or risk consequences."

When Qianze got back to the apartment, she felt as if she had stumbled upon a pocket dimension—a rip in time and space where she became Qianze After Ba again. He'd settled in comfortably, if the full ashtray and the stink of alcohol were any indication.

"You work late," he commented as she closed the door behind her. "It's dark out."

"This is nothing."

"Oh." He frowned and turned back to the TV. It was playing a rerun of some show from the '90s. The laugh track blared through the living room.

"Can you turn that off?" Qianze asked. She rubbed her temples. She felt the beginnings of a heat headache settling in, and the sitcom laughter rang in pulsing throbs.

"Okay," he said. A tense silence followed, with Qianze still standing near the entrance.

She walked in and laid out two takeout containers on the table, along with a sheath of printouts on care facilities for the elderly. "I have some food. And I did some research at work."

Ba stood up slowly, his joints creaking. He sat down in a dining chair, opened the lid, and sniffed warily at the dinner.

Qianze quickly discovered that, like her AC, Ba sometimes shut off without warning. He seemed to pass in and out of lucidity on a whim; one moment he was sitting at the table, listening thoughtfully as Qianze presented a list of possible care facilities and treatment plans in New York.

"If you're interested in any of them," she said, "I can do some more research when work slows down."

The next moment his eyes grew gelatinous—taxidermic—the pupils devouring the whole of his irises until they were a blank black. At first, Qianze thought this was a diversion tactic to avoid telling her about the state of his health insurance and finances.

"What month is it?" he asked.

"It's August," Qianze said, humoring him.

"August," he repeated, "the eighth month. The lucky month."

Qianze couldn't help herself. She let out a snort. August had never been kind to her. The noise startled Ba, who jumped in his seat and turned to look at her, his eyes wide. He squinted at her, and she squirmed under his evaluating gaze.

"What?" she asked, her tone defensive.

"How old are you now?"

She blinked. It shouldn't have hurt as much as it did. "I'm twenty-five."

"Twenty-five," he repeated, chewing the words slowly.

Suddenly, he jolted and leaned forward. His hands grabbed at her arms. She flinched. They had not touched in the past two days, besides an occasional rustle next to each other on the bus. His palms were clammy and tight, and she could see the skin of her biceps turning white under his grasp.

"I went back to Virginia to tell you something. Before it gets lost," he said. His eyes were still crazed, but there was a sober urgency present that hadn't been there before.

She jutted her chin out, refusing to let it quiver. Was this the long-awaited apology? Would hearing it heal her, as she always imagined it would?

"I know why I'm here now. Fate brought me here," he said.

Qianze deflated. More nonsense. "No, Ba. The Tiger Travel Bus brought you here."

"No. What? Tiger Travel?" he asked. "No, no." Ba shook his head violently, his eyes screwing closed behind his glasses. "No," he repeated, sounding less certain. "It *was* fate. It was the prophecy. I came back to tell you the prophecy."

"What prophecy?"

Ba blinked, and he was gone again. His eyes empty.

"What?" he asked. He looked at his hands encircling her biceps. "Oh, sorry." He let go.

She rubbed her hands over her arms, the white marks of his fingers fading to pink.

"You were talking about a prophecy?"

"What did you say? Prophecy?" he echoed dumbly. "I was?"

Frustration built in her throat, tasting of bile. "You said that was why you came back to the Myrtle house."

"The Myrtle house," he repeated. He looked thoughtful. "With the azaleas?"

"Yes, Ba." An unexpected waver in her voice. "With the azaleas."

It was so easy for him to uproot her. One question, and he had reincarnated the seething, grieving girl, the one she thought she'd buried but now discovered was simply rotting within her like gangrene.

They had planted the azalea bushes together. His large, callused palms cradled her child ones as they piled soil over roots.

Two

Qianze
2017: Two Days Since Reunion
Manhattan, New York

LIFE IN THIS TIMELINE TOOK on an unreal quality, like a lucid dream. On Tuesday, August 8, Qianze's express online order arrived: a discreet nanny cam, nestled in the eyes of a teddy bear that she placed on her living-room shelf. On the battered iPhone Ba used, Qianze set his Location Services to be shared with her number. The passcode—7792—was her birthday.

While at the office, Qianze tracked Ba's movements, switching between the camera and Find My Friends. When she left the apartment, he took his morning nap. Afterward, he woke and made his way downstairs with her spare set of keys, where he bought a pack of cigarettes and some more liquor. Along with these, he hauled back cheap plastic boxes of dumplings—the kind that went for less than $5 at the Chinese-run holes-in-the-wall. He did not venture farther than a two-block radius. For the rest of the day, he indulged in his purchases, sometimes with the TV droning on in the background, and scribbled down notes on the back of receipts in jagged Chinese that Qianze could not read. Drunk, he then fell asleep until she returned from work.

Qianze came back to the apartment for a stilted dinner with Ba, who responded to her attempts at conversation with monosyllabic answers.

Did you eat? Yes.

Did you look at the papers I gave you? No. Soon.

Was it too hot in the apartment today? A grunt of dissent.

Is there anything I can pick up for you from the drugstore? No.

This continued until Ba lost his thread of sanity and began to spout Chinese. She could make out some odd words—guǐ, yāoguài, wūshī—which were only familiar to her because they came from the bedtime stories her parents had read to her as a child: "Nezha Conquering the Sea," "Journey to the West," "The Legend of the White Snake." Interspersed in this frenzied slurry were pleas in English for her to "take warning of the prophecy."

Yes, she promised, she would, and this placated him for the time being, though he still had not told her what this prophecy foretold.

When he was somewhat lucid, he told her a story. She listened. She was waiting to hear one particular story: his version of that July night eleven years ago when he left. A night that she'd replayed so often in her own mind—its soundtrack haunting her: the creak and slam of their screen door, a long silence, and then the squeak of his bicycle wheels tonguing the tar of the street, never to return.

Instead, he fed her scraps from his childhood.

THAT NIGHT, WILDFIRES FROM THE Midwest dragged their smog into the city. Outside of the apartment windows, there was little visibility beyond a glimpse of the setting red sun, which bathed the room in an amber light. Ba, who cracked open a window to take long drags of a cigarette, hacked phlegm.

"You know, they issued an air-quality alert. You should really close the window," Qianze said.

He waved her off. "Grew up near iron and steel works. Lungs are used to it."

She didn't even know what province he was from. Only that he, like her mother, was from northeastern China. Dōng běi.

"Your lungs are used to disease?"

His response was a wracking cough that might have been a laugh. "One time, air pollution was so bad in Ānshān, eleven people died in one night."

Ānshān. She filed the name away for later.

He took another long drag, looking out at the orange-soaked streets. The cigarette end crackled as it ashed. "My Ma used to tell me about people in the countryside who worshipped fire," he said. "They said it was cleansing. That something was only pure after it was burned. That wildfires start on their own to rid monsters from the area."

Qianze looked at him oddly.

He shrugged. "Just old wives' tales from the cold provinces."

"You never talked about her. Your mother."

"Didn't I?" He rubbed the stubble of his chin. Finally, he ground the cigarette out and closed the window soundly.

"No," Qianze said, "you didn't."

He seemed thoughtful, as if he were evaluating the truth of her words. "She was a storyteller."

"That's it?"

"What else is there to say?"

"More than one sentence."

He took off his glasses and squinted, wiping the lenses with the hem of his shirt. "It's hard sometimes. To remember her."

Try, she wanted to plead. *I don't even know her name.*

Online, Qianze had tried to diagnose her father, attempting to determine if what he had was Alzheimer's, some other variant of dementia, or some elusive and rare third option. Could it be the alcohol—the smell of which wafted into her face whenever he spoke—eating his memory? The online quizzes were little help in narrowing down an answer. Do you get lost in places that are familiar to you, like your neighborhood or grocery store? Do these difficulties reflect changes from how you were functioning a few years ago? Do you have trouble managing your personal finances? She stared at these questions until her eyes grew dry. She did not know where his money came from, or if he had even held a job during his absence. Perhaps he had returned to sponge off of her. She did not know if his mind had become addled in recent years or if it had started eleven years ago. She did not know where his former neighborhood had been, what his local grocery store was. He could have been anywhere, nowhere—spit out of some portal onto the yard of the Myrtle house, no time having passed for him at all.

They said that when you have dementia, you go backward. "They" were a chorus of WebMD doctors, usernames on Alzheimer's forums, and Quora physicians. A poor substitute for a live doctor, but "They" would have to do for now. Later, Qianze thought, she could look at the out-of-pocket costs of genetic testing and diagnosis. If only so she herself could have peace of mind.

They explained that recent memories got subsumed by the dementia or never formed at all. Instead, the patient returned to the crystallized memories of the past. They called this phenomenon time-shifting. Think of it, They said, as time traveling. A return to childhood or adolescence. It's important, They stressed, to allow the patient to live inside their delusions.

Ba ebbed back into his past, and Qianze watched. The Myrtle house's azaleas, the Tiger Travel bus, the wildfires, the Chinatown apartment, even the estrangement—these all receded, replaced by a deluge of memories that crashed into their lives like whitecapped swells. Ba's eyes turned filmy—jellied like the belly-up fish in the seafood stalls on her street—caught in the current of another reality.

The first story he told was about famine.

The winters up in dōng běi, he began, were seasons of sacrifice.

"You could not fill a child's belly, let alone an adult's. In the fall, we'd dig dirt cellars in our yards to store vegetables. No modern refrigerators, no, we'd have to shovel out three meters of frozen dirt for our cabbages, our radishes, our winter melons—any vegetables we could trade for my family's sorghum harvest."

Fruits were rare jewels. And like jade charms and bracelets, they only passed between the hands of the wealthy. Sweet things were foreign to his family. Their tongues were made for dirt and roots and starvation. But one winter there was an apple.

"A gift," Ba explained, "from a well-off woman. The town physician's wife. But Mama snatched it up before I could take a bite."

Mama wanted to save the apple for his newborn brother. His brother hadn't started teething yet, wouldn't for a few months, and by then, it would be the end of the season. How was she supposed to preserve the precious fruit until then?

"She pickled it," Ba said, answering his own question. In a jar with a solution of brine and sour-smelling mǐ cù. Then she buried it deep in the dirt cellar, where it waited to be exhumed in the spring. But Ba's brother's teeth came in early at the end of the first lunar month. So Mama excavated it in the winter, grinding her fingers down to the bone to dislodge the permafrost.

During fermentation, the apple had plumped up and turned redder. It was soft and bloated with wetness; Mama's fingertips left dents in its skin when she picked it up. She prepared it by crushing it under a cleaver, and that was the first solid food his brother ate. In turn, the apple's bitter milk made his brother bitter and dangerous: always toeing the line with the Japanese soldiers occupying the region. Later, arsons and boyish raids cropped up that could never be traced to a perpetrator, but Ba knew.

"Sometimes," Ba said with a frown, "I think the apple never left him."

Instead—Ba proposed—it sat in his brother's stomach. Weaned

on vinegar, it liked feeding off the miseries of their lives: poverty, famine, colonization.

WAS THIS DEMENTIA? OR HAD Ba waded into the deeper, choppier waters of psychosis? Qianze chided herself for not considering this.

She could not tell what was true. Whenever Ba could not find a word in English, he switched to Mandarin, so that his sentences were a murky mixture of English and Chinese, and Qianze did not always trust herself to translate correctly. Qianze and her mother used to watch Chinese period dramas together when she was a girl. This was like that. She could hold on to the basic plot, but the nuance, metaphors, and details went over her head.

All her life she had never heard Ba or Ma speak about their time in China, except to say that it was better left alone. Ancient history, they said. Sometimes it seemed as if her parents had sprouted up in America with no past: saplings uprooted and replanted in immigrant soil—the only betrayal of their foreignness the flat curves of their faces, their accents, the food they made. To her knowledge, no photographs or evidence of either set of grandparents existed, if they had been brought across the Pacific at all.

How could she separate fact from fiction? Qianze laid out what she knew: Ba was in his sixties. Qianze remembered his birthday—March 28—but not the exact year. She knew that her parents had been older than her friends' by a decade. This placed Ba's birth and childhood in the 1950s. A quick Google search revealed that the '50s had been the era of Mao's Great Famine, but several years after the Japanese occupation. Neither of which she had known about until that moment. Unless Ba had lied about his age and was now in his mid-to-late seventies, he had not been alive when the Japanese colonized northern China.

Upon further research, another contradiction troubled her, wriggling in her mind like a leech. The root cellars. The underground pantries were a real phenomenon, but they belonged to rural landscapes and villages, not the industrial city of Ānshān that Ba had claimed he was from just that night. Most people who lived in Ānshān lived in small rooms in former compounds with a communal courtyard. City folk would've dried their food or stored it in sealed clay jars.

Most damning: Ba didn't have a brother.

THE NEXT DAY, A HEAVY summer storm came in from the south, clearing out the wildfire fumes. Qianze returned home late: her commute time tripled by the flash floods that inundated lower Manhattan, delaying the trains. Her short walk from the Grand Street station felt more like a swim as she trudged past cars stuck in tire-high water. Ba was startled by her appearance; she didn't blame him. She was drenched and caked in mud, resembling some creature trawled from a bog.

The apartment bristled with sound: the roll of thunder, the rattling of the AC, the metallic *twang* of the leak in the kitchen ceiling as it dripped into a saucepan. For dinner, they had damp takeout boxes of catering from the office. No story tonight. The downpour had upset Ba's cycle of lucidity and delusion, and he spent most of the night muttering to himself under his breath—quick Chinese in a heavy dōng běi accent she could not parse—some other timeline wrestling for dominance within his mind.

Afraid of wrenching him out of his time-shift, Qianze silently guided Ba to the couch after dinner and helped him lie down. He continued muttering and staring up at the ceiling as she pulled a thin summer blanket over him. He did not seem to register her presence. Qianze was perturbed by the sight of him, lying corpse-like on the couch save for the rapid stream of Chinese that filtered from his liquor-stinking mouth like a ghostly medium.

She retreated to her bedroom and closed the door, even as the heavy humidity swelled in the small space, threatening to knock the door off its hinges. She stretched out on her bed. Her sheets smelled tart from her recent night sweats. She looked at her phone: a text from Theo.

He was checking in, hadn't heard from her in a few days. Was her boss being a shit? Was she still stuck at the office? He had made too much igado and rice. He could drop some off in the office lobby.

Don't bother. Just left and the office street is flooded, she lied. *Stay safe*, she added. She turned off her phone and smothered her face in a pillow.

Theo was her boyfriend whom she had met at UVA. He had been a year ahead of her and recruited her to the Asian Student Union. Even though Theo was half Filipino, Qianze often felt that he was more Filipino than she was Chinese. Tagalog was his first language, and he had retained fluency into adulthood. Qianze's Chinese comprehension was decent, but she had trouble stringing together a full sentence. Theo visited his lola every month at her apartment in Queens, where they cooked together—the spoils of which he would bring back to Qianze: sun-yellow lumpia fried in vegetable oil; sour sinigang paired with silver-scaled tuyo; rich peanut kare kare topped with tenderized oxtail.

Their friendship in college had always existed in a middling space, oscillating between friend and something more. For the past few years, it had been firmly in the territory of something more. They split their nights at each other's apartments, and Theo cooked for her whenever she was over and sometimes when she was not, dropping food off at the office. A recent conversation about moving in together had left Qianze in the throes of a panic attack. Their other college friends were moving in and getting engaged, but the thought of these changes made her chest hot and tight, and she'd held him at arm's length since.

She hadn't told Theo that Ba had returned. Theo didn't even know Ba was alive. Besides Ma, no one did. Since Ba left, Qianze had hawked the lie that her father had died of an aneurysm until there were days when even she believed it. Mourning a dead man proved easier than mourning a living one. There was a permanence to it; she could put her disappointment and longing away in a casket.

Qianze lay in her bed as the heat lulled her into blinks of unsettled sleep. Without realizing it, she slipped into the dream of the jackalope. But when it came time for the creature to give its practiced grin—lips peeling back from its yellow-and-black teeth—it opened its mouth and screamed.

Qianze sat up. Her eyes adjusted to the night. The jackalope's scream had not been imagined. It was real and deep and coming from her living room. Frantically, she threw open the door of her room and ran to her father, who writhed on the couch in a night terror. His mouth a gaping, dark hole, the guttural cry exploding out of him. Qianze shook him awake.

When he woke, he stared blankly at her. She knew that her adult face was as strange to him as his elderly one was to her. That it was a Frankenstein mixture of features borrowed from his mother, himself, and his wife.

"Who are you?" he asked first, then more frantically, "Where's my daughter?"

Here I am, here I am! she wanted to shout. The tenderness, the want, surprising her.

"She's small, she's only thirteen, she needs her Ba. I need to protect her from . . ." He trailed off, seeming to forget what he meant to say.

She swallowed hard. "Go back to sleep, she'll be here in the morning."

BY DAYBREAK, BA RECOGNIZED HER again. It was Thursday, August 10. It had been four days since their reunion. He was surprisingly clearheaded. Early mornings seemed to be some of the better hours. He went through the motions of ritual: using the bathroom, vomiting up the liquor from the previous day, brushing his teeth, sipping coffee, eating whatever Qianze placed in front of him. Then there'd be a spark of recognition, and he would say something that told her he knew she was his—his blood, his child. When he finished eating, he would drift back to sleep on the sofa while she went to work. Nights were worse, his awareness hallucinatory and gossamer-thin. The chorus of doctors called this sundowning.

That day, he wished her a good morning and called her hái'ér, as if the previous night hadn't happened. Qianze winced at the term of endearment. She was in the kitchen, beating together eggs in a bowl for a steamed egg custard. Unable to sleep after Ba's fit, she'd gone out early to a nearby Asian grocery store and bought a dozen eggs and a metal steamer rack. She looked down and realized she'd whisked the eggs too hard. She pressed on anyway, adding mirin, sesame oil, and soy sauce. Then she let the bowl sit in the pot of boiling water on top of the steam rack. She had a single saucepan. Her stovetop was clean, no visible residue of home cooking. Her firm paid for her takeout meals in the office. Now the carton of eggs sat in the empty interior of her fridge, accompanied by two boxes of leftover wilted salad.

She felt silly as she served it to him, like she was lapping at his ankles for affection. It had been a dish he regularly made for her as a girl when she was in a bad mood. *Remember me? You used to love me!* the custard seemed to cry out as it jiggled. All it had cost to make was a few dollars and her pride.

As they sat down to eat, Qianze saw Ma's name and photo flash on her phone screen. Quickly, she declined the call, hoping Ba hadn't noticed. No such luck.

"Was that your Ma?" Ba asked.

Qianze chose not to answer. Ma didn't know that Ba had returned, let alone that he was staying with her. Qianze didn't know how Ma would take the news. She hastily took a bite of the steaming egg and immediately regretted it, coughing as it slid, burning, down her throat.

"How is she?"

Even though Qianze was housing and feeding Ba from her own coin, she firmly believed he didn't deserve any information about Ma or her well-being. "She's good. She has a cat. So she's not, you know, alone," Qianze said pointedly, refusing to meet his eye. A lie. Ma was alone.

"I used to have cats."

"We never had pets, Ba."

"No, when I was little. My mèimei would feed the street cats. But I would cut off their whiskers with kitchen shears so that they ran into the walls and not the little hide-a-holes they made for themselves."

"That sounds like you," Qianze replied coolly.

He sputtered out something that might have been a chuckle but sounded like a croak: "My daughter is vicious."

She swallowed down the searing words she wanted to say in response and instead shoved her half-eaten bowl of egg toward him. "You can have this. I have to go to work now," she announced, then pushed out her chair with a screech and walked out. Her viciousness was an heirloom she inherited from him.

Some nights there were no stories, only brief recountings of images from his dreams. A turtle growing hair, a red Celestial Hound.

"All omens of war," he mused over a cigarette that Thursday night.

"There's no war here right now, Ba," Qianze said, exasperated.

A frown, a furrow of his creased brow. "I didn't say they were omens for me."

"Then whose are they?"

A shrug. "Someone's. Not mine."

Three

Ba

2017: Five Days Since Reunion
Manhattan, New York

EACH MORNING, WHEN HE BLINKED the thick, crusting sleep from his eyes, he had to relearn the rules of his new existence. Often, he felt as if he had stumbled from one dream into another: the new space he awoke in so foreign and loud and hot. The last space he'd roomed in was—*don't remember, but at least it was cool and quiet.* Outside, a clamor of car horns and the chatter of English from passing pedestrians floated up toward him. But when he peered out the window, he was greeted by the sight of overhangs printed with Chinese characters and Chinese elders pushing their way through crowds, their grocery carts parting the sea of people for them—the landscape and soundscape a surreal contradiction.

The room he was in was small. It had four stained walls and two windows facing the street. One was half-jammed with an AC unit. There was a kitchen in the corner, cordoned off by a thin, long counter and a tightly packed bookshelf. A dining table with mismatched chairs. The couch he had been asleep on, made up in white sheets, ripe with the smell of his body. A television. Three doors. One leading to a small, tiled bathroom. One at the end of a hallway to the outside, framed by an umbrella and a shoe rack.

And the other. He was not sure what was behind it, only that he was *not supposed to go inside.*

It flung open. She walked into the living room in a flurry of motion, one arm in a suit jacket, the other rapidly scrolling through her phone before she shrugged on the other sleeve. Her hair was smooth, bluntly cut at her chin. The sight of her—this, too, he had to relearn. She looked up, and her mouth formed a small O of surprise.

"You're awake. Sorry, I know it's early, I thought I was being quiet. Work wanted me to come in now." She paused. "I could make some scrambled eggs. Do you want any?"

He could see his face in hers. It was his mother's face. Perhaps his grandmother's before that. Round cheekbones like a waxing moon, uptilted eyes like a fox's, a nose that sloped sharply downward. When he had left, she did not have this borrowed face. She had grown into it. This was what he had to relearn: that she had grown.

He blinked.

He was sitting in one of the mismatched chairs, a plate of scrambled eggs before him. This happened more and more. He forgot the in-betweens. One moment here; the next, there. Like the Myrtle house. One moment—*where?*—the next—

The squelch of ketchup startled him. Across the table, Qianze's brows knit together into a look of concentration as she painted a zigzagging line over her eggs in thick, dripping red red red—

There was a word on the tip of his tongue. *Red what?*

Red Army, red badge, red blood, rednecks, all the reds overlapping and accruing, red-surrection, red-incarnation, red-threading the red thread of fate, yes yes yes that was it—red thread.

The red thread was snaking toward him, fast as the glint of a silver fish being reeled in, hooking and pulling his mind out from this foreign space with the too-hot air and the too-piercing eyes of his daughter and back into the past, across the Promised Lands of

America and past the depths of the Pacific, down, down, down into Mao's Steel Town, when he was just a boy and knobby-kneed and not a He but a We.

In Red August, the lucky month, we all went swimming. The Chairman went floating down the Yángzǐ, so we, his comrades in Ānshān, Liáoníng, went looking to emulate him in any watering hole available to us. Park lakes and reedy little streams—anything not too polluted from the steel factories. We would float on our backs in the shallows and let the sun warm our bellies, which were empty, save for a hunger for blood. We were resplendent in our youth, in our bloodlust. No room for remorse.

"Ba, did you hear me? I asked if you wanted the rest of my food. I've got to leave for work."

Her face came back into focus.

"Fine." She pressed her lips into a line. "I'll leave it out if you want it. Put it in the sink when you're done."

He blinked. There, again, those two piercing eyes, glittering and hard, and they left the taste of curdled bitter melon in his mouth because he knew that he was the one responsible for that resentment, and sometimes his daughter's eyes and face would slip and slide—*or elide*—into her mother's, his wife's, the small hand putting down a bowl of steamed egg custard lengthening, thinning out—the left thumb now his wife's stiff trigger finger—now the dry, cracked hands of his own mother placing a plate of salted fish preserves at the table—now the bony hands of Nǎinai, his grandmother, reaching out to him, the veins jutting out and haunting him. All of their hands culminating into this one holding the plate. Pointing to him, accusatory—

—No. Not right. Find the thread again. The one that leads to the prophecy. Ah. There it is. There's the lure and the line. Reel it in. Start again. Yes.

Mao's *Little Red Book* says revolution is violent, and so we worshipped at the altar of violence. Each morning in our classrooms, our dark heads bowed to the hanging portrait of the Chairman, praying wàn shòu wú jiāng, wàn shòu wú jiāng. Long may he live, may he live for ten thousand years.

Mao wrote to the middle schoolers at Qīnghuá in the capital that to rebel is justified, and so we rebelled, even though we hailed from Ānshān, Liáoníng, and most people who lived in Ānshān were poor, dirty steelworkers. Still, we dug through our relatives' trunks, seeking old military garb. When we came up empty, we scrounged together steelworkers' trousers and jackets, soaked them in bitter tea to make them look like the worn uniforms of soldiers. We ripped off strips of red cotton wherever we could find it—from curtains, from rags, from bloody fabric—and bound it around our left arms. The adults thought we were playing at war, but we were generals, entrusted by the Chairman to carry out his utopia.

We were not born red. We were not the children of revolutionaries, of veteran generals, of the Chairman's inner circle. Some of us were born black, born from bad classes—the offspring of capitalists, rich peasants, counterrevolutionaries. For those of us whose past was stained, the red band and the violence it enabled was a salvation. We would not be targets of this brute horror; we would be the tools for it. Damned if you did, damned if you didn't.

The things we did we tried to forget.

And still they returned to us, lingering in our bodies like a poltergeist. The muscle memory of how it felt to bring a copper-buckled belt down against someone's cheek. Of our kicks and nail-spiked clubs meeting soft, counterrevolutionary flesh until it became corpse flesh. The ink stains on our hands from pouring ink into mouths, into eyes, marking people as black, knowing it wouldn't wash out of the lines of our palms for four, five days. The bulging eyes of an old woman looking at him with fear, pleading, her hand raised to him—

—No. Not that. Anything but that. Bì xū chōu yān. Need a smoke. Gǒu pì. Dog shit, no more cigarettes left. Need cigarettes. Need èrguōtóu. Need to leave the house.

The apartment was a stone's throw away from a liquor store that stocked bottles of Red Star èrguōtóu. His father had been a heavy drinker, and once, when he was younger, he swore off all the things that had made his ba cruel and volatile: cigarettes, liquor, gambling. Now he enjoyed floating down the current of the èrguōtóu, pickling his sorrows in báijiǔ.

Behind the store counter was a small display of Chinese-brand cigarettes, their stock dwindling in their cardboard cartons. He bought a bottle of Red Star and splurged on a pack of Double Happiness cigarettes, the gold box catching the light as the cashier handed it to him. On the pavement outside the store, he tucked himself under the overhang, slipped a cigarette between his teeth, and lit the cheap lighter he had pilfered from the counter.

The smoke got behind his lenses, making his eyes sting, but the smell was comforting. Double Happiness cigarettes were smoked during celebrations, so it was his father's breath coasting over his face at a Lunar New Year dinner, his wife's laughter as she lit the cigarettes of the guests at their wedding banquet, his factory coworkers toasting to his college acceptance—

Someone asked him for a light.

It was a boy around his daughter's age, face still round with baby fat. Chinese. He could tell. He could always tell the difference between Chinese, Japanese, and Korean faces and never understood why Americans couldn't.

"Shūshu," the boy asked in an American accent, "light?" He mimed the flick of the lighter.

He lit the boy's cigarette. The boy slipped his pack back into the front pocket of his jacket. Marlboro, he noted.

"Thanks," the boy said, then corrected himself, "xièxie." He watched the boy amble away, rounding the corner, and returned to his cigarette.

How young, he thought, barely of drinking age. Everything was within arm's reach for that child—cigarettes, sex, capitalism—none of it forced underground. No black markets for simple necessities like radishes and cabbages and aluminum pans. This street, this city, this country was a land of indulgence.

You could buy women online now. He knew this because he still got emails from a site, reminding him of his moment of weakness: "Hot Asian singles in your area!" flashing on the computer screen with a picture of a woman, her hair in two schoolgirl braids. It wasn't about sex. They never had sex. They had coffee once. They spoke on the phone twice. They spoke in Chinese, trading stories like currency. He couldn't remember all the details, just fragments lifted from the fog. A woman, malnourished and pale. She called herself a sugar baby, but he could see that she was nearing her thirties, had a child herself, and nothing about her face was saccharine; it was all angles and bone. They talked about craving connection. They talked about how they missed speaking in Chinese. They talked about the beast.

The beast was within him, its presence an unabating ache.

The beast's existence reminded him that he was supposed to tell someone a prophecy.

She asked who, and he said he didn't remember, only that he had left them in the past.

How far in the past? He didn't remember. The beast was at the center of the prophecy. The beast was devouring its own tale—the memories of its origin—to protect itself, to keep him from finding it.

What do you remember?

He remembered a row of crepe myrtle trees, but not the state they were in. He remembered the sadness of his mother's face but not when he last saw it. He remembered how it felt to be cradled by water, but not the names of the bodies of water he swam in or even if he could still swim. He remembered that Red August reading in the papers about how Mao swam in the Yángzǐ—before it all went sideways. Being too small for old fatigues, being too young to dip his fingers into a fresh corpse and write in thick, dripping blood, "Long Live the Red Terror," but being forced to anyway, because he should've considered himself lucky that the Reds associated with him instead of killing him like he had killed—

He took a deep swig from the paper-bagged bottle in his hand. The esophageal burn of it sank, settling in his stomach. He drank. He smoked. He went back into the store.

Four

Qianze

2017: Five Days Since Reunion

Manhattan, New York

IT WAS THE CREPUSCULAR HOUR when Qianze left the office: the blue period when the city began to speed up. People traded in their office chairs for barstools, and bikers with briefcases raced home along the streets, close enough to take a stray pedestrian's nose off. Qianze had just deserted several of her coworkers, who were clustered in their cubicles, red-eyed and clinging to consciousness by the dregs of the company coffee machine. Their dead-eyed expressions followed her as she tried to slip out of the office as quietly as possible.

Today was the last day of her early exits. It was Friday, August 11: the sixth and final day of her grace period, which included the Sunday she'd flown back to Virginia. Her manager had been unexpectedly understanding about her personal crisis. Qianze supposed that he had aging parents too. To Qianze, the situation at hand sounded like the opening to a bad joke. Stop me if you've heard this before: your father walks back into your life after eleven years and starts playing Scheherazade, and it seems as if his reality is curdling, pooling in waxy drips and stories, and you, his twenty-five-year-old daughter whom he abandoned, are the only one left to tether him to the real world.

On the subway platform, Qianze slumped down on a wooden bench. The heat underground was viscous, and her movements and thoughts felt slow and sticky. Seven minutes until her train. She rubbed her temples. In her periphery, she noted a figure taking a seat near to her.

"You look tired. Are you in pain? Advil?" the figure offered, and Qianze peered at the stranger from the sides of her eyes. The woman held out a bottle with its lid off. Inside was a handful of red, circular pills.

"Oh, I'm all right," Qianze offered a weak smile, "but thank you." She considered standing to avoid further interaction, but her train was still six minutes away. Six minutes on her heeled feet sounded excruciating, and her thighs had plastered themselves to the bench. She went back to cradling her head in her hands. The subway station was unusually devoid of the typical rush-hour crowd of a Friday evening. Besides a man in the distance, the two of them were alone.

"Suit yourself," the woman said, and Qianze watched through her fingers as the woman popped three of the pills into her mouth. That was definitely over the suggested dosage, but Qianze couldn't blame her. It was a three-Advil kind of day. A three-Advil kind of month.

The woman was a friendly looking Asian Auntie, her permed, graying hair tucked underneath a clear visor. Despite the suffocating heat, she was wearing a clasped cardigan and thick socks under her sandals. In the rolling cart in front of her was a wrapped cut of meat, bloody and sweaty, and several leeks bundled in plastic, their fleshy stems peeping out. Qianze willed herself not to linger on the Auntie's face. Her left eye bulged and blinked out of tune with the right one. The Auntie had suffered a stroke; Qianze could tell. She had recently become very knowledgeable about conditions of the elderly.

"You look familiar," the Auntie said. "Do I know you?"

Qianze shot her a polite, close-lipped smile. “I don’t think so.”

“Where are you going?” the Auntie asked. Qianze was surprised the woman was still speaking to her, breaking the New Yorker code of indifference and silence. That was one of the reasons she had left the South: Southern hospitality was always probing and bruising its way into her life.

“I’m going to Chinatown,” Qianze said.

The woman sighed, as if this answer disappointed her. “Where are you actually going?”

“What?” Qianze asked, taken aback.

“You’re going the wrong way,” the woman said. Qianze blinked in confusion, taking a second to look up at the sign, which confirmed that she was on the correct platform. She didn’t have the patience to explain the nuances of the MTA, which had taken her a month to learn.

The Auntie’s good eye flitted to the space behind Qianze. “Something’s following you,” the Auntie said. Qianze furrowed her brows and spun around, but there was no one behind her. The platform was empty, save for her and the Auntie and the man at the far end, his features an unknowable blur. Still, her pulse quickened. She was no stranger to being followed. In her handful of years in New York, she had been trailed on subways and streets by men crooning words in Korean, Japanese, and Chinese. Or ugly, mocking slurs asking her to *love me looong time*.

Qianze smiled politely. “I don’t see anyone following me.”

Auntie pursed her lips. “Something is definitely following you,” she said. “Whether you can see it or not is a different matter. You look tired. Not sleeping well? Nightmares? Want Advil?” Auntie offered again, shaking the bottle. When Qianze turned fully to look at her, Auntie blinked at her innocently, her left eye lagging and spinning in its socket. Qianze decided that this was no longer worth the seat.

She began to stand up but found that her legs were paralyzed, as if her feet were cemented in the subway station floor. The train was still three minutes away.

Her breathing hitched in panic. In her mind, she ran through a list of possibilities, each one increasingly far-fetched. Her legs had fallen asleep, but there was none of the classic static prickling in them, no feeling at all. Perhaps it was spontaneous paralysis. *Was that a real phenomenon?* She moved to check these symptoms on her phone, but her arms were frozen too. Perhaps in her exhaustion, she *had* taken one of the Auntie's proffered Advil pills, only it was laced, and she was now the target of some sick human-trafficking scheme that used old Asian ladies to get their targets' guard down. That must be why the red of Auntie's cardigan had developed a glossy, liquid sheen and her face was vaguely translucent, like a sheet of single-ply toilet paper. The pungent smell of the medicated oil on the Auntie's neck, the green kind that came in the shell-like glass bottle, soon filled Qianze's nostrils—her senses so violently bludgeoned with it that she had to close her eyes. Drugged, definitely drugged. Xanax, possibly, she thought, recalling a long-ago college experience.

"Breathe, girl," the Auntie said. Qianze let out a short, panicked huff. When she looked around, the distant man was gone. It was just the two of them. Her mouth grew dry.

"I—I can't—" *Move*, but the word was lost on her tongue. The overhead lights began to flicker. Auntie was nodding at her knowingly, and as her head shook, her appearance seemed to splinter and mirage. On, off, on, off. Each time the searing yellow light illuminated her, she bore a different face. Now she was the freckled, fresh-faced barista who'd served Qianze an overpriced coffee yesterday (on, off), now the night patrolman at her office whose eyes she always felt at the nape of her neck even when he was looking away (on, off), now an old woman with a wiry head of hair and a blind left eye, blue and sickly (on, off). Now she inhabited the faces of those passersby in Qianze's daily life—the pedestrians that brushed her shoulders in the crosswalks, on the subway stairs, on, off, on, off, on on on on—and *were they all her? Or was this woman some waking dream?*

"You're asking the wrong questions," the Auntie said, leaning forward as if she could hear the thoughts playing out in Qianze's head. Qianze tried to jerk away but found she couldn't do that either.

A crowd began to arrive at the platform, but their eyes slid off of her, returning to their phones. This was not the urge to avoid eye contact but a genuine unseeing, as if Qianze were enveloped in a magic that rendered her invisible. If she squinted, she thought she could make out an oily ripple around their bench, like hot air above tarmac.

"You need to go home, Qianze," the Auntie said. She had not told the woman her name. "Go home now, Qianze. Weihong is waiting for you."

"How did you—" she began to ask, but the train came at last, halting with a screeching whine and a slight breeze that ruffled Auntie's perm. Qianze regained feeling in her legs. She stood up too fast and stumbled to the edge. She pushed herself to the front of the doors, ignoring the affronted looks of those she had cut off, and collapsed on the cold vinyl seat, bringing her head again to her hands. The train began to lurch, and her headache bloomed into a full-blown migraine.

From the grimy train windows she saw the woman with the pills, still sitting in the same spot, with a giddy, frantic gleam to her face, refusing to break eye contact.

Five

Weihong
1963: Fifty-Four Years Before Reunion
Ānshān, Liáoníng Province

THE STRANGE OLD WOMAN WAS sweeping down a cobweb, which had spun itself overnight, from the kitchen corner. Then she swept away the mugwort bouquets his mother had so carefully dried and hung up along the wall. Weihong watched this all happen from where he was crouched at the threshold of his apartment, peeping through the open sliver of the front door. Mother was out on a walk with the baby. Father was somewhere; he didn't know where. Father had been disappearing and keeping odd, drunken hours ever since his own father, Weihong's yéyé, had passed a month prior.

Weihong had spent the day playing outside with some of the neighborhood kids. When he returned to the apartment, he was alerted to the presence of a trespasser. He noted the time on the kitchen clock. Mother wouldn't be back for a while. It was up to Weihong to deal with the intruder in their home.

He observed her while he plotted his next steps. Should he alert the neighbors? Should he go find an officer? He squinted. There was a suggestion of familiarity about her.

The old woman turned, as if sensing him watching her, and looked up from her broom. Her eyes found his immediately. Caught. He flew back as she approached and opened the door fully, staring down at him. They paused, each taking the other in. She had a bloated moon-fish face, worn through with wrinkles and sunspots. Her bovine eyes widened with recognition.

"Weihong? Is that you? I haven't seen you since you were a newborn." She approached, and he scuttled backward on his arms and legs like a crab.

She sighed and smiled sweetly, condescendingly—the way people did at small children. She said, "Weihong, it's me. It's Năinai."

AT THE INSISTENCE OF HIS supposed grandmother, Weihong was sitting warily at the kitchen table while she prattled away at the stovetop, preparing him something to eat.

"I remember the night you were born. I helped midwife you. You were born with all your baby teeth already inside your mouth."

He cocked his head and swung his legs—his toes only able to reach the ground recently after his tenth birthday—as he surveyed her.

The woman who claimed to be his Năinai sniffed the smoke and hummed in approval as she boiled together a simple soup: water, fat from their pork rations, spoonfuls of soy sauce and vinegar, dried herbs from the cabinets. A welcome break from their usual famine diet of dried yams. His stomach grumbled, awoken by the savory fragrance.

"Your father used to beg for my soups as a child. Rabbit stew was his favorite."

He could not imagine Father—stern and immovable—begging for anything. The few emotions he displayed verged on wrathful; even his grief was colored with it.

Weihong's parents had never mentioned any grandparents. Weihong had asked Mother about them once when he was young. Her answer was a sharp flinch and a deflection: "Why do you want to know?" she asked. "Does Ma not take good enough care of you?"

Only when the letter about Yéyé's death had arrived—and Father had plunged into a pit of mourning and báijiǔ, batting Mother's comforting hand away and shoving her against the wall—did Weihong realize his parents had come from parents of their own.

"Your father and mother, when they were children, used to spend all the time they could out in the woods together. They'd hunt rabbits, frogs, fish, dragonflies—all by hand—for me to make into stew."

Weihong found this taxonomy of abundance fantastical. He and his friends made a game of trying to catch fat pigeons for meals, but they had to settle for park frogs and the broken-winged, maggot-infested birds too weak to evade them, or—more often than not—mud pancakes. They gnashed the granular dirt under their molars, pretending it was the flaky, flavorful scallion bǐng from the street vendors that they could not afford.

"Feral little creatures," the woman continued. "Then back to civilized schoolchildren after supper, doing their homework."

He scrunched his brows. "They knew each other as children?"

She gave him a surprised look. "Of course. They grew up together. They've known each other since before they could speak. They didn't tell you?"

Weihong frowned. He began to wonder if some dotty old woman had wandered into the wrong apartment by mistake. His parents did not share this fondness that she described. They did not seem like childhood friends. They were separate planets, orbiting each other, occasionally influenced by the other's gravitational pull. They seemed to lead separate, distant lives. They slept with their backs to each other. They ate dinner in silence. If they spoke, it was about finances. Weihong had thought that theirs, like that of many of his friends' parents, was a marriage of convenience and class.

He wanted to ask more. He opened his mouth to speak, but then his mother's panicked voice came from the hallway.

"Weihong, what's going on in there? Is the stove on? I thought I smelled smoke—" Mother said as she opened the door. When she saw the old woman, there was shock and confusion written all over her face.

"Ma," she stammered, "what are you doing here?"

Nǎinai's warm expression dissipated quickly, her mouth flattening to a straight line. "Fei paid for my way here. I couldn't stay in the village alone, you know. That big old compound with just me."

Mother was quiet for a moment as she considered this. "Fei didn't tell me," she said. "So you're staying with us?" she asked, her arms folded tightly across her chest.

"Yes. Where else?"

"Did Fei leave you here alone?"

"He picked me up from the train station and dropped me off here. He has work."

Weihong's eyes darted between Mother and the old woman. Mother's reaction had confirmed that this was his paternal grandmother. Over the heavy silence oil popped in their sole saucepan. Finally, Nǎinai returned to the stovetop. Mother ducked her head, hiding her face with her sheet of hair.

"Weihong," Mother asked softly, "will you help me with your sister?"

He obediently went to her side. The baby was bound to Mother's back. The baby's name was Kangmei, and she was four, but strangers mistook her for an infant because of her small size. She'd been born premature and was often sick and colicky.

Kangmei was recovering from a fever. Today was the first day she had not been hot to the touch. Mother had taken her outside for fresh air, though Kangmei had been too weak to walk on her own. Weihong unbound the fabric holding Kangmei to Mother's back, then held her awkwardly by her warm armpits as Mother rolled her shoulders, the joints cracking. Kangmei, noticing the close presence of the stranger, squirmed out of Weihong's grasp and darted back to Mother, hiding behind her legs. Only her hair, wispy and sweaty, braided in two buns, was visible from behind Mother's knees.

The sour look on Nǎinai's face faltered, giving way to curiosity. "Is that Kangmei?" she asked. "Fei wrote to me when she was born. She's so big now."

Mother nodded slowly in agreement. The two women faced each other from opposite ends of the room at a standstill. For a moment, Kangmei shyly peered out. Mother's mouth opened, closed. Finally, she asked, "Do you want to introduce yourself?"

Nǎinai nodded, and Mother gently urged Kangmei toward Nǎinai, whose wide mouth began to creep upward into a smile. Nǎinai leaned down, brought her hands to her knees.

"Hello," Nǎinai said, "I'm your grandmother."

"Hello," Kangmei mouthed quietly, her voice barely above a whisper.

"You look just like your father did as a child," Nǎinai said. Mother's nose twitched. Weihong bristled. Kangmei, smarting under the direct attention, retreated back into the safety of Mother's shadow.

"She's shy around strangers," Mother explained. Kangmei tugged at the side seam of Mother's trousers, bringing her down to ear level. She whispered something and Mother nodded.

"She's not feeling well," Mother said. "I'm going to put her in bed to rest."

"All right," Nǎinai said, "sleep well, little one."

Kangmei ducked her head as she and Mother entered the bedroom. A few moments passed, and Weihong returned to his seat, waiting for Mother to reemerge. When she did, she closed the door and sagged against it, her face weary.

Mother was thin and willowy, and her bony shoulder blades curved away from each other. Even with her hunched frame, she was taller than most other women. As a toddler, whenever Weihong tore away from her in the market, he could find her by her bobbing black head of hair, rising above the crowd. She smelled like herbs—both the rarer ones she bought from the market and the ones she grew and tended to in the community garden in the apartment's courtyard. The pads of her fingers were stained green from plants and poultices. She, too, was prone to constant bouts of illness: weak vision, fainting spells, heat headaches, upset stomachs.

Weihong thought she was the most beautiful mother among his friends', even though she was a decade older than them. He was a mother's boy, and for the six years before the baby, they had been thick as thieves, tied to each other as if the umbilical cord had never been cut. Since he could remember, she spoke to him like an adult: no mincing words, no simplifying things, no underestimating his intelligence.

"Would you like something to eat, Ming?" Nǎinai asked, her tone perfunctory.

"Oh, I'm all right, Ma. You made it for Weihong, so he should have it all. It's not every day he gets a treat like this," Mother said. She noted the discarded mugwort bouquets on the counter and hung them back up while the corner of Nǎinai's mouth curled downward. Then sat at the table and playfully pinched Weihong's cheek, giving him a smile. Weihong pulled away from the affectionate gesture, but inside he was pleased.

Nǎinai served the soup. The wafting steam made his tongue prickle. Droplets of oil floated to the top: golden and gleaming. Mother asked him about his day.

In between quick slurps, he responded, "I played with the Wang brothers in the marketplace. Hide-and-seek. I won a spinning top." He reached into his pockets to show her his prize, almost overturning the bowl in the process.

"Slow down," Mother said, laughing, running her hand through the hair on the back of his head. She made appreciative sounds over the spinning top before handing it back. Her fingers pinched a strand of his hair, and she examined it. "Āiyā," she tsked, "it's not even summer, but you're already getting burnt. You should wear a hat." The warm seasons turned his skin a scalded copper red and brought out the auburn in his hair so that in direct light it looked like fox hide.

Nǎinai was standing stiffly in the kitchen. "You let him play in the streets by himself?"

"Oh, all the children do. And besides, Fei and I used to run around like wild animals when we were younger. How is this any different?"

"It's the city. It's far more dangerous than an empty forest."

Mother's eyes stilled at the invocation of the forest. Catching Weihong's curious expression, she blinked and forced a smile to her face. Then, to Nǎinai, she said, "You'll see soon, all the kids play in the city when school's not in session. The city looks out for its children."

Nǎinai frowned. "I don't understand how you can live here. No green, all gray, gray, gray. People crowded in compounds with so little space to live. And the smell." Nǎinai wrinkled her nose for effect.

"What smell?" Weihong asked.

"*Āiyā*, the city smells so bad—like the street cleaners used blood to wash the roads instead of water. You think I would be used to it, all those years of being a physician's wife—"

"*Ma*," Mother snapped, her eyes dangerous and sharp.

"What?" Nǎinai blinked innocently.

"Yéyé was a physician?" Weihong asked, turning his eyes to his mother. "You told me your families were peasant farmers."

Mother winced and would not meet his eyes. His parents never spoke much about where they came from, and most of it was deliberately bland, padded with murky details about the Manchurian countryside. Weihong now tried to recall specific stories of his parents' childhood but found he could only conjure up images: sorghum stalks rustling on the horizon and silver fish flapping about in a seining net.

Nǎinai turned her head, her pupils bouncing back and forth between them. "You didn't tell him? Are you ashamed? Of all the things to be ashamed of—"

"*Ma, don't.*" Mother cut her off abruptly, her voice a warning. "We'll speak about this later," she said, and there was such an authority to her tone that Nǎinai grew quiet.

"What did Nǎinai mean when she said the city smells like blood?" Weihong asked. The image of the street cleaners, pushing their mops into buckets of red liquid and spreading it along the city's alleyways and roads, sent an involuntary shiver down his spine.

Mother sighed. "She means the metal smell of the steelworks. Ba probably tracks some more of it home after work. You'll get used to it, Ma." Nǎinai ignored Mother's words and busied herself with washing Weihong's now-empty bowl. Another long, strained silence—like a whole-note rest—filled the apartment.

"You look just like your mother when she was younger. Before. The spitting image," Nǎinai said to Weihong. She dried the bowl with a dingy rag. There was a reluctant sentimentality to these words, different from the hostile tone she had been using with Mother.

"Yes," Mother said, a bittersweet smile dancing on her lips. Her hand reached out to smooth a lock of hair that had fallen into his eyes.

"That one though," Nǎinai nodded her chin toward the bedroom with a shine of affection, "looks like Fei. Same nose, same eyes."

"Isn't that what the Aunties say? Sons take after their mothers; daughters, their fathers."

The two women shared a pointed look, indecipherable in its mélange of emotions. Weihong squinted, trying to pick them out. Eventually, he had to look away.

Six

Qianze
2017: Five Days Since Reunion
Manhattan, New York

QIANZE GLIDED UP THE STATION steps in a state of half sleep. She had nodded off on her train. There'd been a dream and a jolt as the subway car screeched to her stop, but it was already fading in the recesses of her mind. The more she tugged at it, the more it seemed to elude her. What remained was the final glimpse of the Auntie's smiling face as the train left the station. How that yellowing grin seemed to follow Qianze as the subway barreled away—like the moon from a car window; no matter where or how far you drove, it remained, suspended and omniscient. Recalling the interaction made her skin prickle and her palms damp with sweat. The woman, Qianze decided, was unwell, and she herself was sleep-deprived. What she thought were names must have been Chinese phrases: mumbled nonsense with a tonal mark off, a different vowel. Yes, she thought, though her fear did not ebb away when she replayed the memory with this new rationalization.

She emerged from the Grand Street station to an animal smell in the streets. Her vision had taken on a blurred quality—the result of her dried-out contacts—and it rendered Chinatown a sea of colorful lens flares overlaid with the odor of cooked meat. The hanging duck carcasses seemed to glisten more than usual and she could almost taste the thick fat melting on her tongue, hear the crunch of the brown skin under her molars. Everything was phantomlike and oversaturated.

Absent were the voices of the street hawkers, replaced by the shuffle of people on their way home. The vendors had already cleaned up their outdoor stalls, but the smell of the seafood tanks and fish displays lingered. Qianze was hurled back into childhood weekends spent in the lone Asian grocery store in her hometown, tapping at tanks filled with limping lobsters and frenzied eels while her parents gathered ingredients. Her father had a taste for seafood: blue crabs and oysters that were delicacies in Virginia. Foods she'd only grown to appreciate as an adult—the brine and slick texture unpalatable in her child throat, threatening to swim back up.

Perhaps one of these days she would get a few crabs to cook. Ba used to pick the biggest live ones, fierce and fighting, and he'd let her toy with them with the tongs in their sink before boiling them and shucking the best parts for her.

Something inside her faltered at the tender ritual: the husking, the picking. *No, no crab boil, not yet.* It felt too much like forgiveness, and Qianze wasn't ready for that, didn't know if she would ever be ready. There were so many unanswered questions: where he had been this past decade, how he had become the alcoholic stranger staying on her couch, why he had left in the first place.

What she did know: Ba kept leaving things in the freezer. Gone were the days of returning home to an empty fridge. Now it swelled full with random household goods: a book, a lamp, the modem. Objects placed in the wrong drawers. In the bathtub, she found a nest: throw pillows and the framed photo of her and Ma at her high school graduation. This was also how she ruined her phone charger, which she found in the tub only after she had turned on the shower. Unplugged, thankfully.

Ba was stuck in the distant past: years, even decades, before she had been born. How she longed to wrench him back to the now, to the last eleven years, to that July night. Did she have to wait for him to finish rewinding through his chronological past—like a whirring VCR—before she could talk to him properly? Before he would be the man who had raised her and abandoned her? Or had that man already been lost to disease, existing now only in her memory?

As she opened her apartment door she mentally reviewed her glamorous Friday-night plans. She would see that Ba was fed, and if not, order him food. She would take melatonin, turn the fan and AC on high, and let the rush of cold air sear her brain until it was blank, then sleep for twelve hours, cocooned in a different world where the past week was a lucid dream. At any minute, she would wake and return to being Qianze Before Ba, spending her Friday night at Theo's apartment. Instead, Qianze After Ba opened her door, where she was greeted by a rancid smell and the figure of her father laid out on the floor like a crime scene.

"Ba?" She dropped her bag and went to turn him over, her heels squelching in vomit. There were remnants of sick, which he'd been lying facedown in, clinging to his mouth. Was this what the Auntie had been warning her of?

"You cannot die," she commanded him as she frantically felt for his pulse, "there are still things I need to say." After some searching, she found it: faint, slow, but thrumming. She slumped with relief, which was quickly replaced by disgust and anger. A squall of emotions that made her fingers shake as she peeled them away from his neck. Did he think she was a two-star motel? That he could do as he pleased and she would be there to clean up his messes and turn down his duvet?

She wanted to hurl the leftover eggs from yesterday's carton out of her window and watch them break and dribble down the street. She was taken aback by how much she wanted it; it felt unruly and all-consuming, this yolky mixture of sadness and wrath and frustration threatening to pour out of her. She sat seething in the mess for a few minutes before her body stopped shaking.

She sopped up the rest of the vomit. Then she scrubbed Ba's face until it was red and raw and threw out the stained overshirt he was wearing. She cleaned his glasses, spattered in sick. In a surprising feat of strength, she dragged his limp body by the arms along the wood floor and heaved him onto the couch. For the next hour, she cleaned until her whole apartment stank of Clorox: clinical and sharp.

She discovered other remnants of his presence during her cleaning frenzy: coaster rings, sweat stains, empty bottles stashed away that had begun to attract the beginnings of a fruit-fly swarm. She'd been tiptoeing on eggshells around his addled mind for a week, and all she had to show for it was a line of black trash bags. When she was done, she set a glass of water and some Advil on the coffee table by Ba's side. Then she sank down into her shower and cried. This was her home, and it was not expensive or nice, but it was hers, curated piece by piece, and he had violated it.

WHILE MANY OF HER COWORKERS had apartments that looked like West Elm showrooms, Qianze's place looked lived-in—her friends' polite way of saying that half the furniture looked like it had been pilfered off the street. Which it had.

There was a bookshelf that housed her childhood paperbacks. There was the tufted ottoman with a button missing and someone's old boarding-school steamer trunk with a false bottom. There were cheaply framed prints of paintings that Qianze had bought during a poster sale at her freshman orientation and several stools and chairs of varying heights clustered around a circular dining table. At the center of the apartment was the pièce de résistance: a sleeper couch upholstered in a verdant green velvet, which had become the place where Ba slept, drank, and straddled his thin divide between reality and fantasy, past and present.

It had taken several years to amass the collection. One temporary therapist had called it nesting. Her friends called it stooping. The term brought to mind the bent curve of Ma's back as she leaned over to inspect the leftovers on street medians.

After Ba left, Qianze and Ma were left scrambling to pay the bills each month. Qianze had held a string of mall retail jobs ever since she could work, and Ma picked up occasional waitressing gigs and tutored white children in Chinese. Ma was the one who taught Qianze the art of scavenging. Ma had three rules: Always check for bed bugs. Anything could be salvaged. Nothing should be wasted.

Ma was different now and had been even before Qianze began sending her money. Ma had left pseudo-poverty behind and costumed herself in a middle-class affluence, complete with weekly yoga classes, a wardrobe of athleisure, and a cult fanaticism for Clinique. The mother Qianze had grown up with and the mother she had now were so divorced from each other, so alien. In a recent phone call, Ma was debating whether to get caramel highlights, since all the women in her book club had gotten them.

What book club? Qianze asked.

Her yoga book club, Ma replied, they had started one last month. They were reading *The Joy Luck Club* by Amy Tan, and she was presenting on it. Qianze could imagine it now: the book club ladies' bleach-blond, Botoxed heads bobbing along as if they understood.

Ma was not a practicing Buddhist, but she had a stack of coffee table books on the subject. Gifts from said book club—composed of middle-aged white women, thin and taut and leathery from their daily routines of yoga and lying out beside their respective pools—who spoke about feng shui and karmic cycles. They referred to one another as "the girls." "The girls and I are going to the club for a spot of brunch" or "The girls and I are going to go on a walk around the park with their dogs." They scavenged pieces of Asian culture that made them interesting, but come Sunday, they would be sitting docilely in their pews at church.

A month ago, on a restless, miserable July afternoon, Qianze received a call from Ma.

"Bǎobèi, the girls tell me that if you hold on too much hatred, too much delusion, in next life you will be reincarnate as bug."

"Ma, I think I misheard you, it's loud here," Qianze near-shouted as she picked her way through Times Square. Her office was in Midtown, and she was doing her best to get to the subway without being trampled by a tour group on one side and a flock of *Sesame Street* characters on the other.

"I said my friends told me that if you have too much hatred and delusion in you life, next life you will be reincarnate as bug."

Qianze bit out a laugh. "Where'd they learn that from? *Buddhism for Dummies*? Their guru? They don't even believe in reincarnation." She could hear her mother's stiff, disapproving silence. "How'd that even come up?"

"I was telling them about you—"

"Wait, what did you tell them to make them think that?"

Ma paused before evading the question. "Not bad bug. Like bee, butterfly. Or moth. Not dung beetle or worm." Another pause. "Well, maybe dung beetle or worm."

"Great. Something to look forward to." Qianze exhaled deeply. "So you think I'm full of hatred and delusion?"

"I did not say that."

"Somehow that was the impression your friends got."

Ma let out a sigh. "Qianze, bǎobèi, you just—you just so angry. It scare me, you know? I don't want you be bug in next life. I want you be happy. In all your lives. Why you hold on to all this negative emotion?"

"Ma, it does—it doesn't work like that." Her voice cracked. This was a conversation they'd had before. "I'm not like you, I can't just take a yoga class and breathe it all out or whatever."

"I just want you be happy," Ma said, and her voice sounded so sad, Qianze's chest constricted.

"Ma, I am ha—" She choked on the lie, took a breath, and tried again: "I'll try not to be so full of hatred and delusion, so I won't be reincarnated as a dung beetle."

"Okay, bǎobèi, that make me happy. When you happy, Ma is happy."

Qianze had failed her promise the next month when Ba returned, bringing with him the familiar rage, the childish tenderness, and the constant missing. The missing was always humming, like electricity—something she tuned out—but when Ba came back, the white noise became deafening, thick with betrayal. A pied-piper tune luring in old feelings and a cloud of fruit flies that coagulated around the condensation of Ba's alcoholism. She imagined each fruit fly as the reincarnation of some hateful, abandoned girl who went to the grave unable to forgive her father.

Qianze let the cold water of the shower spray over her face. She did not want to think about the fatherless swarm of daughters in her apartment. She did not want to think about Ba or Ma or the reappearance of the jackalope in her dreams, which, in the past, had been the first warning in a sequence of inexplicable events. Was the strange encounter on her commute a sign of that old pattern reemerging? The Auntie's eerily prophetic warning had burrowed into her subconscious despite her reasoning, leaving a disturbing sense of dread. Perhaps she was going mad. Could Ba's madness be inhaled like miasma? She wanted to scream. She wanted to rent a car and drive far away from Ba and New York and the memory of the Auntie, which filled her with foreboding.

When she opened the bathroom door, the warm bulb above the mirror cast a beacon into the dark living room. She watched her father, now illuminated, sleeping fitfully, his limbs twitching, his eyes rolling around under his lids. As she watched him, she tried to imagine a scenario in which this could've turned out well. In which letting in the stray found baying at her old house and indulging his madness could've turned out remotely well. She couldn't. She went to her room and closed the door and slumped onto her bed, eventually drifting off still wrapped in her bath towel.

One of them was helpless, needed the other, and it wasn't her. *It wasn't her it wasn't her it wasn't her.*

It should've been her.

Seven

Ba

2017: Six Days Since Reunion
Manhattan, New York

HE CAME TO. HIS GLASSES were smudged and askew. He'd been stripped of his baggy button-down, leaving him in his wifebeater, and he was lying on a couch. He had to stew in his memory for a few minutes before remembering whose couch it was. At first, he only knew that the fabric had indented around his body—a sign that he had stayed long enough for the furniture to mold to him. The gray light of early morning filtered through the window and he squinted, struggling to decipher the layout of the space from the dark shapes the furniture made. Then someone entered the room, and he remembered.

For a split second, he thought she was his wife—the outraged eyes flinging him into an imagined reunion—but her teeth weren't as yellow, her skin not as sun-hardened. There was a series of garbage bags lined up beside the door, and she had picked one up, but at the sight of him awake, dropped it. The bag crashed noisily with Red Star bottles.

"You were lying in your vomit in the hallway."

He blinked at her.

"I thought you were dead at first."

They stared at each other for a few moments. Her lips pressed together. She turned away without waiting for a response. She lugged out the bags of bottles, two in each hand, letting the door slam. He winced.

When she came back, her face was weary, aging her. The flights of stairs seemed to have burned the spite out of her. She had the faint smell of bleach on her, perfumed over by shampoo.

"Do you want any food?" she asked tonelessly. He opened his mouth to answer, but his tongue was dry and caked in a rank acidity. He let out a rasp, and without speaking, she nodded at the cup of water and medicine next to him. She watched as he downed it and then sighed.

"You should put something in your stomach," she said. He wanted to protest, but he could only hold his head in his hands as it began to fill again. He missed the vacancy that drink afforded him; already his mind began to pound with the ghosts he had smuggled across the Pacific.

Using the only two things she had in the fridge—a carton of eggs and old frozen microwave rice—Qianze began to make fried rice. His emptied stomach roiled at the smell of sesame oil coating the pan.

He knew that she did not cook: her garbage was filled with takeout containers and receipts, her pots and pans were unscratched, her fridge empty. He watched as she cracked an egg over the rice. Even with his stuttering memory, he knew this was an act of care that he did not deserve.

How often had he looked at his own ba and thought, *I will not be a father like you were a father*. And now his failure was all over his daughter's face, a familiar smattering of disappointment and yearning and anger. It was hard to reconcile the child he had raised with the adult now standing over the stovetop. The image of her as a girl—waist-high with freckled shoulders and a long, trilling laugh, too young to be self-conscious of the sound yet—flickered over this stern young woman. He wished he had seen the transformation play out. But of course, he could not. Better, actually, that he had not.

From Qianze's infant years, he and his wife could tell that their child was deeply empathic, a weather vane for the emotions in the house, able to pick up on any sign of unhappiness no matter how well hidden. *Why are you mad, Baba? Why are you upset? Why do you look sad, Mama?* Even when they pasted smiles on their faces—hiding the reality of their finances and their immigration paperwork from her, and the subsequent strain both of these put on their relationship—Qianze knew when they were false. She'd sing, dance, gift them stones and art projects in an effort to turn them genuine. He wondered, even then, how such a generous child would grow up. A girl who gave away pieces of herself for others.

Now he knew. Now he could see it. He could feel his presence derailing her life, could see how their reunion wrecked her and how she tried to hide that wreckage from him. How she pushed those feelings to a place the sunlight could not touch, where they grew and had been growing since he left—and now all he could think about was that same dark place within himself and how his father had planted his own cancerous seed; now all he could see was his father's face and the feelings of regret and fear, feelings he always associated with the color red. When he closed his eyes, it was red on the backs of his eyelids.

Qianze cracked the second egg, and he was back in the present.

"A double yolk," she mused. "Is that an omen?"

He shrugged, watching as the three yolks danced and bubbled with the rice.

"I thought everything was an omen." She was teasing him.

"I've never seen a double yolk before. When I was growing up, eggs were the most expensive thing in the market. You'd be lucky to see two yolks in as many months."

She was quiet at that. She went over to the windowsill, where she kept a jar of scallion bulbs in murky water—the only plants in the apartment. She cut off a wilting stem, washed it, and chopped it finely to garnish his rice. Finished, she placed the bowl in front of him and sat down. He ate a bite. Before coming here, it had been many years since he'd eaten food prepared by someone who cared for him. It had a specific taste: September, the harvest season, salt, safety. He ate, and he spoke. Stories were the only thing he had, the only thing that he could give her now.

"We were lucky for a while, because our family had a chicken. We named her Xiǎo Bǎobiāo—Little Bodyguard—because she clung to my mèimei's side and would peck if any strangers got near her."

"Had? What happened to her?"

"We ate her. Boiled her in a bit of cooking wine."

He watched as her face screwed up in disgust, her wide, dark eyes refusing to meet his. "That's fucked up, Ba."

"That's famine, hái'ér." There was more to this tale, but he did not know how to say it. Not in English. Some memories were untranslatable.

He put down his chopsticks. His tongue craved some wine with the rice. His hand had a warning tremor. He would take a beer, as a last resort, though it was far too weak for his tolerance.

"Is there any wine?"

Qianze made a face. "The sun's not even up yet. And there's no alcohol in the apartment anymore, Ba."

His throat dried. Desperation clawed at his nerves, lighting up his whole body with anxiety. How to tell her that he needed something to cope with the memories that resurfaced. How to make her understand. How to show her the memory wound, that half-forgotten tragedy that wanted to be fully remembered.

The words "I want to go home" slipped out of him, childish and needy.

"Where's home?" she asked. He could see from her face that she thought he meant the bare shoebox he'd stayed at during this past decade. He did not. He wanted to return to Liáoníng. To the pond, where he lay on his back, the August heat seeping into his skin while reeds tickled his feet. To the streets of Steeltown, where he had played war games with the other boys, where his mother had cooked meals for him, where his mèimei had trailed him like a shadow, where he had done the worst thing he had ever done in his life, that memory now bringing back the irrepressible image of a woman's desperate eyes bulging out of her head like two jaundiced ping-pong balls—

No. Not right.

He wanted to return to Liáoníng, but what he meant was Liáoníng six decades ago. Liáoníng as his childhood playground, before consciousness had its hooks in him. He had done his damnedest to caulk up the violent periods of his childhood. His past read like Morse code: long, great blanks washed down with báijiǔ between brief pinpoints of nostalgic idyll. But those silences crawled back to consciousness now, refusing to be forgotten—

"Ba? Where's home?" Qianze asked again, her voice steely.

He took the easy way out. "I don't remember."

Qianze huffed a sigh, and the wisps of baby hair that curled on her forehead floated up. She sat for a moment, then stood and began to clean: gathering his plate and chopsticks, scraping the leftovers into the trash, running the porcelain under the tap.

"I'm tired," he said as she dried her hands on a kitchen towel.

"Okay. I'm going to go to a coffee shop to do some work. You should get more sleep," she said. Once she left, he returned to the sofa and slouched against the velvet upholstery. His head began to throb, a sign that it had been too many hours since his last drink. What began as a dull ache quickly escalated into a debilitating, thrumming pain, pressing against his temples. He imagined his skull on his neck as a raw, white egg in an eggcup, and something was about to hatch, something was about to give. He put his head between his knees to ease the pain, but it did nothing. He imagined the shell of the egg splintering, the fissures growing, and usually he would have a drink to keep it from cracking, but now there was no drink—*no alcohol in the apartment anymore, Ba*—and so his mind broke open, and he was involuntarily hurled back to the red thread. It was waiting for him. In the attic of his head, it came alive, became a spider with a thorax full of red history weaving a red web, obscuring the memories of the last few years, ensnaring him, yanking him back to the beginning to be devoured by his past, where—

The old gods were dead. They were rotting in the boglands. There was only one God now, and His name was Mao. From our mothers, we were born in blood, but in His revolution, we would be reborn and baptized in new blood until we were all red, red, Red.

The old gods were corrupt and feudal. They played with mankind like we were toys, amusements, poking at us like wild animals until we bit back. And we did. Bite back. Before our revolution, our Red August—that burning, razor-edged precipice—Mao's early followers dismantled the churches and the temples and the monasteries and the mosques and made them prisons, made them barracks. They smelted down sacred objects for metal. By the time we gained consciousness, there was nothing and no one left for us to worship except the Great Redeemer.

See, you must understand: we were children raised on a battleground, and harm was a game we played; bloodletting a sport; terror and rage the comforts that we slept with, draped over us like a blanket. Mao and His administration told us that the counterrevolutionaries were monsters and demons, and that made them inhuman, which made them killable. Most of us did not like our first act of violence. Some of us grew to like it; some of us never did. They shaped us into a blade, into a guillotine, and turned us loose against their enemies, but sometimes their enemies were our teacher mother father sister brother aunt uncle—

No, can't go in there. Too close. Start somewhere else.

When she was little, my daughter grew tired of Chinese stories. She made me read her English bedtime tales—how did they all start?

Once upon a time, hái'ér, my mind started eating itself, spitting out bite-sized memories like breadcrumbs. At the end, a house. A witch. A prophecy. A beast—

The house is wrong—too many ghosts waiting in corners—rooms devoured by termites, locked from the inside—a maze of hallways with no end in sight. One of the rooms has the prophecy. My prophecy. My daughter's prophecy. One of them has—

A good memory: I once built my daughter a cheap bookshelf to house all the books she scavenged. The back of the shelf was flimsy cardboard, more for decoration than structure. There is something like that in the house's scaffolding. A false back with no door. And behind it, I feel something slumbering: sharp and malevolent.

Eight

Weihong

1966: Fifty-One Years Before Reunion
Ānshān, Liáoníng Province

WEIHONG AND HIS FAMILY LIVED in an apartment provided by Father's work. The building, once a compound for one family, consisted of several rooms built around a square courtyard. The space had since been split to house ten families, and each of them had one or two small rooms for themselves, with a shared toilet in the courtyard. It had been nearly four years since Nǎinai arrived, and in that time, she'd become a fixture in their small makeshift apartment. She was too old to work, but she would wake early in the mornings, take a worn wooden stool, and sit in lines at the market as it yawned awake so she could pick out the best of the rations for their meals. Her bed mat, pillow, and winter quilt—a leek-green, heavy thing—were folded and stacked on top of Weihong's and Kangmei's in the corner of the main room. Her cloying scent, warm and heavy, clung to the clothes she hung up in the window to dry. Like a piece of furniture, the unexplainable rift between Nǎinai and Mother remained, becoming part of their household landscape.

Weihong spent many hours with Nǎinai alone, when Father was working and Mother was taking Kangmei out for a constitutional walk. The two traded in a currency of memories. Nǎinai would tell him about his parents as children, and he would puzzle over these tales like they were arithmetic problems. He could see traces of his mother in the recollections, in the child she was. But his father. He would look at Father across the table at dinner and wonder where the boy Nǎinai remembered was. Occasionally, he would share his own memories of Mother.

Mother was the smartest person he knew. She'd learned Russian on her own, and she liked to read borrowed Russian books to him. Her mellow voice melded the rasping syllables into music, the words of Gorky and Gogol lulling him to sleep. When he thought of his childhood, it was their ritual of reading: the way she looked when the afternoon sun slanted in, tinting her hair and eyes the rufous shade of his own. She would hide the books in the apartment upon Father's return. When they completed a book, she would bring Weihong with her to the black market's underground library to exchange it. When there were no books to borrow, she told him stories of her own creation. Her tales hit a pitch between hallucination and magic. There was no room for divinity in his belief system; in their new world, they only worshipped Mao. Still, he recalled her stories of apples and omens and blasphemously called them holy. Sacred.

Once, when he was five, he had gotten lost in the black market. Mother was in her first trimester with Kangmei. She was returning a copy of *Snowy Winters*. He had wandered off, drawn to the ruckus of peddlers with colorful goods. Fruits and glistening red meats with veins of fat he was tempted to lick. Eventually, he found his way to an alley, where the sons of some sellers were playing with a ratty set of Chinese checkers.

He caught on quickly. Beginner's luck, one of the sons sneered. Weihong was winning—just one jump away—when his mother came tearing into the alley, caterwauling as she knelt down before him, her hands patting his convex child belly to make sure he was real, not a story she had spoken to life that had blinked out of existence once she lost sight of him.

"I thought"—her voice came out in breathless spurts—"I thought he—"

She never finished her sentence, sweeping him up into her arms, leaving behind a wake of pieces she'd scattered in her fervor to get to him. She did not bring him to the black market again.

Weihong recalled this incident to Nǎinai: this moment that had fossilized in his brain, indicating some significance he had yet to solve. He safeguarded Mother's secret and did not mention the books or the black market. He changed details: the black market becoming the produce market, the curious "he" his mother feared and never mentioned again becoming a faceless kidnapper at large.

Nǎinai nodded when she heard. "Mothers and their firstborn sons. I felt the same way about your ba."

When he looked at her blankly, she added, "I don't know how to say it in words. You'll know it when you have a child of your own."

Weihong made a face. There were so many answers that required the slow calcification of adulthood.

Nǎinai laughed, jowls shaking. "Oh I remember that look. Being told 'You'll understand when you're older' always felt like a way for adults to avoid answering questions. I guess, hái'ér, if I had to put it into words, it would be like"—she paused, her forehead crinkling in thought—"like drowning."

"Have you ever been swimming?" Weihong asked. Mother had taught him and Kangmei how to swim in the park's trio of lakes.

To his surprise, Nǎinai said, "No. But I can imagine it. When your ba was born, what I felt was so large. Larger than me or the village. Like I could keep sinking in it, and there would be no end. Does that make sense?"

Weihong shook his head.

EACH WEEK, THE FAMILY ATTENDED the city's Recalling Bitterness meetings. Their local neighborhood meetings took place every Sunday. Occasionally, the steelworks would have one, and Weihong would stand in the crowd, brushing shoulders with Father's colleagues and their families. The citywide meetings, however, had no set schedule. One day, the big posters would go up on the walls, announcing the date, time, and venue, and everyone would cancel their plans or risk scrutiny.

In a local meeting, there would be a parade of elderly workers and countryside peasants filtering on and off the auditorium stage. For an hour, Weihong would stand there, rocking on his heels, while they waded into their past, their sea of bitterness, a kǔhǎi created by waves of suffering under the nationalist and imperialist regimes. Weihong had an ear for stories, which is how he knew these were recycled narratives.

Each week, the same scaffolding—life before Our Chairman was only a semblance of living, but then He came and gave us rice and clothing, created the great proletarian dictatorship, and we could not be more grateful to Him. The objects shifted: some stories were punctuated by frostbitten limbs and empty dirt cellars, while those from more southern regions were explicitly violent, containing Japanese faces with garlic-bulb noses—their nostrils flaring with evil intent—bayonets, and amputations.

Once, a man from Nánjīng told a story of how, when his village was overtaken in the Nánjīng Dàtúshā, the soldiers forced the fathers to rape their daughters. How they nailed people alive to walls, how they hung people by their tongues on iron hooks, how they sliced babies into quarters. For a month afterward, Kangmei had nightmares, biting her tongue in her sleep until it became so swollen and bloody, she could not speak.

At the end, the theater would erupt into sobs and grateful cries, and Mother would pinch Weihong's arm so tightly that his ruddy complexion turned bone-white. This was his cue to sniffle and let out a few false tears. This was also her way of warning him to behave in public, which meant not deviating from the story. The story was that his grandfather was not a physician-scholar with a capitalistic practice and his own compound, and his grandmother was not a physician's wife. His mother and father were uneducated peasants: migrants from rural Manchuria, where they had lived and toiled all their life. Father had attended grade school and middle school and was a quick study with numbers, which is how he had picked up work at the factory so quickly. There was not a black smear of landownership or capitalism or higher education to their name. Until he was ten, this was the only narrative he had ever known. Nǎinai's arrival had created a snag in the tapestry Mother had woven, causing the threads to unravel.

Every so often, there were town meetings that skewed more toward inquisition. A landlord or an employer would be brought onstage, forced to answer for their abuses by the crowd. At the end, they'd be stripped of their land, their position, reduced to a street cleaner or janitor. There were rumors that some of these interrogations in other provinces had turned bloody.

Or that was what Weihong overheard that morning when Mother told Nǎinai that she was required to go to the citywide meeting—even if she felt ill—hissing that, farther south, they executed landlords. Farther south, they beat those with black backgrounds. Did Nǎinai want to bring the Party's eyes down onto their family? Did she want her skin to turn as black and mottled as their past?

No, Nǎinai had said, but her eyes were hard.

The impromptu citywide meeting was held in a theater. Weihong and his family were packed into the crowd like tinned fish. Weihong craned his neck to see the stage, but it was empty except for a large lit portrait of the Chairman, which hung in front of the red curtains. Kangmei sat on Father's shoulders, her hands gripping his dark strands of hair like a horse's reins. It had been a cold winter and remained so even as the year edged into spring, but in the theater, it was uncomfortably warm. Weihong began to sweat under his coat.

The chief of Ānshān's Communist Party emerged onstage from the wings. The crowd grew quiet, save for the whispered tail ends of conversations, speculating on the reason for the meeting. At the chief's nod, a few men brought out four people, looking the worse for wear. They did not fight. They drooped, defeated, under the men's arms like sacks of yams.

The chief spoke. He had a metallic voice that carried to the corners of the theater, trumpetlike. "People of Ānshān," he began, "I can see in your faces that you're wondering why you've all been brought here. Why you're spending your afternoon in this crowded, smelly theater, instead of in your homes."

This earned some scattered anxious tittering.

"We are here, as always, to honor our Party, which has instituted our proletarian dictatorship. But," his voice grew cold, "there exist among us those that would threaten our great Party, our Chairman."

He gestured to the four people onstage, their eyes downcast. "There are wolves in sheep's clothing among us. These four represent the four old evils. Old ways of thought, old cultures, old habits, old customs. Remember, before the Liberation, that these four evils, the feudalism that ran rampant, were a rot that plagued our country. And it is our job to weed them out."

He nodded at one of his men. "Bring forward the scholar."

The scholar was a man of indiscriminate old age. He had white hair and a pair of square glasses that pinched the bridge of a beaked nose. One of the lenses was cracked; the stage light that bounced off the fractured lens was a bright gunshot glare that made Weihong's own pupils constrict. Weihong heard his father and Nǎinai suck in breaths as the man was dragged forward. Under his cotton shirt—too thin for the winter cold—the visible sliver of skin was a gallery of bruises the color of a rotting plum.

"This man," the chief sneered, "is counterrevolutionary, intellectual elitist scum."

This announcement was met with jeers from the crowd. At this goading, the men holding the scholar pushed his head down and brought his arms back in the jet-plane position. Pain echoed across his face.

"He is aided by his son, a bourgeois, rightist relic of a doctor." At this cue, the men brought forward the doctor, who looked around Father's age. Weihong snuck a glance at Father and Nǎinai. Their faces had gone bloodless.

"These class enemies are guilty of the following crimes: Study of Western philosophy and literature. Study of Western medicine. Critique of Chairman Mao. Critique of Our Party. Capitalist practice. Class crimes. Interlocution with fellow imperialists . . ."

The list continued. The crowd stirred with each addition, a tempest rippling. The people's disapproval determined the father and son's punishment. They would be jailed for the remainder of their lives.

Weihong's ears rang. He was looking at Mother, whose mouth was moving along with the crowd's, but no sound came out. He was looking at Father and Nǎinai, whose mouths weren't moving, their faces rendered dumb by the uncanny coincidence. He was looking at the stage, the large image of Mao fastened to the backdrop. The auditorium lights reflected off the black of the Chairman's eyes, turning them a glowing yellow. The scripted play between the chief and the assembly continued. Outside, the afternoon turned a waning blue, warning of dusk. Weihong's legs ached from standing. He shifted.

The hairs on the back of his neck rose up. Weihong had the distinct sensation that he was being scrutinized. He scanned the room, but everyone's faces were turned toward the stage, watching the ongoing torture, the same blank expression mirrored across the crowd as they chanted in unison. His eyes drifted to the large paned windows on either side of the space. They had grown opaque from condensation. He squinted, rubbed his eyes. There, outside, he thought, was the outline of a figure, turned toward him. A person of short stature, no taller than a child of five or six, dressed in white in a pale contrast against the gray street. They seemed to sense his stare and tilted their head. In this light, they appeared more animal than human. He thought he could make out spindly arms resting on the ground, a body sitting on its haunches like a dog. On top of its head, two long ears—one drooping that seemed to perk up at his gaze. He did not know how long he and the white figure looked at each other. Seconds, maybe even several minutes.

And then the figure moved quickly, approaching the window, pressing its face right against the glass, and he saw a nightmarish hare smiling widely at him with black human teeth and a pair of eerie eyes the same color as the stage's red curtains. He stumbled backward. All sound receded, leaving only a high-pitched ringing in his ears.

His mother gripped his elbow to keep him from falling over. His panicked eyes met hers. She frowned. *Are you all right?* she mouthed. He looked back at the window. The hare was gone. He let out a shaky exhale. He nodded, straightened. His hearing began to return. Mother gave his arm a squeeze and turned again to the front. He feared what he might find if he looked back at the window, but in his periphery, the spot remained empty—save for a circle of condensation from someone's breath. He shook his head to rid himself of the vision.

He must have drifted off, sedated by the warmth of the theater. Nonetheless, he did not look up until the roar of voices subsided. Only the chief remained onstage, dismissing them. There was blood. There, dotted on the stage. Bubbling with spit. He refused to look at Father and Nǎinai, scared at what he would find in their expressions.

He heard his name through the crowd as they filtered out. He sniffed it out to its source: his friends, who were gathered outside in a small circle, waving him over. They were a pack of scrawny, ration-fed boys, their skin winter-burnt, their hair close-cropped. Like him, they were not children of revolutionary Party officials but also not from ostensibly bad class backgrounds. Neither red nor black but some murky mix.

He did not want to stew in the silence of the apartment with his parents and Nǎinai, their fear thick as smog. In that quiet, his mind would wander to the eerie hare of his daydream, who'd seemed hungry for Weihong's fear. He looked to Mother for her approval to join them, which she granted, surprisingly, with an absent nod and a perfunctory "Be back before dinner."

Wriggling through the crowd, he made his way to the boys. The four of them wandered off, detaching themselves from the people still gathered in front of the theater.

The boys he ran with liked playing war games. That winter, they played the Long March. None of them were Mao—that would be sacrilegious. Instead, they were all soldiers in the Red Army. The temperature was cold enough to pretend they were traversing snowcapped mountains. They clung to the sides of building façades dusted in hoarfrost like they were craggy mountain faces. They wound through the streets, pretending the loops of cement were the treacherous swamplands of the Fathomless Morass, the Ruòěrgài Shīdì. Sometimes, they lost fingers and toes to frostbite. Other times, they died and were reincarnated as new soldiers, only to die again—this time from hunger, from drowning in the mud of the marsh. They encountered imaginary Nationalists and gunned them down, yelling, "Die, traitors! Down, counterrevolutionaries!" Watched as the enemy bodies crumpled in a spray of invisible viscera. Sidestepped the injured, who pleaded for mercy, gripping their spilling entrails. Left them there for the animals as they swung their guns onto their backs.

Weihong stepped over a dying Nationalist, whose pleading hand curled around his ankle. He kicked off the hand and stomped on the imaginary skull, the sound of splintering ringing in the street.

THE TENSION IN THEIR APARTMENT peaked. His parents and Năinai retreated into a state of self-preservation. For Father, that meant unleashing a fresh hell upon their family.

There was a time when Weihong believed that he could earn his father's love. That the mediocre grades he brought home, the chores he did not do, the schoolyard fights he got in were deserving of Father's stern hand. But the sore handprints on his body had evolved into welts on his back and long willow-switch scars. Weihong became a better student and son in the aftermath, but the lashings continued: over a slammed door, over an insolent look.

The belt was new, different—then it began to appear nightly. Eventually, Father would grow bored of doling out punishment and collapse onto the bed, drunk and unconscious. Mother would then apply a warm compress of honeysuckle, mint, and dandelion to the lesions on Weihong's back.

A pattern emerged. If Father did not return home after work—an event that became more frequent—they assumed that he was downing drinks with his coworkers or tangling with fickle Fortune at a back-alley mahjong table. They never sought him out, so they never knew exactly what he was doing. But Weihong watched his mother's pinched face as she did their household expenses, noting when increments of money disappeared, when they magically reappeared. If Father did come home from whatever hole he had drunk himself into, he would be red-faced and stumbling, shaking his fist at the world.

As Father entered the apartment, Năinai and Kangmei would scurry out. Năinai would shoot Father a disappointed look that he did not register in his stupor, and then the two of them would flee to the courtyard like dogs with their tails between their legs. Mother would try to sober him up, ply him with glasses of water, but he would be looking for a fight and Weihong was there.

Weihong was glad, at least, that it was not his mother.

In the aftermath, when Father was in the bedroom, he and Mother would sit in silence in the main room. Mother's voice would be hoarse from pleading for Father to *stop, please*, her weak body bruised from being tossed aside. They would sit at the dining table as she washed her son's wounds in sophora root.

"He's not himself when he's like that. He's someone else."

Weihong bristled. "How?" he asked.

"He's the person he becomes to cope."

"Ma, you're not making sense. Are you defending him?" He pulled away from her touch. The damp rag in her hand dripped in the space between them.

Mother pressed her lips into a thin line. "People do worse things to cope. Become worse people."

Weihong opened his mouth to respond, but Nǎinai and Kangmei returned, and the tension between them was interrupted, left unresolved.

There were moments when Weihong thought his father did love him. Breadcrumbs that he gluttonously gobbled up. Weihong had a bad right ear. There was no childhood ear infection, no injury to trace it back to. He had always had poor hearing in it, like he'd been born hollow on one side. His father, too, had an old ear injury that made him prone to ear infections. There were days when both their ears would flare with pain, and Mother or Nǎinai would make them ear poultices and have them lie down in the one bedroom. They would face each other, their injured ears turned to the ceiling: Weihong's right ear, Father's left. Nǎinai thought that humming a soft tune would help them sleep. It never did, but they didn't have the heart to tell her to stop. Sometimes, while Nǎinai was croaking along, Father would shoot him a comically exasperated look, which made Weihong laugh silently, warmed by the knowledge that they were co-conspirators, despite the shooting pain down his jaw.

Or, when he brought home a math exam, the top ranked in the class, and Father looked it over slowly, the ghost of a smile on his face. The time when Father handed down one of his work shirts for Weihong, a starched, thinning button-down that Mother altered for him. How Father gave a sharp, approving nod when Weihong wore it: the picture of a young model revolutionary.

These crumbs paled in comparison to the wholeness of Father's love for Kangmei, which Weihong envisioned as a round and full mooncake. A delicacy he had seen in store displays but never tasted.

Everyone loved Kangmei. Since her birth, Weihong measured the affection each of them received, and he always came up short. Father had a soft and transformative tenderness for her: one that thawed his exterior, if only briefly. It turned him into the kind of father who picked up his child and swung her in circles when he got home. Kangmei's peals of ensuing laughter rang loud and mocking to Weihong's ears. In those moments, Father called her his Xiǎo Shǐ Pǔ Níkè: Little Sputnik.

Weihong scoured his memory to see if his father had done this with him even once. He imagined the feeling of that lightness. His arms spread like his sister's, imitating flight, Father beaming. But when he tried to recall his father's affectionate touch, he conjured up the violence of the past month instead.

"It's different with fathers and sons," Mother said. "You'll carry on his name. You and he will always be linked. Fathers must raise their sons to be self-sufficient."

IN WEIHONG'S BAD EAR, THERE was a constant low-pitched ringing—like wind whistling through a long, empty tunnel or a river humming with a strong current. Sometimes he thought he heard orchestral music from it: flutes and other woodwinds. Some days it was louder, sounding as if there were a whole country inside his head he wasn't privy to. Based on the decibels, he imagined his ear as a portal to different spaces, increasing in size: a hut, a cave, a theater, a forest, an abyss.

When the sound was small and tinny, he thought it sounded like a snoring, slumbering beast. It was deep, but not dissimilar to the rumbling purrs of the street cats that hung around his sister. That afternoon, Kangmei had lured a small colony of street cats into their compound. Weihong was babysitting her while the adults were out. The cats mewed and pawed at her for attention, their eyes pink and wet.

At eight, Kangmei was fragile and the runt of her class. She had large eyes and weak vision; her wire-rimmed glasses—the pair she'd had since she was five—emphasized the round, teary quality of her eyes. Her head was comically large for her body, like a balloon rising from bony girl limbs, which made her look like a starving stray cat herself.

Kangmei didn't have many friends. She spent long stretches at home from school, too sick to be in the classroom. Weihong tracked seasons by Kangmei's bouts of illness: winter flus and summer colds; she took after Mother in this way. But Kangmei loved the street cats of Ānshān, and they, in turn, loved her. She saved them scraps of food from her meals, pinching them into cloth napkins and scattering them before the gathering crowd of cats in their apartment courtyard. She was the only one in the neighborhood to take pity on the animals, who were as famine-hungry and scrawny as the rest of them. In the streets, she was always surrounded by a cluster of them, as they butted their matted heads against her shins, flicking their tails to curl around her knobby knees.

"You're going to get fleas. Or rabies. And then we'll all get fleas," Weihong said when he saw her sitting in the courtyard, a calico grooming her hairline.

"They're so soft and warm. Pet them, gē," she implored, stroking a scrappy tabby that was vying for her attention. The same tabby gave him a hiss and a warning look, daring him to try. The cats always seemed wary around him.

Sometimes, he imagined wrapping his long fingers around their scruffy necks and squeezing. Once, he told Kangmei this, who told their mother, and for a month, Mother looked at him sadly, as if she hadn't expected anything else. *I wasn't gonna go through with it*, he pleaded to her, *I only said it to scare Kangmei, I didn't mean it*. The most he had done was snip the cats' whiskers off with his friends.

He could still picture Mother's disappointed face in startling detail, betraying a hint of fear. That day had sparked the beginnings of a long-laid plan for vengeance Weihong had been privately indulging.

Since the beatings began, Weihong harbored fantasies of overthrowing his father. Like a young buck, he would defeat the old stag in an upset, his new antlers shearing pelt from skin. These were just whims—seedlings planted in salted land. Despite everything, Weihong knew he could not lift a finger against his father. Father's income was the source of their apartment, their livelihood. Instead, he turned his violence toward Kangmei, both the object of Father's affection and the instigator of Mother's fear.

The plan began with a whiff of an urban legend. He'd first heard the rumors about the Woman in the Alley at school, then at the market and around the streets of Ānshān. Among the red children, the Woman was a test of bravery. It was said she could predict your future and in particular, the most painful moment of your life.

Kangmei had never known real pain. She'd been coddled since birth, swaddled in the unconditional love of their parents and Nǎinai. Besides the annual illnesses, Kangmei had been sheltered from discomfort. She did not know what it felt like to be whipped by someone who was supposed to love you.

The Woman was a diviner. The worst she could do was scare Kangmei. Hawk a false fortune that showed her a future not so soft and spoilt. He hadn't been intending to enact his plan—only entertaining it—but his bad mood had shifted into something cruel.

Mind made up, he said, "Come on, Kangmei, you can play with the cats whenever. Why don't we go out around the city?" He shooed a dirty white cat off the garden patch with his foot. "Go on. Get out," he said, watching as it sulked and slunk out of the compound entrance.

She blinked up at him, frowned. "It's not whenever. It's only when Mama and Baba and Nǎinai are all gone. You know they don't like them hanging around." She paused to dust off cat hairs from her blouse. "I like how warm they are. It's been so cold this winter."

He heaved a sigh. "Kangmei, please. I want to go out. Come on. I'll buy you something from the market," he said, wriggling around in his pocket to find a creased rénmínbì that he'd picked up off the street. He had been saving it for a special occasion. He straightened it out and held it up. The smiling, red-inked face of Liáng Jūn beamed down at Kangmei. She sat up, alert.

"Okay," she gasped, excited, "we can go." She hastily waved the other cats out. "Sorry, sorry, māo mī, another time," she murmured under her breath as they yowled at the loss.

The siblings walked silently past the courtyard to the entrance. Long strings meant for drying laundry fluttered in the wind, waiting for use in the warmer months. Kangmei's breath was uneven and quick as she kept pace with him. He was hitting his growth spurt—the bones in his spine ached as he slept—and now he could see the whole crown of his sister's head, could rest his elbow on it.

"Weihong?"

"Hmm?"

"Where are we going?"

"Somewhere I heard some kids at school talking about."

"But we're going to the market after, right?"

"Yes, Kangmei, you'll get your dumplings after," he said.

"Okay," she said, sounding pleased. She grabbed hold of his hand, which surprised him enough that he almost jerked it away. His arm tensed, but he didn't let go. They continued walking through Ānshān, skirting around the steelworks where their father worked.

They entered the part of town their mother warned them off of. It was where the shantytowns were: a notorious haunt for pickpockets and street urchins. The walls here were so dirty—pitch-black—that, despite the early hour, it seemed as if the two of them had wandered into a pocket of night. This area was home to the black market, and the few streetlamps cast their glow upon a seething mass of people, clustered around rickety tables with wares that Weihong had not seen for years. But this was not where they were going. Kangmei's hand grew clammy from her tight grasp, and she began to inch closer to Weihong. Before they turned the corner, Weihong saw a streak of white dart past them. Another stray cat, he thought, but the bright glimmer of fur was the same shade as the hare from the Recalling Bitterness meeting. That bizarre dream came roaring back, making him stumble, and he caught himself against the wall.

"Are you okay, gē?" Kangmei asked.

He nodded shakily, collecting himself. Something was sinking in his belly: a hot ball of lead that he recognized as panic, as a warning. They could still turn back and go home. But another part of him urged him to follow the white creature to its destination, and it was this part that possessed his body like a marionette, pressing him onward through the streets until they turned into an alley.

At the far side of the alley sat a woman. When she looked up at them, Kangmei squeaked and hid behind his leg. The woman's right eye was normal, dark and slow-blinking, but her left eye, hidden by a sweep of wiry hair, was blind. It was blue and glassy like curdled milk. Surrounding her was an air of rough, rotten magic.

Nine

Weihong

1966: Fifty-One Years Before Reunion

Ānshān, Liáoníng Province

THERE WAS A LARGE MYTHOS surrounding the Woman in the Alley. Weihong had gathered all the stories about her that he could. He was a collector. Living in a decade of poverty, he was forced to collect intangible things: the views from the window as the light darkened from yellow to amber; the different smells of their apartment, which changed and wafted depending on whether his mother and grandmother were cooking or cleaning or brewing herbal remedies; the textures of his life: the plush of his quilt, the sudsy damp of clean clothes on the line, the stiffness of a newly patched jacket; and stories. Weihong gathered stories like Kangmei did strays.

His fascination with the Woman in the Alley began with an overheard conversation between three red boys on the steps after school. They said that she was supposed to be dead, that the Party had tried to kill her multiple times, multiple ways: a bullet, a knife, a broken neck, a forged suicide. But she always came back: each time less human, bearing the scars of the previous attempts. They said that she was the consort of a demon priest before he cast her out of hell and into the mortal world, but that he remained attached to her, lingering around her like a miasma, and this was how she survived. In the right light, they whispered, you might even catch a glimpse of him, his third eye and canine teeth the fodder of nightmares.

On Sunday mornings, Nǎinai would bring Weihong and Kangmei to the produce market with her. While Nǎinai would have Kangmei beg clerks for pork discards, Weihong's job was to stand in the longest line—the egg line—and try his luck there. He gathered his best stories there, slinking underfoot beyond the notice of the adults. Weihong's most consistent sources were the jabbering Aunties, whose stiff collars bristled with excitement when they came across a particularly succulent piece of gossip.

From the Ānshān Aunties Weihong learned that the Woman in the Alley lurked in an offshoot of the black market, which some of them professed to have visited to acquire non-rationed goods. One of them claimed that she had been walking by the infamous alley when she saw the Woman levitating a man against the wall, peeling his screaming spirit from his body. Another Auntie scoffed at this and said that the Woman's method was well known to be sticking her fingers inside of your ears to read your thoughts like tea leaves. Not just your thoughts, either, but your past, present, and future, because for the Woman, all of it was happening at once. Around the market, the older vendors spoke of her as a girl, a child like him, before she became the subject of legend. In one version of the story—snatched from an eavesdropped conversation between the vegetable vendor and the butcher—she was from the countryside, born outside of marriage.

In her village, she was raised solely by her ostracized mother, and the mother-daughter pair spent most of their time in the wild, finding refuge in caves, only entering the village to purchase or trade for necessities. The villagers called her Squash because of her rippled cheeks, striated with red streaks and pockmarks. She was often the target of mockery by the village boys. It was said that her powers were awakened in desperation when three boys cornered her in the caves, their heavy weight pinning her down, their knees against her ribs, their hands tearing at her trousers. In the end, she killed them all. The vegetable vendor ended his story, saying, "Her magic comes from that pain. You can't cultivate seer magic on joy."

Weihong heard a different story between the butcher and the fishmonger. The fishmonger dismissed the vegetable vendor's claims with a laugh. "He said that?" The large man with snow-white hair chortled, bringing his cleaver down on a flapping fish's neck. "He's still fresh, he wouldn't know, but that girl's been here from the start. An Ānshān street urchin. But he was right about her sight." The fishmonger worked the edge of his blade against the fish's silver scales, which rained upon his skin, sticking to his thick arms in a spray of chrome. "That brand of magic feeds off misery, just like the old gods."

The red children gathered in cliques after school before their club meetings, and the Woman in the Alley was frequently invoked as a dare. Those who claimed they'd seen her told tall tales. Lies, Weihong was certain. Like Kangmei, they lived cowardly, coddled lives. One girl said that the Woman had given her a series of dates portending the deaths of everyone in her family, down to the minute.

The longer Weihong listened, the more he realized that the only similarity between these accounts was their disparity. The only testimonies Weihong truly believed were scared confessions, whispered to a confidant. These people claimed that the Woman had appeared to them in visions, where they would see her in all the faces around them: their wife's, their mother's, the vendors'. Finally, she would arrive outside their window for several nights, as if drawn to their future pain, and when confronted, would give them directions to her alley. These people always went, driven mad by curiosity.

Most people who went to the alley arrived only to find it empty, or else overrun by children eager to prove their daring, but no Woman. Weihong had a theory that she only appeared to those destined for true anguish. And so he was expecting nothing—at most, a false fortune-teller making money off myths. Seeing her here before him, reeking of magic, sent a feeling of damnation arcing through his body.

She had the beginnings of a smile that seemed to say, *Found me, didn't you?* And despite all the stories he had gathered, he had the distinct feeling that she knew more about him than he did her.

"Come to get your fortune read?" she asked. "I don't think you'll like it," she added offhandedly. Weihong felt that she must have seen this moment before. Lived it a hundred times, even if for him it was all happening for the first time.

"*Gē*," Kangmei whined, "let's go home. I'm scared." Then, more urgently, "*Gē*, I can't move."

Weihong tried to turn back, but he, too, was stuck.

"You can come forward. But not backwards. Though it's all the same thing in the end." The Woman shrugged.

Kangmei began to cry, the sobs coming up quietly from the back of her throat.

"Sorry, little one," the Woman said, sounding truly apologetic, "but I'm afraid this won't be the most painful moment of your life."

The Woman walked up to them, and she put a hand on Kangmei's arm. "Breathe, little one. It'll pass."

The Woman's eyes met Weihong's—a searing, all-consuming blue—and he felt his soul fold up and out of existence, ripped from his body and tugged and squeezed in all directions like he was being drawn and quartered, then dropped through an oculus, a wound in the fabric of space-time. It was blue all the way down, a watery blueness as he tumbled and rotated in every direction, a world-bending dizziness swirling behind his eyes. He kept sliding, unable to find purchase, pulled by a current of fate—drowning in it, like a twig in a rapid.

Then there was stillness. Then there was the peat.

HE LANDED ON HIS FEET hard enough that his knees buckled and the wind was knocked out of him. When he stood up, he was no longer in the alley but in some other world, an endless fog-clouded bog. It was how he envisioned the Fathomless Morass in his war games. He felt the Woman's presence, tugging at him, urging him to move his feet as they sank in the mud. He could not see her, but he could sense her fluttering at the edges of his mind.

His hearing grew faint, replaced by his racing heartbeat. Around him: flat, liquid topography, speckled with islands of brown-green fenland.

He could feel the bog shifting around him. It was a living, divine landscape: an annex for lost souls—neither alive nor dead—and possible realities, that grew from the netherworld, Dìyù. The Woman told him this. He could not tell if they were sharing one mind or if she was only haunting his; whatever the case, their thoughts were now entangled.

The Woman was a steady guide. She had been his ticket into this half-world, and she would be his ticket out. There was an assuredness that Weihong knew was hers, a fear that he knew was his. The Woman pointed him on a narrow path through the grassy inlands and the silver mirrored pools of stagnant water. He walked the path for several yards.

He kept his eyes trained on his steps, one foot in front of the other. On the surface of the ponds were wisps of bubbles—the kind that tadpoles or small fish made. When he kneeled to investigate, he realized with a shock that there were faces in the water. He leaned over to study one, and he recognized the chapped lips of his mother, only her face was more sallow and less wrinkled, and her eyes were open but unseeing, the pupils constricted and muted.

Unconsciously, his hand began to reach for her shoulder, as if to shake her from her stupor.

Don't do that, the Woman's voice snapped with the tone of an adult scolding a toddler. Weihong was startled by her voice. How close it was. How it pressed inside his right ear. He was tempted to ignore her for her tone alone. He was a month away from fourteen, practically an adult.

He swore he could hear the Woman's amused scoff echoing in his head.

Come along now, the Woman's voice chimed impatiently, *no time for dallying. Don't disturb the bog bodies.*

He followed her directions again, though he now noted the different faces lingering under the surface. Some, he knew. Some, he did not but instinctively felt he would. Some, he would even love. And some were just passersby—lives that touched his for a fleeting second, people whose shoulders he would brush on the street, but their pools seemed to feed into whole other worlds. Each body brought with it brief flashes of his encounters with them in multiple possible realities.

We don't have much time, the Woman chided, *stop sightseeing and make haste.*

He wanted to ignore her voice, but curiosity got the best of him. *Where are we? Did you create this world? Where are we going?*

She ignored his first two questions. *The most painful moment of your existence. I thought you knew that. I've seen you, gathering all those stories about me like a bird about to nest.*

He resisted the urge to ask her which of them were true.

Well, it wasn't the Aunties' stories. Aunties are almost always liars. Gossip-mongering busybodies and false soothsayers.

Is that some fact of life?

No, boy, that was a joke. He heard her chuckle to herself. *There it is*, the Woman's voice said. *That pool is yours.*

He felt her turn his head toward a pond in the distance. It seemed to glint red from afar like a mirage, setting itself apart from the infinite bog, which stretched heathery into the distance, like a peat sea.

Hurry, the Woman urged. He had half a mind to ignore her and drag his heels. Why was he going along with this? He could wander until she grew fed up with him and sent him back. Perhaps it was better to leave this place and return to his life with no warning hanging over his head. And yet, it hung. Like an apple waiting to be picked, blood fat and enticing, mere meters in front of him. So he began to walk toward the pool. Then he ran.

His heels kicked mud up the back of his trousers, and he was running so quick on the spongy turf that the green and gray of the world blurred.

At the lapping borders of his pond, he stopped and panted to catch his breath, his hands on his knees. His lungs strained for air in wheezy breaths. At the edge of the water sprouted a wildfire bed of spider lilies, their thin scarlet petals the only true color in the morass. He looked into the pool, then recoiled.

What is that?

Boy, it's you, can't you recognize yourself?

Inside the water was him at thirteen, only wrong and horrific, in the midst of a violent metamorphosis. There was something growing inside of him, blossoming from his stomach. Like an unborn child, it was the size of a winter melon, and lay upside down, curled around itself. Weihong could see it through the translucent, stretched skin of his belly.

The thing had two horns, a head of wild hair growing from its scalp, and three eyes, which were closed. Its small hands were curled to its chest, and they each had three fingers. The eyes twitched, as if sensing Weihong there, revealing yellow irises, rolled back in slumber. Its mouth was slightly open, drooling, and Weihong could see its full set of teeth: serrated and predatory.

That's not me. What kind of sick trick is this? I thought you were supposed to show me the most painful moment in my life.

What, a seer can't deviate?

His fists curled until his nails left bleeding crescent marks in his palm. Surely, this was not him.

A trick, he repeated, trying to convince himself.

It's gestating, she continued with the congratulatory tone of the Aunties whenever there was a newly pregnant mother in town. *I'd say forty years until it's hatched. Give or take. Divine things take time to form. Gods don't pay mind to the snapshots of human lifetimes.* He felt her presence too close to him now, probing and examining him. *You, however, could* almost *pass as human. Ten-month gestation. Mostly normal birth. The full mouth of teeth gave everyone pause, I'm sure. Yes, that mother of yours did a good job hiding you.*

What did his mother have to do with all of this?

Well, you could ask her. If you remember this. But you won't. Not really. Flashes, if you're lucky. A sense of foreboding and immortality that you'll chalk up to regular adolescence. A shame. You came all this way. But there's divine qì at work against you, within you. And I'm just a guide with a drop of power to the gods' reservoir.

His thoughts were a jumble. *It's a trick it's a trick trick trick*. But he was still trying to decipher what he was seeing. Was this thing truly a part of him or some cancerous tumor? A curse from the Woman?

It's your whole self, your inheritance, both halves—like a forked tongue. The seer sounded baffled that he hadn't grasped this yet. *In forty years, once your other half matures, that's when the trouble starts. It'll hurt everyone you love. It'll destroy your life.*

How? How will it hurt everyone? Tell me, he pleaded.

Time's up, Weihong. I'll be seeing you. But for now you need to—

Ten

Weihong

1966: Fifty-One Years Before Reunion

Ānshān, Liáoníng Province

WEIHONG WOKE UP.

He had landed on all fours, dropped back into the mortal world with no warning. Immediately, he dry-heaved the contents of his stomach until a trickle of acid came up. It froze as it dribbled down his chin. His hands grew numb from clutching at the cement, fingertips chafing under the grit as he tried to ground himself. Nearby, Kangmei was sitting against the wall, holding her knees and rocking back and forth. Her eyes darted from him to the wall in front of her, spinning, unfocused and wild. They had resurfaced too quickly. A few minutes passed by as their breath evened out. Weihong checked his trousers, his shoes, but they were clean of mud. There was no physical evidence of where they'd just been.

Only the two of them remained in the alley. There was no trace of the Woman.

"What did you see?" Weihong asked.

She looked up at him. "She told me I can't tell you."

"Was it the most painful moment of your life?"

She nodded slowly, like her head was too heavy to hold on her neck.

"You can remember it?"

"You can't?"

"No." He frowned. "Not exactly."

A pause, then, "Lucky," she said. Her voice broke in the middle of the word.

Weihong ran his hands through his hair and tugged hard at the tangles. Slammed his fists against his temples. Already the last minutes of his time in the morass were fading from his memory. From the shock or the brute barotrauma, he didn't know. Just a moment ago, the bogland was so real. There was the texture of mud and the soreness of his muscles. But now, when he prodded at the memory, it dissolved, puddling in his mind. Snatches remained, but the crux was lost.

"What are you doing?" Kangmei asked.

Weihong lifted his head. He hadn't realized that he'd pulled out two small clumps of hair, the tendrils dangling loosely from his hands. He let them go, watching as they fell on the ground. He stared at them like they were animal entrails and he was a haruspex—if he looked at them long enough, perhaps he could divine the memories from the pattern they made.

"I'm trying to remember."

"Why would you want that?"

"It's worse. Not knowing," he said. Kangmei looked skeptical.

"It's like . . ." He paused, thinking of a way to explain. "It's like how we go to the photo studio once a year to take a family portrait. And we don't know what it'll look like until a week later. It's like that. Like there's some dark shape in the background, but I can't see it until it gets developed. But I know it's there. Even now, I know it's there."

Kangmei asked, "What do you think it is?"

"I don't know. I just know it's bad. And it's going to cause a lot of pain."

Kangmei chewed on her lip. "I think I'd like that better. I keep seeing it. I see it but I don't think it's me because I wouldn't do that."

Weihong shook his head. He'd rather know than be wary for a lifetime, to have that dark shape hanging over his head like an executioner's blade, not knowing what form the prophecy would finally take. Kangmei, at least, could prepare. He began to check himself again for a scarlet spider-lily petal, for a strand of yellow-green fen grass, for a trace of damp acidity on his upper lip from the fog. Again, nothing.

"Was it a dream?" he mused.

"It was real, Weihong. It was the realest moment of my life." Kangmei's voice was firm. For a moment, when Weihong looked at her, he did not see an eight-year-old girl but someone older. There was a haunted quality to the set of her chin that he had only seen in the elders at Recalling Bitterness meetings. Even if he forgot what had happened, Kangmei could not. This moment was a tether, binding them together.

Her lip wobbled, and she was a child once more. "I want Ma," Kangmei said.

Weihong crawled to sit on his knees in front of her.

"You can't tell Ma. We can't tell anyone," he said.

"Why? So you won't get in trouble?"

"No," he said instinctively, though she wasn't wrong, "you know why. Who would believe us? If we told anyone, people would call us mad pagans. We'd be putting our whole family in danger."

Kangmei looked up at the patch of sky between the two buildings that bordered the alley. She leaned her head against the brick of the wall behind her. She began to bang her head against it. Softly at first, then with increasing force.

"Stop that," he said, alarmed. He held her head still between his two palms. "Kangmei, look at me. Do you understand?"

She glared at him. He let his hands drop back to his sides. "Yes, Weihong. I saw things. I'm not stupid. I just wish—"

"What?" he asked.

"I wish it didn't happen, even though I know it was going to no matter what. I wish I could tell Ma or Ba so you could be punished for it. I wish I could hurt you. I wish we could go back to an hour ago when I was just happy my gē wanted to spend time with me. I wish—" She paused to catch her breath, and her words dissolved into tears.

Weihong slumped. She had seen it too. In every lifetime, they had come to the Woman in the Alley. Always because of his spite. Their journey to limbo was the knot at the center of their realities: all paths led there, and all paths diverged from there.

"I wish that too," Weihong said.

"You haven't even said sorry."

"Of course I'm sorry," he said, his brows wrinkling. How did she not know that?

"You didn't say it."

"I'm sorry. I am so sorry, Kangmei."

"I know," Kangmei said weakly, "I just wanted to hear it." Awkwardly, Weihong put his arms around her and rubbed circles on her back, like their mother did when they were upset. At first, she flinched from his embrace, but slowly she relented, settling her face into his shoulder.

They sat like that for what felt like hours. The winter day darkened into a purple afternoon, threatening to spill over into night. Kangmei's tears subsided into sniffles.

"I know why you did it. Because of Ba." Her voice was muffled, her face still buried in his coat.

Weihong stiffened at the invocation of their father.

"I don't think it's right," she said, "and neither does Nǎinai. When Ba comes back like"—she paused, searching for a word that captured the barbaric transformation that báijiǔ caused—"like that," she finished weakly. "We sit in the courtyard, and we talk about how we don't think it's right what he does to you."

Then, she added, "I didn't ask for it. To be his favorite. I don't know why I am. I'd give it to you if I could."

Guilt burst in his stomach, threatening to overflow like bile.

"Don't be silly. That's not why I did it."

She shot him a weary look. "Don't lie to me. It's not right. But it's not my fault."

He blinked. When had his sister hatched into a person without him noticing? Somehow Weihong had overlooked Kangmei's maturity. Kangmei, the baby. Kangmei, whose sympathy magnified his shame.

"Neither of us can make it right, can we?" he asked.

There was a saying among the Aunties: One's family is not a brief tempest but a lifetime of mist. A constant fog, whose wet texture of hurt would always be there.

"We're the only ones who can understand," Kangmei said.

Weihong straightened his aching knees to stand. He offered a hand to her. "Let's go home. We can get dumplings on the way."

IT HAD BEEN A WEEK since the alley. Mother seemed surprised by the newfound closeness between the two siblings. She'd taken to looking at Weihong with softness, as if he'd done something deserving of it. It was a look that said, *That's my boy, I raised him well*. He could not bear to see it.

At school, Weihong sat in the classroom. His mind wandered. How was he expected to continue with his life as if nothing was amiss? As if he had not skimmed the borders of a divine plane? The quotidian routine of breakfast, school, lunch, school, and homework felt insignificant and wrong. He stared at the green chalkboard behind his teacher's head until the surface of it rippled, grew murky with a dark, underwater shape.

The sound of the class packing up their books for the end of the school day jostled him awake. The world solidified. Weihong shuffled his empty notebooks into his bag. In the hallway, his friends asked if he wanted to play war games. He declined. He said he had to help Mother with errands. While he was within their sight, he walked slowly toward his apartment. When he turned around and saw that they were gone, he doubled back and began to make his way to the black market. Every day for the past week after school, Weihong had made this pilgrimage.

Small buds dotted the trees of the city streets, harkening the arrival of spring. The weather was warming slowly, almost imperceptibly. He pulled the edges of his hat down until it rested on his eyelashes, making himself smaller and less noticeable. He wove through the pedestrians and the stalls, which sold everything from highly coveted bags of white rice to gold-encrusted family antiques deemed too dangerous to possess. He slipped past whiffs of conversations between haggling buyers and vendors as he wound his way through the labyrinthine streets toward the alley.

He did not know what he would do if he saw the Woman again. Could he barter with her over his fate? Could he see it again, just one more time? Could he receive another destiny, like an unhappy customer with a damaged product? Could he escape it? *It* was unclear. *It* was a dark outline of dread: a latent image soaking in its chemical bath under the darkroom's red light for the next forty years. The subject a glaring absence that made Weihong's chest tighten every time he thought of it.

The alley was empty. There was a scent of ammonia that hadn't been there the day before. Weihong followed it, but it was just an alley cat in the trash, its hackles raised at the intrusion. He was reminded of the warning he should've heeded, that animal blur of white. But he knew now that there was no use in regret. Weihong ignored the cat and began his ritual. He took off his glove and ran his hand along the walls of the compounds that comprised the alley. His fingertips grazed every brick, every crack. He didn't know what he was looking for. A hint of the divine. A sizzle of acidity. Something that rang different from the banal fabric of reality. He worked his way up from the bottom row of bricks until he could no longer reach. Then he repeated his actions on the other side. It got dark. His fingers grew numb. No one had come by in the time he had been there.

He heard a loud *bang* that made him jump. It was one of the building's windows slamming shut, a glimpse of its owner's wiry hair disappearing from sight. The cat, startled, ran out of the alley, its belly close to the ground. Weihong looked back to the window. It was the farthest one down the alley. Perhaps its owner had seen something. Tomorrow, he resolved, he would go into the compound, knock on the apartment door, and ask if they knew anything about the Woman. If they knew what hours she kept, when she might return.

When he returned the next day, the window was somehow gone, bricked up.

PART II

Eleven

Ming
1924: Ninety-Three Years Before Reunion
Rural Manchuria

IN THE EARLY MORNING OF the third day of the third lunar month—the peach month—the midwife pulled a child from the small hips of the grain farmer's wife. The neighbors, kept up by the screams of labor, thanked their gods and went to sleep for the few meager hours before dawn.

Outside, the new father sat on the steps of the mudbrick and earth house, smoking a pipe, waiting for the bloody ordeal to be over so he could welcome his son into the world. Several of the town's fortune-tellers had divined from his and his wife's horoscopes that their union would be blessed with a boy. For the past nine months, his wife had followed all of the physician's advice: avoiding spicy foods and taking a daily broth of Siberian motherwort and white peony. They trusted the physician. After all, hadn't his wife just given birth to a healthy, plump baby boy a few months ago? A son would help the grain farmer during harvest season and take over his lands when he became too brittle to sow them himself.

They had done everything right. They'd prayed daily until their knees bruised at Guānyīn's altar. All the portents—the divinations, the egg shape of the bulging belly, round as a kettle at the bottom and slim at the top—had pointed to a boy. So, the slit between the baby's legs was a damnation, and when the new mother laid eyes upon it, she muttered an "*Āiyā*" and refused to hold the girl. It was the midwife the child saw first in this world, her disappointed parents second.

The midwife wetted a rag from the water vat and cleaned the blood from the girl's body under the light of the bean-oil lamp then wrapped her in cotton.

"She's a beautiful child," the midwife said, "she takes after you."

The mother had been a town beauty back in her day. Stiffly, she held out her arms to receive her daughter.

"She's lovely," the midwife added, stroking the full head of dark hair.

"Then she will make a good wife," the mother said with a sniff.

The next day, it was arranged that the child would marry the newborn son of the physician. She was no longer their problem. Born and bridalled, as they say.

Twelve

Ming

1929: Eighty-Eight Years Before Reunion
Rural Manchuria

THERE WAS ONLY ONE SUMMER left before they would have to start school. It was the fifth summer of their lives, and they were spending it on the riverbank, catching dragonflies. Their quick arms snatched the wings before the insects' kaleidoscopic eyes noticed them. Ming was very good at the game, but she always shared her winnings with Fei, her betrothed. This went for mushrooms when they were sent to dig in the loam, kindling from the nearby forest, and slippery catches from the river.

Their thin cotton shirts, shoes, and willow baskets lay abandoned on the shore. In the stream, they stuck to the shallows, their trousers rolled up to their knees, the hems damp. They'd squat in the reeds and pounce when they saw the dragonflies land. Fei laughingly dared Ming to eat one, so she did, her teeth sinking into its body, her smile leaking its green blood.

The sun had started setting earlier—a warning of fall—so the children abandoned their prey, wading back to the shore for their original task. They collected their baskets and began to fill them with shrimp and small fish, whose silver bodies reflected little lines of light in the brown water. They worked in silence. Ming raked her hands through the grasses, grabbing at writhing creatures. Fei had a small net his mother had woven, and he was seining it through the deeper waters, his trousers more than half damp now.

The sky shifted into a rich summer blue. The sinking orange sun lengthened their silhouettes: two shadows swinging full baskets, walking back toward the village. Amidst the crickets and frogs, they padded along in a companionable quiet. Tonight, Ming's future mother-in-law, Fei's mother, would stew the shrimp in a broth and serve it with fresh-pulled flour noodles; she'd promised them this treat if they would gather the shrimp and some small fish to grind and garnish. Neither of them had tasted true salt in months: only the brackish minerals stuck to the scales of fish.

They returned to the house dry, the day's sweat washed clean off of them. Ming's long, damp hair was plaited, pooling in the small of her back. She had two mugwort branches tucked behind her ears to ward off mosquitoes.

"Back with the bounty?" Mother-in-law greeted them at the lit entrance of the physician's compound. The compound was a gray brick building made up of four outer walls and one circular main entrance. Half the compound was for the family, while the other half housed their clinic and apothecary.

Fei lifted his basket to show off his spoils, and his mother chuckled, running a hand through his hair as the children bounded past the door.

"Ming, you'll help me with the stew, won't you?" Mother-in-law asked.

"Yes, Zhou Āyí," she said. Zhou Āyí and Zhou Shūshu were their proper addresses, but Ming always thought of them as Mother-in-law and Father-in-law.

Ming put her basket in the corner of the kitchen, laying a piece of cotton over the top to keep out the flies and gnats. Her own mother pickled the best kills in brine to save them for Dìdi, her younger brother and the prized son. Mama had even done this with a succulent red apple Mother-in-law had gifted Ming last winter. Dìdi had teethed on that sour fruit. He was now two, born in the Year of the Rabbit, three years younger than she was.

"Should I do anything?" Fei asked.

"Go assist your father with his inventory so we can eat," Mother-in-law said, shooing him away. He crossed the courtyard into Father-in-law's apothecary.

In the kitchen, Ming and Mother-in-law boiled the shrimp, cut up leeks, and washed the narrow little fish. Ming descaled them into the stew, which had already been started, filled with the boiled and bled bones from the butcher. Even the physician's family could not afford to splurge on meat for their daily dinner. Noodles were a treat and only possible with flour from Ming's parents—a sign of goodwill between the two families.

Ming liked spending the evenings with her future in-laws. Mother-in-law would sneak her small treats: dates, candied ginger, a hard-boiled egg. After dinner, Father-in-law would steeple his hands under his chin and read aloud from what books he had: a medley of traditional Confucian texts and May Fourth books he'd had imported from the nearest city. Father-in-law was a scholarly looking man with neat hair and a pair of circular, wire-rimmed glasses. They left a permanent indent on his nose. A year ago, Father-in-law had started teaching Ming and Fei how to read.

Ming liked evenings at the compound more than evenings in her own house, where Mama would glare and grumble that Ming was selfishly taking food away from her growing Dìdi when she had another family she could eat with.

"Stop working and come eat," Mother-in-law called across the courtyard as they finished setting the table.

"*Wa*," Father-in-law exclaimed as he entered, "kàn qǐlái hěn hào chī—I'm salivating." The steam from the stew fogged his lenses, and he wiped them with his sleeve before giving his wife a smile.

"It's really the children you should be thanking," Mother-in-law said, nudging Ming's shoulder with her hip. "We'd be on the brink of malnutrition without them," she joked. Ming smiled down at her bowl. She had been alive for a series of good harvest years. Malnutrition and famine were not yet a part of her vocabulary.

Fei tore into his bowl ravenously, slurping up the noodles, spooning soup into his mouth. He tilted the dregs until they slid onto his tongue. The whole affair took five minutes, at which point he held out the dish to his mother.

"More?" he asked, the edges of his mouth stained wet with hunger.

Mother-in-law chortled but didn't hesitate to dole out a second serving. In the humidity of August, the combination of soup and the warmth of the soybean-oil lamp made Ming sweat. There was something delightful about the night's swelter—how it shrouded her like a quilt. Mother-in-law asked after Father-in-law's day, and he told them about his patients: an elderly woman who couldn't feel her feet, a newborn with two bumps on its head, a little girl with a trigger finger. They whiled away the evening like that.

There was nothing holy about the evening ritual. It was the simple act of stirring and slurping and storytelling. And yet, if Ming knew the meaning of the word *sacred*, she might've described it as such.

MING'S PARENTS' HOUSE WAS ONLY a lǐ away through the village, and after the meal she walked the familiar path guided by the lamplights that shone through paper window coverings. Most families were finishing dinner and preparing to retire to bed. The grain farmers lived at the outskirts of town beside the acres of wheat and sorghum fields. Ming slipped inside the door, hoping to escape notice. No such luck.

"Do you have anything for me today?" Mama asked, not looking up from her mending. She was sitting in wait at the table like a guard dog. Baba was already snoring heavily on the brick kang after a long day's work.

Ming presented her basket of shrimp and fish, which Mama took without a word.

"*Āiyā*, so little. What did you do all day?" she scolded. Ming bowed her head and apologized.

"Go to bed." Mama sent her off. "Useless slip of a girl," she muttered.

With flushed cheeks, Ming ducked inside the second room of the two-room house, only large enough for the kang that Dìdi was sleeping on and a hutch for storage. She lay down and curled around his small body, the baby fat on him supple. He had kicked off the summer quilt, and she rearranged it over the two of them. Between them, she and Mama shared only a face and a love for Dìdi.

In the market, she'd overheard the Aunties gossip about Mama—Ming's thin, reedy frame slipping underfoot through the throng of vendors and hawkers. The Aunties said that Mama was bitter because her feet had been broken and bound when she was too young, and she'd been weaned on pain, growing vinegar-hearted and full of rage. They said that Mama's father had pawned Mama off like a rusty antique to the homely grain farmer when he lost the family fortune.

They said that if Ming hadn't slid out of the womb the spitting image of Mama, Mama would've abandoned the baby girl in the reeds for the animals and said that it was stillborn. But Ming was undeniably Mama's. They said that the physician's family was very kind to feed the unwanted, half-starved girl promised to their son. They had questions about the betrothal though. *Surely the physician's son could make a better match? Wasn't it odd that the physician hadn't adopted the child yet?* Most daughters-in-law in the countryside were adopted by the betrothed's family at a month, a year. Ming was five and a half with no sign of an upcoming adoption. Was it the physician's progressive city education that made him ignore country customs? Stipulate that the girl should be raised with her birth family up until menstruation to guarantee she could give his son children? This was a bargain that begot only more bitterness on Mama's part. *He is cheating me out of years of food and warmth, more than Ming's dowry*, she told anyone who would listen.

Ming had begun spending days away from Mama when she was three, the year Dìdi was born. Like most of the other children she ran simple errands under the watchful eyes of the townspeople. If there were no errands to run, Baba would deposit her at the physician's house in the mornings, where she'd spend her days with Mother-in-law and Fei. Anything to get her out of the house while Mama was nursing Dìdi. Ming still did not know what "betrothed" meant, but Mother-in-law had explained it as her and Fei being bosom friends for life.

It was Ming who invented their game of collecting when they were four. It began at the riverbank when Mother-in-law was doing laundry. Ming's quick hands snagged tadpoles and lean fish straight from the water. At the end of the afternoon, when Ming showed Mother-in-law her full basket, Mother-in-law had exclaimed delightedly, called Ming her "clever little magpie," and promised to fry the fish in oil as crispy snacks.

Mother-in-law's reaction had sparked an idea inside Ming: a flicker that fanned into a flame. The next day, Ming and Fei went into the nearby woods, where Ming enlisted Fei to help her find wild herbs. She sought out medicinal herbs she remembered seeing in the compound. They were everywhere: drying in bunches in the kitchen, growing in the garden, ground in jars on the shelves of the apothecary. Fei, who'd been outdone at the river, excelled in the forest, having tagged along with his father on foraging trips.

When Ming went home that night, she presented Mama with a basket, teeming with the anemone yellow-orange blooms of safflower and the earthy roots and bark that Fei had pried up.

"What's this?" Mama asked, confused.

"Herbs. For a foot bath," Ming said shyly. She'd heard Father-in-law prescribe herbal soaks to his patients before.

Mama's face softened. Ming's heart swooped.

"I can get water?" Ming offered, but she did not wait for Mama's response, scampering through the door to the well outside. Ming filled up a small basin with the water and herbs, watching as Mama placed her bare, broken feet inside, sighing as the medicinal water lapped at her ankles. Mama's eyes fluttered closed in relief. With her face relaxed and free from pain, Mama looked young. Almost kind.

"Good?" Ming asked hesitantly.

"Yes," Mama said, "good, Ming." Mama's mouth crinkled into a half smile, which faltered and withdrew at Ming's face, split open in a beaming, hopeful expression. But Ming didn't notice, because in her head she was singing the words *good Ming*.

Ming continued to bring gifts to Mama—damp moss bandages and river eels—but after the first bath, Mama seemed immune to these gestures. Mama's face did not soften. Instead, it shuttered in a flat, blank expression.

Ming did not want to belong to Mama. She wanted to belong to Mother-in-law and Father-in-law. One day, she'd be bound to them by blood. It was what filled her thoughts as she blinked off to sleep. Dìdi rolled around and nestled his head in the crook of her shoulder, the heat of him spreading through her body.

"HAH!" FEI SHOUTED, TACKLING MING from the side. They landed in a heap of limbs and wild sorghum. He pinned her, her stomach on the ground, her shoulder blades under his bony, boyish knees.

"Empty your pockets, and I'll let you live."

"*Fei.*" Ming rolled her eyes. "I can't reach my pockets."

"My name isn't Fei. I am the Great Bandit of the Sorghum Fields. You will obey me, or I'll shoot you in the eye. *Bang!*" He mimed firing a shot into the sky. The stalks rustled as a summer breeze drifted by. He leveled his imaginary pistol at Ming, who defiantly turned around to stare down the length of his finger. At last, she looked away and sighed: a sign of her surrender.

Fei let up, and she grumbled as she emptied out the treasures she had with her: flat, smooth stones for skipping; a lint-covered piece of candied ginger; the abandoned shells of river mollusks, worn smooth by her anxious fingers. Fei gathered up his winnings, shoving them into his pockets gleefully, and popped the ginger into his mouth.

"Not fair," Ming complained, adjusting herself into a sitting position on the smothered sorghum. "Why couldn't we play bandits in the forest?"

He shot her an exasperated look. "You always win in the forest."

"That's not true!" she protested.

"I know when you're lying, Ming," he singsonged. Sometimes he put on airs because he was half a year older. Her *senior*, he'd taunt. He was right, though. She did always win in the forest. Whereas Fei's pale skin darkened only to the golden color of wheat in the summer, Ming turned a rich tan, able to blend in with the tones of the trees. On top of that, she was sneaky and sly, and Fei, his paleness as radiant as a ghost's, didn't stand a chance.

"Sore loser," she muttered under her breath, unaware of the irony. She dusted herself off and began to make her way out of their killing field. Fei, who liked winning more than anything, was still gloating over his victory, examining the shells, turning them this way and that in the sunlight.

"Don't be mad, Ming," he said, running to catch up with quick, deliberate strides.

"I'm not mad," she sniffed.

"*Mi-ng*," he dragged out her name, "want to go swimming?" He offered this as a truce. She turned away as a bitterness too large for her body washed over her. Ming didn't own many things, and what she did own could never be described as pretty. There was no jewelry, no jade stones strung on red string, no stiff-collared silk blouses. Nothing except those shells. Mothers who loved their daughters gave them trinkets, then taught them how to make themselves as pretty as their ornaments.

"I don't swim with stealers," Ming said. Fei looked crestfallen.

Ming, unsure why she felt guilty, relented after a few minutes of spiteful silence. "Fine. We can swim," she said.

"We don't have to," he said softly.

Fei was a spoiled, sensitive boy, but Ming still felt a pang at his expression. In these early, amorphous years—when memory had just begun to stick—Ming thought of her and Fei as One Being: a two-headed snake. Perhaps age would split them into separate entities, but Ming believed they would still echo and enfold each other, like stacked soup spoons.

"You can stay here if you want. *I'm* going to the river," she declared, and started making her way out of the maze of stalks. Fei, with the beginnings of a smile sprouting on his face, followed her.

The day was punctuated by a scorching heat, and the two kicked up a cloud of dry dust in their wake. It was, Ming grudgingly admitted, a perfect day to swim. Along the riverbank, there were housewives with washboards and other village children, who'd had the same idea as them. By silent agreement, Ming and Fei made their way to an abandoned stretch of shoreline.

Ming, stripping down to her underwear, plunged headfirst into the cold water. Fei waded in slowly—a grimace giving away his discomfort. She laughed at him, smoothing away the wet hair pasted to her forehead.

"You're such a baby," she teased.

"I'm older than *you*," Fei said, affronted. To prove his courage, he sank into the water and emerged in front of her, his eyes hovering above the surface, reptilian. She shrieked and sent a drenching splash in his direction, then kicked herself into deeper waters before he could retaliate. Behind her, she heard him sputtering and coughing. Underwater, the only thing that tethered her to the surface was the line of mercurial bubbles that escaped from her lips. They floated upward, ensnaring a fingerling of a fish and sending it spinning.

The sun warmed her rippled, browning skin. Her toes grazed the surface of a turtle's shell—the hardness of it coated in a soft, algae-like hair. She did not want to go home. She did not want to start school. She only wanted to stay in the river forever, until her body was pruned and preserved.

Thirteen

Ming

1929: Eighty-Eight Years Before Reunion
Rural Manchuria

MING WAS SURPRISED BY HOW quickly her skin settled back into a pallor from the weeks cooped up in the classroom. Both the fields and the forest had changed their colors with her, donning different clothes for the new season. As Ming and Fei raced through the trees—their padded cotton jackets discarded, tied around a trunk to let them sweat freely—the woods seemed pithed of their summer life, all the plants half-dead. Some trees had begun to leak amber-red sap, bleeding into the ground.

Ming's thin soles skimmed the underwood, always several steps ahead of Fei. The other schoolchildren knew not to play games of speed with Ming, who trounced them soundly each time. Springy and surefooted, Ming thought that she was made for running—that if she ran off a cliffside, her feet would carry her through the air until it might be called flying. She stopped abruptly. Fei did his best not to crash into her.

"What's wrong?" he asked, panting from the exertion. She silently pointed out what had caught her eye: a distant rabbit with white fur. It seemed aware of the children's presence and tipped its head to the side as if appraising them. The rabbit had a pair of searing red eyes, the color of a spider lily. Its whiskers twitched in such a way that it looked as if its mouth were spreading in a one-sided smile.

"We should catch it," Ming whispered.

"Are you crazy?" Fei said. "You think you can catch up to a rabbit?"

Ming sniffed. Earlier that fall, she'd caught a wild pheasant.

"Don't you want rabbit stew?" she asked, knowing his mother made an excellent rabbit broth. Fei's stomach let out a low, traitorous grumble at the thought, and Ming grinned. The rabbit sat back on its haunches, daring them to follow as Ming's calves tensed.

They both set off at once—a ribbon of color winding through the woods, leaving Fei far behind. Down they went: down the wooded alley, the rabbit hole, down, down, down, where mere mortals could not keep pace.

It was a hare. Ming could tell now by how wiry and long its limbs were, how its pupils were not a soft, liquid black but an unsettling, beady pink. It stopped at the base of a tree, skittering across the undergrowth.

Cornered, Ming thought, pleased with herself. She stumbled to a halt as she considered which way the hare might go, preparing her legs to lunge. But as she watched, the fear in the hare's eyes receded, replaced by a look that took Ming aback.

The switch was so quick, Ming barely had time to react. She felt the hair on the back of her neck rise. Her chest grew tight. The hare rose on its hind legs and underwent a transformation. Its body stretched, limbs lengthening until it was unsettlingly large, larger than Ming. Behind its ears, two small horns spiraled upward, branching out into the full antlers of a stag.

What is that? Ming thought as she faltered and stepped back. *Wake up!* she shouted at herself, but she knew better: all her waking senses were magnified by her fear.

The hare seemed amused. It smiled, revealing human teeth that resembled the yellow, rotting, gap-toothed grins of the town elders. It cocked its head. Left, then right. Then it charged at her.

In a panic, Ming stumbled and fell. She could do nothing but hold out her right hand to keep the approaching antlers from spearing her face. At the last minute the hare turned away, but one of its antlers swiped Ming's palm, and the stunning pain of the sharp curve tearing through her flesh made her gasp and cradle her hand to her chest as she pitched backward. Lying with her head on the forest floor, she heard the quick feet of the hare as it bounded away.

She did not know how long she lay there, sucking in quick breaths to quell her panic, clutching her right hand to stanch the blood. She could see the dark-red flesh inside the raw gash. She thought she saw the glint of white bone. Her vision grew dim at the edges. She felt tears pricking at her eyes, her head vacant except for the scream of dizzying pain—so loud, she felt like it could go on for decades.

At some point, Fei appeared, his face a mask of concern. "You're hurt," he said, looking down at her. Dumbly, she let him sit her up and examine her hand.

"Did you fall on something?" he asked, puzzled.

"No, it was the rabbit," she said. Her voice sounded tinny and distant to her ears.

"Did it bite you?" He squinted at the wound and blanched. He pulled out a handkerchief and used it to curtail the bleeding.

"It had horns. Like deer antlers. It charged at me."

He frowned. "Stop playing, it's not funny. What really happened? You can tell me."

"I'm not playing. It was horrible," she snapped. She stopped shaking and glared at him. How could Fei not believe her?

"We should get you to baba. He'll know what to do," he said, mostly to himself.

"I'm not playing. You can believe me or not. It was a hare with horns, and its horn hurt my hand. How else could a rabbit hurt me?" She held up her gored, dirty palm to him as evidence, and he swallowed. He adjusted the handkerchief, tied it tighter, and offered her his hand to help her up.

"We should get you to baba," he repeated.

"Fine, don't believe me," she spat through gritted teeth and stood up awkwardly, refusing his hand.

WHEN THEY GOT BACK TO the physician's compound, there was only a wisp of daylight left. Under the dim light of dusk, Fei's mother greeted them cheerfully. Her expression morphed into one of horror as they reached the lit entry. Ming, bloody and woozy, winced as the physician's wife patted her down, checking for injuries, exclaiming soft *āiyā*s over her hand. She unwound the bandage Fei had put on.

"What happened? We'll have Shūshu look at it now, hǎo ma? Does it hurt badly?"

"Āyí, I'm okay. Please don't get Shūshu," Ming tried to reassure her but flinched when Mother-in-law pried her bad hand open. The torn skin stretched taut around the edges.

"I can't send you back home like this," Mother-in-law fretted, twisting her fingers. "Érzi, go get your ba. I think he's still at the apothecary."

"Yes, Ma," Fei said, and dashed away before Ming could protest.

"We'll wash it out," Mother-in-law said, leading Ming by the wrist to the water vat. When Fei and Father-in-law returned, Ming's wound was cleaned and leaking fresh blood. Her hand was spread in the center of the kitchen table.

Father-in-law sat down, setting a box of medical supplies beside him. He nudged his glasses up the bridge of his nose as he examined Ming's palm, turning and bending it this way and that. At last, he smiled and patted her arm.

"You'll be all right. It'll only be trouble if it gets infected, but I'll give you some salve and bandages for it. I can help you change it until its healed. Fei, can you fetch the Jīnchuāng ointment?"

While Father-in-law dressed and packed the wound, Mother-in-law flitted nervously around the room. She inspected his handiwork when he was done, tightening the knot of the bandage, asking Ming if she still felt the pang of it.

"No, Āyí. It doesn't hurt anymore," Ming lied, hissing through her teeth. Mother-in-law fetched a concoction that she said would help the pain. Ming downed it and winced at the bitter taste.

"You need to be careful playing outside," she said, her fingers still cradling Ming's hand, "*both* of you."

"Mama, it wasn't our fault. Ming says a wild animal did it."

"A *wild animal*," Mother-in-law echoed, aghast. "What kind of animal was it?"

"It was a rabbit," Ming said. "A hare," Ming corrected herself, "with horns on its head like deer antlers."

The silence that followed had its own resonance. Father-in-law looked thoughtful behind his glasses, which was more than Ming could hope for. She knew it was outrageous. But it was true too. She had the antler wound to prove it. Fei and his mother's faces bore twin expressions of disbelief. Ming looked down at her feet, frustrated. Why would she lie to them when her palm still throbbed with the evidence? When her mind kept replaying that transformation?

"You're sure it was a hare?" Father-in-law asked.

Under her breath, Mother-in-law said, "Don't indulge their game."

But Father-in-law had already gotten up to go into the study, from which he emerged a few minutes later with an open book balanced on his forearms. Ming strung together the characters on the cover to read *In Search of the Supernatural* by Gan Bao.

"I thought I recognized her description," Father-in-law said by way of explanation. He flipped a few pages before reading aloud,

"'In the time of Chou of Shang, the giant turtle grew hair and the hare grew horns—signs that arms and armor would soon arise.'"

He looked at the page for another moment before closing the book and turning his gaze to Ming. "Ming, do you remember me reading this to you?"

She did not remember the specific passage, but the book seemed familiar.

"I think your mind was confused, because you were scared and in pain. Do you think it's possible you remembered something from here when you were hurt? Maybe when you fell unconscious?" he asked with an unconvincing smile—thin as a zither string.

She opened her mouth to protest, frustrated at being written off, but he continued before she could speak. "I'm sorry, Ming, I didn't realize the hour, we've been holding you here for too long. You should head home. I'm sure your parents are worried about you by now." They all knew this was a lie. "Have them talk to me if they have questions about the wound."

Father-in-law shot Mother-in-law a meaningful look, one that Ming knew meant the adults wanted to talk privately amongst themselves.

"Look how dark it got," Mother-in-law added, picking up on the shift in the room. "Fei, it's time for you to do your schoolwork. Ming, would you like a lamp for your way back? Should I walk you?"

"No, Āyí, I can go by myself."

"Off you go, then."

Ming waited to see Fei grudgingly go to his room. She left, feeling dismissed, taking with her some bandages that Mother-in-law had insistently packed. From the warm light of the threshold, Mother-in-law watched Ming walk twenty meters down the path before closing the door, hurtling the landscape into complete darkness. Ming then quietly snuck back to the physician's compound, pressing her body against the round door. From there, she could make out Fei's parents' voices.

"You don't believe her, do you? What do you think actually did it? Do you think Fei was playing too rough with her? You've seen how he acts with his toys. And what are you reading to them? Now they're scared and have all these strange ideas," Mother-in-law said, her voice rising in pitch with each subsequent question.

"It's harmless," Father-in-law said, "a book of old myths. What I read was a minor omen prophesying the fall of the Shang Dynasty and the rise of the Zhou Dynasty. Ancient history. It means nothing. She must've hallucinated it when she fainted from the pain."

"A hare with horns," Mother-in-law muttered. "Why a hare with horns?"

"I don't know why she was drawn to that particular image. There are thousands of creatures in this book. Normal animals whose qì has been reversed by the chaos of the world, forcing them into abnormal transformations. Nothing scary about that."

Ming wanted to know more. Could the hare's abnormal energy transfer to her? Could humans undergo a reversal of qì?

"No more filling the children's heads with these myths and war prophecies."

Outside, Ming strained to hear what they said next, but it was quiet for a long while. Instead, there was the whistle of the wind as it neared mid-autumn.

Mother-in-law spoke at last: "It looked bad. Maybe we should take her in and monitor it for infection. We should've taken her in years ago. I hear the ladies in town talk about how untraditional it is, making a daughter-in-law live with her birth parents for so long."

Ming's breath got caught in her throat. *Yes*, she wanted to burst in and plead. *Please, please, please*. If Father-in-law agreed, she would run in there right now and carve a space for herself—as surely as the hare had carved its mark in her.

"I've told you before, it's not right to separate a child from their parents. Especially a girl before womanhood. We agreed that we'd wait until her first cycle. If she's barren, then what will we do? We'll be saddled with another child, a daughter we have no use for."

Ming felt her hope dissociate from her body like a guǐ, a ghost.

"It's not right that we send her back to that wretched woman every night. She's hardly a parent, let alone a mother. Ming feels like my own. Her unhappiness weighs on my soul. Does it not weigh on yours?"

"Lǎopó, you know that my opinion on this matter is final. Don't bring it up again."

She'd heard enough. From her hiding place, Ming slunk out of the shadows, slipping onto the path back to the farm. Shūshu had read her books, and she had mistaken that for love. He had spun her stories, and she had hidden in them, imagining that she was the divine hero, the Monkey King encased in stone, that she was special, but she was just a girl. A daughter.

She did not remember how she got back, only that, by morning light, she was once again under the same roof as Mama.

Fourteen

Qianze
2017: Eight Days Since Reunion
Manhattan, New York

THERE WERE QUIET NIGHTS BEFORE this. Quiet of Qianze's own volition: her muteness stretching and filling the apartment in a comfortable stasis. There were empty trash liners and a clean sink with no dishes. There were windowsills devoid of cigarette ash and tables without sticky rings. There were baths where Qianze would sink down into the yellowing plastic tub until only the ends of her hair floated on the blue-green surface. In the water, a gurgling scream emerged from the darkest parts of her, and afterward there was a deeper quiet.

There was a time when there were no eggs in her refrigerator, no camera in her living room, and no excavated memories—those dusty relics cluttering her apartment, turning it into an archaeological dig. Qianze missed sprawling on the couch in front of the TV alone after a long day of work, her evenings spent with the drone of a sitcom or a procedural in the background instead of Ba's revelations.

It was Monday, August 14, marking the second week of Ba's stay. Qianze had come back from work and was loitering outside her apartment building. She stood under the awning of the front entrance, where she couldn't be seen even if Ba looked out the window. She was gathering the strength to go up and endure another night. She spent a long time watching insects flutter and crowd around the one outdoor bulb, blackened with fly corpses. She found herself longing for a cigarette to hold so that she wouldn't look quite so conspicuous to the people filtering in and out of the narrow lobby. An older white woman with her dog coming into the apartment shot her a look and firmly closed the entry door behind her.

Qianze looked up past the faded awning to the building across the street. Sometimes while sitting in her living room listening to Ba she found her gaze wandering to the brick building that faced her. She'd watch the lights in those windows blink on in the same yellow hue as hers, the apartments looking miniature and dioramalike. The inhabitants would go about their evenings: cooking, eating, drinking, watching TV. The windows were frighteningly transparent, and few bothered to put up curtains. Qianze never closed her blinds either, only hung up sheer half curtains, and until recently, hadn't considered how the other building might see her: her and her father's silhouettes, tensed, as they sat across from each other. His hand, age-spotted and fat, darting out of the window to tap out the end of his cigarette.

How must they look to a stranger? They did not spend time together outside of the apartment. They existed solely in that space, that impossible wormhole where their parallel realities clashed. Would an outsider know he was her father? They both had changed. But Qianze remembered photos of them in her childhood—preserved only in her memory after Ma had gotten rid of them—and comments from neighbors and teachers about how similar they looked. Even though she had thinned and he had bloated, their relationship was inescapable. It had ossified into their bones, their cartilage, the shape of their faces.

When Ba left, Qianze had created a long list of reasons for his disappearance, chief among them a mistress with a swollen belly. Another child whose bones also belonged to Ba's. Whose face had the same features. A half-sibling. That child would be eleven now, around the age that Ba had left her. Had he cycled through another tragedy, left another mother and child in his wake? The more she considered it, the more plausible it seemed. She berated herself for not questioning him more about his sudden reappearance, for letting him time-shift his way out of blame. A mosquito landed on Qianze's cheek. She slapped it, but it was too late. As she went up the stairs to her apartment, she could feel the skin swelling.

QIANZE HAD PLANNED TO APPROACH the question delicately. The online doctors said it was best to treat Ba with kid gloves. So far she had refrained from asking the questions she'd been harboring for the past decade, but her masochistic streak wanted him to press at the center of the wound he'd left in her, gaping and picked over.

She'd intended to sit and listen to Ba's memories, nodding, occasionally making sounds of understanding. Agreeing docilely when he murmured about the prophecy like a broken penny-arcade fortune-teller. Sprinkle in a question or two, then gently guide the conversation to his missing years. It had been a week since his arrival. Surely she deserved—had *earned*—some answers.

Instead, when she opened her door and saw him at the window smoking a cigarette, making her apartment reek of nicotine, she blurted it out accusingly: "Did you have another family?"

He frowned, confused. She closed the door firmly, toed off her shoes, and berated herself for her impulsivity.

"When you left me and Ma, was it because you had another family?" Qianze clarified.

His frown deepened. He put out the cigarette. "Why would I do that?"

Now it was Qianze's turn to frown. "I don't know. Why wouldn't you?"

"I never wanted children."

Qianze recoiled. The new welt on her cheek throbbed.

"That doesn't make sense," she said slowly. Perhaps he had misunderstood. Perhaps he had forgotten. "You and Ma—you had all those miscarriages. And you tried all those years. Ma still keeps those urns, with the twins? From when you first immigrated? I remember you both used to light incense for them, put fruit out for them. You and Ma always called me," her voice hitched, "your miracle," she finished weakly.

He nodded somberly. "That's all true. But that was your Ma. She was the one who wanted children. You were an accident."

Qianze flinched as if slapped. Somehow, he was still discovering new ways to wound her.

In her head, Qianze had been drawing a distinction between the father of the past week and *her* father. Her father made her breakfast every morning. Her father left work early in the afternoons so he'd always be on time for pickup after school. Her father tried his best to give her everything she wanted—for holidays, for birthdays, for accomplishments, for an art-contest prize—insulating her from the truth of their finances. *This* father was an unwanted guest, an infestation.

If she entertained his words as truth, the separation between the two fathers would disintegrate. If she entertained this, then that meant *her* father had not wanted *her*. That her conception and birth had been a rupture. That she might have been the reason why he left.

"If you didn't want me, why are you here? Why am I taking care of you?" Her voice grew wobbly.

"I didn't ask you to do that."

"Is your prophecy even real? Your warning? Or are you just trying to con me into housing you, feeding you, letting you destroy my home?"

"It's real. It's at the end of the thread. I'm getting there. Once I warn you, I'll leave." He nodded to himself, but his words lacked assurance.

"When will that be? What if you never find it? Then I'm saddled with you, with your problems, for the rest of your life?" She took a breath. She could no longer stand to be in his presence. She calculated her next words: "You shouldn't have had me," she said, enunciating each syllable. "It would've been better if I'd died. If I didn't exist. That would be better than this. Having you as a father. Having someone who always leaves."

She refused to look at him. To see how her words had landed, whether or not his mouth was opening to form a response. She went into her room and slammed the door, feeling every bit the lost, fatherless teenager she'd been. Despite her clenched jaw, despite willing herself, *Don't cry don't cry*, she felt tears well up in her eyes. She picked up the ceramic lamp by her bedside and hurled it at the door, watching as it broke in a shower of fragments. Her lip quivered. She was immediately filled with regret; Theo had found her that lamp in his neighborhood, and there was no replacing it. She squatted and began to sweep the pieces into a pile.

During the past weekend, Qianze had started having violent fantasies, brought on by the breach in her home. Qianze would've given her right arm for a week—a *night*—alone. She would've sawed it off herself. *Please leave*, she would say, plopping the bloody thing on the coffee table in front of her father. The bone would be jutting out of her shoulder, and she would be dripping all over the sofa, and Ba would laugh at the offering and light another cigarette. Each night a new jagged limb, Qianze dismembering herself to accommodate Ba. But these were just flights of fancy, because she would never ask him to leave, not when he was sick. She was a Good Chinese Daughter even if he was a Bad Chinese Father.

Perhaps Ba's oft-mentioned prophecy was Oedipal. She envisioned flipping the dining table, the couch. Plates and crockery smashing against the wall beside his head. Dashing his liquor bottles against the grain of the floor. Waving the jagged remains around, sharp enough to slice an artery. Setting his cigarettes all alight until the building caught, Ba's alcohol sending columns of fire roaring toward the ceiling. *See what you have driven me to, what I have become*, she would screech among the leaping flames. *See what ruin you have borne.*

Long ago, there'd been a collection of birthday candles and coins in fountains and stray eyelashes and dandelion seeds all spent on Ba's return. That he might come back to the Myrtle house and tell them that it was all a mistake, that he'd gotten lost, that he'd been kidnapped, that he'd been swept up in a portal to the fairy realm, the Xiānjìng. Something that would explain away his leaving, that would make it not his.

Instead, Ba had barreled back into her life—a bull in a Chinatown apartment—with his blathering and his báijiǔ truths, the most hurtful one that he had never wanted her.

QIANZE HAD BEEN FORCED TO grow up fast in the wake of her father's abandonment. It was like a word problem on a math test. If your father leaves you at age fourteen, reducing your means to a scraping-by, single-income household, and your mother becomes bedridden and doesn't feed you for two days, what age would you mentally mature to? One day, she was a girl, a sapling, green and alive. And the next, she was sweating over the stovetop, making meals of Kraft macaroni and wondering if they had enough that month to pay the electric bill.

When Qianze recalled the house on Myrtle, she landed on an unnamable nostalgia, teeming with possible parallel planes: lives she could've lived if her father had only stayed. Some nights, she found herself returning to the Myrtle house on Google Maps Street View.

She would click "See more dates," and there would be "Image Capture: June 2006." Before Ba left. Each time, she felt a lurch in her chest at the grainy image, felt herself careening into the past. If she squinted, she thought she could make out the silhouette of Ba's shoulders behind the windows where the computer desk was—orange interior light leaking through the glass and onto the asphalt of a dark-blue afternoon, staining their azalea bushes a warm desert red. And where was she? Perhaps she was sitting in the same room, reading a book or sketching, basking in his presence. And she was a girl again, loving and loved.

Ba left in July, the night of Qianze's fourteenth birthday.

Qianze was a summer baby, born around the solstice. High summer: stretched out, bleached, sun-heavy days. The year she turned fourteen, it was a wet season. The marshes were overflowing. The air was so humid, so fraught with damp, that lightning would manifest from stale air without any warning.

Like the cicadas that emerged every fourteen summers, she wanted to shed her childhood skin. At Qianze's insistence, Ma plaited her hair every morning because it felt so luxurious and grown-up. Unlike the towheaded girls at school, whose hair turned a blinding white with exposure, Qianze's dark head drank in the heat, and her scalp was always burnt and blisteringly hot. Qianze was *thirteen going on fourteen*. She would sing this to the tune from *The Sound of Music* in the shower in the weeks approaching her birthday. She wore uncomfortably sticky lip gloss and was now allowed to wear a two-piece to go swimming, even if she lacked the body to fill it. She was above celebrating with her parents. She had gone to the movies at the mall with her friends the day before and gotten her ears pierced at Claire's.

On the morning of her actual birthday, her father came in with a breakfast tray, loaded with a variety of eggs: steamed egg custard, eggs sunny side up on toast, boiled eggs dyed red with sū mù from the only Asian grocery store in town. There was a saucer with red vinegar, scallions, and soy sauce, which was how Qianze liked to season her eggs.

"Do you know why we eat eggs on birthdays?" Ba asked. He sat down on the edge of her bed. Qianze tucked into her breakfast.

"No," Qianze managed to say, her mouth full.

"See the shape?" He delicately held up a boiled egg between two of his fingers. "A full circle. Rebirth for another year." He put it back on her plate. She nodded, barely listening.

"And for dinner, we'll have noodles. The longer the noodle, the longer your life." He pressed his lips quickly to her forehead and said, "Happy birthday, hái'ér." Qianze squirmed away from his touch.

Later, she would go over this moment many times, until it became a memory of a memory. Did Ba say this all in Chinese? Did her parents speak more Chinese or English that year? Qianze of twenty-five had been turning over her childhood memories from every angle. She skewered them, rotated them on a spit, examined them. Would she lose them like Ba had? Even as she returned to her childhood, she could not remember what language it was spoken in, found those memories pasted over with subtitles. Her mother tongue nearly forgotten, plastered in whiteness. What she knew for certain: she wished she had not squirmed away. She wished she had lingered there. She wished she had called him back and given him a proper embrace. Him, the father who existed in this consecrated childhood. Him, the father who had never hurt her.

Ba spent the afternoon making dough from scratch and hand pulling noodles. He gave Qianze the longest ones, leaving the shorter ones for him and Ma.

Qianze drenched them in vinegar, to which Ba said happily, "Qianze xi huān chī kǔ. Like me."

"What does chī kǔ mean?" Qianze asked between loud slurps. The birthday girl was not supposed to bite the noodles, because that might cut her life short.

"It's Chinese saying," Ma answered. "It mean 'eating bitterness.'

Ba plays with words. It means persisting in the face of hard time. But Qianze is lucky, because she lives in good time," Ma said, smiling.

Ba left that night.

Maybe he knew all along that this would be their last birthday together. When Qianze looked back at this dinner, it was tainted with that thought.

He left through the front door. That creaky screen door that could never hide anything. The night he left, she had been sleeping when, over the sound of the crickets, she heard the hinges groan loudly, drowning out all other noise. She woke up briefly to stare at the ceiling and knew something was wrong. That the delicate ecosystem of their family had been upset in some way. In the morning, his bike and a bag of his things were gone.

And then it was just her and Ma in the Myrtle house.

MYRTLE HAD TWO ONE-WAY STREETS, separated by a grassy median, and was made up of one-story houses and yards with chain-link fences. There were only two kinds of people who lived there: families who couldn't afford anything better and college students from the nearby university seeking cheap housing. Qianze had learned the seasons of this world, as predictable as the tide. With the end of the spring semester came the end of leases, and the students would empty their houses of things they did not want into the median. Stained couches, scuffed nightstands, and filthy mattresses populated the landscape.

No one ever mowed the median, so the grass and wild onions came up to Qianze's knees, itching where they brushed against her skin. Before she was born, Ma and Ba had furnished their house with the college students' leftovers, and even when they were better off, supplemented by Ba's university teaching salary, Ma still brought Qianze through the median, weaving around the discards like they were in a department store. At some point Ma had abandoned this ritual, leaving it up to Qianze, who gathered bric-a-brac like a magpie. She scoured boxes for jewelry, trinkets, and pretty glassware. She liked books to keep her occupied while her parents worked. Some summers had slim pickings. Others were bountiful—when a house of English majors moved—and those summers, she would have a bookshelf heaving with worn paperbacks. Her favorite kinds of books were also the rarest: the heavy, hardcover textbooks of the art students, filled with glossy prints of paintings. She had recovered two so far, along with a handful of nubby art supplies—paints with only dregs that she had to roll up like toothpaste, sketchbooks half-full—and these she guarded on her nightstand.

In the years following Ba's disappearance, Qianze would find Ma on the porch or in the living room, staring out at the median. Ma never had to say it, but Qianze knew she was waiting for Ba to wash up on that grassy shore. Occasionally, Ma would claim that she had seen a guǐ threading his way around the junk of that middle wasteland: pale, thin, and exuding a deep-seated yearning. But it always turned out to be some wandering college student, drunk out of his mind, Ba's image superimposed onto him by Ma's desire.

The day after Ba left, Qianze found Ma standing at the stovetop, chopping scallions into ringlets, stirring together a soup base. At the table were two bowls, two placemats, two dining chairs. The third of everything tossed out to the curb. The wreckage of Ba's chair, smashed against a crepe myrtle tree. This would be the last time Ma cooked for them for years. The next week, Ma conjured a story of a sudden aneurysm and Ba's death.

Ma was good at playing the grieving widow. Ma was good at grief, basking in it until she and the grief morphed into another mother, gray and lifeless, who did not know how to go on.

Qianze went on. But she went on as a new person, one who wore resentment like a second skin. Why did she, the child, have to be the adult? Why did Ma think motherhood was a part-time job that she could pick up and put down? Why did Ba leave her to this fate? When she was fourteen, the head of the table emptied, and Qianze took a seat. No one else was going to do it. But that didn't stop her from wishing someone else had.

THERE HAD ALWAYS BEEN DAYS of mourning through the years, days she knew not to bother her parents as they lit candles on the small altar Ma had built on her nightstand. A picture of an ultrasound that sat next to incense holders and votives. A child urn, dusted regularly, placed on top of a yellowing doily, containing ashes they had ferried across the world in a plastic bag. Qianze was her parents' miracle child. She had been born after several miscarriages, when Ma thought she was too old to conceive.

Qianze had always been curious about her ghost siblings, but Ma and Ba had been reticent and dodged her questions. After Ba left, Qianze, alone and rootless, felt their absence even more. She had no other family now, just Ma. The siblings' names were written on the ultrasounds in Ma's neat Chinese calligraphy, but Qianze could not read Chinese. Still, she imagined them: what they would look like, their similarities to her, how they would speak, the pitch of their voices.

The twins were three years older than her. They were fraternal, one boy and one girl—just like Ma and Qianze's late uncle. They were Earth Snakes, born in December of 1989. Because Qianze didn't know their names, she resorted to calling her sister Dà Jiě and her brother Dà Gē.

Dà Gē was strikingly tall: six foot and lanky, the star of the cross-country team. In contrast, Dà Jiě was slightly below average height.

"He stole all the nutrients from me in the womb, selfish bastard," Jiě would often joke. Their banter was easy and practiced.

"I was trying to kill you so I could be an only child," Gē would reply.

In reality, Jiě had died first, and Gē absorbed her before he was delivered stillborn.

In Qianze's head, despite their difference in height, the twins' faces were mirrors of one another. As they grew older, their differences would become more pronounced, especially to Qianze. Gē's hair developed a natural curl to it, while Jiě's was sleek and straight, usually pulled back from her face. Gē's face was more oval, and his features were sharp and stretched out: his cheekbones and jaw jutted out at right angles and his beaked Roman nose flared when he was upset. Jiě's face was rounder, like Ba's, and her brows were thick and straight, giving the impression that she was always worried, emphasized by the natural downward pout of her lips.

Gē was Ma's favorite. "Some internalized Confucian patriarchy, I'm sure," Dà Jiě would say with a roll of her eyes, but they all knew better. In hushed tones, Ba told them that Ma's twin brother had died in Tiān'ānmén during Ma's second trimester, and to her, Gē was a piece of him reincarnated.

In reality, Ma birthed Gē early and stillborn when she heard the news.

Ma's favoritism was fine, Qianze thought, because she had her sister. The girls would share a room: a comfort in the aftermath of Ba's abandonment.

Mostly when Qianze envisioned this alternate reality—the one where the Myrtle house was brimming with messy, abundant life—she pictured one moment. It was more of a sensation. That of being enveloped by her siblings, of knowing she was safe and would be taken care of.

On a weekend in August of 2006, a month after Ba left, when Qianze still hoped he might return, she left the house early in the morning and walked to the nearby river. She stripped down to her bathing suit and waded out into the water, the cold a salve against her skin, until it came up to her neck. Then she kicked out her legs until she was floating on the green surface, her arms stretched outward, her head laid back. There was a soft current that grabbed hold of and cradled her.

The sun briefly broke through the gray clouds. She thought of her ghost siblings. She wanted to pray to them, but their altar and ashes were in Ma's room, and Ma was always there: their sentinel on the underworld threshold, hoarding them to herself. Qianze let the water carry her in its drift and imagined that, just outside of her reach, her siblings were floating as well, their fingertips grazing hers, their heads all clustered together, forming a three-pointed star. She could almost feel the whisper of their dark hair brushing against her arms like kelp. Perhaps this, too, was a kind of praying, of worship.

For a moment, she felt buoyant.

Fifteen

Qianze

2017: Nine Days Since Reunion

Manhattan, New York

BA HAD FORGOTTEN HE DID not want her. Or, Ba had forgotten he'd told her he did not want her. The next morning, Tuesday, August 15, he carried on, business as usual, finding comfort in his routine. Qianze found comfort nowhere, suspended in a debilitating hurt in which she could do nothing, think nothing, without betrayal elbowing its way to the forefront of her mind.

Each morning, she woke and was met with a stranger. He seemed to understand that they were related, there was no denying that. He was driven by his persistent need to recover his so-called prophecy from the recesses of his memory, but little else remained consistent. Qianze never knew how much he remembered, what year or decade he was in. Each day, he regained more of his past but forgot their daily interactions. How could Qianze be upset at him for an argument he couldn't recall? How could she dredge up a fight that did not exist inside his mind? How could she even know if what he said was true? But she was upset. She tried to tamp it down, but she felt it on every inch of her skin. This searing fury that slashed her open like a fault line, made her hands shake, itching to destroy something: the plates, the eggs, the father of yesterday.

The busy season did not care about the recent upheaval in her personal life. Her manager's patience had run out.

"This is a demanding time, and we need all hands on deck, Kenzie."

She nodded.

"A few years ago, before you joined, my mamaw died during the busy season. I had to miss the funeral."

She understood.

"No rest for the wicked, right?" He grinned. She laughed weakly. She focused on his one canine that was more yellow than the rest of his teeth.

That second week, Qianze returned to her fifteen-hour workdays. At her desk, she had her phone propped up underneath her monitor. It was open to the nanny cam. In two weeks, Qianze had gone from a corporate accountant to a helicopter mom. This was the only solution she could come up with besides hiring a caretaker, which would involve several rounds of interviews and a background check. Pawning your parents off onto someone else was an expensive and drawn-out process.

Ba, either out of rightful paranoia or dementia, spent most of the day in the bathroom. Sometimes, he left his tiled refuge and bumbled around the living room and kitchen, muttering under his breath in Chinese she couldn't understand or couldn't hear. Mostly he was quiet as he poked around. If he was lucid, he reshelved books that had been lying out. He snipped the browning stems of her scallions on the windowsill and changed out the water. He gingerly picked up her framed photos and looked at them for minutes. She let herself believe this was him speaking to her. A silent, stumbling language of care relearned after years of not practicing it. Glimmers of the father she remembered that felt like a hook in her gut.

After work, Qianze lingered in Sarah D. Roosevelt Park outside her subway station. She had picked up this habit in this second week, spending midnights at this crossroads: circling the handball courts or sitting on a bench near the Hester Street Playground. She allowed herself a half hour each day to tighten her grasp on her sanity, on reality—caught between two places that demanded more from her than she could give. Mostly, she did not want to go back to the apartment, that claustrophobic site where every unruly emotion was trapped like rotting food in the sieve of the kitchen sink.

Despite it being the last few weeks of summer before school started, the park was empty when she frequented it. No old men near the chain-link fences, no players on the courts, no teenagers sneaking cigarettes on the benches. Her only company was the whistle of the wind, the electric hum of the streetlamps, and a feeling of loneliness tailing her, cradling her in its embrace.

That Thursday, August 17, Qianze was sitting near the playground when she heard a rustle in the bushes beside her, which made her jump. The yellow light of the streetlamp pooled in the new divots of her body: the wells of her collarbone, the sharp jab of her shoulders. Her appetite had suffered from the stress of the past two weeks, and she suddenly felt vulnerable and exposed under the glare. Her mouth grew dry, throat narrowing in fear.

Out from the leaves emerged the snout of a fox. Its red pelt sliced through the dark landscape like a bright wound. Its eyes met Qianze's, and its black whiskers twitched. Qianze stilled. The park was surrounded on all sides by pavement and buildings. There was no logical explanation for how the fox had made its way into the bushes, from where it now stared at her intently. *Not again, not again*, she thought, dread filling her mouth. She realized she'd been waiting for it to appear, for the other shoe to drop.

"A fox loose in the hen house. A bad omen," a voice chimed from behind Qianze, startling her.

She whipped around to find two Aunties, their elbows interlocked, their twin faces round and aged, their hair permed at their jowls. Qianze blinked. Theirs was not the face of the Auntie from the subway, but there was an uneasy similarity to these two women. A sense that beneath their skins was something otherworldly, buzzing to be let out. Their features seemed flat and too precise. A near likeness of women, but not quite.

Qianze wanted to run, but she didn't want to provoke the fox into chasing her. The fox, seeing the Aunties, turned its gaze toward them, its black ears twitching.

"Depends on the breed of fox, sister," the other Auntie responded.

"Who are you?" Qianze stammered out. The women's mirror faces swiveled toward her, and Qianze flinched, causing the fox to let out a low, warning growl, its ears pressed back. The women turned their attention back to the fox.

"Húyāo or húxiān? What do you think?" one of the Aunties asked the other. Their heads tilted to the side simultaneously in curiosity.

"Perhaps something in between," the other Auntie proposed. "Not living, but not all dead. Looks like it had enough strength to burrow here from the Dìyù."

"It *is* that time of the year. Resurrection season." The other Auntie hummed in agreement.

They squatted together, their long floral skirts rising to expose socked feet in sandals.

"What were you before?" one Auntie asked the fox, who had cautiously moved to sit on its black-slippered feet as it peered back at the Aunties. "Healer? Or troublemaker?"

Now that the Aunties sat between Qianze and the fox, she began to slowly edge off the bench, preparing to run back to her apartment. She did not know what was wrong with the women, but there was a wrongness to them, an eeriness that rolled off them in waves and made her skin prickle into gooseflesh.

"Where are you going, girl? Don't you want to hear what it has to say to you?" one Auntie asked just as Qianze stood. She turned around to see the two women, still squatting, their faces angled toward her.

"It's just a fox," Qianze said weakly, but she didn't believe her own words.

"She really knows nothing," one Auntie said to her sister.

Qianze felt her mouth open against her better judgment, then closed it. She knew more about foxes than most.

"Do you want it to leave you alone? It probably will, if that's what you want. It won't hurt you, if that's what you're scared of."

"I'm not scared," Qianze said, the waver in her voice betraying her.

"It doesn't mean any harm. Fox infestations have symptoms like all hauntings. The sounds, the apparitions, the little gifts—"

The Auntie was still speaking, but Qianze heard nothing, her hearing giving way to a rush of blood in her head. *How could they know? How did all these women* know? Fear gripped her, and she couldn't breathe, and she felt herself stumbling away in a hurry, vision blurring, eyes darting back occasionally to see if she was being followed. She made it to her apartment, unlocking the door with shaking hands.

Something was wrong. Ba's delirium was leaking. It had flooded her apartment and now she was drowning in it. Was this the conclusion of Ba's prophecy? A Shakespearean tragedy ending: both of them doomed to madness? The jackalope dream, these empty places, omniscient Aunties with their cryptic messages—and now the reappearance of the fox.

She rushed through the apartment, not bothering to check on Ba, whose presence she felt beyond the bathroom door. She got on her knees and began to dig frantically at the boxes under her bed, unearthing winter coats and luggage, until she found it: a dusty shoebox shoved into the corner to be forgotten. She took a deep, steadying breath and pried the lid off.

Inside was her childhood sketchbook, untouched for the past seven years. She flipped the cover open, and there on the first page was the fox from the park.

THE FOX FIRST APPEARED WHEN Qianze was fourteen. It was the spring after Ba left. Qianze had had trouble sleeping for the half year since. When she did sleep, it was light and easily interrupted: lost to the soft thump of a bird flying into the window, to the muffled sound of her mother's sobs from the next room over.

Then, one night, a sound she had never heard before. A scream in a gravelly pitch that felt neither human nor animal. The reverberations traveled through the backyard and past the windowpanes, where it woke Qianze, her heartbeat quick and afraid. When she pressed an eye to the cold glass, she saw the tawny smear of a fox, its jaw unhinging into a dark, wide hole. It let out another banshee shriek, the sound too large for its body, sending Qianze skittering away from the window. In her haste, she stumbled and fell onto the floor. She untwisted herself, padding over to Ma's room, too afraid to be alone.

Ma spent most of her days and nights tucked away in her room. There, she cocooned herself in her grief. She left the bed only to use the bathroom, and once, earlier that day, to blearily light a stick of incense on the windowsill, imploring Qianze to follow suit for Tomb Sweeping Day. Qianze walked to Ma's sleeping form, the sour smell of unwashed sheets mixing with the lingering scent of incense. She shook Ma's shoulder until Ma groaned and cracked open a heavy-lidded eye.

"Yǐjing zǎoshangle?" *Morning, already?*

Qianze had taken responsibility for managing Ma's schedule of tutoring lessons and part-time waitressing shifts. She was also the one who had to prod Ma to wake up, to shower, to eat, to go to work on time.

"No," Qianze said, shaking her head, "did you hear that?"

"Hear what?" Ma asked.

"The fox," Qianze hissed, "it was screaming just now."

"Didn't hear," Ma mumbled, patting Qianze's hand, "go back to sleep."

At that moment, the fox let out another wail. A desperate, deep-bellied sound that went on for several seconds, like it was trying to scream out its organs.

"*There*," Qianze said, frantic, "there it is again. You heard it, right?"

Ma opened her eyes again. The whites of her eyes were the only color in the dark room. She frowned. "I didn't hear anything."

Fear lanced through Qianze's spine as she stiffened. Ma curled upward to sit. She brought the back of her hand to Qianze's forehead. "You okay, bǎobèi? Feeling sick? Do you want to sleep here?"

Qianze pulled away. Part of her wanted to crawl into Ma's arms and pretend at normalcy for one night. Another part of her harbored too much bitterness to accept Ma's offer. Where had Ma's concern been in the weeks following Ba's departure when she'd needed it the most? She didn't want Ma's scraps of care. She wanted Ma to take care of her and the house and the money. She wanted Ma, but she knew she couldn't have her. Not the same Ma from before.

"No," Qianze said curtly, shaking her head and backing away. Ma's face fell, almost imperceptibly in the unlit room, and she nodded before turning over onto her side. Qianze left the room, closed the door, then went to the living room where the family computer sat. She knew she couldn't fall back asleep, too preoccupied by the fox's caterwauling that Ma couldn't hear.

Under the thick blue glow of the computer, Qianze tumbled down a search-engine rabbit hole. Auditory hallucinations. What are auditory hallucinations a symptom of? Schizophrenia onset age. Sleep paralysis hallucinations. How long do sleep paralysis visions last after you wake up? Are foxes native to southeastern Virginia? Fox migration patterns. Why do foxes scream?

When the morning sun came in through the windows, Qianze found herself hunched over the computer, the keyboard indented in her left cheek. At some point, she had drifted off. She rubbed at her face but paused before she sat up. She began to feel along her shoulders, her breasts, her stomach. Something had shifted inside her body. She couldn't name what it was, only that she felt different, uncomfortably so. She tried searching the feeling on the internet but lacked the words to describe it. Her body today was not the same body as yesterday. Her mind was different, like it was tuned to a new station, and she didn't know how to set it back.

THE APPEARANCE OF THE FOX unleashed a barrage of nightmares. Qianze flipped frantically through the sketchbook, each subsequent page documenting the creatures in harried charcoal strokes that appeared in her adolescent dreams. An eight-foot-long turtle with green sprouts of algae on its shell and prehistoric yellow eyes. A large, mangy-looking cur with wildfire-red fur. Birds with human hair and dark-scaled dragons. Oxen with no legs, with five legs, with two heads. Then, the jackalope.

Whereas the other creatures merely observed her, lurking in the background of her dreams, the jackalope had crossed the threshold of reality, close enough to carve its mark on her. The wound it inflicted blisteringly real, painful enough to wake her. Qianze had filled half the sketchbook with studies of the jackalope. A variety of different mediums and styles—pencil, charcoal, acrylic, gouache, even an attempt at Chinese ink—whatever supplies she had on hand. Some pages dedicated to just one aspect: the curve of its antler, the uncanny smile, the red eyes. She'd thought that if she could capture the jackalope's likeness, dismember it, understand it, then she would no longer be afraid of it.

But even now, the dream fresh in her mind again, there was something missing from her caricatures, some quality she could not replicate.

Finally the jackalope studies gave way to a handful of blank pages. Months in which she threw herself into college applications and test preparation, sleeping in twenty-to-thirty-minute spurts, too short for her brain to wander into the REM stage. She'd kept herself awake on a regimen of black coffee and desperation. Then, a series of drawings from her first semester at UVA. Manic, jagged illustrations made by a trembling hand.

The return of the fox and the jackalope, who had followed her to Charlottesville.

Sixteen

Ming
1931: Eighty-Six Years Before Reunion
Rural Manchuria

AT SEVEN, MING HAD GROWN into a gangly, spindly child, no longer able to carry her brother on her back. She was tall for her age, taller even than some of the older girls in the village, while her brother was a round, fat four-year-old, and if she tried to bind him against her back, she'd topple over. Instead, the siblings took to holding hands and walking around the village: to the physician's compound, where she would read him books out loud; to the river, where she caught him tadpoles; to the hill near the forest overlooking town. They were there now, sitting on the grass.

It was midsummer. Ming was weaving him a crown from the season's wildflowers. She smoothed it over his dark hair.

"A crown for a prince," she said, delighting when he smiled. "This village is your kingdom."

He frowned. "You're a princess and need a crown too," he said, his baby fists grabbing at wilting weeds that bore a slight resemblance to blooms.

"No, no," she protested, "there can only be one royal in our family. You are Mama and Baba's little prince, and you will look after them when you're older."

Dìdi's face contorted in confusion. "Where will you be?"

From the hilltop, she pointed out the physician's compound with Āyí's small garden patch in front of it, alive with Siberian irises, peonies, and yellow witch-hazel blooms. Beyond the four outer walls, the interior courtyard was visible. A laundry line rippled in the wind, bisecting the space. "I'll be there, just a lǐ away. Hardly a stone's throw."

Ming watched as he tracked the distance with his eyes from the compound to their father's fields. The whole town lay between the two.

"When you marry Zhou gēgē, I'll move in too," he declared.

She laughed, clear and true, and swatted him playfully with her unscarred hand. "Silly, you'll be married too, and then you and your wife will live with Mama and Baba. That's just how it is."

"But Yéyé and Nǎinai don't live with us."

"That's because—" She frowned. Yéyé and Nǎinai had died in the Manchurian Plague a decade or so before Ming was born, but she didn't think Dìdi knew about death. Even she had only a hazy grasp on the concept. He was still too young to understand what the spring Tomb Sweeping Festival meant beyond the gifts of kites and congee.

"Well," she finished, "Yéyé and Nǎinai are sick, so they can't live with us."

Dìdi considered this for a moment and moved on to more pressing questions.

"If you leave, jiě, who will catch tadpoles with me and make me flower crowns?"

"You'll be too old for those things." She pinched his ruddy cheek. "And anyway, I'm not *leaving*. You can always visit. And I'll cook you all your favorites when you come for dinner, won't that be nice?"

"I guess," Dìdi said, bowing his head to pull out tufts of grass.

"Sticky buns with pork bone and radish filling, guō bāo ròu, chive dumplings," she sang with a wolfish grin. Underneath her playful tone, she was telling him that they had shared a womb, a home, and a kang, and these were things that wouldn't be forgotten after marriage.

His round face hid a reluctant smile. It faltered as he looked down at the expanse of the town. "Why do you want to leave, jiě?"

"You wouldn't understand. You're a boy." He blinked at her, as if waiting for her to explain. She sighed. "Silly," she repeated, but her heart wasn't in it. She took his hand into hers, his soft palm chafing against her scar. "Should we head back for dinner?"

DINNER WAS A SPARSE AFFAIR. Mama and Baba were preoccupied, the space between their brows perpetually wrinkled. The adults of the town assumed so little of their schoolchildren. They thought that at seven, Ming wouldn't notice their concern: the way they halted conversations mid-sentence and forced smiles whenever she passed. The way the vendors at the market stalls seemed to have less and less food to sell.

Lately, all her classmates had developed an air of worry—the adults' anxiety rubbing off on them. Children, it was said, like animals, often have a preternatural sense for catastrophe.

The shift occurred one season ago. Something ominous had been swept in with the beginning of spring. The méiyǔ—the plum rain—had turned the landscape an immodest green and made everything damp and uneasy. The paper window coverings were still soft and wavy though the wet season had been over for two months. In the village, fear swelled, announcing itself like a monsoon. Ming's long, puckered scar ached like a broken bone before a thunderstorm.

Ming ate her shallow scoop of sorghum rice slowly, even as her hunger called out. She watched as her parents bowed their heads to eat: Baba's sunburnt scalp paired with Mama's dark head of thick hair. Mama and Baba were shoveling the small portions into their mouths, scraping their bowls clean. They did not look at her. Their eyes slid off and hovered behind her. This wasn't unusual for Mama, who tended to look through Ming like she was an evil spirit that had blighted their dining table with her presence. Baba usually treated Ming with the strained politeness given a guest who had overstayed her welcome, asking her questions about her day and nodding absently at her short answers. Tonight, though, they weren't even looking at Dìdi, whom they loved to gaze at, his every action worthy of their adoration.

She felt Dìdi's grubby hand grip her tunic, bunching it in his clammy fingers. He did this whenever she had dinner with them, reassuring himself that she was there. He had been doing it more away from the table. Sometimes at night, she would feel the bite of his nails catching on her skin, waking her from her sleep. Even Dìdi knew something was amiss.

Mama's harried arms gathered the bowls and chopsticks, sweeping the table clean. In her haste, she collected the crockery with grains of rice still clinging to the bottom. Food was precious. Mama was taken to spouting folktales about how each leftover grain translated to a pockmark on their future spouse's face. Absently, Ming wondered if Fei would wake the next morning with pustules on his smooth, prepubescent cheek.

Mama insisted that it was bedtime, even though the summer evening was still bright. Ming and Dìdi, exiled to their room, sat with their backs against the wall on their kang. There was little privacy in the open two-room house, but from a certain angle, Ming could pretend that they were alone in an enclosed room of their own. Baba ducked his head in and told them that he and Mama were going out to inspect the fields. Then they were alone.

Dìdi's lower lip was wet and protruding. Ming could tell he was minutes away from complaining of boredom. The light slanted, bathing his features in an orange so vivid she could taste it on the flat of her tongue. If he were a year or two older, they could've been mistaken for twins. The same eyes, but his were rounder at the edges, the nose a touch more masculine, the chin less stubborn, the jaw softer. She would've made a beautiful boy.

Dìdi turned to meet her gaze and furrowed his brow, as if he could sense her thoughts. He slipped his thumb into his mouth, and Ming jerked it out with more force than needed. His spittle dangled like a skein of string.

"Don't do that," she chided, "it's disgusting. You're not a baby anymore."

But he was, *he was, he was*, and his face screwed into an expression torn between crying and proving her wrong. She didn't hurry to salve over the cruelty. She allowed herself the occasional indulgence. Beside her, her brother choked down a sob, and remorse coursed through her, heavy as a millstone.

"Have you heard the story of the Lis' red sorghum fields?"

"No," he said with a sniffle, "Mama says not to go there."

"Well, the Luan brothers and some of the Yan girls told me and Fei a ghost story about the fields."

A peace offering. A glimpse into the inner circle of the older children—the ones he so doggedly idolized.

He sniffed and turned to look at her with those wide, watery eyes, swimming with unconditional forgiveness. She refused to meet his gaze, looking down instead to where she twisted a stray thread around and around her finger until it became painfully white and bloodless. She began.

THE CHILDREN WERE IN THE forest at dusk—the part of the woods that slopes downward to the Li family's red sorghum fields. On one side of the fields, the forest. On the other, barren salted land, where nothing had grown for more than a decade. They all knew it was haunted, but they didn't know how it was haunted or what haunted it. The Lis owned a pack of seven black and bloodthirsty mongrels. Their baying could be heard all the way from the village, a sign that some unlucky animal was being shredded by their teeth. The Luan boys said they knew someone who had outrun them, crossing the Lis' fields and making it to the barren land on a dare. The Yan girls said no, that was ridiculous, there had only ever been one person who went to the barren land and came back, and she had left the village years ago. They pooled their stories together—a collection of rumors and scraps and warnings.

The older Yan girl had heard the beginning from their great-uncle, whom everyone called Bǎobèi, because he was younger than his siblings by twenty years, even though now he was an old drunk with rotting teeth. He said that a decade ago, before the Lis took up residence, a girl their age had wandered into that land—empty and endless, except for an indistinct shape at the center. She walked to this dark object on the horizon, but it always seemed to retreat and slip away from her. What was it? A house? A grazing horse?

Eventually, the dark shape bowed to the girl's efforts and let her draw near, until she found herself in front of a woman on her back with her arms and legs stretched out. Her body was that of an old crone's, but her face was no older than a woman of twenty.

"A witch," one of the Luan boys proposed.

"No," Fei said, "I heard something different. A demon."

"It must've been a witch. She cast a protection around her, that's why the girl couldn't approach at first," the Luan boys insisted.

Fei sighed.

Ming said that the fish vendor described the woman as having apples in her cheeks and hungry, dark eyes. She did not admit that when she pictured the woman, she envisioned Mama.

The woman—"Witch," the Luan brothers interrupted again, "Demon," Fei retorted—told the traveler that she had been born and raised in their village before she was cast out. She miscarried seven times, burying the stillborn babes in the ground. Miscarriage was the worst crime a woman could commit, so after the seventh, the woman's husband tossed her out and married a girl who gave him a son before the year's end. And so, the woman became a pariah and lived out the rest of her days in the mountains.

Here, they encountered a blank. No one knew what happened between her exile and when she came to the fields, so they invented a life in a cave, imagining the woman living off weeds and a mountain spring.

The Luan brothers told the ending, which they heard from their mother. The Luans' mother had been the butcher's daughter before she married, so her stories were always tinged with viscera, which the boys only played up. Ming could never tell what was real and what was embellished. According to the brothers, the woman stumbled across a house, built into the mountain. This was unusual, because the house was along a path she walked daily, and it had appeared overnight, so that she thought she had conjured it, like how one sees an oasis in a desert.

When she went inside, she found a baby who looked like her firstborn; he curled the same fetal way like a river shrimp, had the same face as her. The woman took this as a sign from the gods, as penance. An opportunity to be a mother, to birth him right. So she swallowed him whole and felt him nestle back into her womb.

Then she saw six children in the doorway, her other stillborns, she thought mistakenly, and she tried to devour them too, chasing them down the mountain and into the field. The gods, fickle creatures, sent down a golden chain for the six children to climb. Then they sent down a rope for the woman, but when she was a hairsbreadth away from the children, they cut the rope and let her fall. The blood that seeped out of her—hers and the boy's inside her—dyed the fields and turned the sorghum red.

"CAN YOU TAKE ME?"

"To the barren land? Mama would kill me if she knew I let you get that close to the Lis' dogs."

"What's it mean?"

"Nothing. It's an old wives' tale to explain why red sorghum is red."

He considered this for a second. "Can I play with you and Zhou gēgē in the forest tomorrow?"

"Sure."

"And the other kids?"

"If they're around and want to."

"Can I have another story?"

"I don't have any other stories. Maybe later if I hear something good."

"Was she a witch?"

"Sort of. Not really. I don't know. I think she was tricked by the gods."

"I thought gods were supposed to be good."

"There are hundreds of gods. Not all of them can be good."

"Why not? We pray to them, we give them things."

"Zhou Āyí says we're like small toys to them. You know those toy soldiers Fei gave to you? We're like that to them. And you're not always nice to your toys."

A brief frown, then an idea flashed across his round face. "Does Zhou gēgē have any other toys he doesn't want?"

"Maybe. You can ask him tomorrow."

Dìdi seemed pleased by his barter and the promise of spending time with the other children. Soon, his eyes drooped with sleep. But long after Mama and Baba had come in and gone to bed, Ming tossed and turned, still thinking of the town's ghost story.

THE FARMERS' SONS BEGAN THE next morning like any other, starting their daily chores in the fields. At high noon, they saw their fathers clustering in the shade. They abandoned their lunches and inched closer to overhear their conversation. The sons listened, hiding behind trees and huts until they were caught and yelled at, at which point they scattered to the four winds, spreading their newfound gossip amongst the village children, trading it like wares.

Ming got it for a slippery eel and the promise to hem a pair of too-large hand-me-down trousers. Afterward, she realized she'd been swindled. She saw one of the Chen boys try to sell it to Dìdi for the lunch Mama packed him and the mugwort candle from their shared room, which kept the mosquitoes at bay. Dìdi was about to take the bait when she grabbed his hand, told the Chen boy off, and walked quickly away, Dìdi stumbling in her wake.

"Why'd you do that?" Dìdi whined once they slowed.

"It would've been a waste of your lunch. And I don't want to wake up with bites all over my arms tomorrow." Ming sniffed.

"Now I'm going to be the only one who doesn't know." He pouted.

"It's no big secret."

"So you'll tell me?" He looked up at her with hopeful eyes.

She chewed her lip. Did he not deserve to know? Had he not sensed it already? That disturbance that had caused his infant behaviors to resurge: the thumb-sucking, the clawed hand-holding? And yet, something within her wished to insulate him from all the troubles of the world. Fictional horrors were one thing, but real bloodshed was another.

As they walked, Dìdi began to swing her arm wildly in anticipation. He began to chant—*jiě jiě jiě jiě*—hoping annoyance would make her relent. He had that first-son overindulgence. Like Fei, he possessed a gnawing need to have everything he wanted.

"All right!" Ming shouted at last. "All right," she said again, softly this time.

Dìdi squirmed gleefully at his victory. Ming heaved a sigh.

"The farmers' sons said that they heard Baba and the other men talking. Some of them have family down in Shěnyáng, and they got letters saying that the Japanese took over the city. Now they want to take over the rest of Manchuria."

He frowned. "What does that mean?"

"From what the boys said, it sounds like"—Ming paused—"we'll belong to them. Like how people own cows and pigs and mules."

"Like how I own the toy soldiers?"

"Maybe. I don't know."

"Will they come here?"

"I don't know."

"Why are Ma and Ba so scared?"

"I don't know."

"Do we have to move?"

"I don't know."

"What's going to happen?"

"*I don't know*, Qian," she snapped. He winced at the use of his name, his arm drooping, deflated.

"I'm sorry," Ming said. "I wish I knew, but I don't. I know as much as you."

"Okay," he said quietly. She sighed and squeezed his hand as a gesture of comfort. She shouldn't have told him. He couldn't understand.

Unlike Dìdi, Ming was beginning to comprehend what being bound to someone meant. She observed and cataloged the assortment of marriages and relationships in the village. A wife bound to her husband differed from how a mother was bound to her son, which differed from how she was bound to a daughter or a stillborn. Ming had been raised with the knowledge that one day, she would be someone's wife, someone's mother. But a wife was not a cow or pig or mule. A wife was not a toy. Ming did not know what being bound to the Japanese would mean. She was realizing that the adults didn't know either. She squinted at the horizon, wondering at what point a dark shape would manifest, when the Japanese army would approach, slinking toward them to lay claim on them.

The sky was bruising purple and yellow, a summer storm front blowing in.

Seventeen

Qianze
2010: Seven Years Before Reunion
Charlottesville, Virginia

BEFORE MANHATTAN, QIANZE'S LIFE HAD been confined to a small cartographical slice of Virginia. Specifically, the southeastern mosquito-bitten corner where she'd grown up, and then Charlottesville for the four years she was at university.

In Virginia, she was pressed on all sides by a suffocating whiteness: boys who pulled their bruise-blue eyes into slits and the coiffed older church ladies who spoke to her and Ma in the pitying tones they reserved for speaking about their latest charity cases. Qianze was not a believer. She was a staunch atheist, who worshipped at the altar of science. For the sake of her hometown—several hours below the Mason–Dixon line—not quite the Bible Belt, but not far from it either—their family pretended. Sundays were spent splaying thin novels between the pages of her Bible. When Ba died, the church ladies offered their condolences. Their Tidewater drawl—those lengthened, saltwater vowels spoken in the rhythm of breaking waves—polite and insincere.

"So sorry 'bout your daddy. Good man. Didn't quite unnerstand him all the time, but ya could see he had a noble way 'bout him.

Ya could tell it in his eyes," followed by a chorus of murmured agreements.

"Yes, so sad," Ma would agree with a nod and a widow's countenance as she accepted platters of collard greens and casserole.

Ma told everyone at church that Ba had died suddenly. Aneurysm. Unavoidable, undetectable. All the trappings of an inescapable tragedy. The churchgoers, who frequently told them in the aftermath "God always got a plan," lapped it up. Over the years, the story would build, with Ma adding on tense hospital-waiting-room scenes and health-insurance drama, ending with a solemn scattering of ashes over the Atlantic Ocean on the Chesapeake Bay Bridge.

Ma knew how to spin a yarn. It was too good a tale to waste on false sympathy and Pyrex containers of macaroni. Qianze aimed for bigger game and made a killing: the story the centerpiece of her University of Virginia supplement, earning her a fully funded ride.

In the months leading up to her first week at university, Qianze painted over the water-stained walls and found college renters for the house on Myrtle. With the students' security deposit and the promise of monthly rent checks, she helped Ma move out and into a one-bedroom apartment. She packed up all the possessions she wanted to keep, which filled two suitcases in the cargo hold of the bus to Charlottesville, and donated the rest.

QIANZE HAD TO DRAG HER suitcases up searing, hilly asphalt from the bus stop but found she didn't mind much. She was free from the grasp of the Myrtle house. She'd even done away with her name, which Ba had given her, naming her after his late uncle. She registered her preferred name as Kenzie: no more confusing Q's for white tongues to trip over. She'd long given up on correcting people's pronunciation. Now even Qianze thought of and introduced herself as "Kenzie" Zhou. There, proudly displayed on her Echol dormitory door, was her new name, along with her roommate's.

Kenzie and Ainsley, written in bubble letters on colorful construction paper.

Kenzie would be the version of Qianze who flourished in college, who had friends. There had been friends from middle school, but they had ended up at different high schools, and Qianze had lost touch with them. She'd deleted their sympathy messages, feeling ashamed at the thought of lying to them about her father. In high school, while her peers were at beach parties and school dances, Qianze had been learning how to balance the household books and budget for groceries. Her senior spring was spent figuring out how to manage a rental property and advertising the Myrtle house on Craigslist. Charming 2 Bed, 2 Bath House with Private Backyard, Azalea Garden, Ghost of Father.

There was only one difference between Qianze and Kenzie. Kenzie's father had died. Unlike Qianze, who'd spent years leaping to the front windows whenever orange headlights cut through the dark living room, hoping that it was him this time, that it was *really him*. There was closure in death. There was health-insurance money and truth. There was a mother who loved Kenzie the way Qianze wanted to be loved: not a pale imitation of it, threaded through with melancholy. Kenzie's mother would never blame her for being her father's daughter, never flinch from the sight of her. Kenzie's mother would've sent her off to college herself instead of regressing into her annual summer grief—the hot months transporting her back to the year of Ba's desertion, the sorrow fresh and raw again.

By the time Ainsley arrived at their dorm, it was late afternoon, and Qianze was finished setting up her side. It was sparse as far as girls' dorms went. When she brought up her belongings that morning, she'd peeked into the other girls' rooms along the hall. It had been a bustle of activity as her classmates and their parents hung up decorations, unrolled tufted rugs onto tiled floors, and stuffed the closets to bursting. Qianze spotted ponytailed mothers making tight hospital corners and rigorously fluffing up duvets as if a photographer from *Southern Living* might come by at any moment.

Qianze had not brought much. Some clean sheets, a blanket, and enough clothes to fill half the closet. There was a small stack of books, which she displayed on the hutch over her desk, and a drawer of scavenged art supplies, at the bottom of which she'd stashed her old sketchbook. She hadn't known what to do with it. Throwing it out felt wrong, unlucky: an act of defiance that might invite something worse to visit her dreams.

On the white cinder-block walls, she taped up posters from the student-center poster sale she'd stumbled upon during a midmorning search for food.

"Discards from the art history department," the boy manning the booth said. Her spoils were *Clytemnestra after the Murder* by John Collier, *Oedipus at Colonus* by Henry Fuseli, and *Cleopatra* by John William Waterhouse.

"You're kind of dark, aren't you?" the boy asked as he rolled up the posters and snapped a rubber band around them.

Qianze shrugged. She liked emotion in her art, an amber preservation of uninhibited feeling. The girls in her hall could have the impressionists' soft brushstrokes, the ornate limerence of Klimt. Qianze preferred the brutal realism of Gentileschi and Caravaggio.

"Do you paint?" the boy asked.

"No," Qianze said before walking off quickly with her posters. She had not sketched or painted in some time. There had always been something more pressing to do: a babysitting job, a shift at the mall, a test. When she set out to draw something, all she could think of was a canvas, slashed through with naphthol: that shade of wrath that colored the jackalope's eyes.

Beside the posters, she taped one photo of her and Ma from her high school graduation on her desk. The photo was taken off-center, and Qianze's eye was drawn to the distinct absence on her left. This was the closest thing she had to a photo of Ba: an empty space next to her hip. Everything else Ma had tossed or burned or hidden away. All Qianze knew was that one day, he was a fixture in every photo album, and the next, nowhere, not even solid enough for her to sketch from memory.

Qianze was lining up her shoes when a pair of Tory Burch sandals entered her field of vision. They were connected to the burnt pair of lobster-red legs of a girl with white-blond hair who introduced herself as Ainsley and was planning to major in communications. She wore a saturated salmon and lime Lilly Pulitzer dress, which showed the angry sear of her freckled shoulders.

"Summer at the Outer Banks house," Ainsley explained with a dismissive wave when she caught Qianze glancing at the rashy patches, pink and prickled like raw chicken breast.

"What are you studying?" Ainsley asked.

"Accounting," Qianze said.

"Oh, interesting," Ainsley said, not bothering to hide the crinkle of her nose. "My parents are coming up now with a load. They want to meet yours," she said while texting on her Sidekick.

"My parents aren't here," Qianze said.

Ainsley looked up, interest piqued. "Oh, did they leave already? Are you all done moving in?" Ainsley took a closer look at Qianze's side, and the left corner of her lip-glossed mouth tugged down in disapproval.

"My mom couldn't make it, and my dad's dead." The lie slipped out so easily. She had repeated it so much that it felt true, and for a moment she stepped into the skin of Kenzie, whose father had died. Whose father had been unwaveringly good and had made her egg-custard breakfasts and bought her colored pencils and helped her with her homework.

"Oh, wow, I'm sorry," Ainsley said, putting on a false pout. "I've never known someone with a dead parent before."

Of the many condolences Qianze had received, she had to admit this was one of the worst: the shallow sympathy, the lack of empathy.

Still, Qianze nodded with the sad, closed-lip smile she'd perfected in the mirror. Reactions to the lie ran the gamut. There were those who seemed paralyzed after, afraid that whatever they said next might cause Qianze to plunge back into mourning. Then, those like Ainsley, who'd never experienced loss or hardship. But always, a snatch of morbid curiosity. Qianze could see it now in the slight tip of Ainsley's head, the small crease between her brows. Very few asked—that would be impolite—but they all seemed to think that if they peered hard enough, they could divine how Ba had died. It was this look that made her nervous, her mind leaping to different possibilities. Had they seen Ba? Did he live in their town? Qianze shifted her weight from one foot to the other under Ainsley's gaze. She felt like an exhibit at a roadside attraction: the shed skin of a two-headed snake, its visitors trying to determine whether it was real or fake.

"I think I'll just get out of your way while you unpack."

"That'd actually be great," Ainsley said, sounding relieved. Her face broke open in a hundred-watt smile. "I have a lot of stuff to move in."

Qianze was already halfway out the door. She passed by a red-faced, balding man—Ainsley's father, she presumed—buckling under the weight of a mini fridge and a blond, ponytailed woman wheeling two Tumi suitcases, a garish paisley Vera Bradley duffel propped on top of each like a garnish. Once she was outside, Qianze let out an exhale.

She walked the grounds, cutting a path through the green of the Lawn, observing the other first years hauling in their belongings. Some had already paired off: roommates walking the campus together, eager boys and shy girls sneaking glances at each other on the front steps of their dorms. Qianze had thought that being Kenzie would be a rebirth. That she'd slip out, slick-coated, into a new life and into the fold of fraternity parties and shows of sororal affection that the movies and TV shows had promised.

She had spent so long cloaked in the costume of adulthood, she assumed the independence of college would feel natural to her, intuitive. Instead, she felt more alone and untethered than ever, like if she slipped through the membrane of reality and disappeared, no one would notice, not even Ma.

BY THE NEXT EVENING, AINSLEY had somehow gathered a flock of acolytes from their hall. Like Ainsley, many of them flaunted sheets of white-blond hair, but theirs came from the salon, betrayed by their brown roots. They flitted around her, unconsciously mirroring her style, toting Longchamp bags and dolling themselves up in chunky bubble necklaces, blazers, and Tory Burch gladiator sandals.

Ainsley was hosting a pregame in their dorm, swanning around in a bodycon skirt, plying the girls with shots of fruit-flavored alcohol she'd acquired with her fake. Qianze sensed that she'd only been allowed to participate because Ainsley couldn't kick her out of her own room. Qianze sat at the edge of her bed while the girls from the hall sat in a circle on the floor, spreading out on the thick chevron shag rug. As the girls drank more of the fruit abomination, they grew nicer and sloppier. One of them squinted at Qianze, as if seeing her for the first time. She snatched a strand of Qianze's hair, which she'd grown out to her waist.

"How do you get your hair like this? What conditioner do you use?" She scrutinized the hair, as if trying to spot split ends. Qianze, confused by the attention after being ignored most of the night, muttered the brand of her conditioner.

"I'll have to try that out. Here, sit," the girl said, tugging at the strand again, leading Qianze down to the circle like a pet by a leash. The other girls exchanged confused looks, but the drunk smiles on their faces seemed genuine, if a bit hesitant.

"You're pretty. I've never met a pretty Asian before," the girl said, tilting her head to dissect Qianze's features.

"Thanks," Qianze said, unsure if this was a compliment.

"Take a shot with me?" She handed Qianze a plastic shot glass and poured, the liquid sloshing over the rim.

"I'll have one too," someone else chimed in, then another. Only Ainsley seemed displeased at this new development.

This was Qianze's first real drink besides the sips of wine offered by winking elders at church holiday parties. It went down burning, sickly saccharine, and she felt tears prick in her eyes, which she blinked back.

After another shot and a discussion of which popular class they wanted to take next semester, Qianze relaxed, her shoulders loosening.

"You should come out with us," one of the girls said to Qianze, which was followed by some echoing nods and the flutter of feathery white hair.

"I'll think about it," Qianze hiccupped, unsure if she was about to be the butt of a joke.

"The frat boys would love you. You've got that mysterious, sad, dead-dad thing. It's very Tumblr."

Qianze's hand, halfway to her mouth with a third shot, froze. It was the way the girl had said it, as if death and grief were glamorous, romantic.

"Ainsley told us," the girl said. Around the circle, the other girls were nodding, their watery eyes wide and pitying, and in Qianze's swimming vision, they morphed, aging into the Tidewater church ladies, who gazed at her like she was their favorite charity case. Qianze flinched, and one of the girls, in an effort to smooth over the moment, poured her a conciliatory fourth shot.

"Come out with us," the girls chimed, "it'll be fun."

"The boys at Chi Phi *and* Sigma Chi put us on their list."

"And then we might go to the bars at the Corner."

"Please come, Kenzie, you'll have a blast," they chorused.

Qianze relented. She would've preferred other company, but she didn't want to be the girl who stayed in her dorm. Not when it seemed like everyone else on campus had spilled out into the night to celebrate the new school year. The girls clapped their hands excitedly, strapped her feet into death-trap wedges, swiped frosted lip gloss on her lips. What came next was a series of still images, brief moments of consciousness when she resurfaced from the swirl of fruit cocktail.

THERE WAS A FRATERNITY PARTY—Chi Phi or Sigma Chi, she couldn't tell the difference—where her borrowed wedges stuck to the floors, buffed to a sheen by years of alcohol and sugar. At some point, Qianze careened into a bathroom, the swinging bulb over the grimy sink casting deep shadows under her eyes as she stared into the mirror. How the girl looking back at her had her face, but not her face. It was darker, thinner. She had her hair pulled back in two braids and wore a fraying cotton tunic. She was mouthing something frantic at Qianze, one scarred palm reaching for her, and Qianze shook her head until the vision dissipated and her reflection returned to normal, her hands bone-white as they gripped the edges of the sink.

Then the Irish pub Trin, whose bouncer shot Qianze a shit-eating grin, his breath damp and revolting as he whispered *konichiwa* in her ear. Then the fullness of a drained Guinness sloshing around in her stomach so she could forget the rank murmur of this greeting. There was a second-year boy in the corner, one she'd spoken to earlier at the student fair when he handed her a flyer for the Asian Student Association. The girls tittered and giggled to her about him afterward, saying how *perfect* he was for her. Probably because they were both Asian. She shouted something to him over the din at Trin and then a blink where memory wouldn't stick, and when she next turned around to find the girls, they were gone.

There was a stumbling, barefoot walk alone, wedges dangling from her hand. She tried to remember which path led back to her dorm through the haze of alcohol and adrenaline, which was replaced by an intense nausea, bringing her to her knees as she retched into a bush. Afterward, her eyes wet and her throat sore, she sat back on her heels and noticed something observing her from the shade of a nearby bush.

Those beady amber eyes and that russet fur, as if conjured from memory. Qianze's vision doubled, tripled, nonupled, the fox's nine tails fanning out behind its tiny black-slippered feet, and she was scrambling to stand, taking off down the brick pathway, her soles dirty and aching. A cold chill of foreboding lancing through her. She had left these nightmares behind, exiled them to the land of her childhood. But the fox had been there, closer than it had ever been, that harbinger of stranger things to come.

The next morning, Qianze found herself in her bed, unsure when she'd found her way back to the dorm. There were bloody socks on her feet and charcoal smudged on her fingers. On her desk was a mess of art supplies, her old sketchbook sitting open. She moved to reach for it when Ainsley walked in, her hair wrapped in a towel, wearing a striped bathrobe.

"Morning," Ainsley chirped.

Qianze sat up, frowning. "Where did you all go last night? You left me."

Ainsley sat down at her desk, which she'd turned into a makeshift vanity. She ran a brush through her wet hair. "I thought you were having fun. Didn't you have *fun*?" Ainsley asked. In the mirror that sat on the desk, a plastic smile spread across her bony features.

Qianze, in the midst of her first hangover, felt sweat bead on her lower back. Every sensation was heightened: the heat on her skin, the sores on her feet, the brightness of the sun bouncing off the floor. Ainsley's presence made her throat thick with unease, so she grabbed the sketchbook and her keys before dashing out of the room.

Ainsley muttered something unkind under her breath as Qianze slammed the door. She walked quickly down the hallway in her socks, telling herself that once she was outside and got some fresh air, she would feel better. But when she was standing on the steps of the dorm, she felt worse: her headache shifting into a swarmlike buzzing that threatened to cleave her skull open. The harsh sunlight drew out a vibrancy in the surroundings that was painful to look at, and that, combined with her wooziness, sent her pitching toward the shade of a tree near the curb. She rested a hand against the bark of the tree to steady herself, her vision splotchy from the heat. When she looked up, she froze.

There, across the road was an albino hare. It had the look of the jackalope, peeled from her mind and dropped into her reality. It was looking directly at her, its eyes boring into hers. Qianze whipped her head around to see if anyone else noticed it, how out of place it looked against the manicured greenery, but there was no one else outside the dorm.

The jackalope edged closer, a hairsbreadth over the yellow lane marks. Qianze's breathing stalled. She didn't know what would happen if she made contact with the dream creature, if it would winnow her away into its reality. The forest. The damp bough. The antlers ripping through her skin like paper.

She didn't notice the car hurtling down the road until it was too late. A thump and then a sickening squelch as the tread of the front tires ground the hare's soft body apart. The rear axle compressing the skull then dragging a cord of torn pink guts along the tar, smearing the intestines into the road where they glittered hotly. Qianze's mouth hung open, a scream stuck in her throat. The decapitated head gaped back at her, one of its red eyes bulging out from the force of the impact.

She took a step back, stumbled over a tree root, and fell, catching herself on her elbows. She let out a hiss of pain as her funny bone took the brunt of her weight, an electric jolt shooting through her arm. Then the secondary, softer sting of her elbows, raw and skinned.

Her sketchbook had fallen open. There, on the most recent page, a messy sketch of the fox: all scribbles of black and orange, save for the yellow eyes, rendered in meticulous detail, which stared out from the page like two headlights. She rolled over onto her side and threw up at the base of the tree.

QIANZE HAD BEEN WILLING TO write off the encounters with the fox and hare as a side effect of the alcohol. Perhaps one of the fraternity drinks had been spiked with a hallucinogen. But the next morning, when she left the dorm, she found a brown cottontail staining the steps of Echols, its insides spilling out onto the sidewalk in a glossy rush of guts and soft organs. At night, she was hounded by the wails of the fox baying at her window in a desolate and yearning pitch.

For the rest of orientation week, Qianze withdrew from the company of others. A trail of grisly gifts followed her. A stolen magpie's nest with a broken, dribbling egg. A gray swallow with its head torn clean off. Little bird bones, bleached and floundering with gristle. Something was wrong. She was unraveling, constantly on the precipice of a panic attack. She felt manic, her body a palpitating, nervous mess. She resorted to desperate measures. She sent in an application to one of the psychology department's sleep paralysis studies, only to be told they were full. She made an appointment with the student health center for an antipsychotic prescription, but was informed the next available appointment wasn't until late October. A sidewalk psychic on Charlottesville's main street told her a spirit was trying to commune with her but refused to say more unless Qianze paid $250 for a séance.

Out of options, she went to look for answers in Shannon Library's East Asian Collection. The library was empty, save for an occasional student tucked away at a desk. Qianze, lost, wandered up to a circulation desk. To her surprise, she found the boy from the student fair and Trin, wearing a pin that read, I'M A STUDENT LIBRARY ASSISTANT. ASK ME ANYTHING!

"You're everywhere, aren't you?" Qianze asked.

The boy looked up, surprised. His face smoothed into a smile. "Kenzie, right?"

"Right," Qianze confirmed, "and you are . . ." She trailed off, realizing she'd forgotten his name.

"Theo," he supplied, a faint flush spreading across the bridge of his nose. "How can I help you? You do know classes haven't started yet."

"I'm doing some research. For a personal project."

"Ah, okay. What are you looking for?"

"The East Asian collection."

He looked apologetic. "It's not really centralized, but if you let me know your topic, I can pull some books and articles from the catalog."

"Can I search on the catalog?"

"Sure," he said, nodding toward a monitor at the end of the desk. "Let me know if you need help finding anything."

The first thing she searched was "jackalope nightmare." No results. The next, "jackalope demon," only came up with a history book on Wyoming, where the myth of the jackalope originated. Still, she jotted down the call number on a slip of paper. Her search "nine-tailed fox" yielded more: a book on East Asian fox lore and an old, translated copy of *Fēnshén Yǎnyì*. She wrote those call numbers down then returned to Theo, who had been reading a dog-eared copy of *Dracula*.

"Here." She held the paper out to him. "Can you help me find these?"

He scanned the list and nodded. She followed along, feeling awkward as they walked in silence along the deserted floors. He raised a brow when he pulled out *100 Years of Wyoming History*, his expression shifting into full confusion at *Chinese Fairy Tales and Fox Fables*.

"What kind of project is this anyway?"

"Don't worry about it," she said quickly, snatching the two books from him.

"Shouldn't you be enjoying your orientation week instead of reading about"—he skimmed the back of the last book—"ancient Chinese court politics?"

"You're very curious." She frowned, taking the last book from him.

His face fell. "Sorry. You're right. It's none of my business. Here, I'll check these out for you."

She stood there, studying his features. He had such an unguarded face, earnest and open. He finished scanning her books and opened his mouth to say something, then seemed to think better of it.

"What?" Qianze asked sharply.

"Nothing," he said, shaking his head, "just, have a good day."

"You were going to say something."

He hesitated. "It's not my place."

"What is it?" she demanded.

"Those girls you were with at Trin. You should be careful of them. They didn't leave you behind by accident."

Qianze blinked. She felt shame rise in her cheeks. She'd suspected as much, but part of her hoped that they'd been too drunk to realize she was missing. She should've listened to her fear that she'd be a laughingstock among them.

Theo was still talking. ". . . first years will do anything to fit in, to make friends. I'm sure they're not all bad people, and some of them just went along with it so they wouldn't be the odd one out."

Qianze hated that he had borne witness to her humiliation. She had just wanted a normal college night out, but even that had gone wrong. Everything had gone wrong. Every other first year on campus seemed to be having the time of their life—a slice of the All-American College Experience—and she wasn't, and she didn't understand why this was happening, why nothing ever went her way. All the wrongness was frothing over, and she wanted to scream or run for the hills or both.

"Hey, are you okay?" Theo asked, his brows dipping together

in concern. She realized she hadn't spoken in some time, and her breathing had turned shallow.

"Fine," she said, swallowing.

"Look, what those girls did was messed up, but I'm sure it wasn't about you. Everyone's just eighteen and scared and homesick."

Homesick. The word almost made her laugh. Yes, she'd brought some sickness from home onto campus.

In the months before orientation week, she'd systematically packed away her past. The Myrtle house. The furniture. The childhood toys that Ma had asked twice if she wanted to throw out. *You sure, bǎobèi? What if you want later for your own children?* She wouldn't. She didn't want to be a parent; she didn't think she was cut out for mothering, not the way she thought a child deserved. She wanted a clean and cold severance from her past: a fresh January of her life. She didn't account for the fox, the hare—these violent poltergeists that she could not make sense of, but that reminded her of the grief that she wanted to forget.

"Hey," Theo said softly, breaking her out of her reverie. "I bet your luck will turn around soon. Ghost month's almost over."

"Ghost month?" she echoed.

He looked embarrassed. "I guess it's a Filipino thing, something my lola talks about. It's supposed to be an unlucky month. She's superstitious like that." Theo paused and caught her questioning gaze. "I'm only half, but she practically raised me," he said in a rehearsed way, as if he was used to explaining this.

She frowned. "August is a lucky month. That's what my dad used to say."

"I think it's lunar. But all to say, it'll get better."

"Right," she said, skeptical.

"Look, if you want, you can come to dinner with me and my friends tomorrow night. We're going to get real Asian food. Not the fake stuff they serve in the dining halls."

"I'm not a charity case," she snapped.

"Who said you were?" He looked genuinely taken aback by her reaction. "Maybe my friends and I are just interested in Wyoming history." He tapped the book on her pile.

She considered it. He had already seen the vulnerable, animal side of her. Her, drunk and abandoned. Her, falling apart at the seams. Part of her never wanted to see him again because of it. And part of her knew that if she continued on the way she had in high school, she'd evolve into a wholly solitary creature with no room for the possibility of friendship, tailed only by her apparitions and their bloody offerings.

"I'll think about it," she said at last.

Eighteen

Ming

1939: Seventy-Eight Years Before Reunion

Manchukuo

MING WOULD NOT BLEED.

At fifteen, she was late, fulfilling Shūshu's fears of betrothing his son to a barren girl. This would not do. Mama had clothed, housed, and fed Ming in anticipation of a wedding, of one day being rid of her. As a last resort, Mama took Ming up to the Manchu wise woman. Ming had chafed at the idea, but Mama was insistent and threatened to beat the blood out of her if she would not go. So they went.

The wise woman lived up in the mountain caves and had shamanistic powers. No one in the village knew why she'd been cast out from the nearby clan. Those who traded with the Manchus believed that they'd squirrelled her away for her own safety. Fearing the Japanese and their violent distaste for shamanism, they harbored her and their idols in the caves, where the clan brought her food and supplies.

It was a two-hour journey by mule through forest and up the mountain, and Ming and Mama sat together on the animal's back. Mama flinched every time their bodies jostled together, every time Mama's mangled feet bumped against the mule's hide. Mama's breath grew raspy as they steadily climbed up the mountain, the air becoming thin and cold.

The natural circular entrance to the cave had been bricked up, and there was a yellow wooden door, pasted with paper cutouts, set within the brick that beckoned them. Mama and Ming stood there, taken aback by the strange doorway. Sensing the two pilgrims, the wise woman cracked the door open and called them in. She surveyed them at the threshold with her pale, otherworldly sight. The wise woman's eyes were cloudy from years of darkness—eight since the Japanese occupation—and tinged blue and nocturnal. She was dressed simply in a robe patterned with clouds and a headdress of magpie feathers.

Ming's gaze darted around the cave, unable to settle as she took in the busy interior. Vertical wooden columns reinforced the natural cave space. There was a brick kang built along the side of the cave, a fire burning underneath, providing warmth. Behind the kang were baskets and coffers, too many to count, from which Ming could see the heads of wooden idols peering out, their carved eyes following her. Ming thought they looked sad and neglected, longing to be worshipped. An altar, filled with heady incense and colorful silk spirit cloths, sat to the right of the entrance. Hung up everywhere around the cave were lanterns, bronze mirrors, and crystals, which reflected Ming and Mama, multiplying and fracturing their images.

The woman took in Mama, looking her up and down. "I remember you. Sixteen years ago, you and your husband came to the hala asking for fertility medicine." Mama stiffened. "I hope you're not here to ask for my help with another baby. A bit old now, aren't you?"

"It's not for me," Mama said, pushing Ming in front of her.

"Your daughter?" the woman asked, squinting at the two of them.

Mama gave a sharp nod. Side by side, their features coalesced: the slope of their noses, the pout of their mouths, the upturned corners of their eyes. One young and one old, as if Ming had siphoned the beauty and youth out of Mama's body, taking it in the afterbirth.

"Sixteen?"

"Fifteen," Mama said quietly.

"So. This is the baby that you came to the clan to pray for."

Neither Mama nor Ming said a word.

"Are you trying to get pregnant, girl?" the woman addressed Ming.

"She hasn't bled yet. I was hoping you could give her some medicine," Mama spoke for Ming.

The woman frowned. "Don't you have your own physician for that?"

"He's the father of her betrothed. I didn't want to worry him."

The woman murmured a sound of understanding. "Can I examine you?"

Ming nodded, squirmed as the woman's hands flitted gently around her body. The shaman paused for a long time as she held Ming's scarred right hand palm side up.

"You have strong shén qì, here," she said softly, tapping the scar left by the gash from the hare.

"What does that mean?" Mama asked.

But the shaman did not answer, just gave Ming a knowing look. She patted the hand and dropped it, where it hung limply at Ming's side.

"I have some herbs I can give you." She rummaged around in the dark back of the cave, sidestepping the many idols, and emerged, holding up two large pouches. "This one is for drinking. This one is a powder that you should massage into your body. You don't want to confuse them. It would taste very bad." She laughed. "Use the herbs and the powder and pray to your ancestors and fertility gods. You seem healthy. I suspect the reason you haven't bled is malnutrition."

"Everyone is malnourished," Mama protested.

The woman shrugged. "Well, if you want her to bleed, you have to feed her."

On the way down the mountain, Mama grumbled about this diagnosis, bitter that she'd paid a valuable bag of sorghum flour to hear a truth she already knew.

For the next month, Ming experienced the foreign sensation of being full. With the sparse ingredients they had, Mama made Ming three hearty meals a day of catfish, skinned frogs, and wheat congee. An outsider might've seen this as a kind gesture, a farewell, but the town knew better. Mama was fattening Ming up for marriage like a livestock farmer about to bring his animals to the butcher.

If the proverbial butcher's block was the physician's family, so be it. Ming patiently swallowed down the herbal remedies, ate until her bowl was empty, massaged the rancid powder into her inner thighs and belly before bed, and prayed daily to her ancestors and Guānyīn. Her days left in Mama's house were numbered, and this gave her comfort when her knees began to ache from the hours of kowtowing.

ALMOST A MONTH AFTER THE visit to the wise woman, the woven grass mat on top of Ming's kang remained spotless. Each morning, Ming checked the seams of her trousers and was disappointed. She'd begun to notice other changes in her body, which she took as a good sign. There was the wiry sprout of pubic hair that matched the growing dark patches on her legs and armpits. There was new fat that had begun to settle—on her arms, on her hips, and most notably, on her chest—that Fei and the other boys took notice of.

As Ming and Fei hurtled into adolescence, their peers showed a vested interest in the unusual circumstances of their betrothal. The other girls crowded around Ming, asking her questions. *How'd your parents arrange such a match? Did you see the matchmaker? Have you kissed? Have you talked about your marriage night? Have you started planning your wedding? Do you think it'll hurt?*

They followed her like a flock of birds, pecking her with their curiosities. Always, the unspoken question: *How are you marrying above your station?*

Ming did not know the answer. Neither set of parents was forthcoming with the truth. The popular story among the town gossips was that Zhou Shūshu owed Baba a life debt from the days of the Russo–Japanese War. Another was that Baba was blackmailing Shūshu. The boys in town weren't interested in the origins of the arrangement. They made whooping, suggestive noises every time Ming came by to fetch Fei for dinner. They shouted innuendos at the pair as they walked back to the compound. Ming hadn't been aware of the effect of her looks beyond how much they angered Mama, but in their bloom, Fei had grown different: tentative and wanting.

Their friendship shapeshifted. Their childhood games became juvenile, and their parents grew wary about leaving them alone together. They no longer spent every hour by each other's side. Fei went to school with the other boys, while Ming helped Mama with chores or Mother-in-law with apothecary errands. She'd stopped attending school when she was eleven. That was when the Japanese reforms were put in place, turning the girls' education into a sham: nothing more than housekeeping lessons that were better taught at home. Girls, the Japanese said, were meant for the hearth, not the classroom. Ming tried to keep herself sharp by reading Shūshu's books and doing sums on his abacus when she had spare time.

In Shūshu's medical texts, she read that humans developed in phases of seven years. For females, at age seven, their kidney aura grew strong, their baby teeth fell out, and their hair grew. At fourteen, they began menstruation and could conceive children. Ming was over a year late. Any later and Shūshu might end the betrothal, calling her damaged goods. Then no one would marry her. Then she and Mama would live out the rest of their days shackled to one another.

As the days passed, the anxiety of failure blossomed within her stomach. Within her head, a chorus of the women that came before her—the ancestors she prayed to—pressed against her thoughts, wondering if she could bear to, bear it, bear a child, if she could just—be a good girl and—*bleed*. They wombed inside her, a Russian nesting doll of wives and mothers, all asking if she was a real woman or not.

MING SPENT THE DAY BEFORE the month was up helping Mother-in-law prepare herbal remedies. On days spent at the compound, Mother-in-law invited Ming to stay for dinner, just the four of them. Ming went to fetch Fei. He was walking back from school. The boys he was with jostled him as Ming approached.

"Hi, Ming," they chimed, straightening their backs, their voices cheery and innocent.

"Hello," Ming said. "Āyí wanted me to get you for dinner," she said to Fei. He nodded. The boys pushed him forward. Since Ming had started filling out her clothes, the boys had gotten cruder. When they thought she wasn't looking, they would thrust and grope at the air like it was her new breasts. On the dim, wooded path to the apothecary, Fei's cheeks burned.

"What do you see in them?" Ming asked. Fei was smart and well read. Ming didn't understand why he chose to spend his time with those boys, who spat on the road and leered at her.

"What do you mean?" Fei asked. Ming shot him a pointed look, and his face reddened more.

"They're just playing around. They can be idiots, but they're also good friends. Loyal. They're happy for us, that we're going to get married soon."

Fei threaded his hand within hers, squeezed her fingers.

"Happy for us," Ming echoed in disbelief.

"They've been listening to me talk about you for years."

Ming hummed in acknowledgment. Fei had been the first person to love her. When they were children, she'd been desperate for affection, and Fei had given it to her freely. He promised her a new house, a new family. That had been a lifeline for Ming. Still, marriage was daunting. Ming did not know how to be a wife to Fei. As her body had so stubbornly shown, Ming barely knew how to be a woman.

"Do they ever ask you questions? About us?"

"Like?"

"The girls in town ask me questions about our betrothal, our wedding," she paused, "our wedding night."

The tips of Fei's ears turned a vibrant pink even as he said, "Not really, no."

She jabbed him in the side with their linked hands. "I know when you're lying."

He winced. "They're not questions. It's nothing you should hear. Nothing serious. Just them joking around."

"I want to know."

"No, you don't. You'll get mad."

"How do you know?"

"I know you."

"And I want to know." Ming peeled their hands apart, standing in the path, unmoving, until he answered her.

"Fine, fine," Fei said at last, heaving a sigh, "they say that if we're going to be married anyway, we should just sleep with each other now. To see what it's like." He said this nervously, but Ming saw something in his expression—an implicit question and a hunger lurking behind his pupils—that set her on edge. She turned around and began walking the path without him.

"Don't be upset, Ming. I told you you wouldn't like it. They were just joking around," Fei called out, catching up to her.

"I'm not upset," Ming said.

Fei sighed again, and they walked back to the house in silence.

True to her word, Ming wasn't upset. She was thinking of how many ways she could be ruined. She was thinking of how many paths would lead her back to a life spent with Mama. If she didn't bleed. If she slept with Fei before their wedding night, because he wanted to, because he found her new body attractive, because he was a boy and a firstborn son on top of that, who always got his way. If Shūshu changed his mind. Her body was trying to ruin her. How she wished she could shed it and clothe herself in a new skin. An animal, an insect.

She was thinking of who the boy she was promised to was. Whether he was more similar to his friends than he'd like to admit. How well did she really know him, this older, different version of him? Still, she didn't have other options. As they neared the compound, Ming reached over tentatively and gave Fei's arm a squeeze, and he shot her a relieved smile.

As Ming lay in bed that night, she started devising contingency plans. If she did not bleed within the next week, she'd slice her thigh open with the kitchen cleaver and hand the bloody bedding to Mama and Mother-in-law and Shūshu as proof. Or she'd find a wounded bird in the forest and let the carcass pool red on top of the kang. Or—

"Are you still awake?" Dìdi asked. *Qian*, she corrected in her head. Dìdi, twelve years old and in the midst of a growth spurt, had begun to scowl at the use of anything but his given name.

"Yes. Why?"

"You're tossing and turning everywhere."

"Oh. Sorry. Did I wake you?"

"No," he said, but his voice sounded weary.

"Sorry," she repeated. He grumbled.

"Qian?"

"What?" he whined, his voice heavy with sleep.

"What's Fei like at school?"

Dìdi turned to face her, his eyes glinting in the dark. "Why? Don't you lovebirds spend all your time together?" he asked, mocking.

"I was just wondering," she huffed.

"We're not in the same year," Qian said. Then, slowly, "Did he do something to you?"

"What? No. Why would you ask that?"

"No reason."

"What would he do to me?"

"Can we talk about this in the morning?" Qian groaned.

"No," Ming said, sitting up, "we're talking about this now."

"You're so stubborn."

"I know. Now, tell me."

Qian paused, heaved a sigh. "I just don't like the way he talks about you with his friends."

Ming's blood went cold. "Like what?"

"Like he won you in a game. Like a prize."

"What'd he say?"

Qian rolled over, his back to her. "Nothing specific."

"What else?" she asked, but Qian didn't answer. She poked and prodded at his back, but he gave an obnoxious fake snore, letting her know he was done talking.

Ming flopped onto her back, staring at the ceiling. Her heart beat a twitching, rabbity rhythm, the words *like a prize* winding around her mind. Qian, Ming reassured herself, was just being overprotective.

In the morning, there was hot blood between her legs, running down her quilt in rivulets, the answer to her month's prayers.

Nineteen

Qianze

2011: Six Years Before Reunion

Charlottesville, Virginia

"OF COURSE, THERE'S MORE TO Baba Yaga than a child-eating witch in a chicken-legged shack haunting the forest. Beliefs about witches were really fears of women destabilizing the male social order."

The clock struck three. The students, antsy, began to pack their bags.

"Tomorrow, we'll wrap up Slavic spirits with the female swamp demons, the Dziwożona. Then we'll look at the anthropology of lore in Malinowski's essays. Readings are up on Blackboard!" the professor called out futilely to the half-empty lecture hall, students already filing out to the dark winter afternoon.

For spring semester, Qianze had snagged a coveted spot in the university's popular Dracula class, which surprisingly did not teach *Dracula* but a series of twentieth-century monster films and an introduction to Slavic folklore instead. She'd signed up for the class at Theo's suggestion, hoping that learning about monsters and folklore would shed new light on the nightmares that had plagued her in August.

THAT LAST WEEK OF AUGUST had passed much the same as the week before: littered with a succession of bodies. A rat, a starling, then several rabbits. At least three of them, their white bellies turned upward, their necks askew. When she was not in classes or in the dining hall, Qianze remained cooped up in her room, scared of setting foot outside. She pored over the books she'd gotten from the library. The book on Wyoming was quickly discarded, containing only a paragraph about the taxidermic origins of jackalope mounts.

The second book, *Fēnshén Yǎnyì*, turned out to be the basis of a Chinese period drama she'd once watched with Ma. She hazily recalled being seven and tucked underneath Ma's arm as they watched the drama from the '90s. Ma thumbing the thick case of DVDs, one for each episode. A friend of a friend had brought it back from China, and it was passed around the circle of immigrant wives in the area: their version of a romance paperback, full of court intrigue and gauzy, floral clothing.

The series had followed Dájǐ, the favorite concubine of King Zhou, the last emperor of the Shang dynasty before the rise of the Zhou dynasty. She was often blamed for King Zhou's downfall as the invisible hand behind his tyranny. In the drama, Dájǐ began as a sweet girl, who underwent a cruel transformation after being possessed by a fox demon—one sent by the goddess Nüwa to topple the king. The rest of Qianze's memory of the show had been lost to mistranslation or Mama covering her eyes for the adult parts: grainy-quality seductions and cruel torture scenes with bad special effects.

The third book contained a handful of old fox stories, all centered on fox demons and possession. Foxes inhabited a body for a brief time, sowing discord and mayhem within their host's household. Occasionally, a fox like Dájǐ would consume the host's soul—the body now both coffin and doppelgänger. It was believed that foxes drained the luck from a home, leaving in their wake a generation or two of poverty and misfortune.

Qianze, who found herself standing on a crumbling cliffside overlooking a descent into madness, did not know what to make of this information. Was she haunted? Possessed? Was this why she drew omens and misfortune to her like insects to summer flypaper? Despite the terrifying visions, Qianze still sought out a rational answer: mold exposure, narcolepsy, some scientific explanation.

Sleep-deprived and tearing her own hair out, she had been a day or two away from checking herself into the psychiatric ward when the apparitions stopped. The second week of September passed. Qianze spent those days vigilantly cataloging her surroundings, her senses heightened and paranoid, jumping at the squeak of a shoe, at a distant red object that turned out to be a Solo cup. After a few days of this, she tentatively accepted that the sightings were gone, leaving as quickly as they came. Qianze could not trace what was remarkable about that week. Had she done something to exorcize them? All she knew was that, by mid-September, her life had returned to normal, as if nothing had ever been amiss. The only difference was a subtle shift in the air, as if the caul of her reality had grown thicker, less prone to strange slippages.

The fox and the hare disappeared, and Qianze warily settled into her college life. By late fall, she had lost the bruising dark circles around her eyes and gained a small circle of friends from the Asian Student Union whom Theo had introduced her to. She spent Thanksgiving in Charlottesville with them, the experience all new to her. Cooking for one another. Laughter over the dinner table. Having friends. Having Asian friends, who understood how it felt being on a campus with so many rich, white classmates who jangled past her with their tennis bracelets and their generational wealth.

She returned to Tidewater for the first time after finals. She took the bus and packed a small bag, not wanting to unsettle the space she'd made for herself in the dorms. Ainsley had been spending less time in the dorm, preoccupied with cozying up to second-year sorority sisters before spring rush. In her absence, the room had started to feel more like Qianze's, her photos and memorabilia collecting, forming a portrait of a full life.

After a three-hour drive, the bus pulled into the gloomy lot of the Tidewater station. Qianze immediately noticed Ma through the darkened windows. How eerie the woman at the Greyhound bus stop was. How unfamiliar. Her, with the trimmed dark hair gleaming from a recent salon trip. Her, with the lithe limbs and athletic clothes of someone who regularly attended workout classes. Her, with the winter-flushed cheeks and beatific expression, jumping and waving to Qianze excitedly—the motion drawing leering glances from the men in the parking lot.

Qianze, despite her best intentions for the trip, felt bitterness flood her body at this sight. She had been worried that Ma was lying during their calls throughout the past semester, shielding Qianze from the truth of her well-being. Some nights, when Qianze was supposed to be studying, she would be preoccupied, wondering whether the rental property was covering all of Ma's living expenses, whether Ma was eating regularly, whether Ma was going to work and if she'd need to get another job if the books didn't balance. All this time, Ma had been flourishing in Qianze's absence.

"Bǎobèi! Your bus here early!" Ma said as she came up to Qianze, taking the duffel bag slung over her shoulder. "I've been waiting for you, so excited to see you."

"Ma. You look different."

Ma beamed, the apples of her cheeks lifting. The skin of her face looked plump enough that you could bounce a quarter off it.

"You notice! Ma has been taking yoga. A client's mom offer me free class. I love it. Make me feel like new person."

Ma's tutoring clients were primarily private-school children who lived in gated neighborhoods. Their mothers thought Mandarin looked good on college applications. These children cycled through a revolving door of extracurriculars, clubs, and tutors. Their mothers were the women who ran the PTAs and dance committees, hoping to recapture their lost youth.

Qianze did not know how to respond, still in shock at Ma's metamorphosis. Where was the woman she'd left behind in August? The mother of her adolescence, whose negligence was a secret she had to safeguard from the risk of Child Protective Services? How many mornings had she lingered on the threshold of the Myrtle house's master bedroom, watching Ma's chest rise and fall in the tangled sheets before having to get herself to school? How many times had Ma looked at her, deerlike, unable to understand someone's English? She'd thought Ma had needed her.

"Let's go home, bǎobèi. You can see how I decorate the apartment."

It felt odd not driving to the Myrtle house. Instead, they made their way into the downtown area where Ma's apartment was. This was the first time Qianze registered that the Myrtle house was not home anymore. It still belonged to them in name, but she could not go back inside as anything more than a glorified housekeeper. She could bite and bay and scratch like a dog at the door, but she could never go back, not really.

Ma's apartment was a one-bedroom, a second-floor walk-up in a brick building. Qianze remembered the space from when she helped Ma move in at the end of summer. "Decorated" was an overstatement. There was a candle here, a framed yoga slogan there. The effect was a minimalism that felt sterile. In the living room, a gray pullout couch was made up in cream linens.

"Do you like it?" Ma asked.

Qianze nodded, pasted on a smile. It felt like a showroom, the place stripped of all personality—only the gleam of fluorescence reflecting off the enamel polish of the few sparse decorations. When Ma left for her evening yoga class, Qianze skulked through the apartment, seeking traces of the mother she knew.

Her search was interrupted by the *ping* of a text message from Theo, who'd just landed at LaGuardia and was headed to his lola's in Queens. It was Theo and their friends who had encouraged her to spend the holidays with Ma. They didn't know the full story, but they'd gathered that Qianze and Ma's relationship was strained. When Qianze called Ma, their conversations would often peter out to silence, humming with unspoken resentment. With her friends' support and the distance college afforded her, Qianze had resolved to put aside her past grudges and start anew with Ma. But she hadn't anticipated coming home to find this version of Ma, modeled after the shallow yoga mothers she worked with.

Have you talked to her yet? Theo texted.

Not yet. Things are weird here.

To Qianze, the other members of the Asian Student Union seemed so in touch with their mother cultures. Throughout middle and high school, Qianze had only been aware of her Chineseness as something to be sloughed off in order to fit in among her white classmates. Only at college did she begin thinking about her identity. With it came a slew of questions that only Ma could answer: What had her parents' childhoods been like? What were her parents like? Where had she and Ba met? Why had they immigrated? Was there anything she missed about the old country?

Do you want to talk about it?

Despite a semester of friendship with Theo, Qianze was still taken aback by his empathy and concern. Lately, their friendship had developed a different texture. At dinners or parties, she'd search around for him, only to find him already looking at her, his gaze sending a thrill through her. If they were sitting next to each other, she would let her head rest against his shoulder, her thigh touch his. All of this made her nervous and scared; wanting was not new to Qianze—often she felt like a raw, open wound of wanting—but being wanted back was. Sometimes she would linger too long in a hug, daring herself to pull back and press her lips against his, but then she'd stumble away, her heart in her throat, afraid that, if she did so, she'd lose the first true friend she'd had in years.

Not right now. I'll let you know how it goes.

QIANZE DISCOVERED REMNANTS FROM MYRTLE in a shoebox under Ma's bed. The box had contained Ma's new pair of Nike sneakers, which she'd been wearing when she left for yoga. Now it housed the urn of Qianze's siblings' ashes and their ultrasound. A black-and-white photo of Ma and her twin brother, standing in front of the white columns of the Old Gate of Qīnghuá University, their solemn expressions mirrors of each other. Ma's wedding band.

She stared at the box for several minutes, feeling a deep gust of emotion rise in her ribs. She recognized it as a tangle of envy and frustration. When Qianze was in high school, all she'd wanted was for Ma to pull herself together, to be the adult of their family. Instead, Qianze had spent nights on the computer being raised by a forum of strangers on Yahoo! Answers, asking questions on how to pay the bills, budget for groceries, and apply to jobs as a teenager.

Why was it that when Ma did something wrong, her annoyance was so needling and sharp? Resentment, jealousy, condescension: it felt like all these emotions were heightened with Ma. Qianze wanted to swallow them down, but they prickled at the back of her throat. Ma had emerged from her depression, but she'd done it too late; she'd left her past behind, and all that remained was a hollow shell with Ma's face. Qianze couldn't understand this. She had created herself around the hole Ba had left—like a storm with an eye. The loss of him was woven into her being, unable to be packed up and tucked away. Qianze wanted to rip off Ma's new veneer and get to the innermost part of her. There, she would find her and finally understand her.

Ma returned from her yoga class in time to prepare a dinner

of salad with lentils and bland chicken. She was on a Mediterranean diet.

"Ma?" Qianze asked.

"Hmmm?" Ma responded, focused on cutting through the rubbery skin of the chicken.

"What was it like for you, growing up in China?"

Ma's head snapped up. "Why you want to know that?"

"I'm just curious," Qianze said. "You don't talk about your life there. What your parents were like, what your childhood was like, your college life."

Ma frowned. "That was another life. We are American now. We don't need hold on to old things."

"But those things didn't disappear when you immigrated. Your parents, your childhood, your brother." Ma winced at the invocation of her twin. "They didn't just go away when you came here. I want to know about them. How they made you."

Ma shook her head. "No, I make myself. I make new self."

That's not how it works! Qianze wanted to scream. What was the harm in letting Qianze know who she came from? How could she move forward with all this unknown past jangling inside of her?

"Qianze, bǎobèi," Ma said, sensing Qianze's distress, her voice sweetening and stretching like taffy. "You were born in America. You live American life. It is a better life. No use in looking backwards."

"What if looking backwards is important to me?"

Ma's brows knit together as if Qianze had said some English phrase she could not translate. "But why?" she asked.

How could Ma not understand? Ma was Qianze's only family. There were stilted minute-long conversations on the phone during Lunar New Year with Ma's parents: Qianze's lǎolao and lǎoye. But Qianze did not even know their names, what they looked like, only the crackling static of their voices as she wished them xīnnián kuàilè. Beyond Ma, Qianze had no roots. Where had she come from? Where had she gotten her chin from? The texture of her hair? Did she resemble her late uncle? Had she inherited anything from her grandmother?

"Never mind, Ma," Qianze said instead, deflating, not wanting to start a fight.

"Okay," Ma replied. "It for the best, bǎobèi. Past is full of bad memory. We only make good memory now."

Qianze murmured a sound of false assent. She scraped the remaining lentils and the blue chicken bones into the trash can, where they fell with a squelch, feeling Ma's eyes on the back of her neck.

Twenty

Ba

2017: Eleven Days Since Reunion
Manhattan, New York

THE TEDDY BEAR SAT ON the top of his daughter's living-room shelves, beaming down innocently at him. Except he knew better. It was brand-new, still had a loop of plastic that had once held the price tag. He knew what it was to be watched—his whole childhood had been a lesson in surveillance—and so his intuition told him that through those glassy, black eyes, his daughter was peering out.

He got smarter about his indiscretions: knew to hide the liquor in unassuming paper bags, to drink in the bathroom on the outskirts of the camera's periphery, to lug his empties to the dumpster outside the building rather than hide them in the apartment. When his daughter returned from work, there was no evidence of his drinking, save for the smell on his breath that he could not scrub out, though his gums bled from trying.

He spent his days sitting in the plastic bathtub with his knees drawn to his chest, the space too small for him to stretch out his legs. He was sifting through his memories for the prophecy, but the seed of it was buried deep—deep enough that he could feel his bones singing with it.

He wanted to purge his being and search on the floor for it amongst his slippery pink organs. Instead, he was forced to relive his past, memories arising and subsuming him—never knowing where he would wake next. He hoped that this time, the alcohol would cut the thread to his emotions. *Snip*, and he would be cast off: a spectator and not an actor. No such luck. He was damned to continue circling his wounds like tub water around the drain, the old emotions still raw.

He became disoriented looking at himself in the bathroom mirror, spending long minutes wondering who the stranger looking out at him was: the jaundiced eyes, the beer paunch, the way the skin of his face was always swollen like a water-bloated corpse. Some days, while walking in the streets, he would catch a glimpse of his reflection and stop, bewildered by it. *That's not me, bù rènshí.* In his mind, he was still the man he was eleven years ago, before he left.

He thought he had made the right choice by leaving. Seeing his daughter, feeling his wife's absence from her life, cast doubt on that decision. Witnessing her barely contained fury—her wanting in spite of it—was like seeing himself: twenty-one and grieving for the father that would never exist.

A lesson he had learned: his past resisted chronology. It looped. It wound. It spiraled like a Fibonacci sequence. Some ages felt closer to him than others. Multiples of seven, he'd noticed, consumed him, felt uncomfortably, inexplicably real. Fourteen. Twenty-one. Thirty-five. He did not know why. What he also knew: his mind coiled, serpentine, suffocating those memories he most wanted to forget—the same ones he now needed.

His memories had become slippery. He thought he could remember his mother's face, but when he held it for too long, the features slid off, becoming the features of the other women in his life: a monstrous collage of body parts. Their faces overlaid on top of one another, a transparent Russian nesting doll, the expressions of his daughter, his wife, his mother, his sister, his grandmother overlapping in a palimpsest, enclosed in one another, smaller and smaller, until they blurred into one alien entity, all of their eyes spiteful—

Stop this—no more—mind dipping back into regret like a swimmer's arms into water—over and over—

I want to feel solid again. I want to be fifty-three sitting down to dinner—hand-pulled noodles, I remember, I remember the chew of them, the afternoon spent pulling dough apart until they were the length of my wingspan. We were celebrating fourteen years. The others did not make it past seven months in the womb, but Qianze did and then seven more and on and on. I want to be fifty-three sitting down to dinner. I have been fifty-three for the past eleven years. Come autumn, I think I will become something else. Nonetheless. I will follow the thread backwards. Summer 2006. I remember that—

HE HAD NO PLAN. ONE day—no, one hour—all was well. They were sitting around the dining table, laughing as Qianze slurped her fourteenth birthday noodles one by one. And then the Woman's voice was ringing in his head like the air after a gunshot, the intrusion of it after decades a shock that almost made him drop his glass. She reminded him, *It's been forty years.*

The sound of her voice flung him back to when he was thirteen, shaking as he emerged from the bog. The memory of the Woman's words echoing inside him, her warning having come to fruition. How he would hurt everyone he loved. How he would hatch into some *thing*, some beast, which would destroy his life.

He grew desperate. He bartered. *Things are good here. Nothing's happened to me yet. I won't hurt them. I won't let myself. I won't leave.*

She was quiet. She did not need to warn him what might become of his family if he stayed. The dread of the Woman's prophecy lived inside his house. He would turn a corner, open the pantry door, and suddenly, he would imagine the awful possibilities for a fleeting moment, pressing against his ribs, wanting to claw themselves out.

He had damned his family. He realized this, sitting at the table, the ripples of predestination catching up to him, making his breath hitch in his throat. He'd fooled himself, believing that he was safe, but he had created a life that his prophecy could touch, and now he had set the fox loose in the henhouse, the beast upon his family.

His wife brought the cake from the kitchen to the round dining table. It was a cheap sheet cake from the grocery store with bright piping that read *Happy 14th Birthday, Qianze!* He wanted this moment to last. But already the wicks of the candles were burning down and the wax was melting, pooling blue-green on the surface of the cake. He wanted to build a refuge in this sliver of time—a suspended cross section for him to hide in. His palms were sweating, the realization of what he was about to do thudding heavy in his chest, and they were singing and Qianze was blowing out her candles and tearing through her gifts—too excited to notice the mournful quiet he'd settled into—and it was over, over, over and outside it was summer dark, a sharp indigo blue, the afternoon gone so fast, he had not yet finished committing the details to memory.

When his wife and daughter were asleep, he gathered up some of his things. A family photo, his documents, some savings in cash, pilling sweaters, the sleeping bag Qianze had used once before deciding the outdoors weren't for her. He was headed north. Where, he did not know. He did not linger on the threshold. He walked out, his steps resolute. If he lingered, he wouldn't have been able to leave.

He biked to the local bus station. Best to leave the car. They would need it more than him. There was not a hint of wind that night. He could see swarms of blood-bloated mosquitoes and moths crowding around the streetlamps. He focused on these circles of orange light on the tar, illuminating his way. This was duty, he told himself. Not the violent, revolutionary duty to country he had once known, but familial duty. Harder, demanding of more sacrifice. He arrived at the bus station. The next bus north was not for two hours. He waited.

All the stations and buses looked the same. They lent themselves well to anonymity. In these liminal hubs, he grieved. He watched as other weary travelers ducked their faces and floated to their buses, like lost souls being ferried to the afterlife. Over the next two days, he would hop eight buses, until at last, done in by claustrophobia and his own stench, he got off at a stop somewhere in Vermont. He began again.

HE HAD NOT DISAPPEARED. HE could hardly forge a new identity after fighting so hard for citizenship in this country. He went by an American nickname, Wayne. Neither Qianze nor his wife tried to find him. His wife, he knew, would think him better off dead. Perhaps that was what she was telling everyone. They had grown up together. They had survived a revolution, an immigration, a harsh culture where everything that came out of their accented mouths was sneered at. To leave when things were good was a crime worse than dying. When he searched his name, he found himself buried in Google, a blank page amidst half a million results. "Wayne" Zhou, assistant stock crew manager, Hannaford Supermarkets. No picture.

He lived in a shabby apartment, the cheapest place he had found on Craigslist: cash up front, no questions asked. It was a five-minute walk from the grocery store, the second floor of a neglected house with its own set of rickety stairs in the backyard.

"It's a fixer-upper," the man from Craigslist said in a gruff voice.

There was no full-sized fridge, only a mini one that sat under the counter, appearing to have been plucked from a campus's discards. It had fraternity stickers on it that could not be scraped off. The shower was standing room only, and the ceilings were blooming brown, watery splotches. The floor was wood, which would've been nice had it not been warped by the water damage. But he did not need nice. He needed cheap and convenient, and it was certainly that, even if it was lacking in everything else.

"It's fine. I'll take it." Both he and the Craigslist seller seemed surprised by this decision. They exchanged cash, keys, and numbers.

He began to drink to keep the beast from surfacing. Then he began to drink to escape the life he had haphazardly created for himself. There were memories from his past that he had cast aside, things he had shoved in boxes and up into the dusty attic of his head that he did not dare open, but there was also his wife and his daughter and their house. He often thought about how the garden at Myrtle looked in bloom, with its bushes of azaleas in a combustion of red, the crepe myrtle trees shedding their accordion petals. In his mind, in a place where he had excavated and razed all he wanted to forget, he rebuilt the house.

First, the yard, which he had faithfully mown every week. Then the flowers, the perennials and annuals, which he planted in their careful beds of fertilizer and mulch. Inside, he painted the rooms: maroon for the living room, pale green for the kitchen, sunny yellow for the bathroom. Slowly, he moved in the furniture, the photographs, the pencil lines along the corner where he had measured Qianze's height over the years, the chip in the paint from where his wife's dining chair hit the wall when she pulled it out. He mapped out how the sun slanted in through the windows at different times of the day; how, at dawn, its musty light exposed the suspended dust motes. And once, in a drunken stupor—when the veil between reality and dream grew filmy and sheer like cellophane—he went inside and found his wife and daughter sitting at this make-believe kitchen table, waiting for him. They were not angry. They welcomed him back from his travels. He was home.

From that night forward, he became a regular at the local liquor store: another drunk seeking refuge from reality inside a daydream.

He spent a decade as a checkout clerk at Hannaford Supermarket. The white customers barely gave him a passing glance, their glazed eyes flickering over him like he was part of the store scenery. He enjoyed the invisibility. All that wasted education, his life reduced to a monotonous rhythm, as persistent as the barcode scanner that marked his days. Work, home, drink. Until he realized that no one paid him any mind, and it became drink, work, home, drink.

Later, he would find that the house he built had warped into something else, an architectural labyrinth of dead ends and graveyards and strange rooms. Doors that opened into nothing, walls that should've been doors. Later, the scaffolding he built would become something wrong and haunted, and the house would become a cage for the beast. *When had it become this way?* But that was later. For now, he was just happy to sit at the table.

It was July. They were eating hand-pulled noodles. On the kitchen counter, a sheet cake sat waiting. The candles never melted.

Twenty-One

Weihong
1966: Fifty-One Years Before Reunion
Ānshān, Liáoníng Province

IT WAS THE END OF July. There had been no school for two months. Weihong was fourteen and supposed to complete middle school the following year, but there would be no school come fall. It would be that way for the next two years. Out on the streets of Ānshān, the children were running lawless and rabid. Little tyrants, Nǎinai dared to call them once over dinner. Mother and Father had quickly shushed her and made her swear not to say it again.

"We're going to let children run our lives now? What we say in our own homes?" she asked.

"Ma, these children are dangerous," Father said. "They think they're carrying out justice, following the Chairman's orders. If they heard you, they'd . . ." He drifted off, either at a loss for words or unwilling to voice the punishments that they might inflict.

Mother nodded slowly. "I heard from our neighbors that they've killed publicly. Do you remember Weihong's elementary school teacher? Teacher Xing? They boiled her skin off, left her sore-ridden corpse out for the dogs."

"They're *children*," Nǎinai echoed, but she sounded like she was trying to convince herself of their innocence.

"No, Ma," Father said, "they think they're soldiers. And they'd kill you for far less than you calling them—what you did."

Nǎinai blinked in surprise at her son's refusal to repeat her words. From then on, Nǎinai was careful. They all were. They went through their daily errands with their heads bowed and their mouths shut. Citywide, an undercurrent of terror simmered. Mother had insisted that Weihong accompany Kangmei whenever she left the apartment and instituted a curfew for both of them. By all accounts, Weihong and Kangmei were regarded as the descendants of poor, rural farmers, which shielded them for the time being. They walked within the city, ignored by the red children, who had taken it upon themselves to be the ringleaders of the city's eclipsing violence. Not so lucky were the black children, the targets of their abuse.

In the summer mornings, Weihong and Kangmei went to the park while the air was still cool. It was an untenably hot month, and Nǎinai said that the August weather was only good for swimming or retreating to shady corners. Nothing else could be done in heat like this.

It was early, the light of dawn just trickling in. Kangmei hadn't been able to sleep well—the night outside their compound heavy with screams and pleas and worse, the discomfiting silence that followed. Her thrashing, sweating body jostled Weihong awake, and he lay there, staring at the ceiling for hours. They blearily made their way to Yù Fú Park, home to a trio of small lakes and smaller watering holes good for swimming. The water was cold in the mornings, but they liked to float on their backs as the sun rose and began to warm their exposed bellies. Sometimes they'd bring some laundry and a crumbling bar of soap. They'd been going to the lakes since they were young, when their mother had taught them to swim. This summer, she did not join them.

"We're going swimming," he informed her the first summer day it was hot enough to warrant it.

"That sounds refreshing, bǎobèi," she said, the creases of her eyes wrinkling. "It makes me happy to see you and your mèimei getting along. Will you wash this shirt for me while you're there?"

Weihong looked at her, confused. "You're not coming with us?"

"Oh, I don't think so, bǎobèi. I'm not feeling very well," she said.

She gave the same answer until Weihong learned to stop asking. It was true that she looked paler and thinner than usual. Last month, she cut all her hair off to a boyish length before the Red Guards could do it for her. Long hair was a feudal indulgence. On her unframed face, her cheekbones jutted out wrongly and her lips were chewed raw.

Since the newspapers had splashed photos of the Chairman swimming across the Yángzǐ River over their pages, the siblings' routine at the lakes had been disrupted. Hundreds came to swim, hoping to prove their own prowess. Weihong and Kangmei steered away from the daily clamor of swimmers. At dawn, the dark water was empty and beckoning. There, Weihong and Kangmei could pretend it was any other summer, any other year.

They floated in their old gym clothes, their limbs stretched out. When Weihong turned to look at his sister, her face looked its age, smooth and unworried. Her glasses were left on the shore along with their basket of laundry—damp bedsheets and clothes yellowing with summer stains. She opened one eye, like a flounder, squinting to make out the shape of him. The illusion was broken. Weihong dove, kicking himself deeper. Even underwater, the image of his sister floated in his mind. Her face was a child's, but her eyes were not, not since the alley. He had done his best to forget what happened, but sometimes an image would remind him—Kangmei's eyes, milk gone blue, the foot of a hare disappearing into bushes—and he would return to that moment, standing outside the alley, willing himself not to go in.

When the skin of their fingertips became pruned, they waded back to land and dried off in the sun as they scrubbed the sheets against the shoreside rocks. They were walking back to the apartment when they came across one of Weihong's classmates.

His name was Xiaoli. He was quiet and kept to himself. Weihong did not know him well besides the fact that he came from a black family and outperformed the red students on their exams, which was a point of resentment. He wore glasses like Kangmei, and his quarter-moon eyes were often bloodshot from nights of reading. To the reds, this made him an INTELLECTUAL! A RUNNING DOG OF CAPITALISM! And this is what the wooden placard around his neck said.

They had tied him to the tree with wire and then pissed on the deep wounds that the wire had left in his flesh. When Weihong and Kangmei encountered him, he reeked of excrement and infection, having been left out all night. His face was bruised, one quarter-moon eye shut from the beating he'd received. When he saw Weihong, he murmured a sound, which could've been his name. Weihong couldn't tell since his jaw was badly swollen. Weihong swallowed. Kangmei darted forward, moving to free him. Luckily, there was no one around to hear or see when Weihong grabbed her and carried her away, kicking and crying. If Kangmei freed the boy, she would be next, and it would be her—CAPITALIST SYMPATHIZER!—strung up on the tree. Didn't she realize that?

That night, after Kangmei had told Mother about what they had seen, Mother kneeled at the foot of their bed mats. She wrapped a stray thread from the hem of her tunic around and around her finger until the tip of it became white and the thread snapped.

"Kangmei, Weihong," she began, "I don't know what will happen in the coming days, but this is a time for survival. And sometimes," she paused, "sometimes survival is difficult. If the government wants you to do something, then you do it. If the Red Guards want you to do something, you must do it. Okay?" At this, she held Weihong's gaze, beady and hard, and he knew what she was saying. *Do what you must. You have my blessing.* He nodded. He understood.

Within a week, Kangmei's compassion—that same instinct that drew her to the local cats—cowered away, replaced by self-preservation. Weihong's self-preservation manifested differently, which is to say, terribly. Weihong had been hurled into a vortex of violence so cavernous, he did not know where the outer lip of it was, whether it had swallowed the whole country, the whole world. It had become the fabric of their existence.

This was what his family did not know. Lurking under Weihong's skin was a grandiose sense of immortality, one that ran deeper than that of his fellow classmates. Death would not come for him, at least not for the next forty years; he remembered this much from the bog. The consequences of his actions would not come for him this month or the next, but at some distant point in the future, forty years sounding like a lifetime. By that time, his skin would begin to wrinkle and sag, and his mind would start to forget what he had done to survive when he was fourteen.

He would use this survival as a weapon. To be the person who ensured his family's well-being, Weihong would have to sharpen his innate violence, the violence he had inherited and learned from his father, honed and barbed like a fishhook.

The pack of Red Guards he'd sidled up to were red students from his middle school who deemed him, an engineer's son, fit to assist them in their dirty work. At school, he was known for his sleepy, amused expression, which teachers mistook for insolence. He had hit his growth spurt early, and in grade school, he had gone through a period of playground brawls that left his angular jaw slightly asymmetrical. This was what they needed, the reds agreed, someone who disliked the teachers as much as they did, because they'd set their sights on the teachers. The reds called them monsters after the recent *People's Daily* editorial, which urged revolutionaries to denounce the bourgeoisie, to "Sweep Away All Monsters and Demons!"

They did not so much sweep as raze. The reds had been raised by brutality, had suckled at its teat. They had held their rifle-club meetings after school, where they shot at posters of Chiang Kai-shek, and all the while, their fingers itched to shoot at something alive. Mao had told them that to rebel is justified, and so they unleashed their sleeping sadism, and in its wake, left bodies in the streets.

On the afternoon of Weihong's initiation, the reds had gathered him and some of his other classmates outside of their school. The reds were wearing their parents' old military uniforms: oversized and in a shade of green dulled with age. They'd adorned the uniforms with badges of Mao and new red strips of cloth tied around their arms.

Their de facto leader was a petite thirteen-year-old girl with war-hero parents and a deceptively innocent pixie-like face. At her command, the Red Guards led out a line of teachers and administrators, their arms bound, and made them kneel before them. Weihong recognized them even though they wore dunce caps over their shaved heads and placards around their necks that revealed them to be BLACK GANG ELEMENTS! IMPERIALIST SPIES! and COUNTER-REVOLUTIONARY MONSTERS AND DEMONS! They had been locked in a classroom for the past few nights, the leader informed them proudly. They smelled of waste, their clothes soiled.

"The revolution is not for the faint of heart. Our new world is only for the strong. Who among you has the strength?" the girl asked.

Her comrades handed out nail-spiked clubs, bats, and whips to the new recruits. Weihong was given a haphazardly nailed club, the spikes rusty. The students stood silently in front of their teachers. The girl next to Weihong looked like she was about to cry. She'd been given a hammer.

"Well, go on," the red leader said, arching a daring eyebrow.

The first blow was the worst.

After that, butchery became easier. They lost sight of themselves, fusing together, becoming one: a slaughtering mob—a multiheaded beast. The reds quoted from Mao's *Red Book* amidst the cacophony of screams, their polyphonic voice chanting, "A revolution is not a dinner party; it cannot be so refined, so leisurely and gentle." Shreds of stringy flesh showered their faces as they hacked and lacerated. *How easy*, the beast thought as one, *the body gives, the blood spills, the bones crack.*

Their main target was the principal, and when they came apart, came back into their separate selves, they saw that he was at death's door, and the other teachers, battered, cried for mercy for him and for themselves, vomiting at the sight of fat and gristle and muscle. *We did that*, they thought, awed.

"And who will give the killing blow?" their leader asked gleefully.

It must be someone, Weihong thought, why not let it be me? And so he brought the club down against the principal's shaved, exposed head, where the nails embedded themselves into the bone, and he told himself that this strike would buy protection for his family. When he stepped away, he watched as the reds forced the other teachers to beat the dead body with their weak limbs.

Weihong stepped back. His palms were wet with cruelty. The sky was flush with the ground, and when he raised his face to the warm waning sun, he felt—*Divine*.

His mind offered the word in a voice that was not his, but deep and layered, practically primordial. This other being inside of him was pleased. Weihong was pleased. He could not tell the difference. And then, another voice that was not his.

Got caught on the hook of your own monstrosity, I see.

It was the Woman's.

Twenty-Two

Qianze
2017: Twelve Days Since Reunion
Manhattan, New York

THE MORNING AFTER HER BRUSH with the fox and the Aunties, Friday, August 18, Qianze spent an hour in the shower. She'd been unable to sleep the night before, her body both aching for rest and too alert to succumb to it. She'd given up trying to sleep at five in the morning and locked herself in the bathroom before Ba could claim it. She stood under the steam of the shower. She scalded herself down to bone and sinew and scrubbed at her skin with a pumice stone until it was pink and blotchy, ridding herself of the dead skin of the past month. She wanted to crack open the eggshell of her skull and dig out the ribbons of her thoughts, then let the water rinse away the delirium of last night's events.

At the office, she kept herself awake on a combination of coffee and paranoia. She felt like she was being watched, that her coworkers were looking at her, gossiping about her, but when she turned, everyone's back was to her. Wired, her hands shook on the keyboard, resulting in a series of careless mistakes. By lunch, she felt unclean again, so she slipped away and bought some floss. In the office bathroom, she pulled out string after string, flossing until the cords came away red and her gums were tender and sore. She leaned forward and gave her reflection a bleeding smile.

She felt like she was tight-roping on a thin thread of sanity, and that, at any moment, a stray wind might knock her over and send her spiraling into madness. Perhaps she was already there, in the world of foxes, jackalopes, and Aunties that existed side by side with civilization, hidden away from everyone else behind a veil of lunacy.

The afternoon stretched before her, time passing by slowly. How had she spent so many days like this? She'd been in the office for three years and, before Ba's return, had hardly noticed that time. Her world had been a string of numbers: reviewed, verified, analyzed; wrestled into spreadsheets and datasets and documents; cleaned and reformatted and submitted and reviewed once again. But now all she saw were sums that would cover Ba's healthcare and Ma's apartment, that would resolve her problems a thousand times over. Now she was all too aware of how this past month had meandered, her routine collapsing, giving way to two fevered weeks.

Qianze was sent home early. Her manager said she looked unwell, and that she'd be better off resting rather than forcing herself to work through it. She knew he was dismissing her because of her earlier mistakes. She packed up her things, feeling chided, and left the office, the possibility of a promotion dissipating in the face of the day's failure.

On the way home, Qianze chose the most packed subway car and pressed herself among the throng of people, hoping their presence would ward off any run-ins with the Aunties or whatever other creatures might crawl out of the woodwork. She opened the nanny-cam app. Her eye caught movement, but it was just a passing police light slicing through the dark room. The bathroom door was closed, but the sliver of space underneath the door was illuminated by the warm overhead light.

Before she got off, she checked the app again. No changes. But when she unlocked her front door, she found all the lights on in the apartment. Ba was sitting on the couch, awkwardly fidgeting. And leaning against the kitchen counter was Theo.

"Hi," Theo said while she stood frozen on the threshold. "You weren't answering your phone, and I know it's one of your busy seasons, so I came by to drop off some food, but I heard someone inside. So I knocked and your"—he cleared his throat—"your dad answered."

On the table was Theo's offering of food, wrapped in a plastic smiley-face bag. The smile wilted under Qianze's stare. She numbly peeled off the heels that had been blistering her feet and toed on her slippers. Her mind, exhausted and dazed, was still coming to terms with the rupture of her two worlds: Ba and Theo colliding in her living room. A long minute passed before she spoke.

She asked Theo, "Have you been here long?"

"Just a few minutes. Your dad was telling me about his visit."

"Really?" She eyed Ba, who avoided her gaze, nervously cleaning his glasses. "Theo, let's talk outside."

"All right," Theo agreed, his voice clipped.

The two of them walked through the hallway, out the apartment, and down the four flights, the air between them choked with tension. When they reached the lobby, she crossed her arms protectively over her body, hands clutching at her biceps.

"You shouldn't have talked to him. He'll get confused."

Theo's face contorted in disbelief. He took a step back. "You're upset with me? Up until half an hour ago, I thought your dad was dead. Is this why you've been so distant? Ignoring my calls and texts? I thought you were still thinking about us moving in together, I wanted to give you space to make that decision, but I don't—I don't even know where to begin. Is that your real dad?"

"Yes, that's my real dad," she said, sounding as drained as she felt.

"Has he been alive this whole time? Have you known?"

She flinched, turning to look down at her slippers, and he let out a long, slow exhale, his nostrils flaring. "Yes, he's been alive this whole time," she said faintly.

"Why'd you tell everyone in college that he was dead? Why didn't you tell *me* at least? We've been dating for, what, five years now, friends for seven, and you couldn't tell me this huge thing? Every time I think I understand you, you pull something like this, you hide away from me, and I feel like I don't know who you are all over again."

She tried to defend herself. "I didn't tell you because he was dead to *me*."

A muscle in Theo's jaw twitched. "That's not the same thing, and you know it. So your story about the aneurysm, that was all a lie?"

"It was an exaggeration—"

"An exaggeration?"

"Can you give me a moment to explain?" Qianze interrupted. "He left us. That grief was real. My grief was real. He felt dead. He was as good as dead. I wished he was dead! He disappeared, on my *birthday*, and I hadn't heard from him in over eleven years, not until this month."

"You could've told me that! Why didn't you tell me that?"

"I was scared you would react like this! I knew you wouldn't get it," Qianze said. She was thinking of how Theo once encouraged her to mend things with Ma. How his heart had been in the right place, but how he couldn't understand the fissures of her family, the dysfunction. Theo's family was not without problems, but he and his siblings spoke to each other regularly, and he went to Queens twice a month to see his lola and his extended family.

"What's there to get? You lied to me. You didn't give me a chance to get it. You could've told me that he was here, that he was back. That would've been better than what happened just now. I was so caught off guard, I didn't know what to think. I almost called the police. I didn't know who he was, if he was a fucking robber or murderer. What else haven't you told me?"

"Nothing!" Qianze said. Her voice sounded high and desperate. She was scared she would lose him over this, and she knew that the loss of him in the midst of everything else would be her undoing. "What happened with Ba, it happened so fast, I've barely wrapped my mind around it myself. I was going to tell you when I got the chance. But you know everything else."

A lie. There were the Aunties, the jackalope dream, the fox sightings, the strange string of dead animals that had followed her during her first weeks at UVA. But how could she explain those? She worried that if she tried, she would still lose him. She loved him too much to chase him away with the terrifying truth. She didn't know if this was the way other people loved, if it was the right way to love, if her ability to love had been ruined before she met him. Still, the emotion of it washed over her.

Theo's gaze was wary. It needled at her, and she shifted from foot to foot. "How do I know? How can I trust you? If I didn't find out, would you have just kept lying?"

"I would've told you. You have to believe me," Qianze said. But even as she said it, she wasn't sure it was true. To her, Ba's homecoming felt like a fugue from which she would wake at any moment to find that he was gone, had never been there, and that she was the one who was mad. She let out a huff, turned her gaze up to the ceiling. She felt tears prickle in her eyes. "I can't do this right now, I've barely slept in weeks, and my manager's upset at me, and Ba, he's not okay, he needs real medical care or a caretaker, but I don't even know where to start to get him help."

The crease between Theo's brows softened. "Hey, take a breath."

She followed the pattern of his breathing until her chest no longer felt like it was about to burst. Theo sighed then slowly pulled her into an embrace. She sunk into his grasp.

"Are you still mad?" she asked, her voice sounding small.

"Yeah, I'm still mad," Theo said, and she winced. "I don't know how to trust you right now. How we're going to get that trust back. But I'm worried about you too. And I don't think we're going to get anywhere with this conversation right now, not until you get some rest."

"Okay," Qianze said, burying her face in his shoulder. "I want to fix this. I want to make this better."

"Worry about yourself first. You need to sleep and eat and then we can talk." Theo let go of her and stepped back, and Qianze's chest sputtered in panic at the loss. He frowned. "Is there someone who can help you take care of your dad?"

"If he has other people in his life, he's not telling me. Or he's forgotten them. And I can't leave him."

"Maybe you could put him up somewhere, check him into the hospital, I don't know."

"I can't find his health insurance. And I can't leave him—it's hard to explain."

"Go on," he said, "try."

She had been trying to make sense of it herself. Ba was more trouble than he was worth. Still, she couldn't let him go. Even when he was gone, even when he was dead, she couldn't let him go.

"I'm not like you. I never got to go to China. I can't read Chinese. I can't speak it that well. I can understand it, but only as much as a kid. After Ba left, my Ma never taught me how to make Chinese food. I burn my rice almost every time. My parents never told me what their lives were like in China. I don't know my grandparents' names. I don't know my aunt's name, my late uncle's name. I don't know my dead siblings' names. They don't talk about them. The only homeland I have is him and my Ma. I don't belong anywhere, just to them. How can I toss him aside?"

"WHO WAS HE?" BA ASKED, his ears perking up in curiosity. He was waiting near the door for her when she came back to the apartment. She and Theo had promised to talk in a few days after they had cooled off and processed the events of the night.

"No one." She brushed him off. "A friend."

"Boyfriend?"

"Do you care?" she asked. Ba looked hurt and withdrew back to the couch.

She sighed and relented: "He's a friend from college. I went to the University of Virginia."

"I know," Ba said.

Of course, Qianze chastised herself. Her degree was framed in the apartment.

"I remembered something."

"Yeah? From your childhood? More Red Guard stories?" she asked, weary.

A few nights before, he had begun to tell her about the beginning of the Cultural Revolution. She had never learned about it at school. Her Virginia education had spent multiple months covering the Civil War, including a field trip to Gettysburg, but had rushed through international politics in the span of a few weeks. At first she was doubtful of the violence he described—this widespread, abject bloodletting on the streets, heralded in by teenagers. A cursory glance online and skimming a few Red Guard memoirs on Google Books proved her wrong. Ba was somehow telling the truth.

The Cultural Revolution was Ba's sore spot: the core at the center of the wound that was his memory. The more Qianze pressed him to continue, the more Ba tried to remember—his eyes screwed up until they became two long Morse code dashes—the more his memory seemed to unwind and tangle, catching like a thread stuck in a whirring sewing machine. Eventually both he and the accounts would disintegrate, their throughline snapped, the needle broken, until there was no Ba, no "I," only a "we."

We, we, we. He had condensed his childhood into a collective. Qianze knew better.

Own up to it! she had screamed at him two nights ago. *Stop saying "we," stop it stop it stop it, what did* you *do?*

She watched as his mouth formed the words silently. What did *you* do. What did you do. And his face crumpled and his head fell into his hands and he was gone.

What she wanted was for Ba to stop hiding behind his pain. *What about my pain?* she wanted to yell. He had hacked a hole in her life the size of him, but she had plowed on, and she had done it without alcohol or cigarettes or running away. She wanted to shake him. She wanted to pry up the boards of his memory, the rusty nails screeching in their unwillingness to let go, and excavate the hurt, bleed the bad blood out. Maybe then he could heal. Maybe then he could let go. Maybe then he could admit to his own faults, his own leaving. Maybe then he could return to her in a true homecoming: her Ba, her real Ba.

Ba now peered at her in a way that made her fidget. "No, not that, something else," he said. He smiled down at the floor. "Your one hundred days. In China, we celebrate a baby's hundred-day mark. Your Ma almost put it off. Didn't think we were ready to celebrate you yet. Not when we didn't know if we would lose you. But we were lucky. You were such a healthy, cheerful baby. Fat too." He laughed. "Your arms looked like a bag of those—what are they called?—Hawaiian rolls."

Qianze, unable to help it, smiled begrudgingly. She imagined herself as a baby, crawling on the floor of the Myrtle house: her four limbs looking like bags of hamburger buns. After so many days of Ba's stay where she had been drenched in bitterness—chī kǔ, as Ma might say—the sweetness of this image felt foreign on her tongue, and her throat dried up. It was tainted by Ba's revelation that he hadn't wanted her in the first place. She swallowed thickly.

"We did a zhuā zhōu for you too. Five months early for the tradition, but grief made us paranoid. You had lived seven months, but we didn't know if you'd make it to a year."

"What's a zhuā zhōu?"

"It's a tradition for a baby's first birthday. You put objects in front of them. Books, a stethoscope, a calculator, money, whatever you have in the house. And then whatever the baby crawls to and chooses, that's their future."

"Well, was it right? Did it predict I'd be an accountant?" Qianze asked, amused. "Was it the calculator? Or wait, the money?"

"No." Ba laughed. "A paintbrush. We thought we had a little artist. We said to each other, 'We must start saving now.'"

Qianze's smile dropped. She thought of the prints she had fingered at the student center, prints she now hung in frames in her apartment. The sketchbook tucked away under her bed. Who could she have been had the possibilities not been stolen from her, amputated in the height of her adolescence?

Ba's brows knit together as he sensed her pulling back. "Qianze—hái'ér—are you okay?"

She searched for the right words.

Qianze often thought of adulthood as a layering, each year growing a new skin. Ba had a way of knifing through those years until only the child was left, vulnerable and exposed.

"Ba, do you know when you cut wrapping paper, and your scissors begin to glide like you're slicing through nothing?" She paused and waited for him to nod. "Sometimes, you feel like that. Like scissors gliding through me that don't stop."

Twenty-Three

Weihong

1966: Fifty-One Years Before Reunion

Ānshān, Liáoníng Province

WE WERE A WAKE OF vultures circling Ānshān, hungry for a corpse. We patrolled the streets at night and searched homes, overturning them for something suspect. If we found it, we bared our teeth, our bite worse than our bark.

We did not believe in the old religion, the old gods. Religion was FEUDAL! NEO-BOURGEOISIE! ULTRA-RIGHTIST! But we believed in worship, and we worshipped Mao. We did not think ourselves better than Him; that was ANTI-REVOLUTIONARY BLASPHEMY! But we were more. More than human. "Godling," we would say, because we'd been fed on sacrifice, on that obscene, first color: red. We proved our faith to Him in droves of it, so many offerings of its thick wetness on our hands, and we'd been rewarded. We were given a little kingdom where we did as we pleased. Our god-body was red and multi-legged like a spider's.

We made class enemies kneel on glass and crawl. We discovered we liked the way exposed kneecaps looked: shiny and white and split. We poured ink down people's throats until they choked, their eyes rolling back from the viscosity of it. Once, we buried a grandmother and her granddaughter alive. Once, we doused a teacher in petrol and set him on fire. Once, we put a father in a chaff cutter and watched his body get minced into small pink pieces.

WE HAD BEEN OUT ALL night. We liked to commit the worst atrocities in the dark. Come daybreak, the aftermath would sit half-baked under the summer sun like a reckoning. In the still hours after midnight and before dawn, we basked in the thick silence of the city, heavy with fear. Before dawn, we parted—our body separating—to be formed again the next night, bound together by our blood-letting.

We—*no*—Weihong entered the compound in the early morning. He crept toward the shared bathroom in the corner. Under the bathroom light, his eyes were bloodshot. He had been awake for the past two nights in a row, high on the thrill of brutality. His clothes were stained. Fresh streaks of scarlet layered over the tokens of the previous nights: brown splatters that had settled into the fibers. The first night, he'd scrubbed the shirt down to its threads, but the blood refused to budge. He closed his eyes, cracked his neck from side to side. When he was alone, the chants and hammering of drums still filled his ears. Lately, another sound joined them. A rustle, a footstep, someone following him, a half beat behind. But whenever he turned around, there was no one there.

When he opened his eyes, he saw Mother in the mirror, standing behind him in the open threshold. Her eyes were wide. He hadn't heard her open the door. She closed it behind her.

"What did you do?" she whispered.

He turned around to face her. She shuffled across the yellowing tiled room, approaching him: her eyes blown out so wide that her pupils looked like pinpricks in a sea of white. She reached out a shaking hand and cupped his face, patting it a few times softly, as if unsure if he was real, tangible. Her brows dipped. Her thumb rubbed at his cheek, and when it came away, there was a smear of blood coating it like ink. She grew silent and stared at her hand for a long time. Weihong watched her face leap through a series of emotions that he tried to discern: shock, fear, disgust, grief—all of them colliding in the downturn of her mouth, the tremor of her eyes.

He wanted to defend himself. *You told me!* he wanted to say. *You told me that people become worse people to cope.*

Mother's mouth thinned. Her eyes grew hard and steady. She brushed past Weihong and washed her hands roughly.

"Ma—" Weihong began.

"Save it, Weihong," she said. Her head was bowed as she lathered and scrubbed. "I remember what I said." She looked up, her eyes holding his in the mirror. "I meant it. Morality is a privilege we can't afford right now. You're alive. Our family is alive. Everything else—" She did not finish her thought. Her hands turned raw and pink under the water.

Mother squeezed her eyes shut. Her mouth opened, hesitating. "What did you do, Weihong?"

"I—"

"No," she interrupted before he could say another word. "I shouldn't have asked. I don't want to know."

Mother turned to face him. With her damp hand, she caressed his stained cheek clean. She dried her hand, stained once more, on her pants. The blood looked wrong on her. She turned off the light and opened the door. Weihong watched in the dark as she padded off into their apartment.

THE QUESTIONS MOTHER SHOULD'VE ASKED: What did *we* do? What would we do in the following days? What were we capable of? Anything. Everything. When we were together, we could slip off conscience like it was a piece of clothing and slide into the skin of our god-body, which did not meddle with mortal matters like righteousness.

Our god-body was multi-armed and each of its hands was the hand of a butcher. Hands shoving nails down throats. Hands shoveling shit into mouths. Gloved hands strangling necks with wire. Hands callused by the grip of a whip, dirt under the nails from burying, burying, burying. When we tired of burying, we threw bodies into disused wells, letting them slosh and pile up, bloating blue like a bruise.

We were a clamorous swarm. Our sounds harmonized with the insect-infested summer: our chants, our gleeful shouts, our revolutionary songs, our drums and gongs. They warned of our approach. Other broods of Red Guards floated through their cities silently and methodically. Let it be known that we warned them. We could have been less merciful.

We did not discriminate. Blood was blood, and we'd developed a hunger for it. Anyone could be a monster, a demon, a class enemy. We sniffed out traitors. Teachers, landlords, imperialist allies from past wars: soldiers, comfort-woman whores, informants. We were bloodhounds, following the scent of treason to gaps in floorboards, unearthing foreign currency, old land deeds, portraits of Chiang Kai-shek. We eliminated bloodlines. No use in leaving a child festering with revenge.

Our violence was not literate. There were no words to describe what we did. *Atrocity. Massacre. Bloodbath.* They approached but did not capture. They missed the essence of our savagery—which was that we enjoyed it. The lawlessness. The godliness. The Chairman had dug out a dark seed within us and given it permission to bloom.

In mid-August, the Ānshān Communist Party declared cats a BOURGEOISE DECADENCE! We grabbed every stray we came across. We rooted them out from their hiding spots. We left the streets littered in carcasses.

Once, we came across a trusting, long-haired white-and-gray thing. It twined its tail around our kneecaps and wove around our legs. When we crouched to pick it up, a girl in glasses came running to stop us, threw her bony body over it. It purred, nudged its head against her wobbling chin.

Weihong, please, the girl pleaded, *just not this one.*

Who is Weihong? we asked. *No Weihong here. Just We.* We laughed.

NO ONE IN THE APARTMENT would speak at family dinners, the silence thick with Weihong's misdeeds. Kangmei must have told Mother or Father about the cats. Even if she hadn't, the evidence was strewn across town, the cats' soft bodies turned rigid, their pain taxidermized for everyone to see.

Father seemed both gloating and wary. He had to have heard the stories of children denouncing their parents; it was impossible not to. The streets were lined with the fluttering pages of big character posters: clumsy child's calligraphy identifying their own parents as class enemies. But there was a smugness to Father—like he was holding an unknown crime over Weihong's head. Some mutually assured destruction.

Mother lied to Nǎinai. She told Nǎinai that Weihong didn't participate, that the red children allowed him to beat the drums with the other grays, the non-reds, in the back of their procession. Nǎinai's heart, Mother said, couldn't take it if she knew.

Mother picked at her cuticles, opening small raw holes. Her fingers twisted. Her teeth worried at the loose skin of her lip.

"You regret it, Weihong, right? The torture. The killing. The cats." Her voice broke over this last word. "You have remorse for it, right?"

Weihong didn't know. He knew what answer she wanted, so he nodded. Mother's shoulders slumped, the tension leaving them.

"That's good, Weihong," she said softly, "that's good." She gave him a weak smile. She kissed his forehead, and when her dry lips touched the thin skin there, he was thinking: *Did* he regret it? Did he have remorse? That was what Mother wanted. He was doing this for Mother. But he could not deny that something roared to life whenever he swung a club. When that club met the soft pillow of a cheek and the flesh rippled with the force of his strike, sending molars flying, jolted out of their gums, roots and all. This living thing that craved violence did not feel altogether like him, but he did not know if he should fear it, if he wanted to be rid of it. He was drunk on power, dizzy with it. And the city accepted it. It let him and his comrades freely deal out the fates of its denizens. Who else could say that? Not Father. Not Mother.

Perhaps the Woman.

IN THE THIRD WEEK OF August, Father brought home a chicken for Kangmei. He did not say it was a consolation for the loss of the cats, but Weihong knew. The chicken, Father explained, came from his colleague, whose wife, the sister of an egg vendor, had hatched a brood that had gotten too large for the wife's coop. The chicken was not yet fully grown, a week or two shy.

"It's a girl," Father said. "Soon we'll be able to have eggs at every meal."

Kangmei took to the bird immediately, coddling it like a baby. She made it a nest from newspapers and straw. She tied a ribbon around its neck in a bow and took it on walks around the courtyard. She groomed its feathers, which were a pale, downy yellow, and tweezed out the ingrowns. She even bathed it with her own splintering bar of soap. Mother and Nǎinai started calling the bird Xiǎo Bǎobiāo, Little Bodyguard, because of how it trailed Kangmei's heels.

Weihong was determined to ignore Xiǎo Bǎobiāo. The chicken was a reminder of the growing gulf between him and Kangmei, the paths they had chosen, the wrongdoing he'd committed. But whenever Weihong crept back into the apartment before dawn, Xiǎo Bǎobiāo was the only one awake. She would stand up from her nest next to Kangmei, ruffle her feathers, and approach him. The first time, he'd attempted to shoo her away, whispering for her to go back to her nest. She'd ignored him. He left the apartment to use the bathroom and when he returned, she was still there.

She tipped her head. Her eyes were black, wet, and round. She stepped forward and hesitantly rubbed her beak against his shin. He relented a little. He ran a hand through the feathers of her neck. She rubbed the other side of her beak against his fingers. She was not afraid of him. This surprised him. His own mother was afraid of him.

One morning, he woke to find Xiǎo Bǎobiāo pecking and grooming his hair.

"She likes you," Kangmei said. There was disappointment in her voice.

Weihong was just rising. It was almost noon. He'd gotten in during the dark hour before sunrise. Kangmei was sitting at the kitchen table, the summer light flooding into the room. Weihong blinked. This was the first time Kangmei had spoken to him since the incident with the cat.

Weihong rubbed hard at the sleep that had crusted in the corners of his eyes. "I guess," he said, gently pushing the chicken away so he could fold and roll up his bedding.

"I shouldn't let her near you," Kangmei said.

"Why?"

"You hurt everything around you."

He raised his head to meet her gaze. It was swimming with spite. Adult spite—kilometers past the territory of sibling spite. She held his gaze for one blink, two. She looked away. She picked up Xiǎo Bǎobiāo and went out into the courtyard.

Xiǎo Bǎobiāo was small for a chicken her age. She'd been raised on meager rations, just enough for her to survive. Weihong didn't tell Kangmei that he'd started lining his pockets with delicacies, food he found squirreled away in the cabinets of the homes he ransacked. He and Xiǎo Bǎobiāo would split his rewards in the morning. Other Red Guards took radios, bicycles, golden heirlooms. He was allowed this: his mornings; his portions of cooked white rice, oranges, red-bean buns. Xiǎo Bǎobiāo's feathers darkened to the golden color of sesame oil. Even with Weihong's crumbs, she did not grow any bigger, though she did seem more content.

In early September, Xiǎo Bǎobiāo laid her first egg.

Weihong was woken up by Kangmei's high-pitched scream. He sat up as if electrocuted, scrambling to untangle himself from his bedding.

"What, what!" Weihong shouted, and Kangmei's scream turned into a hiccup of a wail.

Had his comrades turned against him? Had they found out about his family's past? When he looked at the door he found it closed. He let out a heavy exhale. He saw Kangmei standing, holding Xiǎo Bǎobiāo in her hands. The nest was red and bloody, and Xiǎo Bǎobiāo was making distressed squawking sounds. Hanging between her legs was the out-turned, veined sack of her insides, stretched taut by an egg.

Weihong gaped for a moment. "What's wrong with her?"

"I don't know, I found her like this," Kangmei said, still holding the struggling bird in her hands. Her face became still and mean. "Did you do this?"

"What?" Weihong asked, taken aback by the question. "No!"

Though the sight of the spilt flesh dangling limply invoked images of—*our hands slicing open bellies with kitchen knives to watch the gush of intestines*— "No," Weihong repeated. "I wou—" *I wouldn't*, he wanted to say, but his throat dried up at the look Kangmei gave him. Her eyes flashed, narrowed and feline.

"I didn't, Kangmei. I swear. I don't know what's wrong with her. Can we fix it?"

She worried at her lip.

"Where's Mother? Nǎinai?" Weihong asked.

"They're out picking up herbs. Father's working." Kangmei frowned.

Weihong began rummaging through the kitchen cabinets, finding a market basket that Mother and Nǎinai had left behind. He dumped the bloody cloths from the nest into it.

"Come on," he said. He put a hand on Kangmei's arm. She flinched. "Put the bird in here. We can go to the egg vendor in the market. He might know what to do."

Kangmei hesitated.

"Come on!" Weihong said, urging her toward the front door.

She relented. "Fine, let's go," she said. She might not have liked him ordering her around, but it didn't seem like she had a better plan. Weihong slipped on his shoes.

They wove through the streams of pedestrians. Kangmei tried to run, but the jostling made Xiǎo Bǎobiāo caw out in pain, so the pair settled for a brisk walk, winding through the crowds and streets to make their way to the market. Kangmei stiffened at the sight of the red armbands that marked the clusters of Red Guards. They were joking with one another, leaning leisurely against each other, stretching their faces upward to enjoy the sun. No one knew when school would be back in session, so they were enjoying this borrowed time. They weren't his comrades, his Red Guards. But Weihong knew them, understood them. The look in their eyes, the red band threaded around their left arms mirroring his own. Kangmei tugged on Weihong's sleeve. He'd slowed down without realizing. He nodded, and they continued on their quiet, breathless walk.

The line for eggs was long, as it always was. Kangmei walked straight to the front, earning an outcry from those who had been waiting for hours.

"Back of the line! No priority for anyone, I don't care who you are," the vendor said, though his eye snagged on Weihong's red band.

"Shūshu, please," Kangmei said, holding out the basket with Xiǎo Bǎobiāo. "Your sister, her husband works with my father at the steelworks. She gave me this chicken. Something's wrong with her, with her egg."

The vendor scanned Kangmei's face. "You Fei's daughter?"

She nodded in earnest.

The vendor sighed. "I heard you've been taking good care of her." He squinted at Xiǎo Bǎobiāo. "Fine, come here. Just for a minute."

Kangmei and Xiǎo Bǎobiāo slipped behind the counter as an assistant took over. Weihong followed. In the back, the vendor gently lifted Xiǎo Bǎobiāo and grimaced slightly.

"She's prolapsed. Her egg's been caught, because she's too small, see? So her insides got blown out when she tried to lay the egg. It'll probably happen again. Common nowadays. Expensive to feed a chicken right. You should soak her in some warm water, then use some oil to get the egg out and push her insides back in."

"Can you do it?" Kangmei asked. "What if I do it wrong? What if I hurt her?"

"I can't. I have customers. It'll take time and care. Better if it's you. Cover her eyes. They tolerate the pain better when they can't see."

The siblings, shooed away, walked back home. The apartment was warm from the windows they'd left open. Mother and Nǎinai still weren't back.

They followed the vendor's instructions. They soaked Xiǎo Bǎobiāo in the washing tub they used for laundry. Weihong held her down, covered her eyes and beak with a washcloth. Kangmei tried to pry the egg out. They used kitchen oil. They used soap. They used whatever they could find. It was slow work. Kangmei sniffled and pretended she wasn't crying. Weihong offered to try, but she snapped at him.

"You'll do it wrong!"

He backed down. He held Xiǎo Bǎobiāo even as she writhed and clucked and kicked. Kangmei got the egg out. She set it aside on the floor, where it wobbled and rolled. She did her best to push the insides back in. Weihong let the bird go. They sighed, slumping. The egg was small. It fit neatly in the cradle of Kangmei's eight-year-old hand. She inspected it. She ran a finger over its textured, translucent surface.

"All that hurt just for this?"

Weihong didn't answer. He didn't think she meant to say it out loud.

That night, Năinai fried the egg. They split it five ways.

The next egg was prolapsed too. And the next. And the next.

THE ĀNSHĀN PARTY COMMITTEE CONTINUED their campaign against the city's animals into September. Dogs were next. Once the streets grew rancid with the smell of mangy carrion, they targeted fowl. Ducks and chickens, they said, were a public health crisis, and laying hens were a BOURGEOISE INDULGENCE! No one was entitled to additional eggs beyond their rations.

Everyone in the compound had seen Kangmei with Xiǎo Bǎobiāo. She walked the bird in the daylight in circles around the courtyard, leashed on its shiny ribbon. When Weihong heard, he knew they did not have more than a day or two before someone would come to check on them. Kangmei knew this, too, but couldn't accept it.

"We can hide her somewhere. Then we can get her back later."

"Where? With who?"

"We can ask the egg vendor. Or his sister."

Weihong shook his head. That was still an act of defiance against the Party.

"We could give her to someone going to the countryside so she can live on a farm, or, or—" Kangmei's voice grew pitchy, threatening to dissolve into tears.

Kangmei couldn't make an exception of the chicken. She knew it. Everyone was watching everyone at every moment: eyes everywhere, mouths itching to condemn someone else to spare their own skin. And Father had started to resent the bird. He complained drunkenly about the long hours of her screeching as they wriggled eggs from her disgorged parts. The payout—three eggs—was not worth the food, water, and supplies the hen needed. Certainly not worth the wrath of the Party.

When Father came home from work, he was whistling. His cheeks were flushed rosy with liquor.

"Chicken for dinner tonight," he said gleefully.

Kangmei's lip quivered. "Ba," she began, "what if we gave her back to your coworker? Or his wife? Or the egg vendor? He's still allowed to raise chickens, right? He can take care of her, he's the one who taught us how to fix her."

Father frowned. "Kangmei," he said, "you need to grow up. This is what must be done. Did you think we'd raise this chicken until it died of old age? It was always meant for our plates sooner or later."

"That's not what you said when you gave her to me."

"Kangmei," Father repeated, his voice taking on a warning tone. His cheeks were turning the bright red of Xiǎo Bǎobiāo's crown. "The thing is a sunk cost. It can't even lay eggs properly."

Kangmei turned and burrowed her face into Nǎinai's shoulder. Mother gave Father a nasty look that he ignored.

"Come along, Weihong. Bring the bird to the courtyard," Father ordered.

"Me?" Weihong asked.

Father narrowed his eyes. "Yes. You. All I do, day in and day out, is work and provide for this family. It's time you show a little responsibility. Isn't killing what you're good at?" He laughed.

Weihong froze. Everyone else grew still, the only sound Father's shaking laugh bouncing off the walls like a loose ping-pong ball. Father strolled toward the kitchen and unsheathed the kitchen cleaver from its block, which let out a metallic *zing*. If Weihong did this, he and Kangmei could never come back from it. The fog between them, that damp hurt, would churn into an unceasing tempest.

"Come on, it's getting dark, and I'll be wanting dinner soon."

Weihong went to pick up Xiǎo Bǎobiāo, who clucked softly.

"I want to say goodbye," Kangmei said. She held the bird's face in between her hands, cradling the wattles that hung from her beak.

"I'm sorry," she said. Then, "Be good."

Outside, it was dusk. Weihong's hand shook. He straightened his fingers to stop it as Father handed him the cleaver. Father leaned against the door of their unit. He pulled out a cigarette and lit it.

"Hold its wings down. Firm. One clean strike. Then you drain the blood and defeather it."

Now both of Weihong's hands started shaking. Xiǎo Bǎobiāo rubbed her beak against him, and unaware of what was going on, squawked cheerfully. In the bird's features, he saw Kangmei's face, Kangmei's beaked nose and wide eyes, and under his breath, he repeated her words, *I'm sorry.* He brought the cleaver down. The blood that erupted from her gullet was as red as the crown of her decapitated head, her dark eyes—Kangmei's eyes—wide in shock.

THE MOON BATHED THE COURTYARD in a pale blue like an underwater scene. It was late, the middle of the night, and Weihong was digging.

It had been a week and a half since he'd killed Xiǎo Bǎobiāo. No one had warned him that chickens could run after they were beheaded. Her body had spun in circles as if looking for her missing head, before collapsing. Weihong's mouth hung open in horror. Father laughed. He looked on as Weihong drained the blood, ripped the feathers out. Weihong could feel his eyes, hot on the back of his neck. He could feel other eyes, too, peering out at him as he stood in the pool of blood.

At dinner that night, Kangmei sniffed, refused to eat. Father yelled at her, said, *You're wasting good meat, did you know that? You're lucky to be eating it.* Weihong had never seen Father like this with Kangmei. She ate small bites. Weihong forced himself to eat the stringy, pale poultry, but it tasted rotten, spoiled by the image of the blood leaking from her neck, splattering around the courtyard as the headless corpse ran amok. His body knew what would happen before he did, his skin becoming warm, drops of sweat beading. He threw up on his plate, the bile white and meaty. Father stood up, his face curled into a snarl, and he began beating Weihong at the table with his belt. *The insolence of this boy!* Weihong's back and arms were still bruised and welted nine days later.

Father made him eat it after. The vomit.

They stretched the meat out for those nine days. Weihong still couldn't keep it down, but he waited until Father was secluded in the bedroom to purge it. In the bathroom, Mother would rub his back in circles until it was all gone.

His fingers were caked in dirt. Into the newly dug hole, Weihong placed a bundle of chicken bones, tied with ribbon. He'd saved them. He'd scraped them off plates after meals, stashed them under a floorboard he'd pried up. He began to cover the hole. He buried her deep enough that no one would find her even if they dug up the surface to plant seeds.

Suddenly, he felt another presence behind him. She squatted down, the moon reflecting off her glasses.

"I heard you leave the apartment," Kangmei said. "Here, put this in too."

She handed him a wishbone. It had been washed and polished clean. He placed it with the others. When they were done, Kangmei placed a hand flat on the earth.

"Was this it?" Weihong asked. "The most painful moment of your life?"

"No." She swallowed. "I do something worse."

He could not imagine that, and he had done everything.

Twenty-Four

Ba

2017: Sixteen Days Since Reunion
Manhattan, New York

HE KEPT TIME BY THE number of cigarette stubs in the ashtray, perched on the lip of the bathtub. This method wasn't always reliable. One moment, he was lighting his first cigarette of the day, and the next, the ashtray was a graveyard for a pack's worth of stubs he didn't know he had smoked. He liked the bathroom the most for its blankness, its yellowing tiles that made him feel like he could be anywhere, nowhere, in the fog bank of his own memory.

At times, he was filled with an urge to draw a bath and submerge himself—let his memories develop underwater, like blank photographs in silver nitrate, until they were whole again. Once, he'd caved in to this impulse. He did not know what led him to it, only that he had blinked, and when he next opened his eyes, he saw bog water, murky with aquatic fauna, and in the distance, the shapes of floating bodies, just out of reach. He'd remembered something crucial: the bog and the shape of the Woman's prophecy, which had come flashing back to him when he recalled the night he'd decided to leave the Myrtle house. And another memory had been surfacing—the final piece of the prophecy: something about the beast in the bog that was just out of reach—when he'd been pulled up with a choking gasp, greeted by his daughter's panicked eyes and drenched sleeves, the sound of the bath still running, his wet clothes pressing him back into the tub. Now he faced the dry spout, whose mouth his daughter had wrapped up in duct tape. Written on a Post-it above it, *BÙYÀO DǍKĀI!!*

There was a persistent sound in the room that carried on for a while. A low growl that seemed to emanate from the dark of the drain. He realized belatedly that it was his own stomach complaining of hunger. He'd begun to feel disconnected from his body, consciousness and clarity houseguests that passed through only every so often. He decided he'd scavenge the kitchen for leftovers. He put his hands on the side of the tub, pushed himself out of it. Lightheaded, he staggered through the smoky interior toward the bathroom mirror, clutched the sides of the sink as his spotty vision cleared. When he looked up, he did not see his own reflection but another face, round and eerie, filling the glass of the mirror, standing in the same bathroom.

He scuttled backward, his body slamming into the door as he opened it, momentum carrying him as he fell sprawling onto the floor of the living room. In the mirror, Kangmei looked down at him and raised her brows. He scrambled to his feet, closing the door, his back resting against it as he tried to steady his breath. He shook his head from side to side, trying to rid himself of the hallucination of his sister.

It was the afternoon, the sun glaring at him through the window, and he stumbled into the kitchen to get a glass of water. But when he opened the cabinet with the glassware, he saw Kangmei's face peering out, prismatic, from each cup. He slammed the cabinet shut, the glasses trembling at the force. Everywhere he looked, there she was—in the sink, in the faucet, in the curved sides of the pots and the tines of the dirty forks lying on the counter—her face crowding his vision from all sides until he had to squeeze his eyes shut. Still, when he opened them, there she was again, tilting her head at him from the stainless steel of the microwave—

—No. Not this. Another memory. Any other memory. Cast it out. Send it back to the deep.

He dove into the bathroom, her reflection still floating in the mirror where his should have been, and shouted, "Go away!"

She looked taken aback, and the two of them peered at each other in the ensuing silence. The Kangmei inside the mirror was not fifty-eight as she should've been but fifteen, the age when he last saw her. When he leaned closer, he could see with unsettling sharpness the details of her face: the small moles on her cheeks, the crook of her beaked nose, and his own aged reflection in the lenses of her glasses.

"What are you?" he asked at last.

She looked affronted. "I'm your sister."

"A ghost? A demon? A god?" He squinted. "A hallucination?"

She looked thoughtful. "None of those. A memory. But you knew that. A ghost, if I had to choose."

"What do you want from me?" he demanded.

"I don't want anything from you," she said, frowning. "You found me, remember?"

"No," he said, shaking his head frantically, "no, I wasn't looking for you."

"I know. You didn't want to find me. You were trawling for your beast, and I got caught up in your net instead."

Who's the fisher and who's the catch, this wretched memory trapping me like a fish on a line, lancing through me like a hook through an eye—rénwéi dāozǔ, wǒ wèi yúròu—

His head pounded painfully—a warning that his liquid courage was seeping out. He was sobering, which made the sight of Kangmei before him more disturbing. He leaned over the sink, gripped its sides with white knuckles, felt like he was going to dry heave. Sweat beaded on his upper lip.

"I don't need you. Go back. You're not part of this," he said.

"I know what memory you are looking for."

At this he looked up and said desperately, "Show me."

She shook her head. "Not in my power. But I can tell you this: what you're looking for doesn't exist in isolation. It's the last in a succession of events, including me."

"I don't want you," he said weakly.

"Of course you don't. Who would?"

A pregnant pause filled the bathroom as he considered this. "Do I have to?" he asked at last, his voice sounding so much like a child's whine.

She shrugged. "Up to you. You could go back into the living room, fish out your hidden báijiǔ and drown me away. That's what ba would do. Or you could follow me."

A mean line, one she knew would hurt. But it had its desired effect. The Kangmei in the mirror seemed to retreat further into the background, into the living room behind her, turning the corner into the hallway. He leaned in closer, and he felt the mirror give, felt the surface envelop him in its cool chrome as he stepped through.

SPRING OF 1974. WEIHONG'S TIME as a Red Guard had ended six years before back in 1968. In Ānshān, the two years between the Red August of 1966 and 1968 had been carnivorous, marked by infighting among different factions: Red Guard bands, workers' federations, local Party allies, People's Liberation Army units. Everyone scrambling to accuse the other of being COUNTERREVOLUTIONARY REVISIONISTS! Echoes of these same turf wars in every city across the country.

In Weihong's memory, these years blended together. His recklessness drove him to commit ruthless acts for his comrades. There'd been the taste of war in the air—guns circulated widely, daily burials at the martyrs' cemetery, shoot-outs in buildings—when the Chairman had the military restore order. Weihong had been fifteen at the time. He hung up his club and completed his middle school courses.

Once more, he became what the Party needed him to be, tamping down the violence churning inside him. Other students and workers who weren't as compliant were sent down to do labor in the countryside or mass executed by PLA soldiers. The local Party Committee regained authority, and life returned to a faltering normalcy with only the occasional struggle session. Weihong passed the next six years settling back into civilian life, trying to repress those red years.

March of 1974 was kind to Ānshān, warm and soft, bathing the scaffolding of the city in the promise of a good spring after a long winter, but Nǎinai was living in a different season from the rest of the family. She forgot what day of the week it was, then the month, then the year. On warmer days, she pulled out winter layers from deep in the hutch where they were stored, and donned thin summer clothes when there was a chill in the air. She lost words and would snap her fingers trying to find them—simple words like egg, bed, daughter, laundry—and then the ends of her sentences, pausing mid-phrase before looking around with glassy eyes. She confused Weihong and Kangmei with their parents, often calling Kangmei Fei. To this, Kangmei would smile, shake her head gently, and lead Nǎinai back to bed, plying her with calming tea.

They hadn't realized the extent of her deterioration until one early April Sunday. Weihong, Kangmei, and Mother had been in the apartment when a small boy, one of the children who was always running underfoot at the market, burst into their compound, pounded on their door, and said that he'd been sent to fetch them. They rushed to follow him and were greeted by the sight of Năinai, curled fetal in the shadows of an alleyway. When they approached, she withdrew, refusing to be touched. She didn't recognize any of them. A small group of Aunties had witnessed the ordeal. She'd been normal one moment, the next, in hysterics, batting everyone away who tried to help, crying about wanting to go home before crawling on her hands and knees to the alley. Father arrived, brought by another market boy from whatever hole in the wall he'd been drinking in, and his ruddy face seemed to spark recognition even as it drained of color at the sight of his mother.

"Are you related to my betrothed?" she asked hesitantly, "the doctor's assistant in Hā'ěrbīn? Is that where I am? You look like him. Can you help me find my way back to him? I think we got separated."

Father made quiet promises to take her to the physician's assistant, to help her back to her village. All the while, the muscle in his jaw twitched.

They could not go see a doctor or visit a hospital. Doctors were INTELLECTUAL REVISIONISTS! BOURGEOISIE RUNNING DOGS! They weathered Năinai's decline on their own. Mother and Father combined the knowledge from their past lives to brew teas and traditional remedies for Năinai to drink. They couldn't tell if these helped—if these concoctions kept the madness dammed up—or if they were tossing a leaky raft to a drowning woman.

After the market, Năinai chafed against her house arrest. She sulked, rattling around the apartment with her bad mood, insisting she was fine, that she'd been lightheaded, that she'd just gotten heat stroke and didn't need everyone treating her like she was an invalid. They gave in one day and let her go out to the market on her own, but hours passed, and she still did not return.

They were ready to form their own search party when one of Weihong's friends from the steelworks factory where he worked arrived at their apartment, Nǎinai in tow. She'd been wandering the train station, looking at maps and mumbling nonsense. Weihong's friend pulled him aside on his way out and told him that Nǎinai had said strange fictions about his family on the way back to the apartment. That her husband had been a grave robber, taken to dissecting corpses in the middle of the night before he'd been caught. That her son did not always seem like her son, that he seemed to crawl back to their apartment each night a possessed animal. And the most absurd: that her daughter-in-law was a fox demon, a whore, a wèi ān fù. Weihong's spine stiffened, hot panic flooding his gut. *Of course it was all nonsense*, his friend reassured him quickly, *and I know none of it was true.* He said his goodbyes, wished Nǎinai a quick recovery, and left. Weihong watched his silhouette, long and lean, hands in his pockets, lope down the street.

WEIHONG SPENT HIS SPRING SUNDAYS studying for the upcoming wén huà exam that would determine if he'd be going to university that fall. He was a good applicant. After completing his middle school courses, he'd done two years of labor on the steelworks factory floor. His workmates had given him approving referrals. All he needed now were good exam results and a favorable endorsement from the Ānshān Party Committee.

Weihong was studying at the kitchen table when he heard a rustle from behind him, followed by a drowsy question: "Who are you?"

He turned in his seat to face his grandmother, who was sitting up, rubbing the sleep from her eyes. She looked at him as if she were trying to place him, and he stilled under her gaze. Nǎinai spent most of her time in bed. Mother and Father plied her with medicated teas that kept her suspended in sleep like a fly trapped in amber. Without the medicine, Nǎinai would run through the course of her life in the span of a day: girl, wife, mother, crone—constantly mutating.

Lately, Weihong had felt hyper-auditory, his bad ear picking up echoes, things no one else could hear; underlying Nǎinai's familiar voice was the hum of her past, all her memories buzzing inside their apartment like insects battering themselves against a bulb. If he listened carefully, he could hear in the timbre of her words that this was not the Nǎinai he knew but a younger woman.

"I remember you," she said, familiarity dawning upon her face. She frowned. "But as a newborn. You were born with all your teeth in your mouth. Unlucky. How old are you now?"

"I'm twenty-one," he said. He poured her a cup of tea Father had brewed that morning.

She sipped at it and frowned. "Has it been that long? Strange, I can remember the night when you were born. How you were red all over even after we washed you, but nothing since."

She brought her hand under his chin and turned his head. "You grew into Ming's face. Her Mama's face. Sharper though. The kind of face that asks for attention." She released him, the place on his jaw where her fingers had been now pink.

The way Nǎinai said Mother's name shifted alongside her memory. Sometimes, it was soft and drawn out: a sacred prayer. Other times, it was hard and spittle-laced. Through tone, Weihong could track the evolution of their relationship, the degrees of spite that had built up through the decades.

By late April, Nǎinai's descents into the past were no longer chronological. She retained the memories of her seventy-year-old self but was taken to throwing the temper tantrums of a child. When she missed home, she dissolved into tears, bartering to return, and when she was angry, she became wild and unbridled. Mother was the target of her fits and was subject to hurled pots, pans, and treason. *Traitorous whore!* Nǎinai would wail, flinging objects at Mother's head. *Imperialist bitch!* The yelling would devolve into crying—no language left for the eddy of emotions seething within her. And Mother would ball her fists by her sides, then unclench her hands and slump, bowing her head to clean the apartment.

End of April. The beginning of summer hung precipitously. Nǎinai was making a scene at the dinner table. Kangmei tried to calm her, but she shrugged her off and squirmed like an infant. She wanted to go home. When she was told she couldn't, she yowled, swept her crockery off the table. Nǎinai accused Mother, claiming she was the one responsible for her exile. *Monster! Demon!*

She pushed back her chair, the legs shrieking against the floor, and then held it, brandishing it like a weapon. She threw it at Mother, who dodged it by scuttling out the front door, the chair falling a meter short. *Wèi ān fù!*

Through the open door, one of their neighbors was emerging from the courtyard bathroom, her mouth a dark circle of surprise. The family stared back at her, frozen. She closed her mouth. There was a glint in her eyes and a faint curl of her lips.

Weihong had heard this term, wèi ān fù, before. During the daily struggle sessions when he was fifteen, this accusation had condemned a handful of women and their families to prison or hard labor.

It was hard to distinguish one struggle session from another; all of them collapsing together in the red maw of memory. Slurs elided into one another, the same phrases bandied about: OLD-LINE COUNTERREVOLUTIONARY! CAPITALIST PIG! IMPERIALIST PUBLIC ENEMY! But this term, wèi ān fù, the arpeggio of its intonation, conjured a specific memory.

The Party chief on the stage, his footsteps as he walked across, listing the perpetrator's crimes—how she served as a comfort woman to the Japanese soldiers, surrendering her body and her virtue wholly to the enemy. The crack of her shoulders as they were rolled backward in their sockets, forced into a jet-plane position. Her confession. The chief's smug voice as he revealed that it had been the woman's own daughter who denounced her, how such impudence could be bred out from the youth. Then, a flare of jealousy, which Weihong remembered as a roar of noise in his ears, drowning out everything else. How he wished he were the one to be praised, to be revered.

WEIHONG SAW THE NEIGHBOR'S KNOWING smile in the pale crescent of the moon, in the hangnails he found littering the ground—which belonged to Mother, who had broken them off, leaving her fingers raw and bleeding. In his restless sleep, he saw the grin, large and wide, through the window, exposing two rows of teeth that yawned open, a dark tendril of a tongue darting toward him, threatening to bite off the apartment and drag it down into the pink column of her throat.

As April bled into May, Nǎinai worsened. A series of sleepless, delirious nights passed, the family kept up into the early hours. Nǎinai frothed at the mouth, shouted, screamed, bit at the arms of anyone who tried to pin her down. They had to stop giving her teas: she would throw the boiling water at Mother if given the chance. Father drank more, and Kangmei grew sullen and distant. Mother wrapped her arms in gauze, the deep bite marks on her skin weeping through, forming red sickles.

Sometimes he would wake in a panic, convinced that Nǎinai's delirium was catching, worming into his body. The sounds in Weihong's right ear grew louder, condensed into overlapping voices. He caught snatches of conversations he'd never had, in English, which he recognized by its sounds but did not know. Conversations between a younger Mother and Nǎinai he had never overheard. But mostly, he was unable to parse the voices, which crowded in his skull, battering against each other. He did not let himself admit that he was afraid: of what was happening inside his head, of what was happening inside his house.

Whenever he remembered the night with the chair, the stark fear on Mother's face at Nǎinai's accusation, the voices stopped their chatter, coalesced, and chorused together, asking the one question that he could not ask. If he asked it, the question would curdle on his tongue and plop on the floor, rotten, and they would never get the smell of it out. It would splinter the fragile ecology of their family. If he asked Mother, he would know the truth about her past. Knowing was dangerous. There would be no deniability or safety in knowing. Instead Weihong focused on one fact: Nǎinai was going to endanger them all, but mostly she was going to endanger Mother, and he couldn't let her do that.

HE DID NOT REMEMBER THE last time Nǎinai was Nǎinai. She'd been someone else for an entire season: a threat to the family. He wanted to talk to someone about her, but Mother and Father liked to pretend that Nǎinai wasn't sick. They treated her as if she had a bad cold, something that would pass with time. Kangmei knew her best. For the whole of Kangmei's childhood, Nǎinai had watched over and accompanied her. Kangmei wouldn't pretend.

Weihong was waiting outside the compound for her, leaning against the wall near the entrance. Kangmei had been disappearing after school and returning home late. When she saw him, she wilted and shrank away from him.

"Where have you been?" he asked.

"Out for a walk," Kangmei said, moving past him toward the compound. He shifted his weight, blocked the entrance with his body.

"I need to speak to you. Here, outside."

She frowned. "Can it wait? I have homework."

"Are you avoiding me?"

She tensed, folded her arms in front of her. "I'm not avoiding *you*. I don't want to be in the house any more than I have to be. You of all people should understand that."

"That's what I wanted to talk to you about."

"Whatever you have to say, I don't want to hear it right now," she said, and she squeezed past him toward the courtyard. He grabbed her wrist, and she recoiled. He held on fast.

"I want to talk about Năinai," he said. She stilled. He let go, and her arm fell to her side. She sagged.

"There's nothing we can do. We just have to hope it passes, and that she gets better."

"She won't get better. You know that. She's not the same," he said, "the grandmother we knew is gone. That's not her. And she's not just a danger to Ma, she's a danger to all of us, she's this—this stranger living in our house, screaming out accusations that could send us all to prison or the countryside."

"And what are we supposed to do about it?" Kangmei asked.

"I don't know," Weihong said.

But he wanted her to fix it. He was tired of being the one to make all the hard decisions to protect the family. He wanted Kangmei to take up the mantle like he had when he was fourteen.

"What could we even do?" Kangmei asked.

They both knew what they could do. They were dancing around it, but they knew. They could denounce Năinai before she denounced them. A few minutes passed in silence.

"There's only one thing we *could* do," Weihong said at last, sounding defeated.

"No. We can't. I don't want to," Kangmei said, her voice sounding small.

"No one's making you do anything," Weihong said.

She looked at him with haunted eyes, a look that he knew, and suddenly they were thirteen and eight again, staring at each other in the cold alley, knowing they had no choice before them, and knowing they could not come back from this.

IT WAS SUNDAY, WEIHONG'S DAY off at the factory. Father had left early to indulge his vices. Mother and Kangmei had done the washing in the morning and then headed out to the shops to pick up their food for the week. Kangmei was to keep Mother busy while Weihong carried out the plan she had come up with. She told Mother that she'd come across an underground herbalist who sold the herbs that were good for memory: ginkgo leaf, milkwort, língzhī mushrooms.

Once they were gone, Weihong convinced Nǎinai to take a walk with him to the park. The cherry blossoms were in bloom, and the air was heavy with spring. It seemed that everyone had poured out to enjoy the weather, and the pathways were crowded. Weihong led Nǎinai to a quiet part of the park and helped her sit on a bench.

She gave him a smile—her crow's-feet wrinkling—and he felt ill. She studied his face.

"We know each other, don't we? You feel familiar."

His throat bobbed, and he nodded. "I'm your grandson. We care about each other very much."

"Ming's boy?" she asked, and he nodded again.

"Can I ask you something?"

Nǎinai nodded, inclined her head as if to say, *Go on.*

"Why do you hate my mother?"

Nǎinai frowned. "I don't hate Ming. Not at all."

His forehead creased. "Then why do you act so awful to her?"

"She came back, and she trapped me in this situation, and I was angry at being trapped."

He looked at her, wanted to ask more, and he saw that she was suddenly very lucid. He'd gotten her back, but it was too late. She was angry at Mother, and he was angry at her. He wanted to tell her how angry he was, because now *they* were trapped in this loop, and he had to see it through. Now he had to give up another piece of himself—the goodness in him—and he'd done this so many times, he didn't think he was good anymore. But just as quickly as it had come, the lucidity was gone, and Nǎinai was scrutinizing him.

"I know you, don't I? I don't remember you, but I can tell that I know you."

"Yes," Weihong said flatly, "we care about each other very much."

He got up and offered her his arm. They walked together to city hall. They are walking together to city hall. They have always been walking together to city hall, this moment stretching before them, Nǎinai's grip encircling Weihong's left arm for support, the scratch of her nails in the crook of his elbow as she shuffles alongside him. They could turn back, go home, return to the park, but they won't, because Weihong feels—felt—that he has done this before, that he is only a vessel through which something larger is acting, and that they always wind—wound—up on this road, one of them the farmer, the other the lamb to slaughter.

City hall was controlled by the Party and was home to the offices of the Party chief. Inside, there was a bare-bones staff running things, everyone else enjoying their day off. Weihong went in, Nǎinai in tow, and had her sit in the hall. He went up to one of the staff members and told him that he was there to denounce someone. To his surprise, he was led to the chief's office. The chief was standing behind his daunting desk, looking rumpled.

"Come in," the chief said, and Weihong entered tentatively. He had not been expecting an audience with the chief; he'd assumed the chief of all people would be taking the day off. Fear flared in his body. What if the chief discovered he was lying? He was the most powerful man in the city, and the consequences could lead to execution.

"You caught me coming in for some paperwork," he said. "Now, what's this about?"

"I came here to denounce someone," Weihong said. His voice broke, and he cleared his throat. "A traitor to our Party."

The chief gestured with his hand for Weihong to continue.

Weihong opened his mouth and found, for a second, that no

sound would come out. He would not be able to take his next words back. But his body was no longer his body. It was a mollusk shell, hollowed out for a creature of fate that had burrowed inside. It was possessing him, pressing itself outward against the underside of his skin, against his eardrums, his vocal cords. It whispered that he had been here before, had been here time and time again, and then it went through the same actions and words that it had always done—Weihong unable to do anything but watch as fortune played itself out.

"My grandmother. She was a comfort woman during the Second Sino–Japanese War."

This was the accusation he'd decided upon. Not a capitalist, not a landowner. Nǎinai's condition would only get worse, and Weihong would not be around to censor her. If he labeled her a comfort woman, then her ravings about Mother being a wèi ān fù could be seen as a desperate diversion of guilt, as a manifestation of her own shame.

The chief made a low whistle. "A comfort woman. That kind of offense would warrant a struggle session."

This was the anticipated response, but Weihong could not have that. He spoke quickly.

"She's sick. Her mind's almost gone. She gets people and times all mixed up. You won't get a confession from her onstage. I doubt she'd even know what was happening. But it's true. She has some sober moments here and there—fewer now—and she told me during one. After she did, I came to you."

The chief crossed his arms, his face closed off. "Without a struggle session, the people can't choose her punishment." He paused. "What would *you* choose for her?"

Weihong licked his lips. "Send her to prison. She can spend the rest of her time there as penance for what she did, for hiding her crime all these years."

For a moment, he did not speak, but then the chief's face bloomed into a slow smile. "Imprison your sick, deranged grandmother? Even with the possibility that her confession was just some delirious rant?"

"I couldn't live with it if it was true. Having a traitor under the same roof as me."

The chief pressed his lips together, then reached for a folder within a tall stack of files.

"Zhou Weihong, isn't it?"

Weihong nodded. His palms grew clammy.

"I recognized your picture. You're applying to university. I have your application here." He shook the papers in his hand, then flipped through them lazily before speaking again.

"What you've done is very admirable. I respect your generation, how far you are willing to go for our country, for the Party. You exemplify the revolutionary fervor that universities need, and I'll write as much in your recommendation."

Weihong stared at the file. He had traded in his Nǎinai's life and gotten a recommendation from the chief, which was as good as a university spot. The chief was waiting for his reaction, but Weihong was no longer in the room. He was thinking of how he'd gotten here. He was standing in the Woman's alley. He was watching his neighbor's smile through the open door. He was sitting on the bench with Nǎinai. Cherry blossoms raining down petals.

Weihong smiles back hesitantly at the chief. The chief is saying something to his staff now. Weihong watches as the chief's mouth moves silently. Then, from the doorway, he watches as two Party officials bring Nǎinai to her feet and begin dragging her away. Her eyes are darting around the hallway, bulging out of her head like two ping-pong balls, landing on him.

"I know you," she says, and Weihong startles because he can hear her. "I know you! Help me! Please!" Her hand breaks free from the officer's grasp, and she is pointing at him—she will always be pointing at him in this hallway in city hall—and she is thrashing and screaming, always thrashing and screaming, "You! Please!"

Weihong turns away. He was always turning away.

THE NEXT FEW HOURS PASSED by in a frenzy. Weihong went back to the empty apartment and upturned everything in it. He ripped the quilts and smashed the chairs. He threw bowls against the walls. He splintered the table with a curled fist. He heard a knock at the door and opened it to let in an old Red Guard comrade who owed him a favor.

The comrade's fist smashed into the bones of his eye socket. Then, a hook to his bad ear that sent him stumbling to the side, the ringing in his head clanging into a cacophony of bells. He spat out the blood that had started filling his mouth. From where he knelt, he raised his face to meet his deliverance.

Later, his comrade leaned over, his face swimming in Weihong's vision. He told Weihong that he was leaving now, and Weihong weakly nodded, clutching his bruised ribs. He stared at the ceiling and waited for Mother and Kangmei to return.

When they did, Mother cried out and rushed to his side, her hands flitting around his injuries. She asked him what happened, and the words came out, as they always did. He'd been looking after Nǎinai when two Party officers came in. Someone had reported Nǎinai for saying counterrevolutionary propaganda. He'd tried to keep them from taking her, telling them she was sick, that she didn't know what she was saying, but he'd been beaten and left on the floor while they dragged her away to be imprisoned.

Mother's legs gave out from underneath her. Her face went blank, and she was repeating, *No, no, no*, and he was standing in the Woman's alley. He was watching his neighbor's smile through the open door. He was in that hallway, Nǎinai's eyes bulging out at him, her finger pointing at him, accusatory.

IN THE MIDDLE OF THE night, he climbed out of his blankets in the empty, wrecked living room to follow Kangmei to the courtyard.

She kept staring at his bloated, bruised face. When he raised his eyes to meet hers, she turned to look at the ground.

"What did we do?" Kangmei asked, her voice choked.

"We didn't have a choice."

"This was what I saw in the bog. Us, standing here."

He watched her profile. He'd suspected this from their conversation before, then at the park with the cherry blossoms. There had been something larger at work.

She continued, "I spent years of sleepless nights thinking through every possible scenario. What would happen if we just let her be, if we sent her off on a train by herself, if we settled her back in the countryside, if, if, if, and always the Party found out and came after us, or Ma died, and it never worked out right for our family, and everyone ended up hurt or dead or both."

She buried her hands in her hair. "It was me. I brought her to city hall, not you. In the bog, that's what I saw."

Weihong looked up at her. So she had changed her fate, had deflected the worst of the blame onto him. He knew he should feel anger at this, indignation, but he just felt tired.

She continued, "I changed other things, too, but we're here again. I never wanted it to come to this. But there wasn't another way. I thought it all through, and there wasn't, because if we sent her down, then the Party would trust us, and the rest of us would be safe. You see that, right?" Her voice was raw and hysterical, and he was unsure of who she was trying to convince, him or herself.

Kangmei's eyes were wet. She looked at him. "I loved her."

"I loved her too," Weihong said defensively.

"I know." Kangmei nodded. "But I love Ma more. And you love Ma most."

PART III

Twenty-Five

Ming

1940: Seventy-Seven Years Before Reunion
Manchukuo

THEIR WEDDING WAS HELD IN the fourth lunar month: one month after Ming turned sixteen, half a year since she started menstruating. The date had been divined by the town matchmaker from Ming's and Fei's horoscopes. The ceremony would be simple, and the arrangements had been straightforward.

The palanquin the village used for its marriages was rented, as were the red silk wedding robes. A group of musicians was hired to play at the banquet, which would be a small affair: family, friends, respected business partners. Mother-in-law had been saving rations, stretching bones into stew, turning foraged goods into a hearty spread for the dinner guests. The red Double Happiness symbols were cut from paper and pasted to the entrance of the Zhous' compound. Ming's trousseau had been delivered several days ago by Qian. Mother-in-law had redone Fei's room, turning the boy's room into one suitable for a newlywed couple.

The morning of the ceremony, Ming woke alongside the winter dawn's warblers, unable to sleep. She sat with her back against the wall, breathing in tune with Dìdi's snores. Gone was the little shadow of a boy. In his place was a brash adolescent who was still adjusting to his new body. Qian, thirteen, had recently constructed a divide down the center of the rectangular kang, creating a plush wall out of pillows and a folded summer quilt. Relegated to separate square spaces of bed, they slept curled inward like river shrimp.

At night, Qian would wedge himself against the far side, desperate for distance. But by morning, he'd have drifted over to the divide like he was missing her. Sometimes, with his face so close, she would forget herself and reach over the wall to smooth his hair away from his eyes. He hated it when he was awake, fleeing when she licked her thumb to slick down stray hairs.

"You're awake."

Ming startled at the voice, ripping her gaze away from Dìdi's face and finding Mama at the threshold.

"I couldn't sleep," Ming said as she sank against the wall.

"Lucky day."

"That's what the matchmaker says."

Mama fidgeted, looking awkward. "If you're not going back to sleep, we can get started on the day's preparations."

Ming frowned but got up, her bones cracking into place. There was not much to do besides getting dressed. "Did you need me for something?" Lately, it had been even harder for Mama to get around on her bound feet. She'd started using a cane, complained often about her hip and back. She could no longer reach the highest shelves in the kitchen.

Mama hesitated, looking down at the floor. Her thin brows furrowed together.

"Is something wrong, Ma?" Ming braced herself for the worst: a tempest of spiteful emotions, set loose on her last morning in the house.

Instead, Mama said, "We should dress your hair. If we're both awake."

"Sorry?" Ming managed to get out in her surprise.

Mama looked up, her eyes flinty in a way that said she wouldn't make the offer again. She hobbled into the main room, which was empty. Ba was out in the fields checking on his seedlings. Ming, in a daze, followed her, wondering if this was a dream from her girlhood, back when she hadn't yet given up on winning Mama's love.

The wedding was far from lavish. They'd forgone many traditions. Traditions were for rich, prosperous years—not frugal winters under the Japanese occupation. All the best rations went to the handful of Japanese families and colonial officers who had settled nearby. Ming and Fei made the best of their leftovers. They picked and chose what they could afford. Ming hadn't even considered the bridal hair ceremony—a farewell ritual for mothers and daughters—and Fei hadn't brought it up.

They didn't have the proper ceremonial objects: the headdress, the hairpins, the candles, the red bridal seat. Instead, they had the dining table and a worn chair. They had the house's scratched, warped mirror, a moon-shaped wooden comb, and leftover joss sticks. Ming watched as Mama collected these items from their places on the shelves.

"You can have a seat," Mama said to Ming, who was still standing at the doorway of her and Qian's room.

Ming sat down at the table, where the mirror was propped up by a bowl. Mama lit a few joss sticks, and the heady scent of incense filled the room. Mama stood behind her—sitting had become hard on her hips—and her long fingers gathered Ming's hair to her back, the nails scratching against her scalp. Mama's fingers were thin and spidery, longer than Ba's.

In the mirror, Ming watched Mama fixate on her hair, avoiding the reflection of her face. If their eyes met, they might peel apart, suddenly aware of the intimate ritual they were performing.

Mama pulled the comb through Ming's hair once, gingerly working out the tangles. "I was married when I was nine." Ming jolted at Mama's voice, at its vulnerability.

This was not new information, and Mama suspected as much. In the mirror, she pursed her lips. "I'm sure you've heard this from the town busybodies. That my father's business was ruined by the war, and he began to sell things off: our heirlooms, our treasures, our compound, and last of all, me. He left after the wedding to remake his fortune, and I haven't heard from him since. The wedding was simple, like yours. Wartime." Mama shrugged. Ming worried that if she spoke or moved, the spell would be broken.

"We didn't have our wedding night until I was eleven. And then, more than a decade before I had a baby that took." Mama paused, working through a knot at the base of Ming's skull. Ming did her best to keep her head still.

"Ming," Mama said quietly. Mama was silent for several minutes, and Ming wondered if she would speak again. Mama took a breath and said, "I was promised a different life. Luxury and leisure, days resting my feet up on a chaise. My mother died in childbirth, but that wasn't supposed to matter at my station. I was taught that childcare was a task meant for the servants. I couldn't have imagined then that my life would look like"—Mama gestured with the comb to their small, mud-brick hut—"this."

Ming stared in the mirror, wanting to commit this image to memory: this still moment of armistice in their long-waged war. Her mother's face in the background, hers in the foreground: the same face doubled and inherited, the distance between them a no-man's-land. Ming knew this confession was the closest Mama would come to an apology. Mama ran the comb through the now-smooth sheet of hair a fourth and final time. Her face softened, crinkled into a half smile at her work.

Ming, feeling a surge of bravery, asked, "Mama, could you braid my hair? Just this once."

THE DAY FLEW BY IN a flurry of well-wishers and kowtows. Finally alone in their new room, Ming sagged on the thick quilt of the marriage kang, a mantle of exhaustion weighing her down, as she extended and bent her legs. Her knees ached. The apples of her cheeks hurt—shooting pains running up and down her jaw—from her frozen smile as she accepted the congratulations. Ming, suddenly very aware that this was the first moment that she and Fei had been left unattended since childhood, felt anxious and shy, like she was in the presence of a foreigner.

Fei was rubbing his eyes, weary from the long day. Ming wondered what he was thinking. He'd been stiff and quiet since they came in. The room was different from how she remembered it, back when they played with toy soldiers on the rug. Back when it was a child's room—primary school homework and open books strewn on the table, toys scattered every which way—not an adult's, not a couple's. The room was hellishly red. Intricate paper cutouts were plastered on every wall, and every surface was upholstered in red fabric: the table, the pillows, the sheer curtains that cordoned off the kang. Even the ceramic bowl, filled with dates and oranges, gleamed in a fluid crimson glaze. The candles cast a sheen on Fei's form, lengthening the shadows of everything in the room, creating a saturated wildfire landscape.

Fei turned around, and Ming relaxed. It was just Fei. It was just his room: their room. He walked to the kang and sat next to her, hesitant. Fei first put his hand over hers, and the familiar weight was comforting, a gesture from the old country of their childhood.

It began slow and unsure. Fei helped her undress, her rented robes pooling in a liquid pile of red silk. There was the first married touch of his hand on her shoulder, which made her spine jerk involuntarily, canting her hips toward him. Hard, inexperienced kneading of her breasts, like her body was flour to be made into strips of noodles.

"Is this good?" Fei asked, breathy. "I want it to be good for you."

Ming knew from the stories that this was far more than most girls got.

"It's good," Ming lied. It would get better, she'd been told. She believed that. They would learn. She and Fei had once been One Being, and this was a natural evolution—a culmination—of the course. They would learn. She repeated this narrative to herself: a chant told to her hammering heart in her head.

She sensed an impatience girding his actions, so she surged forward, her hand curling through the thick hair at his nape, her mouth clashing with his. His hand tangled in her hair, undoing her tight braid. His hot, quick breath lingered in the hollow of her neck as his hand ran up her body, feeling the hips that had become supple from Mama's feeding all those months ago. His animal longing emerged, his hunger to know and claim every part of her, which dug and bit into her skin, leaving fresh nail marks on her waist and the flat indents of teeth on the shell of her ear, marking her as his. Desire rising to a fever pitch—insensate, inchoate, immolating—as he pressed their foreheads together, bone against bone, murmured *lǎo pó* for the first time into the crescent of her jaw, him keeling into her. An erratic thrum in Ming's ears drowning out all other noise.

They were children again: a two-headed snake. No Ming, no Fei, just those four letters—*them, them, them*—the sound of it rocking their bodies. Her eyes fluttered shut. This was the life she was promised.

Twenty-Six

Ming

1943: Seventy-Four Years Before Reunion

Manchukuo

THE WAR BEGAN SIX YEARS ago in 1937. Back then, the stories from farther south—ferried to their village by migrants, letters, rickshaws, trains, and boats—were thought to be tall tales. But in the spring of 1938, the birds that'd flown south in the winter returned to make their nests, carrying their scavenged southern treasures. Rather than their usual loot of feathers, lichen, and spider silk, they carried human hair, skin, and bones. Gory bundles of soft intestines and hard twigs spun together decorated the trees. Later, they would rot, leaving dark streaks of decomposition like sap down the bark.

The villagers considered themselves fortunate. Japanese policing and battlefields were centralized to the thin swaths of the budding railways. They'd never seen Japanese soldiers in their parts. At the beginning of the occupation, a few colonial officials swept through their small town and declared it Manchukuo. The townspeople did not resist, giving up their weapons to spare themselves any bloodshed. The Japanese farming families and colonial officers who settled in their rural region received the best rations: rice, flour, sugar, milk, cooking oil, matches, salt, and cotton. The rest went to the

Japanese war efforts farther south and in the West. Education was upended; living costs rose; inflation, poverty, opium addiction, and malnutrition ran rampant—but this, they told themselves, was bearable. They had only to remind themselves of that season when flocks of birds had flown overhead, their beaks bloody from their macabre foraging. They had only to whisper *Nánjīng Dàtúshā* under their breath with a shiver, like it was a curse, before they pasted false smiles on their faces, told themselves they had it good.

In the fourth lunar month of 1943, Ming and Fei celebrated their third anniversary. There'd been one early pregnancy in that time. It had terminated that past autumn. Malnutrition, Mother-in-law said, shaking her head; she'd seen it more and more in the clinic since the occupation. Ming only remembered the blood. So much blood, it soaked through both the thin mattress and the bed mat, where it finally pooled on top of the tile of the kang like a lake of red vinegar. The nest of bloody bedding, stripped and lying on the floor, waiting to be washed. The undergarments lost to the sporadic bleeding in the months that followed. The damp shirts from her breasts leaking milk for a child that was not there. Ming spent that winter curled in on herself, ashen-faced, feeling like she'd been expelled with the fetus. She turned away visitors, even Qian, who wrote letters and notes, asking after her, telling her how worried he was.

That fourth lunar month found Ming out in the village for the first time since the miscarriage. At Fei's gentle encouragement, Ming decided to go on a walk through the main street. She'd grown weak and wasting in the half year of mourning and was trying to rebuild her strength. Winter had thawed. Early sprouts promised a large harvest that year. There might be enough to feed everyone even after the Japanese took their share. In the heart of town, vendors gave her pitying smiles and nods, which Ming returned halfheartedly. There were no secrets in their community. Still, Ming wished she could shroud herself away from the curious onlookers.

She was halfway down the main road when she saw her brother's familiar figure. Only, it looked like he'd been stretched out like an elastic. He'd shot up to a gangly height since she last saw him, his limbs a lǐ long, hanging off him awkwardly. He was talking to two boys her age. The Chen boys. There had been rumors that the Chen brothers were responsible for a small series of fires and thefts from the neighboring Japanese homes. Ming remembered them being troublemakers in primary school and rabble-rousers as teenagers. They weren't like the lewd boys who once hung around Fei. No, the Chen brothers once had family in Nánjīng. When the Japanese were finished with them, there hadn't been anything left to bury. They told anyone who would listen what the Japanese had done to their maternal grandparents, their uncle, their aunt, their baby girl cousins, but most of the town, including Ming, did not want to hear it.

Ming stood in the road and stared at Qian. He and the brothers seemed deep in conversation. Qian lifted his head, closed his eyes, and rubbed his temples. When he opened them, his gaze flickered past Ming, then returned, and his expression changed, moving from surprise to confusion to delight. He quickly bid the brothers goodbye and bounded over to her, almost skipping.

Ming opened her mouth to apologize. For not writing back. For turning him away. For not seeing him in half a year. For meeting him in the street like they were mere acquaintances. But he collided into her in an embrace, squeezing her tightly, and she knew this was his way of telling her that there was no need.

"Are you well?" he asked first. She nodded. She glanced behind his tall figure and saw that the Chen boys were hurrying away. One gave her a backward glance. It bothered her for some reason, but she didn't know why.

"Look at *you*," she said, holding him at arm's length. She had to strain to look up at him—an ache in her neck that went deeper than muscle and ligament. He let out a throaty laugh.

"What are they feeding you? You're taller than everyone else in the village."

"They're feeding me whatever they can."

"Good. You should come by the compound. I'll cook dinner for you. Scrounge up some of your favorite dishes and—"

He put his big, boyish hands over her shoulders. "You don't have to do that."

"I *want* to."

"Ah, jiě," Qian said, his eyes glittering with tenderness, "you haven't changed much. Always taking care of everyone else. And you? How are you?"

"I can't complain. I'm all right," Ming said slowly, mincing her words. The truth was her body complained for her. There was the constant hunger and malnutrition. She remembered what it felt like to go hungry for years, to be a ghost, a wisp. But her body was older now, and the hunger kicked and screamed within Ming's belly. She slept poorly, kept up by the empty gnawing: another reminder that her insides were as barren as the old, salted battlefield behind the Lis' land.

"You're not all right. You have a tell," Qian said, frowning.

"What?"

"Your teeth don't show when you smile. And you pick at your scar."

Ming saw that her left hand was worrying the raised scar on her right palm. Her hands fell apart.

"You're teasing," Ming said, making a point to smile with her teeth, her lips pulled back over her gums. "I lied to you all the time when we were kids, and you couldn't tell the difference to save your life."

"You're my older sister. I took your word as scripture," he said softly, not looking at her false smile, which slid off her face. *Took*.

"But not anymore?"

He shot her a rueful schoolboy grin. "I've picked up a couple things in the last few years. How to tell a lie, for one."

Her forehead puckered. She was keenly aware of the child he once was, nestled in this young man: in the spoilt way he carried himself, in his generous forgiveness. And yet that child was harder to find, a silver-winged bird swallowed in the belly of a fox.

She shook her head. "I don't want to hear the rest of it. You're still the little boy I strapped to my back and carried around the village."

For some reason, this caused Qian's eyes to harden. Perhaps at the implication that he'd once been a baby, that he once needed her. Ming knew this well: boys at sixteen refused to admit they'd ever been helpless, hiding it behind posturing.

But instead, Qian said, "You're still stuck in the past."

"What?"

"It's okay. Baba and—" He faltered, stumbled over the invocation of Mama. "They're like that too. Nostalgic. Dreaming about our lives before the Japanese but not willing to do anything about it."

"Qian," Ming said lowly, wondering how her words had become so twisted, "I don't—I didn't—what are you saying?" She knew those Chen boys were bad news.

He sighed, looked at his feet. He kicked a rock in the road. "What no one else is willing to say."

Ming's eyes darted around her and her brother, seeing if there were any stray ears. The vendors were busy straightening their stalls, entertaining customers who had come for their share of vinegar, nails, dishes, shoes, fabric—whatever the Japanese didn't want. That didn't mean no one was listening. When she was a child, Ming had been good at slinking between stalls to find the most tantalizing gossip of the market.

"Hush, someone might hear you. You're scaring me."

"*Ming*," he said sternly. His hands returned to rest on her shoulders, but there was an urgency in his grasp. "What should scare you is the way we're living now. No food on our tables, treated like second-class citizens in our own home. Families down in the southern provinces are treated far worse—like animals. The Japanese textbooks tell them that it's their right to rule over us, that we're a backwards, dirty people. They cut us down without a second thought like trees in a forest. You're always terrified, so scared now, you're censoring yourself in the market. Aren't you—aren't you tired of it all?"

Qian was using dangerous language. Treasonous language. Beneath the skin of her brother was a burgeoning radical. The revelation terrified her.

"You sound like a revolutionary pamphlet."

"Do you think that's a bad thing?" he asked slowly, each syllable carefully slipping through the slots of his teeth.

"Was it the Chen boys? Did they teach you all this?"

His face grew dark. "So what if they did?"

She shook her head again, clenched her jaw. "You shouldn't listen to them. They're troublemakers. You can't say these things. If someone heard you, if they reported you, there'd be consequences. They've put people to death elsewhere for less. It's not so bad where we are. We just need to keep our heads down and play along. It'll be over soon. The war—the Chinese will win."

"And if they don't? We live our whole lives under the boot of the Japanese?"

She repeated her words, "It's not so bad here. No soldiers in our town, no deaths."

"No deaths?" he echoed, and pointedly looked at her stomach. Her blood ran cold at the implication. He seemed to realize his mistake, his eyes widening in remorse.

"Jiě, I—"

"That's too far, Qian."

He nodded. "You're right. I'm sorry, jiě," he said, then softer, "I just wanted to show you how deep the rot goes."

"*Don't*," Ming snapped, and he faltered, "don't use my loss to justify your political misgivings."

"Jiě, I want better for you. For everyone."

"You don't even know what better is! Your whole life has been war under the Japanese. Why can't you just bite your tongue and live with it?" *Like the rest of us*, she wanted to say.

"You're three years older than me, don't pretend like you've known better."

"Old enough to know that what you want isn't possible. There'll always be someone looming over us. If not the Japanese, then the Russians, the warlords. Why can't you just be content with being alive?"

They stared at each other. Ming's chest rose and fell with indignation.

"You're right," he said at last. "We've never known anything besides the occupation, the war. But that doesn't mean I can't want better. For you, for Zhou gēgē, for our families. Can you imagine? No starvation, better taxes, fair wages, sovereignty by our own people."

His eyes shone with idealism. It made her sick.

"*Qian*," she said, part admonishment, part plea.

He squeezed her shoulder with such tenderness, it made her breath hitch. "I'll save you a place in the new world. When you're ready for it." He squinted at the horizon. "I have to go now. Let's have that dinner soon. I'll call on you."

He gave her a smile and wrapped his wiry arms around her tightly. Ming reacted too slowly. She was thinking of everything she wanted to say. *Don't go. Stay here. Let jiě watch over you. Don't be brave. Be cowardly like me, like the rest of us. Let me protect you.* But by the time her arms came up to embrace him back, he was gone—bounding away as quickly as he came—her wrists circling empty air.

She saw him join the silhouettes of the two Chen brothers in the distance. They'd been waiting for him in the shade of a cluster of trees. As Qian sauntered up to them, their three heads bowed together conspiratorially. She watched them walk off like that, until they disappeared from sight. Qian didn't turn back. For a long while after, she stood in the sun. She looked until her vision grew blurry, and then she went home.

Twenty-Seven

Ming

1943: Seventy-Four Years Before Reunion

Manchukuo

HOW FAST THE SEASONS ELIDED into one another, chūntiān slipping into xiàtiān. As a girl, Ming remembered summers stretching for decades. Now months passed by at an annihilating pace, each day the same—hours of worrying about their dwindling supplies of food, artemisia incense, thread—seasons of living ration to ration. There was clothing to starch and animals to feed. There were patients to take care of, medicine to order, bandages to be stripped from scrap fabric.

Today was the summer solstice. It was the beginning of the wet season, deep into the dog days of summer. The harvest had been gathered, and the village's local tradition dictated that brides return to their parents' homes to pass the longest, hottest day of the year. Most wives would be carrying bundles on their backs or clutching the clammy hands of toddlers. Ming had decided long ago that she would not go back to Mama and Baba, unwelcome and empty-handed as she was. Perhaps that was a blessing in disguise.

Ming slept on her right side, a remnant of her days from the old house. In her and Dìdi's room, the kang was built alongside the left wall. In the evenings, Dìdi would be asleep already on the inner half of the platform, and she would curl herself around him like a dumpling skin. In the compound, the kang she shared with Fei was also on the left side, but her husband was her protector, and he was the one who slept on the outer half, his body the barrier between her and the outside world. Ming lay awake, unable to leave bed without waking Fei. In his sleep, Fei nuzzled his head near the crook of her exposed throat, their skin not quite touching.

Ming had woken early that morning and then spent the better part of an hour staring at the ceiling, trying to grasp the edges of a dream before it slipped away.

In her dream, she remembered being in the forest and being thirteen. Distinctly thirteen. So much longing, too large to be housed in her body, which was caught in an in-between: sprouting limbs and the small swell of new breasts. She'd been making her way through the sun-dappled forest, foraging for scraps, when in the canopy, a dark bird let out a low, discordant whistle, warning of an approaching predator. The midsummer air shimmered with heat, and a red beast—more wolf than dog, more hellhound than either—loped through the mirage toward her.

She knew she should've been scared. She knew she should've run, that that was what any rational person would have done. But instead she watched, transfixed, as it trotted toward her with the slow and languid gait of an immortal creature. It walked right up to her and sat, resting on its haunches. Its head was eye-level with hers. It sniffed at her hand, at her scar. Then it smiled, panting, its wet, red tongue lolling out of canine jaws, before it turned and left, bounding off to deeper parts of the forest.

Nineteen-year-old Ming did not know what to make of the dream. There was a familiarity to the creature—she'd read about it in some book or scroll, but she could not recall which one. Likely, the dream was a reflection of the omens that had cropped up around town. There had been dead rabbits found amongst the tassels of the sorghum fields, boiled fish seen floating belly-up in the river, and amphibians that surfaced with fanged teeth to bite at swimmers' ankles. Children's nightmares tearfully confessed to their parents, inhabited by birds with human hair and dark-scaled dragons. The townspeople were perturbed, but they chalked up these strange incidents to abnormal migration patterns from the heat of the summer, which scorched hotter than the years prior.

Fei rolled over, his chest curled against her spine. He was hard and pressing into the small of her back. She twitched, shifted away, and he woke.

"Sorry," he said curtly.

"It's okay," Ming replied.

She'd been reluctant to share a bed again after the miscarriage. Last year, on the threshold between qiūtiān and dōngtiān, Ming spent a month sleeping in the clinic alone. When she'd come back to their kang, she withdrew to the wall.

Ming and Fei's honeymoon period had been dedicated to a frenzied learning of the other's body: the jut of a bone, the tender flesh, the thin skin that, when pressed, elicited groans from the other. Fei had been an avid learner, fueled by his adolescent needs. But then the miscarriage. Then the ripping, the excavation of a part of her that had tumbled out with the fetus. The cool emptiness. She was no longer half of One Being. Perhaps a quarter. She didn't know. Just less.

She wanted to be more. She wanted to be the wife and mother she always envisioned she'd be. Someone like Mother-in-law—caring, doting, kind. The antithesis of Mama. But she was nineteen and failing at wifehood like she'd failed at daughterhood. Three years of marriage and what did she have to show for it? A miscarriage. An absence. A husband who did his best to hide his frustration at his imposed celibacy, but who would occasionally boil over, his upbringing lending itself to childish temper tantrums. *I have needs! It's been half a year, how much longer do you want?* he asked. And then after the yelling, *I'm sorry. I love you*, the words like a balm, like a bandage wrapped over a broken bone.

Fei cleared his throat. She looked over at him. His eyes seemed apologetic. He knew it would be a difficult day for her.

"Have you been awake long?"

"No," Ming lied, "just a few minutes."

"Sleep well?"

"Yes," Ming lied again. She gave him a smile, stiff at the edges. "It's going to be hot today," she observed.

Fei hummed in agreement. "Are you going to stay here?"

"I think I might go to the market."

Fei sat up, his fumbling hand seeking his glasses—he had started needing them in the past year—then putting them on. He blinked. "You don't want to stay and help at the apothecary?"

She crawled out of the kang. "I think I'll browse the stalls to see what's in. Wash some clothes by the river, maybe."

His forehead scrunched. "I'll come with you—"

"No need," Ming said hurriedly. "Father-in-law needs you. I could use the time alone. I'll be fine. I'll be back before dinner preparations."

"All right. If that's what you want." Still, Fei's concerned look followed her through the room as she buttoned a cotton summer tunic over her trousers, gathered the market basket in her arms. Stiffly, he got out of bed and pressed a kiss on her cheek, lingering there, unsure, his breath on her jaw.

"I'll see you at dinner then."

She nodded.

Outside, the day had all the indications for a scorcher. There was an uneasy silence as the animals and insects sought refuge in the shade. Shielding her eyes from the sun's glare, Ming made the walk to the hawkers at the center of the village. She was hoping to pop into the market to show face—to show she was a good wife—before the new mothers and brides began their annual pilgrimage.

"Ming!" an Auntie called out, and Ming followed the voice through the throng of the other early market shoppers.

"Hello, Auntie," Ming greeted her, surveying the slim spread of fish and vegetables at the table.

"You're in luck today. We just got some of Fei's favorites. Are you looking for anything special?"

"Anything caught this morning?" Ming asked, turning over stalks and stems for inspection.

"Here." Auntie nodded toward a basket in the shade filled with fish giving off a ripe odor. Ming picked through it, wrist deep in the smooth-scaled bodies.

"I saw Qian the other day passing through the market. Leaving town with the Chen boys."

Ming stopped, withdrew her arm. "The Chen boys? Are you sure?"

"Oh yes," Auntie confirmed. "Qian's gotten so tall. Couldn't mistake him for anyone else. And those Chen brothers. Reek of trouble. Can smell them over the fish. No mistake at all, it was them."

"They left town? Not just passing through?"

"Didn't look like it. They had satchels under their arms. Water, food. Left a few days ago. Haven't seen them since. Bad news, those Chen boys. You should tell Qian not to hang around them anymore."

"I have," Ming said quietly.

What was Qian doing outside of their village? He had to help Baba with the fields. Briefly, Ming considered going to ask Baba if he'd sent Qian on an errand. But that would have to wait for tomorrow; Ming spotted a blushing bride, promenading proudly with her newborn son. The glow of birth stuck to her, gleaming like a sheen of sweat. Ming paid the Auntie for one fish and the news of her brother and began making her way home before another new mother could pass her. The baby began to cry. Soft at first, then louder. The sound cleaved into her chest.

Some of the Aunties gathered around the new mother, cooing at the wailing baby.

"Such a strong cry," they fawned, "means a strong boy."

Ming watched the gathering circle from a few meters away. That could've—*should've*—been her. She was so caught up in the display that her ears pricked when they sensed another sound below the boy's crying.

Dogs barking. But not the Lis' dogs, who'd grown soft with old age. Rabid barking. A hunting barking. Underneath was the gallop of horses, a low, insistent thrumming of hooves, quiet enough that she almost mistook it for her heart within her breastbone. The sound drew closer. Fast, with no promise of stopping. They didn't get many visitors, few on horses. Rarely in a group. Except that one time when the—

The town crier began shouting, jolted from his nap in the watchtower. Fear in the tremor of his voice.

"SOLDIERS! JAPANESE SOLDIERS ON THE HORIZON!"

All was still for a moment. Ming barely registered his words. How unreal they sounded. Then, the smell of human fear settled in.

Vendors abandoning their wares, tipping over their displays. Families running out of their houses, still in the undergarments they wore to sleep. Wailing children yowling at an inhuman pitch. And all the while, the noise of dogs and horses was getting louder and closer, louder and closer. A swell of terror bubbled behind Ming's lips as she stood at the side of the main road, frozen.

They told us they'd leave us alone. They told us we just had to listen to them, and they'd let us be.

It took only a blink for the platoon to descend upon the road, cutting through the space, ripping it open like the sex of a virgin, from which blood and dying brays and falling limbs sprung forth. In the few minutes she stood paralyzed, she saw the families who had been too slow to react pierced by the same spear—four, five people bladed together—bayonets jabbing at the fetuses of the pregnant newlywed wives, women whose weddings she had attended, women she had resented just this morning. Steel whined as the soldiers whetted their swords on stomachs, turning the landscape into a field of corpses. *They're not supposed to be here. They could take what they wanted without this.* But they were here and corporeal and violent, letting out gleeful shouts, these warmongers, war mongrels, so war hungry they worshipped gore in every form, letting it rain down on her home with no remorse.

Finally, she felt a toe twitch, then the arch of her foot. Her limbs unfroze. *Run*, her mind urged, so she did. In the time it took for the basket to hit the ground, she'd already made it to the other end of the street.

Ming pushed forward, her legs complaining as they stretched taut. She was not as strong, not as fast as she once was. Her face grew hot with exertion, her lungs heaved. She wove along the roads between huts. The Japanese had kicked up dust, and it clouded her vision.

Her soles hit the ground hard, thin slippers useless as she pushed her legs past soldiers who were dismounting, past houses where screams emanated from within. She heard the cries grow small and tinny. Heard the sounds of her heart and heavy breathing plug up her ears.

Deeper into the village, where the houses were more spread-out, she continued to run, even as her chest lurched painfully. There was no shade, only sorghum fields lining the paths. All she could see were those endless yellow stalks.

Farther ahead was the dark shape of the forest on the horizon. If she could just make it there, she might be safe. She could hide there for days. Sweat dripped into her lashes, turning her sight watery. She grew aware of two dark unmounted figures following her. Two more came to join them. Cats conspiring to snatch up a wounded bird. Her head grew woozy.

All you're good for is running. The voice inside her head was hers. The voice inside her head was Mama's, was Qian's. She wanted to stop. She wanted to take deep gulps of air instead of these shallow, scared huffs. Her calf was cramping, causing one leg to drag behind the other. Up ahead was the border of the forest, shaded and beckoning.

As she entered the woods, she felt branches crack under her feet. It hurt—the broken debris digging into skin. She tried to spend as little time on each foot as possible, flying past the trees, even as the soldiers got closer, clumsy and noisy as they breached the unfamiliar terrain. Her body was becoming heavy. Her ribs throbbed.

But she had the advantage. She was intimately familiar with the landscape. Knew the buckled roots that would trip the foreigners, the placement of the trees, the slopes and dips. Farther that way, she had been gored by the hare. And there was the tree that she and Fei used to tie their jackets around when they got too hot.

Fei. The thought came to her and made her stumble. In her mindless self-preservation, she'd forgotten him. Her right hand grabbed at the tree for balance, and its bark scraped her palm as she righted herself.

Fei. The image of his face poured into her mind. Surely, she would have felt it if he had been killed? She felt her legs slow. The only thing occupying her head was the image of *Fei in the apothecary, beheaded on the counter, blood leaking onto the wood. His glasses smashed, his sleepy eyes accusatory.* Fei unable to hear all the things she'd wanted to tell him since the miscarriage: that she hoped one day they would move past this tear in their marriage. That they would relearn each other, adapt, grow together, like the kissing trees they'd seen in the forest: fused at a common wound.

She tripped over another root, one that she'd always avoided as a girl. It had grown buckled and snarled. She cursed. The approaching soldiers were a roaring presence, tearing through the underbrush, sending all the animals skittering. The men were panting. They were frustrated. She knew what would happen if they caught her. It was what made her push herself up off the ground and continue.

But her heart wasn't in it. In fact, her heart was creating gruesome scenarios like *Fei skewered, him and his parents rotating on the end of the same spear like three pigs on a spit.*

Farther back, she heard the dogs. Panic rose. She needed to move. She needed to go where they couldn't follow. There was a steep crag up ahead where the forest approached the base of a mountain. Plants grew between the rocky cracks. She began to climb up. The dirt crumbled, showering down onto her face as she grasped at a hard root, but it held and she pulled herself up.

The dogs were closer than the men now. A bird sliced through the air above her, letting out a warning call. The dogs growled, clustering below her as she continued her ascent. Her hands blistered as she grabbed for her next hold. She was halfway up and could see the soldiers beginning to gather at the bottom.

"Little bird," one of them called out tauntingly in broken Chinese, "come down and we promise to feed you well." Cruel laughter echoed through the canopy.

Her hands grew slick with sweat. She reached for another root, slowly inching upward. The muscles of her arms shook from the effort. She heard the mechanical sound of the men below loading their bayonets. She reached for the next root.

In the space of a moment, it split under her grip—her hand still holding a jagged half—and as she began to fall, she realized that this would be the end of her. Her arms and legs sought whatever purchase they could, nicked and torn as they caught on small roots and branches.

She hit the ground on her back, stunned by the impact.

Above her, the leering faces of the Japanese soldiers crowded her vision. The spittle of thrashing dogs, restrained by their masters, landed wet on her cheek. She let out a shuddering breath.

She remembered, then, where she'd seen the red dog from her dream. *The Tiānquán is a red dog called the Celestial Hound. There will be war wherever he descends*. She wanted to laugh, but a wheeze came from her aching chest instead. After the hare with horns, she'd memorized Shūshu's bestiaries, seeking answers. How could she have thought the forest would protect her? It had warned her once before. She had a scar spanning her palm proving these woods were no sanctuary.

"The little bird had her wings clipped. We should nurse her back to health, make her feel better," one soldier taunted.

"I think I know a way we can help her," another said, grinning as his hands reached to undo his belt. The clink of the metal ringing in tune with the shaking of her body.

She tried to move, but she could only let out a pained groan as she shifted to her side in a fetal position. Large hands came down to pin her on her back, clutching at her ankles. As the shock wore off, she fought against their grip. She lashed, she screamed, she frothed at the mouth.

The ones holding her were talking. Angry, harsh words heavy with want. Their foreign, sharp syllables were uninterpretable, but she recognized the language for what it was: male pride. She'd wounded it. She, a starving nineteen-year-old girl had almost gotten the better of them. She had to pay. She would do so fighting.

The belt unwound from its loops and fell to the forest floor, the sound muffled by woody detritus. She squirmed, clenching her thighs together as the men pried them apart. The soldier, his trousers pooling at his ankles, gave her a feral grin. He was lowering himself onto her, his breath hot at the crook of her neck, the place that Fei had nestled in, untouching, and she decided she wouldn't—couldn't—allow that. She would rather die.

Her mouth gaped and blindly searched for purchase, until she suckled at his ear, and when the round, soft thing was fully in her mouth, she bit down hard. Briny, metallic blood filled her mouth. The soldier screeched, flailed above her to get away, but she held fast like a dog, a hellhound, teeth relentless in their grip as she shook her head to and fro. The other soldiers tried to get her off him, reaching for her jaw. He was screaming. It was a feminine, high-pitched wail—like a woman giving birth—and she felt the vibrations of it in her throat. Her teeth ground against each other. The soldier pulled away, the abortive sound turning into a whine, then a whimper.

She spat out the smooth flesh.

The men released her for a moment, shocked, staring at the severed ear. The soldier fell away, his hand clutching the empty, bleeding hole in the side of his head.

"You vicious bitch."

Now it was her with the predatory grin. She wiped the taste of satisfaction from her mouth with her sleeve, smearing the blood across her pale face. The soldiers looked uneasy. The leader of the group, however—a commander by the looks of the insignia on his uniform—laughed, revealing two rows of canine-like teeth. He said something in Japanese that made a few of the men chuckle uncomfortably.

He met her eyes, his wicked and gleaming, and switched to Mandarin for her benefit.

"So, the little girl has teeth."

Twenty-Eight

Ba

2017: Nineteen Days Since Reunion
Manhattan, New York

HE WAS WOKEN BY SHIVERS that wracked his body. He was on the couch, the velvet slick from his night sweats, and it was dark out. There was a tightness in his chest. His heart was beating quickly, skipping every few seconds, and his stomach clenched in pain. Beneath these physical pains were those deeper, chronic injuries inflicted by fate, tender and clotting.

The last thing he remembered was stepping through the mirror to follow Kangmei and plummeting downward into the past, forced to confront what he had done to Nǎinai—the horror of recalling this crime now splitting his head—wishing he could unremember, undo. His hand reached for his hidden stash of báijiǔ, only to find the bottle empty. How much time had passed since he'd gone through the mirror? Was he still on the wrong side of it?

Lightheaded, he staggered toward the bathroom, but when he opened the door, he found himself in the Myrtle house kitchen, only everything was liquefying around him, and he turned around to go back, but the door had disappeared, and the floor was melting, giving way to a darkness, and then he was tumbling—

HOW IT ALL STARTED GOING wrong. It had been a year in Vermont, a year since he left. Qianze was now fifteen. He often wondered if she looked the same as the Qianze he remembered at fourteen. In the Myrtle house he'd built in his mind, Qianze's features began to liquefy, shapeshifting into variations of how she might look once she was grown-up. One moment, her face chiseled, the next, a wide moon face with full cheeks. Her hair short then long. Each one a stranger to him.

In the Myrtle house, the candles began dripping wax. The scene of Qianze's fourteenth birthday unfroze. The weather grew hot, no longer July but a true Virginia August, and with this change, the backdrop began to shift like a mirage. He tried to stop it by drinking more, using his hands to cup the melting drops of wax, but the candles continued to burn to the quick, and now the house had a sickening smell: liquor and burnt flesh.

His memory became moth-eaten—holes in the logic and sequence—and some days the only moments he could recall were the minutes before he topped up his coffee with the small bottles of liquor tucked up his sleeve. He began losing time. He would come to, withdrawal rearing its ugly head, and find himself standing at his register, in the apartment, in the liquor store checkout. He imagined himself sitting still on a revolving stage: the same actors, props, settings, rotating behind him and then—something new emerging from the wings.

THE SILVER CAR HAD BEEN appearing on his street over the past three weekends. From his broken blinds, he could see the dark silhouette of the driver, the shift of their head as they seemed to direct their gaze toward his window. Weihong reasoned that the driver could be waiting for anyone on his street, but each weekend, he would observe the car pulling up quietly across from the house, idling for an hour or two, then driving away with no passenger. He could feel some peripheral presence studying him. A glimpse of a figure darting into the tree line as he turned around—a shadow standing in the front yard at night peering up at him—that disappeared when he went outside.

By the fifth weekend, he was unsettled, tempted to tell someone: his landlord, his manager, even the local police. But he could not shake his uncertainty. What if this phantom was a hallucination of his own creation? Or worse, the beast of his reckoning? He kept quiet, tried to ignore when the hairs on the back of his neck stood up. Once, at work, feeling watched, he'd turned around several times in an hour, but each time, he was greeted only by the glazed eyes of his coworker Felix, staring dumbly at the wall behind him.

Weihong had given very little thought to Felix. They did not overlap often except when Weihong clocked out and Felix clocked in. Weihong usually worked the opening shift, but when he covered an evening shift, Felix was at the register two aisles behind him and occasionally worked as a bag boy. Felix had long hair that he wore in a low bun at his nape, and he had a distinct vegetable musk. *Marijuana*, one of Weihong's coworkers had whispered under her breath, sounding scandalized.

It wasn't until Weihong was in the parking lot leaving after his shift that he saw what kind of car Felix drove, watching him pull into the parking lot in a silver car with a missing fender and faded stickers on the back. The same car that had been stalking his apartment each weekend.

THERE WAS NOTHING OUTWARDLY DANGEROUS about Felix. He was scrawny. He had long arms that dangled almost to his knees. Until that fleeting moment in the parking lot, Weihong had been certain that Felix hadn't paid him any mind. But Felix's car was unmistakably the same one that had been appearing outside his apartment. He made excuses. Felix knew his downstairs neighbors.

Felix parked on his street to get high because it was a block away from the grocery store. All plausible. Still, Weihong made sure that the two of them didn't share any shifts that next week.

The week passed by uneventfully. The silver car had not appeared that weekend, and Weihong had convinced himself it was a misunderstanding, unrelated to him. It was mid-September, and by the time he clocked out, the sun had mostly set. He made his way across the gray sea of the lot, drifting through the occasional oil-spill cast of a streetlamp. He approached the apartment. His downstairs neighbors weren't home. The windows were dark, the porch light off.

He went around the back to his own entrance and was surprised to find Felix, sitting on the steps, smoking. At his arrival, Felix sprang to his feet, and Weihong lost his footing, taking a step back.

"Wayne! Just the man I wanted to see!"

"What are you doing here?" Weihong sputtered, refusing to come closer.

"I just want to talk," Felix said.

"We can talk at work. This is where I live."

Felix took a step forward, and Weihong could see his face clearly in the moonlight. All the excuses he had made for this abrupt appearance dried up, replaced by unease. Felix's glassy-eyed mask had lifted, and now his crazed blue eyes looked at Weihong with a certain fascination, as if he wanted to take him apart, dissect him piece by piece.

"I've been looking for you for a long time," Felix said.

Weihong's mouth went dry, his mind darting to different possibilities. Had his wife and daughter been searching for him? Had they sent Felix? Fear and hope coursed through his body, cutting him to the bone. Maybe something had happened. "Did Qianze send you? The Woman?"

Felix frowned. "What? No, who's that?" He shook his head and continued, "No, I've been looking for someone like you. Like me."

The man was high on something stronger than marijuana; Weihong could see it in how his body moved, unsure and delayed. He seemed harmless at the moment, more of an annoyance than a danger. Weihong decided to call an ambulance so Felix would be someone else's problem.

"You don't know me," Weihong said slowly, "you're not well. I'm going to call for help."

"No!" Felix exclaimed, and Weihong, startled, dropped his phone. He reached down for it, but Felix interrupted again.

"Wait! Listen," he said, and licked his lips. "I just want to have a conversation. Then I'll leave, I swear, okay?" His voice had grown feathery and desperate.

"You need help. You don't know me. We're not alike," Weihong said, his hands outstretched, one in front of the other like he'd stumbled across a feral animal.

"We are!" Felix insisted with a jerky nod. "Can't you see it?"

"See what?" Weihong asked.

"The *blue*," Felix whispered reverently, as if this were obvious.

"The blue," Weihong repeated.

"You can't see it?" Felix asked. For a moment, he seemed disappointed, but then he shook his head and continued. "I've always been able to see them, since I was a kid. Auras. The colors around people. Every color. But no blue. Weird, right? But then I'm in second grade, and my gramps is dying, and I'm in the hospital, and the moment before he dies, right before his aura goes out, it turns blue. So my mom's crying, and I slip out, and I see the trauma bay, and it's like a light show: blue lights everywhere, blinking out. And you," Felix breathed out, looking at Weihong with that strange gaze, "you're just covered in blue. Blue all the way down. You crossed over and came back. Like me."

He froze. Felix was out of his mind, was unstable, was on any number of drugs, but he was looking at him with those blue eyes—

seer eyes—and he could see Weihong: not as he was now, but thirteen and crawling on the floor of the alley looking for answers, for a way back.

"You crossed over?" Weihong asked incredulously.

Felix's face lit up. "That's why I wanted to talk to you. I've never met someone like me before. Someone"—he gestured wildly to the air around them—"blue. You understand now?" Felix laughed, short and loud. "I could hardly believe it when I saw you, had to wait and make sure it wasn't some trick of the light."

Weihong had doubts, but they were outweighed by his curiosity. He broached his questions hesitantly. "How did you cross over? What was it like?"

Felix nodded again with the exuberance of an evangelist on the verge of converting someone to their faith. "Wet. Humid. One moment I'm on shrooms staring at the patterns on my bedroom carpet and the next I'm lying on a shore, and it was like I had woken up. Like my whole life up until then was just some shadow dream, and I was awake, and it was all so real, realer than real. Man, there was knowledge of the universe there that people have been looking for forever, I could feel it in the air, in the salt, in the water, but then I woke up back in my room. But when I did, my aura had changed, it was blue, so I knew. I knew I'd crossed over and that it was real."

Since Weihong had left China, he'd often wondered if the Woman and the bog were real, or a bizarre dream he'd clung to that made his past easier to bear. But her voice had intruded in his mind on Qianze's birthday, and now this—Felix with this knowledge of him: these breadcrumbs that pointed to divinity. He didn't know whether to believe Felix. The shore, the salt, the blueness of that other world: this all rang familiar, dredged up muddy memories from the slough, but he wasn't fully convinced that Felix's story wasn't some drug-induced vision.

Still, Felix had known. He could see the memory inside of Weihong, and that felt familiar too: this ability to know, this strange sight. If Felix could cross over at will, then that made him like the Woman. A seer. And that meant that he could take Weihong along with him, and there, in the bog, Weihong could find someone, anyone, to barter with—a god, an underworld demon, the details didn't matter to him—and exchange his fate altogether for another. Then he could go *home*.

"Have you been back?" Weihong asked breathlessly.

Felix's face fell, which told him what he needed to know, and all the night sounds of the yard receded, replaced by the sea of blood in his head. The hope that he'd briefly nursed fled his body, and he felt ridiculous for imagining that Felix might offer an escape from this exile. He crashed back to reality. Felix was still talking, rambling on about something—Dreamtime, blue lotus, peyote, ayahuasca—but Weihong was now sharply aware that he had work early tomorrow morning and that he hadn't had a drink in a few hours, and that his palms and temples had started to bead sweat, and Felix was still going on about holes in skulls.

"What did you say?" Weihong interrupted him. "About the holes?"

"Trepanation?" Felix asked. "It was a practice the ancients used. They'd cut a hole through your skull to commune with the spirit world. They used to think that the skull was blocking divinity from coming through."

Something was swimming up to the surface along with his withdrawal. A memory from the deep waters inside him, one he'd spent years trying to forget that Felix had hooked and fished out. He grew pale. Felix must've seen it because he grew excited. "You know something. About trepanation. Does it work? It must work, right?"

"I can't talk now," Weihong said, climbing up the stairs two at a time, "we can talk later."

He closed the door and lurched toward the mini fridge, his hands trembling as he opened a bottle. He poured the contents down his throat, felt the discomfort ease. He let out a sigh of relief, sinking down to the floor and curling on his side. His head felt light, like he was falling in open air, like the floor had mawed open, swallowing him.

And then he sank deeper, down into the past.

YEARS BEFORE WEIHONG WAS BORN, Father suffered a hard blow to his left ear, which caused it to bloat and bloom. Huā shì ěr, they called it. Flower ear. With age, the damaged cartilage and tissue seemed more susceptible to infection. The summer of 1974, the summer Weihong would leave for university, was the worst infection yet. A screamer, Mother called it.

During these months of infection and hearing loss, the balance of the apartment grew fraught. Father had violent outbursts, triggered by the smallest things. A track of mud in the kitchen. A missing coin. The temperature of a meal. No one was exempt from his temper. Weihong did his best to keep out of Father's path, throwing himself into work in his final days at the steelworks before university. Evenings were spent drinking with friends and coworkers or anything that kept him out of that apartment, fetid with the smell of Father's ear, Father's festering grief, and the cause of that grief: the cloying ghost of Nǎinai.

She was everywhere. Her absence blanketed the apartment. She was in the stitches of their torn quilts, in the seams of their hastily repaired furniture. Weihong wondered how she passed her days in the three months since he'd last seen her. What her living conditions in the people's prison were like. If she was still in Ānshān or had been transferred to another city. If she remembered him, if she hated him. If she was dead.

He kept his distance from Kangmei, from Mother, from anything that reminded him of what he had done. This proved impossible. He would be walking and see something, hear something—a green blanket in a shop window, a kettle whistling—and he would tumble back down into the throes of guilt. When the Aunties congratulated him on his university spot, on his fervent loyalty to the Party, he remembered what this achievement had cost him.

The tail end of August. Weihong had finished at the factory and had one week to himself to get his affairs in order for university. He packed his suitcase. In it, he had two changes of clothes, a pair of reading glasses, a crumb of laundering soap, a toothbrush, a water flask, a towel, bedsheets, a summer blanket, a pen, a pencil, a slide rule, two bowls, a soup spoon, a pair of chopsticks, and his copy of *The Little Red Book*. The luggage sat by the door, waiting. He spent the next few days out of the house: falling asleep in the park next to the glittering waters he once swam in and then waking up, disoriented and hot.

At home, Weihong and Kangmei ate meals in silence, the presence of one reminding the other of their treachery. Mother mistook this as mourning, and she would serve them their meals and cup their cheeks, look at them with an encouraging smile. Weihong would shrug her palm off, eat quickly, then go on evening walks around the city, losing hours tracing the streets of his childhood. He counted down the days to his departure, craved the space and time away that he needed to forgive himself, to forgive Kangmei, who had made him do her prophesied dirty work.

Two days before his train, Weihong returned from a day in the park to find the apartment empty. Mother had left him a note on the table, saying that she and Kangmei had gone to the shops to pick up some of his favorite vegetables for a send-off feast. It was a languid summer day, limp and feverish. The apartment was quiet, uncannily so. No flies in the kitchen, no mosquitoes in the apartment, lured in by the smell of Father's blood, which dribbled from his ear like a faucet.

Then, Father's voice from the bedroom: "Ming, is that you?"

Weihong hesitated before answering, "No, Ba, it's me."

A long, brooding silence followed before Father asked, "Where's your ma?"

"She went out to the market with Kangmei. Do you want me to fetch her?"

"No," Father answered brusquely. "Come in here for a second."

Weihong swallowed down the warning that radiated from his gut. He opened the door. He reminded himself that, soon, he would only see Father on holidays and summers, and that he could stomach whatever Father had in store for him now. Perhaps it was an innocent request: he just needed water or more of Mother's tincture for the infection. The room's window was open to air out the stench, but Weihong could still smell the disease in the air.

He cleared his throat. "Did you need something, Ba?"

Father struggled to pull himself up into a sitting position. "Weihong," he said slowly, as if weighing the name in his mouth, "you leave for university soon."

Weihong nodded in confirmation. "I leave in two days. Ma and Kangmei are going to come with me to the train platform to say goodbye." He paused. "If you feel well enough, you can come too—"

"Don't come back here. After you leave."

It took Weihong a moment to understand what Father had said. He felt his body and the room grow distant, and he barely heard himself ask, "What?"

"You heard me, boy. I said don't come back to Ānshān after you leave."

Weihong's stomach bottomed out and he was a boy again, standing in the threshold watching Father toe off his work boots, wanting to edge closer to him, hoping for one gentle hand through his short hair, one grin that was his, *all his*, and wondering why his father did not love him—his firstborn son—like other men loved their firstborn sons, and wondering why his father had not made him good enough to love in that way.

Father continued, "I know you think you got away with it, but you didn't. I know what you did to my mother. That woman loved you like a grandson. You denounced her, and I know why."

"Why?" Weihong asked numbly, not bothering to deny it.

"Your ma thinks I don't know, but I know. You're a mutt. You're a mongrel."

"I'm what you made me, ba."

"I don't know whose you are, but I'm not your ba, you're not mine, guī sūn zi."

He had suffered many abuses under Father's hand, but this was the worst: the denial of him, the rejection of his blood. Father was looking at him, smug and victorious. It made Weihong recoil and close the door, muffling Father's tirade. He felt lightheaded, unmoored, fatherless. The implication of Father's words—no, not Father, not *his* father—sliced to the bone. It meant that Mother had betrayed him. It meant that Mother might've known that this was why Father acted the way he did toward him, and still she had lied. It meant that she had hid him away from his real father.

Something was draining from him, from the mess of his chest. Trust? Love? Either way, he could feel it slipping from him, browning like rotting fruit, replaced by anger. He loved Mother, he had killed for her, there was blood on his hands *for her*, and all this time, she had been spinning an arachnoid labyrinth of lies, so many lies he'd lost count of them.

He shoved the wreckage of emotions deep inside himself. Buried them to face another day, a braver day. He picked up his suitcase, left the apartment, and walked through the courtyard. He did not turn back. He did not think. He made his way to the train station, pushing himself through the crowds. He exchanged his ticket for the next train to Běijīng and boarded. He would do as the man requested. He would not come back to Ānshān. There was nothing left for him here.

He had thought that Father had loved him. All along, he had believed that, that Father had loved him in his own cruel way. That Father's violence was a corrective reaction to seeing his son, his reflection, repeat his mistakes. But no, this was not the case, not the case at all.

The train began to pull away from the station. Weihong closed his eyes, leaned his head against the window. He did not see the blur of two figures chasing after him on the platform. Could not hear through the thick pane of glass the plea of his name, asking him to come back, to take the next train home. Could not see his mother collapse at the edge of the platform, having followed the train to the end of the station, her vegetables from the market spilling out from under her like a green skirt: a sea of leeks and cabbages. His favorite.

THE OFFICIAL MEDICAL DIAGNOSIS OF Father's ear would not come until years after the Cultural Revolution when people could freely go to hospitals and see doctors without fear of associating with INTELLECTUAL RELICS!

This was what the doctors said. When Father was nineteen, he was bashed in the head in an attack by the Japanese Kwantung Army. One of the blows landed on his left ear, damaging the cartilage, causing it to swell with fluid and blood in a condition they called cauliflower ear. For several days, he was written off as dead, and when he was found, it was too late to drain the ear. The fluid inside had become infected.

In the summer of 1974, his chronic infections led to the formation of a tumorous, pearl-like mass of skin in the attic of his eardrum. Over the next four years, it continued to accumulate dead skin, eroding the bones around it. It invaded the middle ear space behind the veil of the eardrum. It tunneled through the bony and membranous labyrinths of the inner ear, then the scutum—the last shield of the temporal bone—and bored a lacuna in the mastoid bone behind the ear, causing mastoiditis. Toward the end, the infection ate through bone indiscriminately. The infection spread to the meninges, the membranes cradling the brain, resulting in meningitis. After the onset of meningitis, it was only a matter of hours before brain swelling, sepsis, organ failure, and finally, death. Weihong would not learn of Father's passing until years after the fact.

Father died of an infection that had eroded a path from his ear to the brain. Trepanation, you could say. That summer, in that passage newly vacated of bone and tissue, voices rushed to fill the vacuum. They told Father the truth about Weihong, about the circumstances of his birth, his lineage.

Which was why, after his evening of drinking and remembering, Weihong was willing to believe Felix. Perhaps they could help each other after all: pool their meager knowledge about spirits, trepanation, the Woman, and the blue place and find a way back together. He went to work humming with this possibility. Felix was a seer, Weihong was sure of this now. He tallied his evidence as he scanned a customer's items at his register, his chest brimming with tentative hope. He overheard two of his coworkers talking in front of him, shaking their heads. Cold lanced through him, sharp as a current.

"What did you say?"

His coworkers looked at each other before one spoke: "You haven't heard?"

"Heard what?"

"About Felix," the other supplied.

"No, what?" Weihong asked, trying to suppress the urgency in his voice.

"He's been hospitalized. Brain-dead. Put a power drill through his skull. Can you *imagine*?"

Weihong's mouth grew dry. He could imagine. He wondered what Felix had heard in that moment when the drill bit burrowed through bone, what spirits were gathered at the site of the wound waiting to speak to him. He wondered—

"What the fuck."

Weihong turned back to his register. Standing in front of him, clutching a carton of eggs, was Qianze. Not fourteen, not fifteen, but older, wearing heels, a tailored pinstripe pantsuit, and an expensive, short haircut. Her face pinched in an expression of horror.

"Hái'ér?" he asked. "What's going on?"

She frowned, put the eggs down on his conveyer belt. "You've been saying all this aloud."

Twenty-Nine

Ming

1944: Seventy-Three Years Before Reunion
Manchukuo

THE MAN CAME OFTEN. SHE couldn't tell if it was every night because the windows were all boarded up so that the two-story house was constantly suspended in a nocturnal era. She kept time by the rhythm of the soldiers in the nearby barracks: daybreak, or so she was told, chores, her two measly meals amounting to little more than gruel, and the men's nights off. There had been 407 days like this. A record, she thought, for her occupation.

Ming was lucky that the commander favored her. She was told this often—by the management, by her friends, by the other women who hissed it under their breath. *Lucky, lucky, lucky*. She heard the word so much that it had lost its meaning. The management liked to save her for him, which meant that some nights, they took her photo down from the entrance hall where all the women's photos hung like a menu for the soldiers. The other women could be handed off to their regular clients with wounds and broken bones. The commander's favorite could not.

During chores, the women would whisper amongst themselves about ways to escape. They only spoke about it when management couldn't eavesdrop, but they thought about it each minute of each hour of their inexplicably endless night. When they woke, hungry, to find themselves in the same filthy beds in the same foul-smelling prison. When they did their chores for the station and the soldiers. When they went to sleep, the soldiers gone at last. Even in their dreams, they thought about the bright-white light of the outside, burning their corneas, turning the landscape into a nuclear winter.

For morale, they told each other stories they had picked up. There were girls who had cut off all their hair and escaped the women's fate by looking like boys. There were baby girls smuggled out of the country in cloth bundles, their weight dangling off bamboo yokes digging into their parents' shoulders. There was a girl whiling away the war in a room her mother dug under their house, where she had lived for the past few years; she survived on roots, and she was slowly laying down roots herself—morphing and twisting into the trunk of a Manchurian ash. There would be women who survived this, even if it seemed like all the girls of the country had been damned to the same destiny. They did not speak of the ranks of women and girls who had slept in their beds before them, the ones they had replaced. The virginal girls, barely thirteen, who would inherit their beds after they passed. All of their dead skin and hair and blood gathering and settling on the same bed mats as the only evidence of their brief presence.

There will be women after this. There will be innocence after this. There will be girls who won't know how it feels to be split by a monster crawling between your legs. Ming chanted these words to fall asleep, the way some might pray.

When Ming slept, she dreamed of having shamanistic powers. With the ability of the gods, she could shapeshift, and so she turned into a white-winged moth and slipped out the tear in the black paper window covering and the layers of wooden boards beyond it. Always, some bird snatched her up before she could reach her village—sometimes a small thing like a gray-winged shrike, sometimes a larger predator like a hawk or an owl—and she'd wake with a start to another day in the long night of the comfort station.

MING AND HER FRIEND MOUSE sat silently side by side as they rubbed soldiers' uniforms against washboards in deep basins. Her friend was called Mouse because the two braided buns she wore resembled the ears of a little field mouse. She was petite, made smaller by her starving peasant frame. She looked younger than she was, verging on preadolescent, which many of the men liked.

Their hands were raw and red from scrubbing a regiment's worth of clothing. Next to Ming, Mouse was fighting off sleep, her head bobbing up and down in short blinks. They were both grateful to be sitting; Mouse's stomach was distended and swollen. Ming knew this meant gang rape even if Mouse wouldn't say it outright.

In Ming's first month at the station, she'd been taken by ten men at the same time, their crowded bodies like a school of fish in the small space designated as hers. Smothering her—rutting—ravaging—like it was their right, their reward. She'd succumbed to unconsciousness, and when she woke, her stomach had looked like Mouse's: perverse and warped, bearing the burden of her violation. The abscess had led to infection and a few fevered days. Management rarely called doctors for them, so the other women had looked after her, and she learned that this caretaking was a rite of passage. She returned the favor later, teaching others what she'd learned in the clinic: how to brew herbal remedies for their ailments, how to make preventative mixtures for when the men refused to wear the station-issued protection, how to get rid of a seed that had taken root.

The soldiers came to them high on bloodlust, though now they were often enraged and humiliated, violently frustrated, which was how the women came to suspect that Japan was losing its wars.

Ming wanted to press a tender hand to Mouse's belly, wanted to gut the men who had done it, strangle them with their own entrails.

Instead, she lathered another uniform with the station's dirty soap bar, rinsed, and repeated.

They didn't talk about the number of men or the shame. Mostly, they cried if they were given the opportunity to be alone with one another.

Mouse was a few years younger than Ming and unmarried. Sometimes Mouse worried no husband would want her now, but that was during the rare times when they believed that there was an ending to this that wasn't death. Infection would likely lead to death. Pregnancy would most certainly lead to death. And for women like them, it was one or the other. The few who tried to escape were killed by the guards as an example. If they made it as far as the well, they threw themselves down. That was why there was so little water for drinking or bathing; management had to go out of their way to find a clean well. Most were thirty meters deep in corpses.

Ming still thought of Fei. Wondered if he was alive. Imagined the son she would have had with him, with hair that would curl in tendrils around his forehead. The sons of farmers shaved their heads to keep the heat of a day's work off their scalps, but Fei was the son of a physician and grew his hair long. As a child, his eyes were a large, inky black and his nose the charming beaked shape of a bird's. Lately, her image of him as an adult had become corrupted, worn by her handling of it. But her memory of him as a boy was an obstinate thread. She imagined a son who took after him. During her chores, she played at naming him, but by evening, she'd forget what she had christened the child. It would be lost to exhaustion or hunger or opium. When the men thrust into her rigid body, she went through a list of names, trying to see which one of them sounded right.

Mouse jostled her with a bony elbow, and Ming looked up to see one of the station's managers at the threshold, beckoning to her. Ming put down her washing and followed him as he made his way back into his office. Behind him, she turned to see Mouse giving her a look, equal parts quizzical and concerned.

The manager's office was a stark contrast to the barren and dirty rooms the girls lived in on the second floor. It was clean, airy, and showed signs of the wealth he was making off of them. Lying on his desk was a folded garment in a luxurious blue fabric. Underneath, a glimpse of startling crimson satin.

"The commander sent this for you."

Ming eyed him skeptically. It was well known that all the men's gifts went straight to the manager's coffers. He returned her gaze with a blank one. He was Chinese, but he spoke a strained Japanese and wore Western-style suits. Because his eyes bulged out of their sockets, the women called him Goldfish Eye.

"He asks that you wear it tonight," Goldfish Eye clarified.

Ah, Ming thought. *So that is why I'm even seeing it at all.*

"Afterwards, you will return it to me. Understood?" She nodded.

In the station, everything that had once belonged to her was not her own.

Goldfish Eye waited, which she took as a sign to disrobe. Off came the ratty tunic on which a faded, white square of cloth with the red character yī was pinned. Discarded were the rancid trousers.

The silk press of the blue robe against her ribs was searing. Despite the perfect fit—the drape of the wide sleeves, the tie of the soft red sash around her waist—she could not shake the sensation that she was being squeezed into a false skin. Putting on a pretty thing to perfume over the stench of her disgrace.

She waited for the commander in her room. It was small—she could press her fingers on both sides of the walls with little difficulty—and pitch-black, which she had grown to like. There were no mirrors in the station, so the only time she caught sight of her reflection was in the watery surface of the basins, in the latrine, in the water vats. She could see herself getting thinner, her skin becoming scaly from the dryness of the station's soap. She looked like the fish of the river's underbelly: pale and primordial. She harbored memories of the river—colorful and rippling and brimming with life—in her light-forsaken head, but those, too, were becoming less saturated.

He came in without knocking, just swept in in his uniform and dirty boots, bringing the dim light of the hallway with him. His eyes landed on her, and it made her feel obscene. He smiled, exposing his canine teeth. He closed the door.

"Little girl. You look lovely," he said. "You remind me of the old country."

She screwed her eyes shut, her short lashes grazing her cheekbones. She fought off the desire to vomit up the boiled radish reserves the station tried to pawn off as food.

"Do you have it?" she asked after she swallowed down the bile.

He chuckled. "Little addict." He patted her cheek like an owner with his dog. She did not deny it. His hand trailed down the veins of her neck, settled in the bow of her red obi.

She wiped the emotion off her face and let him unwind the knot. She watched him strike a match against the dirty wall, light the single lamp that sat next to her bed mat, and drink the sight of her in—her in the enemy's clothing, in the enemy's bed.

Satisfied for the moment, he began to prepare her reward. Using two yān zhēn, he knitted and kneaded the gummy wad of opium, which lightened in color over the heat of the candle. After molding it, he presented the full pipe to her with a knowing smile.

She pressed it to her lips and inhaled the vapors. She let the poppy bloom within her body. Her mind settled—became placid, then empty. She could've cried from the relief of it. Like the smoke of the pipe, her pain evaporated, thinning out and curling into wisps. *More, more, more*, the bliss cried out. And she was away and away to a ways away and nothing was in her but a silk moth flapping its wings, the halves touching and parting, touching and parting.

WHEN SHE WOKE, THE COMMANDER was gone, and she felt the telltale signs of last night's opium indulgence. Her thoughts and pains broke through the smoky dam and flooded her head, filling the space vacated by her high. She rose from her bed mat uneasily and noted the throbbing between her thighs, the discarded layers of the kimono. Haphazardly, she folded the thing up to give back to the manager. She did not want it in her room—haunting her, taunting her. Its brightness seemed to wink in the damp dark.

Goldfish Eye had left her clothes outside her door. On all their backs were pinned dirty, white squares of cloth with their numbers printed in red. Among the inhabitants of the station, she was First Girl, the one who had survived the station the longest. The few men besides the commander who paid for her cooed and called her gū niang. She preferred this. Her name was not something given lightly, and only Mouse called her Ming.

Whenever the commander brought the pipe, she had only one aim: to consume as much opium as possible. She was greedy with her inhales, looking to suspend herself above the mortal world, becoming a ghost in the rafters, looking down as her body was abused. In the mornings after the opium and the rape, she felt odd. Like someone had taken her apart, then put her back wrong. There were pieces missing, or pieces that had been shoved back incorrectly. How often, she thought, could this happen before she became something else entirely? Before she was no longer Ming?

Sometimes, to distract herself from her thoughts, she would cup a palm around her ear as she lay on her side—like she was listening to the interior of a shell—transmogrifying the sea of eddying blood into the sound of her village river at dusk, lapping slowly, populated only by the sleepy fishermen. She could pretend she was standing at the riverbank, her toes damp. The waters would pour into her until she was just the fossil of a shell that the river flowed through. If they killed her now, she would leak river instead of blood.

Thirty

Ming

1943: Seventy-Four Years Before Reunion
Manchukuo

ON HER FIRST DAY IN the station, the women welcomed her. They were kind, nodding along in understanding as she cried and mourned for her husband, her family, her baby brother, her village. *Yes,* they echoed as a chorus, *we were there too. Yes,* they said, *we know what it is to be stripped of everything that made us.*

As was the ritual for newcomers, Ming was allowed to bathe first. The women said their water was rarely changed, unlike the water for their male visitors, but it was lucky that she'd come when she had, since it was only a few days old. Ming sank into the cold water clutching her knees, and the other women helped wash her hair and clean her wrists and ankles, bruised by her rope restraints. *The Chinese forces will beat the Japanese soon and free us*, they told her—like a folktale a mother told to put a child to sleep—*and if you can't last that long, there is always the well.* At night, before bed, the women gave her her first taste of opium. To help you sleep tonight, they said.

And she tumbled down to a poppy underworld, her body heavy and her mind a distant glimmer. On nights when there wasn't enough opiate to go around, or when Ming had nothing to trade for it, her sleep was restless and her dreams uncomfortably vivid. These were markedly different from the blissed dreams of her high.

The opium dreams followed a similar narrative. Ming would blink awake and find herself nestled in Fei's arms. They had taken a nap in the forest, and she would be wrapped in his warm body, sitting against a tree. Outside, the landscape was warm, caught in the liminality of xiǎo chūn. She tilted her head upward and could feel the sun on her face and the tremor of Fei's chuckle in his throat as her smile widened. His hand was close enough to grab, and it was so real—fleshy and callused and warm and safe—that she would delude herself into thinking that the station was a bad dream.

The dreams during withdrawal were a different matter. Her body would be racked by an aching combination of shaking, sleeplessness, and starvation. In these nightmares, she would be woken by a cacophony of growls and the tearing of flesh. She'd press her face close to the blackened window, where, through a slit in the boards, she could just make out a small, dark huddle of men around the well. As if feeling her eyes on them, one man would look up and meet her gaze. It was the commander who had brought her here. She recognized the wolfish face that had loomed over her in the forest. Only, his eyes and canine teeth were horrific, were dripping thick liquid down the front of his shirt, and his shadow was all wrong: too tall and warped with horns protruding from the head—

She flew back from the window so quickly that she fell. The next evening when she was called to the entrance, the commander greeted her in the lobby. Goldfish Eye introduced him as her new client.

"We've met already," the commander said, the familiar predatory smile spreading across his face.

AFTER A FEW MONTHS, THERE was a routine to their encounters. If he was feeling generous, he would bring some opium. When she felt her mind descend into some other world—a limbo where she was half-dead, half-alive—she let him do what he wanted to her.

Sometimes, once he was spent, he lingered for an hour or two. He became confessional. The women had warned her about this. They were disposable. At any moment, they could be dead—drowned gutted broken infected—so they lived on a knife's point, which was no place to tell the men's secrets.

"I'm not human," he told her during one of these moments. It had been seventy-seven days.

Wearily, she lifted her head up to look him in the eye. In the candlelight, the color of his skin puddled into a murky amber, the color of a fox's coat. She had to bite her tongue to keep from spitting out treason. To her, none of the Japanese soldiers seemed human.

"So what are you?"

It was the question he'd been looking for, and he seemed delighted she had asked: a cat about to pounce.

"In my country, they call me yōkai or oni."

"Which means?"

"Shifting thing. But you would probably call me a demon—yāoguài."

She scoffed, but something in her animal sense prickled with fear. An image of an old dream rose up to her mind. "Think highly of yourself, do you?"

He raised a brow. "You think I'm lying?"

Despite her instincts, she turned her back to him, exposing the knobs of her spine. "I think that I have met enough men that I would call yāoguài."

He seemed amused by her response, and his cold fingers traced her exposed back. She repressed a shiver.

Against her better judgment, she asked, "If you're a myth of your country, what are you doing off the island?"

He shrugged. "War is good living. Plenty to eat."

"Funny," she said coolly, "most people starve during your wars."

He chuckled. "They're not our wars. They're not divine at all. War is a purely human invention. If there are gods of war, then they were only born from human prayers." She grew silent at that. She turned back to face him.

"What do oni eat?" She hated how her voice stumbled.

"I could eat you, little girl," he said, smiling. She tried not to flinch and failed. He laughed. The sound, the way he carried himself, reminded her of a lynx toying with the carcass of a deer.

"We like human flesh, alive or dead. Blood to wash it down." He shrugged casually, but in this movement, Ming saw a glimmer of his true self. How little he valued human life. How superior he considered himself to be. It was like she was seeing him for the first time—like the hare undergoing its monstrous transformation, prey becoming predator.

She skittered backward from him, but the room—if you could call it that—didn't allow her to go far. The memories of his lips on her body, on her own mouth, of his teeth as they indented her shoulder, leaving raw rings on her skin, returned in a barrage. His tongue on hers after he had— She vomited. The thought returned, persistent: her dream of the men feasting around the well had warned her. She heaved again and only stomach acid came out. He laughed.

"Are you going to eat that too?" she asked hoarsely, looking down at the sick coating the floorboards.

"Why eat the offal when you could have the prime cut?"

"You're a monster."

"Am I?" He looked thoughtful. "To us, mortal things are fleeting. Your life-spans are the blink of an eye. Mayflies. Do you feel monstrous when you swat an insect?"

"Why haven't you eaten me?"

He frowned, as if confused by this question. "We are not entirely unlike humans. Our hunger wants for carnality as well as bloodlust."

She shook, choked down the urge to dry heave. There was nothing left inside of her. At what point did his lust want for more than her living flesh? When would his need demand a blood sacrifice? Her trembling hand reached for the pipe. He put out an arm to stop her.

"I know what you're doing," he said, his fingers tightening around her bony wrist. "You're not very subtle about it."

"I wasn't trying to be." She wanted him to know that she did not want to be here with him, that if she had any choice in the matter, she would take a hatchet and pound it into his monstrous skull until it fell apart into halves—divinity be damned. But he seemed to enjoy her spite. Perhaps he found it amusing to play with a resentful quarry.

He did not let go. "I've seen poppy addiction before. I've lived several centuries longer than you. The more you try to forget me with poppy, the more you become bound to me."

"I won't," Ming said weakly through clenched teeth, and he loosened his grip. She wouldn't let herself reach that point when she would need the Oni and his opium.

"Let it be known that I warned you," he said. *Go on then*, he gestured, smiling. *Go ahead and yoke yourself to the pipe.*

She'd seen opium addicts pass through Father-in-law's clinic and had always wondered how they'd let themselves become so emaciated, their senses blunted, their eyes listless. She always turned her nose up, believing that she would never degrade herself like they had. Now she wondered if they were laughing at her hypocrisy. They were probably all dead. *Lucky*, she thought.

She took another deep inhale, a killing inhale. Could one die from too much opium? That's how she'd like to go: in a daze, cocooned in another reality. She had learned from the station that the only way to escape the depravity was to let it engulf her.

AT DAYBREAK—OR ITS EQUIVALENT IN the station's black time—she woke alone and sat up, static dripping out of her eyes as the blood left her head. Her stomach ached. She found a large, sickly green bruise on her tailbone. It was a minor injury, a pinprick of shame compared to past, more serious injuries, but it felt like a breaking point. It made her want to slough off her skin. Let the Oni eat the mauled husk, she would be somewhere else.

What she really wanted was to wake and find that she was a girl again, five years old, her feet soaking in the cool water of the river, her back warmed by the summer sun. Just out of sight, she would hear Fei exclaiming over a silver-skinned eel he'd caught with his bare hands and the sound of splashing as it tried to wriggle out of his grasp.

Sometimes, sunlight pressed through the slots of the boarded windows, and it was the same shade as it was when she was a child. She wanted to follow it, rip it open, and crawl through until she emerged on the path of her in-laws' home. Mother-in-law would ask, "What are you doing on your hands and knees in the garden like that?" and she would stand and be welcomed inside. There would be a bowl of noodles and cooked eel on the table, the fragrance calling to her. Her childlike self would be reflected in the glint of Father-in-law's glasses, and she would no longer hurt.

ON DAY 656, A YEAR and a half after she'd entered the station, Mouse was dying. Her girlish face was pale, always breaking into a cold sweat. Her body reeked of infection. Ming and the other women did their best to dress the abscesses that had formed, but they had run out of clean dressings and water, so all they could do now was make her comfortable.

Mouse lay on her side on her bed mat. It was early morning, and the station was empty of male visitors. Ming was holding vigil, sitting by her, brushing out her hair, matted from the fever sweats, and rebraiding it into her signature buns.

"Ming, I'm scared," Mouse said weakly.

Ming didn't know how to respond to this. "It will be all right" felt like a weak platitude and could be wrong for all she knew. She did not know what awaited Mouse; it could be anything: from an empty oblivion to the Dìyù. All she could do was plait her hair, wipe the sweat from her forehead, and give her a bit of opium.

She squeezed Mouse's clammy hand within hers.

"Do you think they'll send word to my family? I have two younger sisters. Maybe one of them survived. I think it'd be nice if someone knew. Then, come Ghost Month, they could set out a lantern on the water for me so I could go home. Do you think Goldfish Eye will write to them?"

"I'll know. I'll tell them. I'll write to your village," Ming said, exuding a confidence she did not have. Her promise relied on an increasingly unlikely set of circumstances: that Mouse's family was still alive, that the war would end, that she would live through it, that she would escape from the Japanese—angry and embittered at losing what they had seen as easy, backwater territory—and find enough safety to write and post a letter.

"I'll burn you joss paper," Ming said, trying to imbue lightness in her voice. "A paper house. Paper dumplings and white rice. Whatever you want."

Mouse made a soft sound of assent and her left dimple rose as she closed her eyes, picturing it. "I don't care much for a big house, but I'd like a garden. Not just vegetables, but flowers and trees. I've heard about all sorts of flowers from the girls from the Southern provinces. Plum blossoms and bright-red azaleas. I think I'd like them there with all the yellow witch hazel and peonies from home." She squeezed her eyes shut. "I am so sick of death. I want a garden teeming with life."

Ming nodded. "I'll burn you paper seeds. Paper flowers. A bouquet of them. Paper trees—a forest of them. A rice paddy if you'd like."

In her mind's eye, Ming could see Mouse's garden. A place ruled not by climate but imagination. All color and the swirling, woody scent she'd grown up with but could no longer conjure up, her sense of smell snuffed by the station's sewer reek.

"I'll miss you," Ming said, her voice cracking to a higher pitch. It turned her words childish and young, and for a moment, she was transformed back into that wild country girl who went around silently asking everyone for love.

Mouse squeezed Ming's hand as tight as she could, which wasn't very tight at all. "I'll look out for you. You won't be alone here."

When Mouse drifted off to sleep, Ming considered these words. A small, selfish sliver of herself found it comforting to imagine Mouse's ghost alongside her, but mostly Ming did not want Mouse to ever think of the station again, let alone haunt it after death. Ming wanted Mouse to have her garden. She could envision her there, her braided buns soaking in the sun as she bent over the dirt, her smooth hands breaking off herbs for supper at the foot of a thatch-roofed hut. Those same buns bobbing as she ran through her spring fields and rice paddies—*free, free, free!*—gathering a bouquet for her dinner table.

Suppressing a sob so she wouldn't wake Mouse, Ming whispered low in her ear, "I want you to go. Leave me and go on. Don't come back here. Don't you dare."

In the morning, Mouse was dead.

MOUSE'S ABSENCE DEVELOPED A PHYSICALITY. Her vacancy grew its own body—spindly, long phantom legs of grief that nudged against Ming when she was hemming or laundering. Life continued without a second thought for Ming's mourning. There were chores to be done. At night, there were men to be serviced, which left Ming no time to cry or pray or trade for incense to burn for Mouse.

The Oni did not even give her a full day before climbing back into her bed. Afterward, he lay by her side: his sweaty skin sticking to hers, his shallow breaths in her ear making her shudder. Slowly, she sat up and shrugged on her discarded tunic. She wanted him to leave. If he insisted on staying, he would have to pay the price in poppy.

But he did not present the opium. He looped his arm around her waist, and she recoiled. To her surprise, he withdrew and said, "I'm sorry about your friend."

"No, you're not." It was instinctual. But to Ming, it was also fact. The Oni did not have the capacity to feel sympathy or grief. The yāoguài seemed to take offense at this.

"I've lived much longer than you. How many comrades do you think I've lost in that time?"

"You're a killer. A flesh-eater. A monster. You can't imagine how I feel."

"I *can* imagine how you feel. I felt the same long ago in my first century. We're the same, you and I, Ming. That's why I like you. That's why I keep you alive. I see a twin rage and hurt underneath that human shell of yours. So much of it. From the moment you bit off my soldier's ear. Do you think I was born cruel? I was made this way. Just like I am making you."

"Then unmake me." Ming moved to face him. All her grief morphed into hot anger, and she found it comfortable—like soft, worn slippers. "If you're a demon, a god, then kill me. I don't want this body anymore. Eat my heart and all my muscles. You can have it if you want, if you can swallow your own cruelty. That's the natural order of things, isn't it?"

Her chest heaved, heavy with the plea in her words. He responded in the worst way he could. The way she knew he would. The Oni laughed. His eyes grew watery in his mirth.

"You think I would let that happen? Ming, don't you understand by now? The only thing humans have that's worth having is death. Living, immortality—these are the hard things." His grin subsided.

"But that is why we have poppy, for when living gets hard. You want your reward, don't you?"

And Ming, whose wrath had been building with each word he uttered, her resolve to jump in the well strengthening, felt all her other emotions dry up in a flood of desperation. *Yes, yes, yes, I want my reward*, everything in her screamed shamefully.

Tonight, he gave her a syrupy solution in a stoppered bottle, and she willed her hands not to shake as she took it and brought it to her lips.

"You see, Ming? We both have unruly appetites."

She swallowed. The glow of the hallway faded into a deep throat of blackness.

IN HER DREAM, SHE RETURNED to the near past, rather than the distant past. A month ago, perhaps, if her timekeeping in the station could be trusted, which she knew it could not.

She and the Oni were lying in bed. The single candle in her lamp cast quick, fluttering shadows. If she squinted, they seemed to take the shapes of living creatures—forest animals that skittered around the boundaries of the room, trapped within the walls. The Oni traced the white scar from the hare with horns that stretched across her right palm. Ming let him. Intimacy was the only survival tactic the women had. The scar prickled under his touch. He frowned then pressed her hand to his nose and sniffed it.

"Where'd you get this one from? It smells wrong," he said. "Divine," he clarified.

"This one's from War."

"Oh?" He raised an amused brow. "I have one too."

He showed her an old scar, which lined the back of his neck—it looked like someone had sawed at his neck or tried to garrote his head off and failed. She wondered what they had used. She wondered if she could find something sharper.

Here was where things diverged from reality. In her mind, she did not continue to brood over the weakness the Oni had shown. She did not wonder. She did not grudgingly go back to sleep, lured into dreams by the opium. Instead, she became something sharper.

She molted.

From her torso exploded additional legs—all bent at the wrong angle and green like sapling shoots. Her spine stretched: the tailbone bursting through the skin of her back in a riot of furious red flesh. Her jaw narrowed, grew meaty palps at her mouth. Her eyes bugged. She greened. She grew wings. The room could not contain her. And for once, it was the Oni's face that flashed with fear. She laughed, and the sound of it was like rain, her narrow mantis body writhing in joy. She was unmade and remade.

Mantises started with the head of their prey. Lucky, Ming thought, someone had already begun the work for her. Her mouth opened.

You see, she thought, *I, too, have an unruly appetite.*

Thirty-One

Qianze
2017: Nineteen Days Since Reunion
Manhattan, New York

"YOU'VE BEEN SAYING ALL THIS aloud," Qianze said.

Ba startled from his time-shift. She watched as he frowned and blinked, taking in her living room. How different it must've looked from the grocery store aisles he'd just been standing in, learning of Felix's death. How jarring to be hurtled years, a decade, into the future. Qianze knew she shouldn't have interrupted him. The online doctors frowned upon this. She hadn't meant to; she'd bitten her tongue and listened quietly to more appalling memories. The curse had slipped out of her, beyond her control.

His mouth opened, and he faltered for a few moments, his English just out of reach. His first attempts were in Chinese, then: "Have I really?"

Qianze blinked. How had he not realized that he'd been speaking these memories aloud?

"Yes, Ba," she confirmed, weary.

His face split in confusion, the dissonance catching up to him. Surprise and alarm flitted in equal measure across his features. Qianze felt a swell of relief. *He didn't know*, she thought to herself. *Thank god, thank god*. She'd been wondering if a small part of him knew, if he'd sputtered out these stones of madness to unburden himself, saddling her with their heavy heirloom weight.

Ba looked lost for words. His face was red and sweating. Over the past weekend, Qianze had observed that he drank much less than when he first came. She realized that he'd inadvertently tapered his drinking. Lost in his time-shifts, Ba sometimes forgot about his physical body. She did not know whether his symptoms—the confusion, the feverish delirium, the hallucinations—were a result of his withdrawal or his disease. She wasn't built to be a caretaker, but she'd stayed home the whole weekend, supplying him with water and foods to settle his stomach. On Sunday, August 20, she tried to drag him to an urgent-care clinic, lack of health insurance be damned, but he'd been too sick and disoriented to come with her.

Now it was Friday, August 25, and Ba was still wrestling with withdrawal. He'd improved slightly. That Monday, she'd come home from work and found Ba in a full tub, water all over her floors, his head submerged. She'd pulled him up, afraid that he had drowned himself, but he was fine, only wet and dazed. Since then, she'd placed another nanny cam in the bathroom and taped over the faucet, but the setup was far from sustainable. Leaving him during the day was a risk, and she spent evenings monitoring him closely. She just needed him to last another week, when her busy season ended, and then she would finally have the time to get her life together. Did Ba know it had been more than two weeks since she found him in Virginia? That August was almost over? Doubtful, she thought.

"How much did I say?" Ba asked.

"A lot," Qianze replied. Too much.

Ba deflated, looking small. "You were never meant to hear it. No one was. But especially not you."

Ba did not *tell* her stories. In the past week, his memory had been all-consuming. Immersed in his past, Ba treated Qianze as an understudy, speaking to her in a one-sided conversation as she assumed the roles of his conversation partner: his father, mother, sister, grandmother, wife, coworker. Sometimes she lacked the vocabulary to understand. Words she'd tried and failed to look up on Google Translate: chāojiā, mígōng, pēnqì shì, mílù, wèi ān fù. Her thumb lingered over the different tonal marks. Had he used the first or the third? She was never sure, and she couldn't interrupt the torrent of memory to ask him. From these conversations, she'd pieced together a tentative timeline of Ba's life, but she still hadn't come close to unraveling his so-called prophecy.

How much wrongdoing could someone commit before they became undeserving of forgiveness? Ba might forget his sins, but Qianze did not have that luxury. She had to carry them around at night before bed, on the subway, at her office, where they clattered against her own disturbing memories. The incidents with the fox, the jackalope, the Aunties—these all had to take a back seat while Qianze cared for Ba amidst her fears of her own fledgling madness.

Earlier that morning, on her walk to the subway, Qianze had received a call from Ma.

"Bǎobèi," Ma said, "you haven't called in three week now." Ma sounded accusatory. She'd neglected everything else in her life for Ba: Ma, Theo, work, her friends, even herself.

"I'm sorry, Ma, it's my busy season, and I've just been working all day and night."

There was a pause as Ma considered this, then accepted it, saying, "Okay. You work too hard. You come visit me soon, I take you to yoga and spa, okay?"

Qianze had to stop walking. Ma's offer made her chest twinge. She felt horrible for lying to Ma, for not calling her.

What did she owe Ba? All he had done was take from her. He'd taken her apartment, her food, her care, her money, her time. He'd taken her childhood, her mother, her financial freedom. In return, he'd given her his past, which still felt like taking. Qianze had wanted to know about her parents' lives, only now she felt she knew too much. Like she'd glimpsed her father's body on the slab with his chest butterflied open, only inside it was diseased with memories like the one of him denouncing his grandmother. What had Ma once said? *It for the best. Past is full of bad memory.* Was Ma right?

"Bǎobèi? You still there?"

"Yes, Ma, I'm here." Qianze started walking again to try to shake off her discomfort. As she passed the seafood vendor across from her apartment she caught sight of a girl, no more than five, who was kneeling to watch the crabs shuffling sideways in their tubs while she waited for her parents to finish shopping.

"Do you remember that one Asian grocery store we used to go to when I was a kid?" Qianze asked Ma.

"Yes. I still go there," Ma replied.

"Do you remember taking me?"

"Yes," Ma said, "you were always so bored. Just sit and watch fish. Why you ask?"

"No reason," Qianze said. But she was looking at the girl, and she wanted to switch places. This time, she would luxuriate in childhood. In how long each day felt, time stretching out like hand-pulled noodles. Those precious hours spent sitting in the dingy Asian grocery store, both of her parents with her.

"Do they still have crabs there?"

"Some, but not big as before. You want crab when you come home?"

"Maybe," Qianze said. But she was remembering being eleven and Ba letting her play with the crabs in the sink with a pair of tongs. How she asked him, "Do you think it hurts when you put them in the pot?" And he had responded, "I don't think so, hái'ér. I don't think they can feel pain. They're just shells in the end, see?" How he then took the tongs gingerly from her fingers and tapped on one, creating a hollow sound. Yes, Ma was right, the past was full of bad memories, but here and there were glimmers of tenderness to be found.

"You call me when busy season over, okay? Ma misses you."

"I will, I miss you too."

Ma would never be a paragon of motherhood, but she had done her best. A faltering, imperfect best, but her best nonetheless. For so long, Qianze had been bitter that Ma wasn't the kind of devoted mother that Qianze wanted her to be. Adulthood had showed Qianze that Ma was only human.

Qianze understood Ba better now, too, but Ba's past disturbed and unsettled her. When Ba first came to New York, she'd been itching with curiosity. *Tell me where you've been! Tell me why you left!* She wanted to uproot these truths like rotten teeth from mangled gums. *Spit it out!* He had, and she discovered that it was better when she hadn't known.

Ba was the by-product of a violent, terrifying history and an abusive father, but Qianze was a by-product of him, and she wondered if she was capable of those same moral failings. What's more, he had survived it. He had made it out. He'd gotten his PhD in America, held an assistant professor position, had a wife and daughter who loved him, and he'd thrown it away for—what? A decade spent as a grocery store clerk with a bottle as his only companion? A small hand in the death of his ill coworker?

Multiple truths existed at the same time. What Ba had been through was horrible. What Ba did to his grandmother, to her and Ma was horrible. Qianze had wanted to know about Ba's past. Qianze had not wanted to know so *much* of Ba's past. It was good that Ba had said it out loud to someone instead of keeping it inside. That someone shouldn't have been Qianze. Qianze felt like she was going to be sick, all the contradictions clamoring within her head.

Back in her living room, Ba was still staring at her. The room felt too small and too warm and Ba's gaze too sober.

"Qianze." Ba hesitated. "Hái'ér, I'm—sorry," he said.

Qianze's head snapped up to look at him. His brows were drawn, but his eyes seemed genuine behind his glasses. She let out a shaky exhale. He had not said sorry in all the time he'd been in the apartment. Did her parents ever say sorry when she was growing up? She didn't think so. What did she say now? Did she thank him? She could not forgive him. She could not say that it was okay, because it wasn't. But he had said he was sorry, and that meant something.

In Qianze's silence, Ba spoke again. "I am sorry," Ba repeated, this time without the stutter, "for telling you so much. I wish I could've protected you from those things."

Multiple truths existed. Qianze wanted to protect her father from experiencing hurt again. Qianze wanted to protect herself from her father. Qianze did not want Ba to suffer anymore. Qianze wanted Ba to suffer now as much as she'd suffered for him.

She still didn't know how to respond, so she just nodded. She wanted to scream until her throat went hoarse. She wanted to evict him. She wanted the father of her childhood back. Only that father was not the man she thought he was. That man's acts of adolescent butchery had always lived just beneath his skin. These damp thoughts drenched her, weighing her down. She wished she could wring herself dry. Instead, she took a deep breath and let herself be dragged back under by the current of memory.

Thirty-Two

Ming

1945: Seventy-Two Years Before Reunion
Manchukuo

MING GATHERED INFORMATION FROM THE Oni: confidences murmured after a whiff of opium, soft postcoital whispers, teasing snippets of his history meant to frighten her. She learned that he was born in the abyss of the Dìyù and crawled out into the mortal realm with a band of his brothers, emerging in Kyoto during the Heian period. The Oni served an oni king, the most formidable of them. He and his brethren settled within the caves of Mt. Oe, where they hosted grotesque banquets with dishes made from kidnapped local maidens and pleasure-quarter courtesans. They feasted on kitchen-knifed girl knees and calves and drank from a never-ending flow of blood, which sloshed over their cups. They cataloged and ate every body part there was.

If Ming had Father-in-law's library, she would've rifled through his texts to find a book that would name him, that would tell her how to kill him. Not how to exile him back to the Dìyù but to obliterate his whole being. It seemed like death was what he wanted: an ending to his immortality. She would gladly grant it to him. But she did not have Father-in-law's library, only the faintest prospect that she might return to it again. Still, this splinter of hope was enough. She would return. She would name him. She would kill the Oni.

The most frightening thing the Oni told her was that female oni were not typically born. They were created. They were human women transformed by a mixture of intense grief, shame, fury, vengeance, and ostracism. The wretched possibility of her own transformation tumbled in her mind, the dread of it seeping through all her other thoughts.

IN MIDSUMMER, THE WOMEN OF the barracks encountered a rare night of no visitors. The soldiers had been called away to handle a series of guerrilla attacks in the area. There were two soldiers posted as guards, but they did not enter the station. Goldfish Eye was locked up in his study, preoccupied with his accounting books and the losing war he'd sided with. The women luxuriated in this reprieve and did what they did best to while the time away: they told each other stories.

They sat in the narrow hallway that ran through the station's second floor like a spine, connecting all their small rooms. It was dark and hot, the humidity rising and leaking in through the floorboards, the boarded windows. The women pooled what opium they had scrounged from the soldiers, and then, when the hallway was heavy with smoke, they began to trade folktales, myths—anything that might transport them from their station life.

In her high, Ming came across a thought she had never had before: she understood her mother. At this, she hacked up an unexpected laugh, which made the women around her titter in a faltering echo, exchanging confused glances. This only made Ming buckle into a painful, stomach-heaving bray that rang down the hall and made all the women look up at her.

"What's so funny?" one of them asked.

"I just thought of a story," Ming said, "that's all."

"Well, tell us," another one chimed.

"Yes, tell us," they repeated in a choir of voices. Ming flushed under the attention and assumed the role she once held on insomniac nights with Dìdi's warm body curled around hers like a cat's.

"All right," Ming conceded, "I'll tell you."

THIS IS A STORY OF women yāoguài. In Japan, they are called oni, though they have other names too: yamauba, ubume, kijo, onryō. These are not the Chinese yāoguài you know; there is no bái niángzǐ in this mix. No, these female demons were all born human. Like you. Like me. This is how you create a woman oni. First, you bind her feet.

When she is four, bathe her feet in warm rabbit blood and herbs. It is winter. It is cold. You do this so that she will feel the pain less. Really, she will feel the pain more, and every winter after, her bad bones will hum with cold. Lather the feet. Run gentle hands over the soft baby soles. Then break the bones. *Snap*. Curl the toes under the ball of the foot and wrap them in tight strips. *Snap, snap, snap*. Tell her to stop crying; *don't you want the prettiest chánzú in town?* Knot the binding tighter. *Āiyā, you will have the most beautiful golden lotuses, every man will want to marry you.* And she does. Have the most beautiful golden lotuses, that is. Only, no man wants to marry her, because the fighting between the Russians and the Japanese has slowly ruined her father's trade, and now the family is bankrupt.

First went the heirlooms, then the silks and jade—quietly enough that she didn't notice at first—but then everything was gone, even her dowry and the family compound that she'd grown up in. Suddenly, she is nine years old and being married off to a grain farmer, who'd had a good harvest that year, and this is the price she is worth now: a few livestock, some bushels of sorghum. The grain farmer is fifteen, and he is a good husband as far as teenage boys go—in that he says he won't bed her until she has bled. So she has two more years of innocence, and for girls like her, bound and bankrupt, this is almost a blessing. Somewhere in all of this, her father flees to a large city, trying to remake his fortune. She never hears from him again.

She marks the passing of her adolescence by seasons through a hut window. She cannot walk very far. She has the most beautiful golden lotuses in town, but golden lotuses were not meant for a farm. She grows herbs outside the window. She prays to Guānyīn for a son. A son does not come. A series of miscarriages arrives instead. She harvests shame and fury and ostracism in droves as her husband harvests sorghum. Her husband grows older. He needs a son to continue the work. She visits the Manchu shaman in the nearby hala. She prays to Guānyīn more—hours bowing at her altar—she has nothing better to do. She becomes pregnant. This one takes. She is twenty-three. She needs a son.

It is a daughter. The spitting image of her. The face mocks her. *This is all right*, the grain farmer reassures her, *I know something that will save us*. The physician is one of the most respected men in the village, and her husband knows his secret. A secret dark enough to secure a promised marriage between his son and their newborn daughter.

The mother resents the daughter for her fast feet, her promised marriage, her stolen face. The woman transforms. Slowly, then all at once—just like how her fortune flipped. She shapeshifts into an oni, into a yāoguài, and no one is any the wiser. Only the daughter knows. The oni mother does not treat her like a mother should. The oni mother is still very much like a child, one that salts slugs. Inside, she is the same nine-year-old girl whose feet were broken before she was sold off. And so she cannot help it that inside her is a brewing putrid mixture of vengeance fury rage grief shame. But these are all the ingredients to create an oni.

THERE WAS A TENSE AIR of understanding as Ming finished telling Mama's story—channeled through her throat like she was a shaman summoning a ghost. One woman offered her more opium, which she took. Another whispered, "Well, I didn't find that funny, I don't know why she was laughing." But they were all sharing the same thought: *Will the station make me a monster? Has it already?*

And Ming was thinking about her mother: her yāoguài mother and her story, pieced together from scraps of gossip and rumors and that one moment of armistice—her spider hands weaving Ming's hair into complicated twists. She had spent numerous nights on the kang with her brother wondering how Mama could be two different mothers in one body. Mama had been a mother to Dìdi and a monster to her. Yes, she thought to herself, her mother had been made into a monster. But now, so had she.

A MONTH HAD PASSED SINCE that night. It was another day blessed by the absence of the Oni, who was away dealing with a string of arsons at the Japanese's supply stores. Ming had seen the fires in the distance through the slats, the flames licking at the night sky in a cleansing red. She fell asleep quickly. She dreamed that the Oni and the other soldiers were burning: immolated figures on the darkened landscape running frantically to put themselves out. The fire continued to consume and gorge even after they stopped struggling. The whiff of smoked flesh filled her nostrils, smelling like deliverance.

From inside her dream, she heard the crackle of a fire creeping closer. Then a voice that gently spoke her name. *Ming*. There was something familiar about its tone, but she couldn't place it. *Ming*, it repeated, now with a hiss of urgency. Someone was shaking her, and she startled awake at the feeling of hands on her arm. These hands were warm, gentle, released her when she jolted. These hands knew her name. She blinked, letting her eyes adjust.

He had hollow pits around hungry eyes, and his skin was sunburnt: a line of raw, red skin and freckles traversing the bridge of a crooked nose. He must have broken it since she'd last seen him.

His hair was sheared off now, just a centimeter of fuzz blanketing his head, that round skull she once cradled in her lap and told stories to.

"Am I awake? Is it you?" she whispered. She extended her hand, reaching for his cheek, half expecting it to pass through, to be a hallucination. Instead, his solid hands clasped her scarred palm between his two callused ones.

"It's me," he confirmed.

Disbelief coursed through her. This was one of the Oni's supernatural jokes or an opium dream, so impossible that Qian was here: eighteen—not yet an adult, no longer a child—but with the same bones and eyes she knew so well.

"It's you," she echoed. *It's you it's you it's you*, her mind was exclaiming, looping like birdsong. Then the reality of his presence sank in. Had he been forcibly conscripted? Had he been in the station for his own leisure? "What are you doing here?"

"I'm getting you out. Come on, hands around my neck. We only have a little bit of time before they put out the fires."

She was lightheaded as he pulled her to her feet, but did as she was told, climbing on her brother's back. He hardly seemed to mind her weight, and she became aware of the state she was in, shame flushing on her cheeks. She had imagined escape since she'd arrived but neglected to think of the reality: her brother seeing how the station had changed her, diminished her. The watery pupils that marked her as an opium addict. If he'd noticed, he didn't comment. Instead, he swung out of her window—the boards that once covered it splintered and sawed off—and made his way across the round roof tiles of the overhang, shinnying down one of the building's columns.

They headed toward the tree line, darting through the shadows.

From this distance, she turned back to look at the station. She had never seen it like this, small and harmless. The light in Goldfish Eye's office was still on, the second floor dark and shuttered.

"The other women—" Ming began.

"The war's almost over. Rumor is that the Soviets are moving this way. The girls will be fine," Qian said quickly.

But if they were going to be fine, then why had Qian chosen to come now? Understanding dawned on her. This was her last chance. The Japanese soldiers, sensing defeat, would raze the station before the West could lay eyes on it. And there was time; she could still plead for the other women's lives, but she knew the arithmetic. Her best chance of getting out alive was now, ferried away before the Japanese noticed, unencumbered by the other women. When it came down to it, Ming found herself selfish. She wanted to survive more than she wanted to save everyone else, and the shame of this burnt in her belly.

He was still carrying her when she saw a figure emerge from the shadows and startled violently, pulling at his neck.

"It's okay, it's okay!" Qian said quickly. "They're my friends. They're helping me."

Ming squinted, making out the shapes of a dozen or more men as they emerged from behind trees and under bushes. Qian's friends looked awfully similar to a guerrilla troop: boys on the verge of adolescence, clutching the discards of other armies—rusty knives and older models of rifles.

"You're the guerrilla band that's been in the area," she said matter-of-factly. Qian gave her a guilty nod. The last time they had spoken, she had begged Qian not to go down this path. How quickly she ate her old words when that path now promised her safety.

"We took out the soldiers guarding the station and the manager," one of the boys told Qian. Ming wondered if this meant that they were dead but found she didn't much care. She disentangled herself from her brother, swayed unsteadily on her feet. The boy looked at her, nodded in acknowledgment, a gesture she hesitantly returned.

"She'll have to take the mule. I don't think she's in any state to keep up on foot."

She nodded again, eyes toward the ground, unable to deny it. Qian helped her mount the mule, which they used to transport their saddlebags of supplies. "His name is Dà Gèzi," Qian told her, tightening the reins, which he took. He patted its hide affectionately, and off they went.

The first two hours or so were silent, the boys on guard for any Japanese soldiers coming their way. They moved quickly and quietly through a forest in the opposite direction of where they had set the fires. From her seated position, Ming watched the back of Qian's head as he led the mule, raking over the memories of him she trusted and the memories she'd lost to the opium.

She was his older sister, his jiě, but she did not feel like the sister she used to be. That girl was his protector: respectable, whole. This woman did not deserve salvation. She spent the first hour worried that Qian would realize this: that he'd rescued the wrong sister, that the sister he remembered was stranded in the country of their past. At any moment, Qian would turn around and recognize her as an impostor wearing his sister's face, realize he didn't want her. But when he turned, he gave her a tilt of his head—a gesture she knew was him asking after her well-being—and then an encouraging smile. She felt like she'd eaten something sour, blistering all the way down as she swallowed.

After they'd put a fair amount of distance behind them, they stopped to rest. The men relieved themselves and consulted their map. Qian came to help her dismount before giving the mule some water and food. He told her the station was ten hours west by foot from their village. They had eight hours left of their journey. The other boys would part from them in five hours to head north toward a safe house. Qian would accompany Ming all the way to the village.

Ten hours. If she'd known, she might've tried her own hand at escaping. She could've traded in one of those early nights—the most brutal nights, the men cawing after a shiny, new thing—for ten hours of walking, but after those nights, her body and mind were no longer capable of making that journey.

A slew of questions welled up from her mouth. How had he found her? One didn't just stumble upon a station ten hours away across rural, undeveloped terrain.

No, Qian admitted, one did not. The station was located in a town midway on the Jīnbīn line—used for the transportation of military supplies—between Chánchūn and Hā'ěrbīn. Qian and his guerrilla fighters were based on this line, establishing safe houses and a network along it. They had been causing trouble for some time when they heard about the nearby barracks and its comfort station.

"I looked for you everywhere near the village. I'd been ready to give up. The stories I've heard about women taken by the Japanese—I wasn't sure if you were still alive."

It had been almost two years. Still, Qian had gone in to investigate and saw, against all odds, Ming's photo hanging in the entrance hall.

Where was he when the village was attacked? Who had survived? Had Fei? His parents?

Qian answered patiently. Yes, Fei and his parents were alive. As far as he knew, Fei had not remarried. Qian did not spend much time in the village. He passed holidays with Mama and Baba, but they disapproved of the life he'd chosen. At the time of the attack, he was being initiated into the guerrilla network. He learned about the Japanese scorched-earth operation, Sankō Sakusen, that was sweeping through northern China, but by then, it had already passed through their village. He'd gone back and seen the devastation, learned about Ming's kidnapping, and decided his time was better spent fighting than farming.

Ming wanted to ask him more. She wanted to know every detail of his life since she'd last seen him: how he broke his nose, how he passed his days, what he ate. But the band was regrouping, preparing for another few hours on foot. They would rest again in a bit, Qian said, and they could talk more then.

Two hours later, the insides of her thighs were stiff when they stopped. The boys decided on a longer break. They chewed wet sorghum, and some of them nodded off, their palms cupping their chins. Ming fed her portion of sorghum to Dà Gèzi for carrying her. She couldn't look at the food; the smell of it made her nauseous. She began to calculate how long it'd been since she'd last had opium and when she might get her hands on it next. She was anxious to get back on the road. She busied herself with brushing the mule, combing out its mane. She found the animal's presence comforting. Here was a creature that wanted nothing from her, expected nothing.

Beside her, one of the boys was rifling through the contents of the saddlebags, making a list of what they needed from the safe house. He made light conversation with her, asking what Qian was like as a baby. Laughed when she answered, "Fat and spoiled."

She saw the bullet hit its mark before she heard the shower of gunfire. She watched the blood bloom dark on the front of the boy's shirt, his mouth opening to let out a wet, red gurgle, before he fell backward, his eyes still open. Her mouth was agape as she stared at the body, and her knees gave out, chaos quickly unfurling around her—he'd been laughing just a minute ago—and she did not want to die, she had not survived the station for two years and escaped to die, and she thought she might scream, but Qian clapped his hand over her mouth, pulling her down to the ground amongst the shrubs and roots. Someone had moved the mule and tied it low to the ground here, and she could feel it shake, its long ears twitching at the barrage of bullets.

"Stay low," Qian instructed, and crawled forward. Some of the other boys were loading their rifles to shoot back. She heard the howl of the Japanese hunting dogs that had sniffed them out. They'd found her.

Ming pressed her face into the mule's hide, closed her eyes against the spray of gunfire and sparks lighting up the night, ricocheting off trees. She felt helpless, pinned down behind the boys, wondering when and how this would end. When one of them ran out of artillery? When one side was dead? She smelled fresh blood, the sour stink of sweat, dung. All the markers of a fresh corpse.

From her position, she squinted, trying to make out what was happening. Her eyes found Qian up front, rearing up to reload, and she felt a short-lived sense of relief that evaporated on her tongue, because the next moment he was down: rifle dropped, doubled over and clutching at his stomach, hands coming away bloody. There was no one near Ming to stop her from screaming this time and so she screamed—a vixen scream, as loud and swift as a bullet—the sound lost to the bark of gunshots.

She lay there, frozen, watching as one of Qian's comrades packed the wound, wrapped it with a strip of torn shirt, and rolled him behind the front lines with the other injured and dead before taking up Qian's gun and returning to the shootout. Ming cursed Qian's name. Why did he have to be a martyr? Why was she the cause he'd chosen to die for? Qian's eyes were closing, and Ming, unaware of when she'd started moving, was crawling on her elbows and knees like a spider through the thorny undergrowth, inching forward to Qian. She dragged him back, her movements too slow and weak for her liking. The sky was lightening, a dark blue instead of pitch-black, and Ming knew that this was her last chance to get away with the cover of darkness on her side. She summoned the last of her strength and slung him onto the mule's back. She untied the reins with trembling hands, and when they were unknotted, she climbed up behind her brother, his slumped body wedged in front of her.

"Up," she hissed, "up, up!" She kicked the mule's sides, and it got to its feet. She kicked again with all her strength, and it began to trot away. Bullets whizzed overhead, and she felt the mule pick up speed. Behind her, she heard the distant, desperate caterwaul of

Qian's comrades, *Come back! No, please, come back!* She urged the mule to go as fast as it could, clinging to its neck, holding Qian in place as he jostled up and down, up and down, limp as a puppet.

She rode opposite to the rising sun until the sound of the gun fight grew distant. She didn't know how long it had been, but the sun had been inching upward and now sat high in the sky. Ming felt safe. The Japanese were after the guerrilla band, not her. When the Japanese defeated them—and they would, Ming thought, now that she'd taken their mule and supplies with her—they would not risk their resources for one woman. She could not think about the boys. Not when her brother was hurt and sagging against her, and her fingers on the reins were slippery with his blood.

She steered the mule to a puddle of water, where it drank greedily. Ming's legs ached from riding, but she didn't dare dismount, in case she couldn't get back up. From where she sat, she rummaged through the saddlebags for supplies. She found water, which she drank then poured into Qian's mouth. Long strips of cotton bandages, which she used to wrap his stomach again and again. The map, which contained instructions and sketches of landmarks along the paths. They'd had six hours left from where they had stopped. She studied the trail from the railroad to the village. They should arrive at the village by noon. She set off again.

Ming spoke to Qian as they rode. She told him that she'd seen girls come back from worse in the barracks. That when they got to the village, Zhou Shūshu would patch him up. That she'd cook him a feast to help him recover.

"Sticky buns with pork and radish filling, guō bāo ròu, chive dumplings, do you remember?"

She thought she saw a corner of his mouth turn upward at this. Then he spoke slowly, as if summoning up all his remaining strength, "Maybe in my next life, jiě."

She refrained from slapping his arm. "Don't joke like that."

He murmured something: a laugh, a sound of assent, a gurgle.

Ming passed the time keeping an eye out for the landmarks and telling Qian stories she'd gathered from the women of the station. She told him the things she wanted to eat, the books she wanted to read. She spoke to Dà Gèzi. She apologized for riding him so hard and promised that when they got to the village, he could have a life in retirement, lying down for weeks. Her mouth grew dry from talking. She leaned her cheek against the top of Qian's head, nestled backward against her shoulder. As the sun rose higher, her rabbity heartbeat filled her ears, and her vision grew woozy. She swayed. Her body was equal parts adrenaline and withdrawal.

When the village appeared on the horizon, she urged Dà Gèzi into a gallop the rest of the way. She did not pause to notice the astonished faces that turned toward her as she rode along the main road. She followed her memory back to the physician's compound, where she dismounted—her legs shaking—and pulled Qian down off the mule, the weight of his body making her legs give out.

Father-in-law and Mother-in-law, drawn by the noise, came running out of the compound, their faces twin mirrors of shock and disbelief.

"You need to help him!" Ming shouted as they rushed toward her, legs splayed outward on the ground with her brother pulled in her lap. "He's been shot in the stomach. Someone packed his wound, and I applied bandages, but he needs real help, he—"

"Ming," Mother-in-law said, interrupting her. She put a light hand on her arm. Ming shrugged it off.

"It's been about eight hours since it happened," Ming said, watching as Father-in-law examined the sticky mess of Qian's stomach. An expression passed between him and Mother-in-law.

"Ming," Mother-in-law repeated, shaking her head, "we can't help him. I'm sorry, Ming, your brother is dead."

"No," Ming insisted, "no, I could hear his heartbeat just now, he's unconscious, but he's alive."

But when she looked down at Qian, she saw what Father-in-law and Mother-in-law had seen. The open mouth. The cold, blue cast of his face. The blood that had soaked through the bandages, his shirt, Ming's shirt, the mule's hide.

It was her brother's body, but not her brother.

She was wailing and weeping, bartering with the gods to give him back. She was howling, screaming nonsensical grief, asking Qian why he'd saved *her*, why he'd died for her, and she half expected the gods to grant her request since they'd already taken so much, and Qian would warm under her touch, and his eyes would blink open, and he would croak, "Got you," with a small smile as he coughed out the death stuck in his throat.

A crowd had begun to gather at the edges of her vision, watching on. Her eyes snagged on a familiar face.

"Mama," she gasped, "Mama, it's me," she said. Mama began to trudge forward on her bound feet, and Ming, wracked by sweats and tremors, began crawling toward her.

"No," Mama whispered.

Mama, Ming wanted to say, *I understand you now. Mama, it's me. He brought me back. He died to bring me back. Mama, please, I'll forgive you for all of it if you hold me now. Mama, I need you now. Mama, it's me, it's you, it's me.*

But instead, Mama came rushing forward and slapped Ming so hard, she bit down on the soft of her cheek, filling her mouth with rust.

"You killed him!" Mama screamed at her. And it was all too much, just a bad dream, and in a moment she would wake to her brother, who had just come to save her, and he would smile and ask if she was ready to go home, and she would say *yes, take me home, yes—*

HE WAS BORN IN THE harvest season of her third year. Before his birth, there were scattered beginnings of memory: still-life scenes of the house and the fields, images that lacked substance. Her first real memory—the first one with teeth—was the night her brother was born.

She wanted to resent him. She was not in control of her emotions, her childish need for love at the forefront of everything. She resented other things: how her parents' faces had split open in happiness when the midwife announced it was a boy, how her father rushed off to tell his friends, how her mother was looking at the bundle now, beatific and blissful, an expression Ming had never seen before.

"This is your brother," the midwife said, showing off the bundle to Ming.

"Careful," her mother said, but the usual bite in her voice was absent, and she sounded more tired than reproachful.

The midwife settled the baby in Ming's lap, and his wails calmed into a few gurgles, and his eyes blinked away the tears until he was peering up at her face. He reminded her of a newborn lamb—his skin a winter-melon white under the smears of blood.

"Like this, see?" the midwife said, as she directed Ming's small palm to cup the nape of the baby's head. The hair there was downy and damp, curling in the gaps between her fingers, and his eyes were black and glassy, like water that she could see to the bottom of.

She loved him. The feeling was shocking and too large for her body. His cheeks were round jowls that dipped and sprung under her finger like the dough they rolled noodles from. He made a sound that Ming thought was cheerful. Perhaps he loved her too. Perhaps he knew that they were siblings. Everything about him was miraculous.

"Let me see," her mother said, her arms gesturing for the midwife to bring the baby to her lap. Ming felt the loss immediately, the absence of her baby brother leaving her arms cold and bare.

SHE WOKE DISORIENTED IN THE clinic. For a moment, she fooled herself into thinking none of it had happened. She was a child again. She had fallen asleep in the compound after a large meal and experienced a long and vivid nightmare. But she was in the compound. That was what she wanted, wasn't it? Was she not within the homesick homecoming dream that had kept her alive day after day in the station? That constant, urgent fantasy that she nursed until it had grown a life of its own? But the dream was rotten, because she didn't want it like this, she'd rather be in the station than trudging up toward the village with the mule carrying her brother's body, and it shouldn't have been like this *not like this not like this* with her reentering the village as if she were leading a funeral procession.

Thirty-Three

Weihong

1975: Forty-Two Years Before Reunion

Běijīng City

WEIHONG HAD SPENT THE YEAR and a half since he left Ānshān as a hermitic figure lurking in the corners of rooms. In the eight-person college dorm he shared with his classmates, Weihong could be found most often in his bunk—separate from the other boys as they joked with one another and played cards—or studying alone in the library. There was a friend from class, a friend in the dorm, a friend he ate his meals with, but for the most part, his primary company was his own thoughts. A refrain of guī sūn zi hummed in his mind: *bastard, bastard, bastard*—a wretched melody to the hum of his heart. He wanted to prove Father wrong. He combed over his childhood. He assembled what he knew about Mother, which he discovered was not much at all, and most of it from Nǎinai—the memory of her still stinging and sore—from when she told him about Mother and Fei as children.

Mother was the daughter of a grain farmer, who, if Nǎinai's delirious rantings were to be believed, had blackmailed Fei's father into betrothing their children. Mother and Fei grew up together as childhood friends under Nǎinai's care. They were married. They worked together at the family's clinic and apothecary. At some point during the war with the Japanese, Mother had likely become a comfort woman for the Japanese soldiers. He did not let himself think of the lurid and shameful details of what that might have entailed. She had made it back to Nǎinai and Fei, though her return had splintered these bonds. After seven years, she became pregnant with Weihong, and she and Fei moved to Ānshān to start anew. Ten years later, Nǎinai would join them upon Fei's father's death.

Weihong had done the math. If Fei wasn't his father—and Fei had been adamant that he was not—then his father must have been someone in the village. At night, looking at the planks of the bunk above his, his mind rotated outward to worse possibilities. The revolutionary propaganda of his adolescence resurfaced, trawling up narratives, each one more damning than the next. His father was a wealthy peasant: A CAPITALIST ROADER! His father was part of the Kuomintang Army—A COUNTERREVOLUTIONARY TRAITOR!—and was now living in Táiwān. The vilest one was that his father was a Japanese soldier from Mother's time as a comfort woman. A WAR CRIMINAL! AN IMPERIALIST. The thought of it made him ill. But this was not possible. He had done his research. In the library, Weihong examined the books on the War of Resistance against the Japanese. Books with even a whiff of revisionist history had been burned, but what remained said that the Japanese had been decisively driven out in the winter of 1945. Seven years before his conception. This put his self-loathing fiction to bed.

He cut away the threads of his past. He would build a new life in the capital. In his second year at Qīnghuá, he found his future. Her name was Hong. *Red.* When his eyes alighted on her—the dark sheen of her hair plaited taut in two braids down her back—it caused a visceral pang in his chest, like an ax thrust into his sternum. She blew onto campus, bringing a gust of wonderment that felt foreign to his university existence.

"She looks familiar," he said to his friend, pointing her out.

"She's a bit of a campus celebrity. She and her brother are first-year students. Twins. Maybe you've seen him and that's why she looks familiar."

"No," Weihong replied, "from somewhere else." Somewhere with heath and marsh flowers.

The twins were radically, riotously lovely. The boy was slender, waiflike, and the bones of his wrist jutted skeletal from stiff, pressed sleeves. The girl was shorter, but lithe. Their simian faces wore self-assured expressions; their eyes were double-lidded, and the fat, red pillows of their lips curled into pouts. There was a restraint in the delicacy of their features. He felt an immediate Northern camaraderie with them; they were willowy and pale—features that suggested a lifetime of weathering winters.

He was fascinated by them, watching as their long limbs stalked the campus grounds, their steps always synchronized. Whatever had bound them in the womb had only been cut in the physical realm. On another plane, it still held them fast as one entity.

Red was fluent in Russian and preferred Dostoyevsky to Tolstoy. He had seen her toting around thick, yellowing tomes, pages bookmarked with all sorts of objects: pencils, ribbons, free-floating flyers, embroidered lace. Her hair was always neatly braided back. Only once did he see it down when she pulled out the pen holding it in place; it was around exam time, and she looked disheveled and tired, unlike her usual self.

He offered her a rubber band to tie back her hair. He introduced himself.

"My name is Weihong," he said. It meant "protect red."

A sinuous smile swept across her lips, the color of it verging on immodest. She accepted the rubber band. He watched her plait her hair, his eyes catching on her quick fingers, the one strand that escaped to brush against her cheek.

THEY COURTED FOR FOUR YEARS and married after Red's graduation in 1979. There was a brief moment during the wedding planning when he considered inviting Mother and Kangmei but ultimately decided against it.

It was an understated affair. The ceremony took place in the registry office. Red wore a silk, floor-length qípáo, finely sewed with beaded flowers and leaves. Weihong wore a rented suit. They held their reception with their university friends at a small restaurant, a local favorite among the students. Some of Red's family came in by train from Hēilóngjiāng. Her brother poured the couple glasses of èrguōtóu and gifted them the traditional gold-packaged Double Happiness cigarettes, which he lit with a match. A lazy Susan held a rotation of dishes: crisp Běijīng duck pinched in pancakes, piles of creased pork and cabbage jiǎoji, and minced-meat bāozi.

Weihong was getting his master's at Qīnghuá in mechanical engineering. He began studying English. After the wedding, they moved into a family dormitory in student housing. Red laughed when she first entered. It was a long, narrow space—a railroad apartment—and she could touch the sides of the walls with her fingertips. Weihong laughed, too, because Red's joy was infectious. Life with Red made his world warm. There were weekly dinner parties with her brother and their friends, where she served fresh zhájiàngmiàn, enough to fill a vat. In the window, they hung their laundry on a line—his wrinkled student shirts sitting side by side with Red's delicates, embroidered with colorful mushrooms and insects. Red had recently cultivated a window box of kitchen herbs. After she tended to the plants, Red would read her Russian books leaning against the sill, the laundry fluttering above her. Weihong would watch, transfixed.

"My mother would've liked you."

"Of course she would have," Red replied.

"You could talk about your Russian novels with her."

Red smiled, but she never pushed him about contacting Mother.

They passed eight years like this. Weihong finished his master's and earned a job at the university teaching introductory courses. They moved into a larger apartment. Their new home faced the sun, so that throughout the day, it was soaked in light—no corner lost in the darkness where shadows could fester. In 1987, the eighth year, Weihong applied to study at American universities as a PhD candidate—whiling away his evenings writing letters in English to professors, begging to study with them—and was accepted to one in Virginia. He and Red were approved for their student and dependent visas. Red began to learn English. She struggled with the pronunciation, the tenses—*So many tenses! Twelve to Russian's three, to Chinese's zero!*—and the articles. She did her best. It was not always as peaceful as this. There were nine years behind them and no child. There were two miscarriages, frustration and grief crowding their marriage bed.

And then, three months before they left for America, a miracle. Twins. Red was learning about Buddhism, and she thought that the twins might be those miscarriages reincarnated, her sorrow blooming into new life.

"Twins!" she exclaimed, skipping around the apartment.

"Slow down," Weihong said, stopping her with a gentle hand at her waist. "Be careful with them," he said, laughing. The doctor declared them healthy and assured them that mother and babies would be safe to fly to America come the spring of 1989.

Weihong often felt guilty and undeserving of this happiness. It felt borrowed: a loan that would demand payment. Their life was simple and repetitive. They cooked, they washed up, they asked how the other's day was. They sat in silence together, reading, feet pulled into a lap. They lay in bed and traded ideas for baby names. But to Weihong, this peaceful rhythm felt holy.

IT WAS A WEEK BEFORE they left—early March, approaching Weihong's thirty-sixth birthday, most of their belongings sold off or crammed into a suitcase—when they received a visitor. Red answered the door while Weihong was packing. There was a long pause where no one spoke.

"Who is it?" Weihong asked.

"It's for you," Red said softly.

Weihong poked his head out into the hallway to see the open door. And there, somehow, was his mother.

"I'm going to go on a walk," Red offered, and maneuvered her belly around Mother, who looked at it with tenderness.

"Hi, bǎobèi," she said by way of greeting. A tentative smile. She had shrunk. This was the first thing he noticed: that she was shorter, her back more stooped, the hair at the edges of her forehead gray and wiry. She had her hands clasped at her waist, as if she was resisting reaching out to him, cupping his face, touching his hair.

He took a step back, and she frowned.

"Can I"—she hesitated—"can I come in?"

He considered it, then nodded slowly. He led her to their kitchen table, and they sat down.

"Are you well? You look well. Your wife, too, she's pregnant? Do you know when she's due?" Mother asked, her eyes darting around the bare apartment.

"Why are you here?" Weihong asked rather than answering.

She swallowed at the steely shift of his tone. "I call your department at Qīnghuá every month or so. Not to reach you," she added hurriedly, "just to know that you're okay. The receptionist—her name is Guifang, we're friends now—told me you were leaving for America. She said you are going for a PhD program. I was so proud. But you're going so soon, and I couldn't help myself. I know you don't want to talk to me. I always hoped I'd hear from you, but I understand. I've kept my distance. But America," she let out a short, uncomfortable laugh, "is so far."

Weihong was silent. He watched as his mother fiddled with her thumbs. There was a tremor in her fingers.

She continued, "Guifang did not tell me your wife is pregnant. Is it safe for her and the baby to fly?"

"Babies," he added automatically. He cleared his throat. "Twins."

"Twins, how wonderful! A double blessing." She beamed.

"Yes, fraternal. A boy and a girl. We got the ultrasound two weeks ago." This spilled out of him. He couldn't help it. When he spoke about the twins, he became confessional and unrestrained, like a child himself.

"You're going to be a father," she said, awed. She seemed to realize her mistake, because his face hardened at this word. *Father*.

"I don't know how to be one. But you of all people know that."

Her face fell. "Your ba— *Fei*," she corrected herself at the upward snap of his head, "told me what he said before you left. I'm sorry. He shouldn't have said that to you."

She added, "You should know that Fei died eleven years ago. It was an ear infection that traveled to the brain. I brought his records because I was worried that something similar might happen to you. You were always dealing with those infections together." She took a sheaf of folded papers and laid them on the table between them like a peace offering.

Weihong stared at them. Father—Fei—was gone. He could not hurt Weihong anymore. Eleven years. It had happened when he was a fourth-year. Fei must be bones now—everything else food for insects. A perverse mourning ballooned inside Weihong's stomach. He did not miss Fei. He knew Fei did not love him. But he'd spent so long yearning for that love, and when he could not have it, he wanted Fei to acknowledge him.

"Was he right? About what he said?"

Weihong watched as Mother's mouth opened and closed, as she searched for the right words. It was answer enough. He blanched. Somewhere inside of him, he wanted Father—*Fei*—to be wrong. For his revelation to be a sharp falsehood that he'd unleashed like a willow switch, but nothing more. More than that meant that it was Mother who had lied to him.

"I spent my whole life wondering why he didn't love me. I did"—he stumbled—"I did terrible things to fill that emptiness, to make him feel something, anything, towards me, and in the end, I understand him. I understand *him*, but I don't understand how you sat by and watched it all."

She closed her eyes, took a deep breath. "I've thought about this moment since you were born. What you would say. What I would say. I need you to know that I didn't commit adultery. Not by choice. I was forced. Fei didn't know, and I never told him. I was so ashamed. I thought he would raise you as his own son, but he had suspicions. I thought telling him would make it worse, so I stood by and watched it, as you said. It wasn't fair to you. It hurt me to watch him treat you one way and Kangmei another, more than you might realize, but I had no choice—"

"You had no choice? You could've told me," Weihong interrupted. He barreled on, "Who was he? Who's my real father?"

"Bǎobèi, it isn't important, isn't it enough to know that I love you? Wholly, completely? Your sister, too, and your Nǎinai, she did as well, no matter who your father was."

Weihong flinched at this mention of Nǎinai, as if the invocation was enough to summon her vengeful ghost.

"No," he bit out. Her face caved in as if slapped. "No, it's not enough. I deserve to know the truth. Can't you grant me that much? Why must everything always be a half-truth or a story with you? Why can't you just be honest? Tell me, if Fei wasn't my father, then who was?"

"Bǎobèi—"

"The truth. All of it."

She deflated, seemed to relent. "You're right. If you want to know, you deserve to know."

Her words seemed rehearsed, worn smooth like a stone: "Your

birth father was a commander in the Japanese Kwantung Army. When I was nineteen, his unit came to ransack our village, and he kidnapped me to serve as a comfort woman. I spent two years in the station. I try not to think of it, but I feel those years every day. In my bones, in my gut, in my mind. My little brother was a guerrilla fighter, and he helped me escape back to the village. He died on the journey home." Mother took a sharp inhale before continuing, "I didn't want to live. There was so much shame and pain. None of my wounds healed right. My body was all wrong. But my Dìdi had given up his life for mine, so I continued. Fei and I tried to conceive, but we couldn't. My body could barely sustain itself, let alone a child. Then, years later, the commander found me in the village. He—forced me." She choked on the words, looked up to meet Weihong's aghast expression. "But he's not important, he's nothing. You're nothing like him. Please forgive me, please don't think less of me."

She'd said it with her own tongue. It was out in the open now: the truth they had always danced around. It was not a surprise, though it still shocked him that she had admitted to being a comfort woman. But it was the revelation that his father was a Japanese commander that unnerved him. Not a soldier, but a ranking official. Worse than what he'd imagined. But it didn't make sense.

"No," Weihong said, shaking his head, his hands on the table clenching, "no, you're lying again. It doesn't add up. They wouldn't have let a Japanese commander live on the mainland, not for seven years. He would've been caught and executed, he wouldn't have been there in the first place, he would've been a prisoner of war for the Soviets. What you're saying, it's impossible."

She cast her eyes downward. Her shoulders sagged in defeat. "Why do you want to know these things, Weihong? I raised you, and this commander, he doesn't matter. He had no part in who you are."

Weihong wanted to yell. His voice came out in a barely controlled waver, tense with his anger. "Why are you still shielding things from me? What are you trying to protect me from? I'm thirty-five. I'm not some schoolboy. You told me if I wanted to know, I deserved to know."

Mother pulled at her fingers. One of her hangnails snapped off.

"Okay," she said quietly, "the commander. He always told me that he wasn't—human. He said he was something else. He called himself an oni."

Weihong frowned. What was that? A kind of Japanese military rank?

Mother finished, her face glum: "Here we would use the term yāoguài. After those seven years, I prayed for a child. He heard me and followed my prayer back to me."

At the utterance of the word yāoguài, something returned to him. An image. A stagnant pool of water and a grotesque double. Him and Not-Him. Then, a rush of words that made him dizzy with remembrance, words he had forgotten but that had been submerged inside him all along—*I'd say forty years until it's hatched. Give or take. Divine things take time to form—That mother of yours did a good job hiding you—It's your whole self, your inheritance, both halves—*

He felt like he was being split in half, all understanding of the world as he knew it unmoored. Something welled up in him. A hysterical, howling sob. His mother recoiled at the sound. She looked helpless. She moved to hold him, her arms reaching for him, and he was shrinking back like a cornered, feral animal, and he was pushing her away, yelling at her, "Don't touch me!" He could not look at her face, but he watched as her arms dropped back to her sides, defeated.

It was a long time before his sobs subsided. After, he sat at the table, rigid. He said, "I don't know how to live with this."

"It doesn't change you."

"It changes everything."

"No, bǎobèi, it doesn't matter. I see you, and I know you are good."

"It matters. It mattered. The things I've done, the things I could do, it matters."

She reached for his hands again, and he snatched them away so that she was grasping for empty air.

"How do I make you see that it's not important? How can Ma make it right?"

"You can't," he said.

They sat there in a long, taut silence for what felt like an hour. Inside, Weihong's mind grew fetid with fevered thoughts. What was keeping this demonic sire at bay? Would it find him once his other half matured? Was this the demon of the prophesied destruction? He felt raw and alight, felt the sharp ache in his chest—the jerk of something evil within him baring its teeth, yanking against its ribboned leash.

Finally, he spoke. "You should've killed me back in the womb. Now I have to continue, and I don't know how. Why did you keep me? I don't understand that. I don't understand any of it."

She looked at him with wide eyes and shook her head slowly. "Weihong—"

"I want you to leave."

"No, I can't leave like this. I'm sorry, forgive me, forgive me," she repeated. "Please, Weihong, none of it mattered to me, the—the rape"—she stumbled over the word—"the Oni, it was hard for me, but when you were born, none of it was important, all of it fell away and I just loved you, I love you, it terrifies me sometimes how much I love you."

"If you loved me, you shouldn't have let me live with this. I don't know how to live with this."

"Ma didn't tell you because it doesn't matter. You are still you."

"I'm not!" Weihong shouted, "there's something in me that's not human. I don't know what it's capable of, but it's wrong, it's evil, it eats at me."

"Bǎobèi—"

"I denounced Nǎinai."

Mother made a choking noise. He felt a grim satisfaction that he'd finally gotten a rise out of her.

"I denounced her when she barely remembered what year it was. I knew she'd be dead the moment I entered the Party building. I all but killed her. Do you want to know what crime I condemned her with?"

Mother did not nod or shake her head. She just continued looking at him, her breath shallow and gasping.

"I told the Party she was a comfort woman." Weihong continued, "I told them she was a comfort woman, so they wouldn't find out about you. I was so sure she would have told someone at some point, so I did it to protect you. Even though she never hurt me, even though she never treated me any differently than Kangmei. I loved her. And still, I denounced her. Is that not wrong? Is that not evil?"

"Bǎobèi, I . . ." Mother trailed off, seeming at a loss for what to say next.

"I did it for you, but all you've ever done is lie to me. Is that not wrong?"

"I wanted to keep you safe. From yourself, from the Oni," she said. She broke another nail off right down to the bloody quick. "You are not your father. You are not Fei. We have both done hard things to survive, that's human."

"No," Weihong said, "no, the things I did weren't human."

"That's not true," she said. "I did regrettable things in the station and in the years after, and I never wanted you to know about them . . ." She stopped, seemed to come to a decision, then said, "But when my brother rescued me, I left the other women. I didn't even try to save them. I left my brother's guerrilla group behind for the Japanese soldiers to finish off. My brother died for me. I watched Fei beat you and I couldn't stop him." Weihong felt light-headed. This was all *too much* and he felt the strange dissonance of being in a bad dream that was just a shade different from his life, unsure if any of it was real but wanting to wake up.

"I learned to live with it. It wasn't easy, but these things—they're human. You'll learn too. I can help you through it if you let me."

Her face shone with desperation. But Weihong was cataloging his wrongdoings, tallying them up against his mother's list of confessions. He told her under his breath, "It's not the same," shaking his head like a rabid dog and tuning her voice out even as she tried to reassure him. He relived the muscle memory of murder—the misdeeds that would always live inside him, stemming from that evil half of him that hungered for atrocity. Nothing she could say or do would make this right, because something in him was wrong, and she couldn't understand that because she was human and he wasn't. Self-loathing rose and sat thickly in his throat.

"Bǎobèi—" she began again.

He cut her off. "I don't want to hear anything you have to say. Leave now. I won't ask again."

"Bǎobèi, please. I don't care what you are, I love you, I will always love you. Don't do this. Let Ma be there for you. If not now, then later, when you're ready, Ma will always be here for you."

He ignored her and stalked to the entryway where he flung the door open. Red was standing in the threshold, her keys held in midair.

"Oh," Red said, surprised, "are you leaving?"

"Yes," Weihong said, "yes, she is."

"So soon? I was going to ask your thoughts on names—"

"She has to go now."

Red looked between him and his mother, understanding dawning on her face. Mother stood slowly from the table and walked to the entryway. She summoned up a small smile for Red. She took Red's hand and gave it a small squeeze.

"The boy," his mother said, "will you name him Qian? That was my late brother's name."

"That's enough," Weihong said as Red gave her a small nod of acknowledgment. Mother left, and Weihong closed the door with a trembling force, his own body shuddering as he sank to the floor against it.

Then he looked back at his wife, who had placed a hand on his shoulder. He was eye level with her swollen belly, and he felt his stomach bottom out.

The babies. In the upheaval, he had forgotten this crucial fact. He had fathered children. He had made his mother's mistake.

Part of him knew that he should leave right then and there to protect Red, but he couldn't. Even with his lineage, even with his prophecy. Red was the only good thing about him, and the babies were hers—not just his, not just his father's blood—so they would be good, too, and he could not forsake the only goodness in him. Not now, not when he had just learned this truth. Was this evil? This selfishness? He didn't know. He only knew this: Kangmei had altered her prophecy. Perhaps he could alter his too. Perhaps he could delay the beast's prophesied destruction, make it sixty years, eighty years, when he'd be too old to be of any harm to Red or his children. Yes, he would stay. Yes, he had to stay. He couldn't not stay.

I found it. The whole prophecy. The origins of the beast. Your beast.

"I can't understand you when you mumble like that," Qianze said. They were eating takeout.

He looked at her, his eyes wide.

"What?" she asked, wary.

"I remember now," he croaked. He cleared his throat, then louder: "I remember now. The prophecy."

There were tears trickling down his wide, grimace-stretched cheeks, his face contorted in pain, which made Qianze jolt, looking at him alarmed.

"Oh, hái'ér," he said, "you won't like what I have to say."

"I never do."

His expression turned serious. "I came back to warn you."

"Of what? If you came back to warn me about yourself, you came a little late."

His mouth pursed into a thin line. "Yes. It is about me. But it is also about you." Then, sincerely, he said, "Hái'ér, I'm sorry. I am so sorry."

"For what?" Qianze put her chopsticks down, concern crossing her features. "Be more specific."

"For what I'm about to tell you. For how I failed you."

Thirty-Four

Ming

1952: Sixty-Five Years Before Reunion
Jílín Province, People's Republic of China

IN HER OPIUM-ADDLED DREAMS AT the comfort station, Ming had clung to the remembered solace of the packed earth and brick kang she shared with her husband and craved the taste of Mother-in-law's stew. She remembered slow mornings with Mother-in-law. Before her shameful return. Before the first miscarriage.

In her first years of marriage, Ming spent her days constantly by Mother-in-law's side. The men dealt with the apothecary and clinic, diagnosing and treating their patients, while Ming and Mother-in-law were responsible for the household. They strolled together through the market, shopping for medicinal herbs and ingredients. Ming saw how the merchants respected Mother-in-law. Their backs straightened at the sight of her, and they asked after Father-in-law and Fei while she scanned their offerings of meat, bones, fish, and chives.

Mother-in-law told Ming that she was glad to have her company, that she hadn't realized how lonely her life had been before. Together, the two women spent each day cooking three hot meals. Mother-in-law taught Ming how to make the herbal medicines that Father-in-law used the most. How to grind and cut certain herbs until they turned to paste, how to sew together herbal tea bags from sheer fabric, how to clean the acupuncture needles, the heated cups. Ming returned to childhood habits, foraging for mushrooms and moss, seining the river for fish, setting up traps for stray birds. Mother-in-law never faltered in her gratitude toward Ming's contributions. In between cooking and making remedies, they washed the laundry by the riverside along the flat shoreline rocks—weathered by generations of washerwomen—and hung it to dry in the compound's courtyard. The laundry lines ran diagonal, zigzagging through the space, holding billowing linens and warm-weather clothes.

Ming used to stand in the courtyard while they hung the laundry together, the breeze rippling through the landscape of fabric. Soft white sheets that cocooned her in their cleanliness. Beyond a fluttering blanket was Mother-in-law, the silhouette of her visible, and she would think, *So this is what it's like to have a mother who loves you.*

IT HAD BEEN SEVEN YEARS since Ming had returned to the village, since the Japanese surrendered. It was the seventh lunar month of the seventh year: the month of ghosts—the heat so swollen that Ming, too, felt like she was swimming through the air of the underworld. Ming remembered a time when she thought the departure of the Japanese would allow her some small peace. A return to her home and her husband. A quiet life in the countryside. A son one day. She'd been naïve to believe her life would pick up where it had left off—before the morning when the Japanese invaded the village. That in the tapestry of her life, she could cut out the dark, stained years and take up again. That in the wake of occupation, her war-ripped country would stitch itself together—not stumble into civil war and famine. For all the time she spent in the comfort station, those illusions had sustained her when food had not.

In the season of revenants, she paid respect to her dead. It seemed she knew more ghosts than living people. The villagers reacted to her as if she was also a specter, an unsightly demon hauled from hell back into the world of the living. Children were advised to stay away from her; villagers who'd known her from girlhood averted their eyes when she passed, recoiled if she came too close.

That woman is a curse, she heard an Auntie whisper to her young daughter. The girl ducked behind her mother's skirt.

Ming was not the only woman from the village to be taken by the Japanese Army, but she was the only one who'd come back. She'd been childish to think that the rest of the village would be the same after the carnage. Yes, she was home, but home was not the home she'd loved and dreamed of.

There had been safety in her past life. In spaces, objects, people. Those sacred pockets of sanctuary—Mother-in-law's kitchen, Qian's letters, Fei—no longer existed. Or if they did, they did not exist in the same way. Her return was not a homecoming but a homelosing. Ming had survived, but the imagined life from her opium reveries had not. Where was the comfort she'd been promised? Where was her reward for living and crawling out of war? For giving up her baby brother? *Tell me this procession of men ends in happiness*, she used to pray, her mind numb and her body pliant. The parade of Japanese soldiers that disfigured the country was replaced by an army of Communist and Kuomintang soldiers, who led their country back into war and famine.

The day-to-day of the village remained the same, but the village itself was changed. Ming was not the only victim of the Japanese attack. The soldiers had orphaned children and made new brides into widows and new grooms into widowers.

During the attack, Mother-in-law and Father-in-law fled to the caves to hide. In their absence, the compound was ransacked. All the medicine and medical supplies were taken. Heirlooms, food, money—all of it gone. Fei went looking for Ming in the forest, but he'd been found by two soldiers, who bashed in his skull, boxed his ears, and left him for dead. Mother-in-law and Father-in-law hadn't been able to look for him in the aftermath. When the soldiers left, their clinic was full of patients with sawn-off limbs and cleaved bellies. They tried to treat what injuries they could without their supplies. The whole town had been raided. Nothing remained: only the people and scattered objects the Japanese deemed worthless. When the townspeople found Fei deep in the forest days later, he was barely conscious and his left ear was as swollen as a peony—his hearing gone until the ear was drained of pus and blood. After, the ear was never quite the same.

They rebuilt slowly. Supplies were hard to come by. Their harvest stores from the summer had been taken. The following winter brought more losses. Fei and Father-in-law slept little for the next few years, kept up by their stream of patients. By the time the village neared normalcy and Fei began to think of remarrying, Ming reappeared, dragging fresh misery into their lives.

MING SPENT THAT FIRST YEAR trying to live without opium. Quickly, she learned that she couldn't. She was sustained by a constant regimen of herbs and sedatives that suspended her in an aching, troubled sleep. Ming stayed in a small room once used as a pantry. It was big enough only for a straw mat, a stool, and a chamber pot. The door was shrouded in dark, thick cloth, because the light hurt her eyes. Months passed by without her knowledge.

She woke. She shook like a branch in a blizzard, cold underneath the sheen of sweat and the layers of woolen padded quilts piled on top of her. She crawled on all fours to the chamber pot in the corner, unable to stand. She slept. She woke again to her neck being propped up, liquid sloshing on her cracked lips and down her dry throat. Swallowing was hard. Sometimes the liquid came back up, splashing across her front and the blankets. She hurt. All her untreated wounds from the station screamed for poppy, not the jujube and roots that were a dull, colorless balm to the birdsong of opium.

Mother-in-law, Father-in-law, and Fei filtered in and out of her vision. Ming could not make out their features through her heavy eyes. They looked like faceless creatures: their eyes, noses, and mouths smoothed down, like the noppera-bō, the Oni's trickster siblings. They held vigil on the stool, carrying a single lit candle. They disappeared. Voices floated, cresting near her ears, unable to pierce the veil of quilts and palpitations, which throbbed heavy inside her head. She wanted opium, loved it more than Father-in-law or Mother-in-law or Fei. She said as much, screaming and crying and thrashing. In her darkest hours, she yelled for the Oni.

Once, Ming heard Mother-in-law's voice. She tried to make out the words. Mother-in-law had been speaking for a while, the hum of it buzzing on the other side of consciousness. Weakly, Ming tried to blink open her eyes. She could just make out Mother-in-law's face—sorrow lining the grooves of her mouth—through the sliver of her lids. Mother-in-law was sitting on the footstool, her eyes sharp.

". . . I don't recognize you anymore," she said. "What did you do with my Ming?"

Here I am, here I am, here I am, Ming wanted to shout, but her mouth was as dry as the wool blanket, and she couldn't open it.

Mother-in-law leaned close, her breath hot and searing on Ming's ear. "I don't know why you've chosen to prey on my family. To come here as an impostor, a parasite, wearing the face of my daughter. We just finished grieving her."

Does she know? Can she see the oni within me?

"My family used to worship foxes, so I know a fox demon when I see one. My parents taught me how to tell the difference between foxes and fox demons. How you appear suddenly, like a bad dream. How you bring evil in your wake. How you possess bodies. And now you've made my son hope, made him believe his wife has come back. But you're not her. She wouldn't—she wouldn't let herself get this way, become this whore and addict."

No, Ming wanted to croak, *it is me. This is my face. My body.* But when she blinked, Mother-in-law was gone, and she was alone in the room, unsure if the conversation had been real or a hallucination.

Sometimes she saw Fei, who sat by her side with his elbows resting on his knees, his head in his hands. He would lift his face when she shifted in her half sleep and whisper, "What happened to you?"

She could not tell him, though she was sure he had an idea. They all did. Her body could not hide her secrets. There was severe uterine damage—she could feel it deep in her belly—and recurring infections. She could never tell him how many men, how many times, how many ways. He wouldn't understand. When she could speak, she told him it was one man, that she was the pet of a commander. One man was shameful, but much less so than the truth.

Slowly, she got better. Fei began feeding her solid food, which she kept down. She had a proper bath. She began using the outhouse. She started a routine of cupping, acupuncture, and moxibustion. She could walk again. Short distances at first, like a baby taking its first steps, then the circumference of the compound. The craving for opium never went away. It undergirded her every thought. Only the access went away. Authorities were cracking down on poppy fields, on opium dens, on rural trade. Ming was too weak to make her way to a city to find some in a black market, though that did not stop her from thinking about it.

Before she knew it, a year had passed. She moved back into her room with Fei. The first time they were intimate again was in the second year, and it was hard and painful. It got a little better after that, but mostly it was clinical, brief. There were times when Fei tried to touch her affectionately—a stroke of her cheek, a caress down her spine—when she would smile at him, push herself up on her elbows to press her lips to his in a quick peck. There were also times when an accidental brush against her skin would send her scampering backward like a wild rabbit. Fei would look at her then with shock, with wariness: a recognition of the uncrossable difference that had grown between them, thick and knotted with the names of the dead, with the names of the men.

There was so much separate grief. Grief Ming could not share with Fei, even though it clung to her, and it would always cling to her. Some days she could almost forget it, but it would never be gone. She could live with it. Live around it. She had no choice; living was a gift that others had lost for her. He could not understand it. He tried at first. They tried. Gods knew they tried. There were pregnancies: three total, of varying lengths, in the seven years since her return. Three miscarriages. Three times she was halved, quartered, further dismembered by loss. When Ming had her first miscarriage all those years before, Mother-in-law had taken care of her. In these recent years of one stillbirth, two miscarriages, and three burials, Ming watched as Mother-in-law grew distant from her: her, the bad investment that promised no riches. Her, the village disgrace.

After the stillbirth in the fourth year, Ming often snuck away to rummage through the medicinal stores in the backrooms of the apothecary, looking for sedatives. She was there when she heard Mother-in-law at the counter in the front entertaining a customer.

Ming's ears perked up when she heard her name.

". . . Surprised you're still looking after Ming. All that history following her, all that medicine you've wasted on her, and still no grandchildren, no heirs. Has Fei on a hook with the promise of pregnancy, then miscarries." She paused, and her voice dipped into a conspiratorial tone, "You know, my daughter's going to be of age soon. Very healthy, regular menstruation since she was twelve, wide hips. No one would blame Fei if he divorced Ming. Fei should be with someone who can give him an heir. I can speak to the matchmaker tomo—"

The customer's face went pale. Ming had come into the front

room, standing in the doorway of the supply closet behind the counter. Mother-in-law whipped her head around to look at her. Ming folded her arms.

"I have to go," the customer murmured, and scuttled away.

Mother-in-law returned to straightening the jars of herbs on the shelves. Ming watched her for a stretch of time.

"Do you agree with her?" Ming asked.

"Which part?"

"All of it."

Mother-in-law didn't speak.

Ming took a deep breath, summoning her courage. "There's something I wanted to ask you. About something you said that first year, I think. I might've dreamt it." She paused, turning the fugue memory in her hands. "I've been trying to figure out what changed between us, why you can't love me like a daughter anymore. And all I can think of is this time when you told me I was a fox demon, a spirit come to destroy your family. Did that—happen?" she fumbled. "Do you still think that?"

Ming recalled the white landscape of wash day. Standing in the middle of clean linens, holding one corner to be pinned. How a breeze would lift the sheet and reveal Mother-in-law on the other side, smiling at her, humming as she clipped the blanket to the line.

"I didn't think you heard me. You were so . . ." She trailed off, cleared her throat. "I don't think you're a fox demon. I see parts of Ming buried within you. But you're not the Ming I knew, and I can't reconcile you and her. I think you might be something in between."

Ming's throat closed in desperation. "No, it's me. Just me. The things I went through, I did them to survive, but it's still me, I'm still the girl you helped raise." *See me!* She wanted to cry out. *Tear away the ruined body to find me! I am still five years old inside, idolizing you.*

Mother-in-law shook her head. "I have sympathy for the horrors you went through, I do. But they changed you. Replaced you. I can't recognize you anymore. I can't accept what you did. Neither can the town."

"I did those things to be here. To come back to you! To this family!"

Ming wanted to scream until she lost her voice, her throat bloody from the wrathful screech that would crawl its way out.

Mother-in-law flinched. "Ming," she said, "please understand the position you've put me in. I still care for you. Fei and my husband do too. We won't forsake you or exile you. That's the most we can do. That's more than most people would do."

Ming knew there was truth in those words. Anyone else would have exiled her to the caves. They still could.

SHE WOKE EARLY ON ZHŌNGYUÁN JIÉ, the fifteenth day of the seventh month of the seventh year. She and Fei had taken to sleeping on opposite edges of the kang—a canyon of space between them. She slept on the outside so she wouldn't disturb him during her insomniac nights. Often, by the time Fei woke, Ming had already been up for hours, pruning the apothecary herb garden, tending to and feeding Dà Gèzi. On this morning, she quietly sat at the edge of the kang and got dressed, carrying a basket filled with items she'd collected just for this occasion. She went outside and sat next to Dà Gèzi, who lived the peaceful life she'd promised him, only occasionally running errands. She watched as he ate his breakfast. The compound was quiet.

Ming and Fei were cold with each other. There was a learned distance between them. The villagers' distaste for her had begun to rub off onto Fei, who'd grown susceptible to their opinions. They told him that Ming's reputation was an injustice to him. Him, the firstborn son of the only physician. Him, the heir to the apothecary and clinic. He deserved a wife and son worthy of his standing. In the market, Ming heard whispered rumors of divorce, of possible courtship, of affairs—conversations that stuttered into silence when she passed.

She needed a son this year to keep her from exile. She would ask the ghosts for a son. She would ask Guānyīn for a son. She would ask the gods and the demons, the fairies and the monsters, the Mongol and Manchu gods. Anyone who would listen to a woman like her. A woman without a son was as unsettling as a face with no features. The only thing Ming carried in her belly was grief like a sibling slung on her waist. It weighed on her, dragging her shoulders concave.

Ming didn't dare pay her respects at Qian's grave. The last time she'd gone, Mama had chased her off, hurling her shoes, her mean words, her lit incense sticks. In the third year, when she could walk to his grave, Ming had planted a bed of poisonous red spider lilies over the mound of dirt to ward off fox spirits and demons from his bones. Mama had allowed this. Mama, in fact, tended to the corpse flowers yearly, and from a distance, Ming would watch when the bǐàn huā bloomed in late summer—their red, arachnoid petals unfurling in the solstice sun.

Ming set up her altar in a shady spot by the river. She kneeled. She splashed her face with water. Lately, when she looked into the sheen of a mirror or the surface of the river she saw her mother's face, marred with rage.

She began her rituals as she did every year. For Qian, she laid out a plate of sticky buns with pork bone and radish filling, guō bāo ròu, and chive dumplings. One of each—she could not afford to use any more rations. For Mouse, a vase of dried yellow witch hazel and peonies from early summer and packets of paper seeds, which she had labeled. For her four miscarriages: bowls of red bean, gushing sesame tāng yuán, and cups of milk, sweetened with brown sugar and honey. She burnt incense and joss paper for them. For the other dead she knew too: Qian's guerrilla band of brothers, the women of the station lost to the war, the villagers who died in the attack almost a decade ago. Then, she prayed.

On this day, the doors between the living and the divine were thrown open to each other; the veils between the mortal realm, Tiān, Dìyù, and everything in between as thin as gossamer. So Ming prayed indiscriminately. She prayed for a son. She prayed for her brother, who had promised through his gory, dry lips, *maybe in my next life*. She thought about her own reincarnation. *In my next life,* she prayed, *let me be something else. An insect. An animal.* Her time would be brief and honeyed, and there would be no war or rape or mothers' hate. Sometimes she wanted to scream it all out, the whole bloody, bony mess of it. To purge it until she was clean—hollowed and hallowed—and nothing would exist in her but the blank-white beating of a silk moth's wings.

When she was done praying, it was dusk, and Ming set out the paper boats she had folded, the keels strengthened by bamboo, the decks adorned with incense and candles, and set them on the river to guide her ghosts back to the afterlife. She watched as they floated off, little pinpricks of light winking at her as they bobbed on the blue summer current. She watched them until they blinked out of her vision, falling off the darkening horizon onto another plane. She took the shortcut through the forest to get home before true nightfall descended, the time when the malevolent spirits emerged.

HE WAS STANDING AMONG THE blackened trees like a mirage. She wanted to believe he was a hallucination. He was not. The wind that rustled through her hair fluttered through his. The forest was silent, his presence having chased the other animals away.

What she felt when she saw the commander again was that unruly, monstrous hunger. An appetite for his suffering. She wanted to bite off his hands, his lips, his flesh so that he would never hurt another soul. She wanted to hack into his divinity—make him mortal, make him killable. But even as all that rage coursed through her body, she was lock-limbed. The instinct for fight or flight was singing through her, but she could only stand there, deer-eyed, quivering. She was reduced to the addict, that girl motivated only by poppy and survival. Shamefully, her lungs gasped for the opiate smoke she'd always associated him with.

She had tried to find him in Shūshu's library. She had scoured all his texts in the hopes of uncovering a reference to the oni from Kyoto's Mt. Oe. She'd found none. The closest description was the ogre disciple Shā Wùjìng, the traveling companion of Sūn Wù Kōng, but *Journey to the West* did not tell her how to kill such a demon. Ming kept mugwort on her at all times, which she'd read was used to ward off evil spirits. She fumbled for it now in her pockets only to find that she'd burned it all in her rituals. She wanted to howl. She wanted to run. She couldn't do either.

"You called to me," he said. "I heard your prayer."

"I didn't pray to you," she spat after recovering from her shock. "I never wanted to see you again. You ruined me. I hate you."

He bellowed out a laugh. "You were ruined long before I came to the station." She bristled at the truth of it.

"I didn't call for you." Her voice broke.

"Why, Ming, it's the Hungry Ghost Festival. Am I not a ghost? Am I not hungry?" Then his face stretched into that lupine smile that sloshed in the liquid of her nightmares. "You prayed to everyone, little girl. You should've been more specific. If I hadn't come along, something worse might have answered."

"There's nothing worse than you."

He smirked, his yellow canines peeking out from his mouth. "If only that were true. You forget that I'm just a minor god, and others wouldn't be so benevolent."

"*Benevolent*," she echoed. She wanted to scratch the sneer off his face, stain it as red as a butcher's knife.

"Did you think you were free of me? I was sleeping until your voice woke me. Seven years is nothing to me. A night's rest."

She felt so stupid. She had believed her mugwort kept him from finding her, even though he must've known she would return to the village. She ran, her body a slew of panic haring through the trees. She did not make it far.

She had forgotten how strong he was. When he claimed her, it all felt distantly familiar. Like the past few years hadn't happened, and she would find herself in that splinter of a room in the station being woken to do laundry with Mouse. Her life reduced to a hellish loop of the station, the escape, the homelosing. Afterward, she knew that she would never see him again. That he'd finished what he'd once set out to do. He had made her in his image. He had taken her burrowing rage and hurt and added to it, transforming her into something cruel and abnormal.

The next month, she missed her cycle. It was a miracle. It was a monster.

Thirty-Five

Qianze
2017: Twenty-Five Days Since Reunion
Manhattan, New York

QIANZE REELED FROM BA'S REVELATION. When he was telling her about their ancestry, she'd sat on the couch, looking anywhere but at him: picking at her nails, chewing on her lip, looking at the wall past his shoulder. She remembered Ba prodding her out of her daze with "Hái'ér? Are you listening? Do you understand?"

She nodded. Yes, she was listening. Yes, she understood, or as much as she could understand. When he finished speaking, Qianze had calmly gotten up, left the apartment, gone down the four flights of stairs, stepped out onto the street, and vomited into the sewer grate. Head spinning, sick crusted on the edges of her mouth, she then stumbled down Grand Street with no destination in mind, only an urge to keep moving away from the apartment.

Eventually, she came across an empty dive bar. She realized she'd left her keys, wallet, and phone in the apartment, but the bouncer was indifferent to her, barely looking up as she slunk inside the entrance and barricaded herself into the filthy bathroom.

Inside, she closed the toilet lid and sat down, rested her head in her hands to placate her nausea. The floor was wet, varnished in urine. Her vision swam. She tried to even out her breath as she felt the beginnings of a panic attack blooming within her. The quiet of the bathroom contrasted with the loud bass of the music beyond the door. The space had the same texture as other in-between spaces from her past: the Myrtle house computer desk at dawn, the fish tanks in the back of the Asian grocery store. Places that felt insulated from reality, if only briefly. Most important, it was insulated from her apartment, *her* reality.

Qianze ran her sweaty palms through her hair until the strands of it became damp and stringy. Her breath rattled in short spurts. She could not believe Ba. Believing him—this sick alcoholic specter of a father, who could barely separate fact from fiction himself—would be an exercise in insanity. What he'd said was preposterous, her whole self recoiling from it in denial. That his biological father was a Japanese colonial lieutenant. An oni. A demon. This moment bounced in her head like a pinball, echoing and gaining traction with a glowing velocity. Because there were signs.

There were unexplainable moments that only made sense in this new context. Signs that had appeared throughout her life with a neon alacrity, begging for her notice, for her belief. There were the fox and the jackalope, the pair of them always chasing each other, circling her, throughout her adolescence. The Aunties of this August whom only she had seen. The dead birds, the rabbits. Had she not spent the years since she was fourteen afraid of some madness inside of her? She had thought that these visions were the result of her unstable childhood, but she was wrong. Ba had left because of his own encounters with the supernatural, an inheritance he'd passed down to her.

Ba had crawled out of oblivion, out of his failing memory, to tell her this. And she had been naïve, lured in by the bright light of reconciliation, only to discover the jagged teeth of an anglerfish behind it. How did she begin to come to terms with this? And not just this, but the other monstrosities Ba had revealed: the all-too-human ones.

The Ba she knew now was the result of war and rape, abuse and persecution, colonialism and authoritarianism. Thinking about what he had done filled her with a surge of unruly emotions. She could not single them all out; they blended and slid into one another. Horror. Pity. Superiority. But, backed into a corner like a trapped animal, would she have made the same decisions he had? Would her answer make Ba's actions less deplorable? She didn't know. Did that make her good or bad?

Qianze had long held an unshakable suspicion that her life and fate were not hers. That she did not have a selfhood but rather a façade of one, propped up by Ba's desertion: a manifestation of the rage and sorrow from her childhood. Ba's revelation felt like a confirmation: that she was not herself but some inherited anger, some reincarnation, which was why her life never felt like it fit right. And underneath all of these thoughts was a riptide of grief. Grief for the Ba of her childhood. Grief for the Ba of this August. Both men slipping out of her grasp, wrenched from her by disease.

Someone pounded demandingly against the bathroom door, and Qianze, startled, left on wobbly legs, avoiding their gaze. She spilled out onto the street and then began to walk, trying to outpace her thoughts. The bars gave way to the eerie, empty streets of the Financial District: large white edifices bathed in weary orange streetlights. A bus stop by the road told her the time, 4:07 a.m., and the temperature, 72 degrees.

Out of habit, she'd looped back to the apartment. She once again found herself standing in front of her building but could not go in. Instead, she was filled with an urge to flee the city and went to the subway station, descending into its depths. She hopped the turnstile and sat on the bench, waiting for the next D train to pull into the station. One arrived, and she tucked herself into the corner of a car, resting her head against the cloudy window, which rumbled with the tracks.

Ba had left. And now that he had come back, he'd told her things about his past, about their lineage. These things she could not forget. These things she carried inside her; they were bred in her blood. Ba had hurt Ma. He had hurt her. He had hurt his mother, grandmother, and sister, all because of his fear of this beast. Would Qianze do the same? Her monstrosity, would it consume her? It would be so easy to sink into her bitterness. And yet, she did not want to remain in that dark place.

She wanted a different life for herself. One that fit. She wanted to move in with Theo, to spend her future with him. She wanted to be someone worthy of his love and honesty. To learn how to cook more Chinese dishes than just fried rice and steamed egg. She wanted to go to yoga with Ma. To have a job that didn't make her miserable. She wanted to try oil painting at least once. Did she have to abandon all those possibilities like Ba had?

This half-life she was living was because of her father leaving, her father's hurt. But her father's hurt had come from his father's hurt, and now she could see what might become of her life, how it might become a reflection of his. He had left to protect her, but he had made her into an angry person, unable to move on from his abandonment. Was this what would happen to Theo? To Ma? Would it not be better to stay? To try?

THE TRAIN HAD PULLED INTO the last stop on the line. Coney Island. Qianze got off and went to switch tracks, but, at the last minute, she left the turnstile, went down the steps of the station, and stood outside. The sun was rising. In the distance, she could make out the shapes of the roller coasters and boardwalk. The seagulls were crying, and the air was cool, cooler than it had been all month. Farther away, she heard the sound of the waves swelling and crashing, lapping blue against the shore. She felt some of the panic ebb, her breathing even out, following the rhythm of the water.

Maybe—maybe she could sit with it. The knowledge of her past, of Ba's past. Maybe she could learn how to live with it. She could learn a new language of existence, one where the words were softer and braver, less angry. Make peace with it eventually. Because this was what she knew: her father had let this secret control his life. Maybe this was the real warning. That there could have been years—eleven of them and one month, to be exact—where she had both parents, and there could have been graduations and move-ins and university parents' weekends and birthdays and hand-pulled noodles. But there weren't.

Thirty-Six

Ba

2017: Twenty-Five Days Since Reunion
Manhattan, New York

SHE HAD LEFT, AND HE had let her leave. He had let her leave, and she had still not come back, and now the sun was showing signs of rising, the pitch-black night lightening to blue. In his mind, he was replaying the conversation.

He'd seen this exchange before from the other side. Now, in his mother's role, he wondered if his expression had fallen the same way Qianze's had upon hearing the truth—her features collapsing—moving rapidly through a sequence of emotions: apprehension, hesitation, realization, loathing, fear. She'd left so suddenly, she hadn't even taken her phone, her wallet, or her keys.

He'd thought that that conversation with Mother was the most painful moment of his life, but he was wrong. It was this. The waiting. The wondering.

Qianze had to come back eventually. He wanted to stay just long enough to see her come through the doorway, whole and unharmed. He couldn't sleep, eat, smoke, drink. He could only sit on the couch with his strangled breath, his heart lodged in his throat, and wait for her.

QIANZE WAS BORN IN THE summer of his thirty-ninth year on the seventh day of the seventh month.

The doctors called it a geriatric pregnancy. They warned the couple that with Red's past miscarriages and her age, there was a high risk of something going wrong. They hadn't thought they would conceive at their age, and he was expecting something to go wrong. The baby would eat its twin—if it had one—then miscarry, a repeat of what had happened three years ago. The baby wouldn't come to term. The baby would come, but it would slip out looking like the tumorous growth he'd seen in the bog: red-skinned, horned, with its three-fingered hands gripping the umbilical cord. It would open its yellow feline eyes and yawn with a saw-toothed smile, and the whole room of nurses would scream and pile up in their scramble to run away, and Red in her stirrups would look at the puddle of blood between her legs and the beast sitting in it, and know what it was: a proclamation of his monstrosity.

The baby was born in the early morning at half past six. She was crying. The nurse handed the child to Red, and the crying subsided into a gurgling curiosity. Her head was smeared with blood, but she was human. Her face was flushed, and her eyes were a wet fawn-black, large and round in her small, impossible face, which was somehow smaller than his hand. Red offered her to him, and he gently took the baby, who turned her face toward his. She was perfect. She couldn't be his. But she was. He knew because he felt like someone had slit open his chest and scooped out his heart, planted it, let it grow legs and arms, and he was afraid of how much he loved her, of how much she was his, of how much he wanted to protect her from everything—especially himself. In that first moment with his daughter, he was afraid of how much he understood his mother.

Later, once the umbilical cord was cut, once the baby was cleaned and dried and placed in the bassinet in the hospital room, once Red was asleep, Weihong tried to find his mother. He went back to their house on Myrtle Avenue. Red had asked for some clothes and toiletries from home that she'd forgotten to pack in her hospital bag. By the landline in the living room was a stack of calling cards that Red used to phone her friends and family back in China. Weihong went through all of these trying to track down Mother. It was early evening, the morning in China.

First, he called his friends who still lived in Běijīng near Qīnghuá. Did any of them have the number for the mechanical engineering department? Could they get in touch with the receptionist, an old woman named Guifang? *The receptionist retired*, his friends reported back, *but we were given the number of her son, who is taking care of her.* Weihong called the son, who put Guifang on the line. She was hard of hearing and didn't understand his request. She gave the phone back to the son, who gave him a number he found in her old phonebook for a Shang Ming, his mother's given name. Weihong copied it down in shaky penmanship then sank into the couch. What would he tell her? It would come to him, he thought. He would hear her voice, and the words would come. He punched in the number.

It rang and rang. At last, the phone picked up.

"Hello?"

It was Kangmei's voice. She sounded tired, like she'd just woken up.

"Kangmei," he said. There was a pause.

"Weihong?" she asked, sounding incredulous.

"Yes, hello," he said, unsure what to say.

"Hello," she repeated. "Is there a reason you're calling?"

"My daughter was just born."

"Congratulations," she said flatly.

"Thank you. It made me want to— Is Ma there? Could I speak with her?"

A long beat. After a minute, then two, Weihong asked, "Hello? Are you there? Did I lose you?"

"Ma's dead."

His stomach bottomed out. He could hear Kangmei still speaking, but the words receded into a ringing white noise. "She died from the injuries she got during the war. You know how she was always sick, how her health was always bad. It's been two years since then. I took care of her here . . ."

He had thought he would know. He had thought that he would feel it when she died. That his blood—her blood—would hum with this knowing. He had thought there was still time. So much fresh time he could sink his arms in it up to his elbows. He wanted to tell her he understood. That he'd been a parent for less than a day, and he now knew that the web she'd spun was a cocoon to protect him.

He was unraveling the seams of shame and betrayal and revulsion from their last interaction and he wanted to tell Mother that he was wrong, but he'd missed his chance. Now he would always be stuck in this limbo, this place where the words were forever lodged in his throat.

"I have to go back to the hospital," Weihong interrupted.

"Are you serious?" Kangmei asked.

He hung up. He stared at the phone in his hand. It was off-white, yellowed at the neck from use. Mother was dead. She had died, and he hadn't known. What was he doing when it had happened? Was he studying? Was he biking to university? He had an urge to call Kangmei again and ask her to tell him the exact date and time of Mother's death. He'd trace his memory back to that day, that minute, that second. There must have been a twang in his stomach, a pang in his chest. There must have been something that fell off the counter, off the desk, off his bike basket, and he'd know now that it was Mother—the ghost of her flying past him on her way to another plane. There must have been some goodbye.

It had been three years since their last conversation. Of those three years, she'd been dead two. He loved her. Even with the lies and the hurt. Somewhere, part of him believed that his love would sustain her. That she would always be there on the other end of that phone. He had not foreseen this. He felt so ill-prepared for it. What was the last thing they'd said to each other? When was the last time she held him? He remembered her reaching out to him, him recoiling, her arms falling back to her sides. How he wanted to stumble back in time into her arms and say better words, kinder words. He felt her absence as a cavernous ache that kept expanding and growing—a hungry thing—and he felt like a child again with a skinned knee, wanting his mother, who could make all his hurts better.

The phone rang again. Weihong jumped. He noticed the flash on the landline that said he'd missed a call. It was a local number, the same number that he now redialed.

"Are you still at home?" It was Red. He cleared his throat and confirmed that he was. She asked him to bring one of her Russian books. She thought reading out loud would be good for the baby. *It'll make her smart*, she said. In the background, Weihong heard the baby's cry. *Is she okay? Is she in pain? Can I do something? Bring something?*

He swallowed down his two-years-too-late grief. He couldn't make amends with his mother, but his daughter needed him.

NOW THAT THE FOG OF withdrawal had lifted, he was filled with things he wanted to tell Qianze. He had wanted to tell her that being this, being what they were, did not mean an unlovable existence. His mother had loved him. His sister had loved him. His grandmother, his wife, his daughter. It was he who had spent decades licking his wounds and keeping everyone else at bay.

If Qianze wanted him to leave after this, he would. He had done what he needed to do. He'd told her the truth. But he didn't want to leave. He could never repent for those eleven years he had missed, but he wanted to try, if she'd let him. But. The beast. How could he protect her from himself?

You know how. The Woman. Her voice was closer than it had been for a long time, and it pressed tight along the inside of his skull. He jolted. He walked to the window and peered through the dark glass expecting to find her standing there under the aura of a streetlight but found it empty.

You've reached the end of this life.

Panic clawed at his chest. No, not now, not *here*. Anywhere else. Anywhere that wasn't his daughter's home, the image of her returning to his corpse rotting, staining her floors and dribbling down to the apartment below.

Not a physical death. She sounded tired. She sounded the same age she had always been. *The way backwards. The way forwards. How to move past the prophecy, past the fate that binds your life. Kill this life.*

What did that mean if not a physical death?

You have burrowed yourself in your own tomb, your own exile, convinced it's your destiny.

I did it to protect them. From me. From the beast waking.

Always with the beast. It is a half of you, not all of you. You've let it consume you completely. Reincarnate. Gods do it all the time. Become something else. Something braver. Burn the bog. Let something new grow in its place.

And Weihong was remembering the rich, yielding soil of a Virginia autumn. He had just bought a series of potted shrubs, the early beginnings of azalea bushes. He wanted to plant them before the winter so they could take root and bloom come summer. Qianze was four, and she helped him dig the shallow pits for the bushes. *Like this, see?* She nodded diligently and followed his lead. *What color will they be, Ba?* And he told her, *I think they'll be red, hái'ér. That's what the picture showed.* He put his hands over her impossibly small ones, and they piled dirt over the roots.

Thirty-Seven

Qianze

2017: Twenty-Six Days Since Reunion

Manhattan, New York

IT WAS THE FIRST DAY of September. It had been nearly four weeks since Ba had arrived. There was a cool front looming. Outside, Qianze saw that the runners had dug out their jackets from under a layer of summer dust. She had returned to the apartment. She did not know if her father would be gone when she went up the stairs.

She snuck in behind a neighbor entering. Someone in the building was making a large breakfast, the fragrant scent of it everywhere: in the entry, the stairwell, her hall. She frowned. She couldn't remember the last time she had eaten a proper breakfast. Only bodega black coffees and her poorly made steamed egg custard.

When she opened the unlocked door to her apartment, the brunt of the smell—good and warm and sweet—wafted in her face. She stood on the threshold, unable to make sense of the scene. The kitchen, an aromatic mess. The table overflowing with dishes. Her father, sitting at the table, looking up expectantly at her. He nervously wrung his hands, sprinkled in flour. He stood abruptly, the chair screeching as its legs slid backward.

"What's all this?" Qianze asked.

"I went to the market stalls when they opened this morning. I cooked for us."

"You cooked for me?"

He nodded. The table was set with two places of mismatched bowls and chopsticks, filled with scoops of steaming white rice. Tiny saucers with red vinegar, scallions, and soy sauce. Even two mugs of tea, percolating and sweating on their coasters. There were so many dishes on the table glistening with oil, Qianze's eyes could hardly take them in.

Fluffy yellow egg and tomato. Green beans covered in a shaving of fresh ginger and garlic and grease. A whole fish steamed in oil and Shàoxīng wine, the gray scales glinting from its bed of Sìchuān peppercorns. Guō bāo ròu, red and bubbling in texture, riddled with juicy fat deposits. At the center, a bowl—vat, really—of long, floury hand-pulled noodles, drizzled in red chili oil and minced garlic. All of it basking in cool September light.

Dizzy, Qianze pulled out a chair and sat down. Ba followed suit.

"Here." He served her noodles, dropping them into her rice bowl, where they slipped like eels.

"Ba, wait."

He looked at her and put the bowl down.

"Ba, I have to say something first."

He nodded.

"I wish you had stayed. Even when it was hard. Even if you, we, are whatever we are."

"I know. Leaving—" Ba stumbled, his face turned toward the ground as he searched for the right word. "Leaving was the most monstrous thing I did."

Qianze nodded. It was not enough, but it was a start.

"Let's talk about it all later. Can we just eat for now?"

Ba nodded. They sat in silence, save for the clinking of their chopsticks against their plates and the sounds of the city, drifting in with the sharp air from the windows.

After a while, Ba hesitantly breached the quiet: "I found my younger sister. On WeChat. Your aunt. I had—I *have* so much to say to her. I said some of it last night, while I was waiting for you. We spoke on the phone."

Qianze nodded. She ate a mouthful of fish. Ba spoke again.

"I want to make things right. I want to stay with her in Ānshān. I want to visit my mother's grave"—Ba paused, his mouth curved and vulnerable—"and I'd like you to come with me."

Qianze swallowed. Her mind instantly turned to logistics. Visas and vacation days, flights and doctors.

Ba took her silence as a refusal and hurried to say, "You can say no. You can say that you don't ever want to see me again. I would understand. I'll do whatever you want me to do."

"No," Qianze said, "no, that's not what I was going to say. I was just thinking." She studied the table, the worn grain pattern underneath the overlapping dishes. She would have to look after him, be his caretaker if they went. But she would also be a daughter. A niece. A granddaughter. Rooted. There were many reasons to say no, but there was also something brave inside her that wanted to say yes.

"I think I'd like that," she said.

Ba's face softened. He said, "I want to plant flowers at her grave. We could plant them together."

"Like the Myrtle house azaleas," she said.

"Like the Myrtle house azaleas," he agreed.

Qianze smiled, small and timid.

"Her name was Ming," Ba said at last. "My mother."

"Ming," Qianze repeated. *Bright.*

There were things to come. There were real doctors to be seen, money to budget, and care facilities to visit. There were calls to

Ma she would have to make and plans to discuss with Theo. There were visa applications to fill and flights to book. There were spider-lily seeds and joss sticks to buy. There was ghost money to burn. A ghost apology.

But this was for later. For now, it was September. They were eating hand-pulled noodles.

Acknowledgments

I am grateful to my agent, Iwalani Kim, who has possessed an unyielding faith in this novel ever since she first read it in its very early iteration, and my editor, Tessa James, who has innately understood the woven threads of this novel and plucked them to the surface in such a beautiful harmony. I am very lucky to have had my book land at William Morrow and its wonderful team: to Paul Miele-Herndon for giving the book its beautiful face, and Michele Cameron for the interior, as well as to Deanna Bailey, Kelsey Manning, Eliza Rosenberry, Rachel Weinick, and many more at HarperCollins who have championed the work. To Dana Spector at CAA for seeing the cinematic in the novel. To Dorothy Vincent at Sanford J. Greenburger Associates and the Abner Stein agency for bringing this book across the Atlantic to the UK, and my UK team at DeadInk Books: Harriet Hirshman and Bekkii Paley.

I would not have been able to write this book without the support of my friends and loved ones, who saw me through countless caffeinated nights, drafts, and edits; read through the many versions of the book; and have reminded me to stop and celebrate each milestone. Special thanks to Clara, whom I forced to read each sentence of the novel while drafting and always encouraged me—even when said sentences were clearly written while sleep-deprived—and Stephanie, who sat with me through many FaceTime writing sessions during the drafting doldrums. With all my care and thanks to—in alphabetical order—Armand, Avni, Chemeche, Cindy, Crystal, Francesca, Genevieve, Grace, Helen, Joe, Kellina, Nafisa, Natalie, Rachel, Sabrina, Sydney, Taylor, and Yulan. And to my cat, Kimchi, who sat with me through the long nights of writing and editing while everyone else was sleeping. Thanks as well to the writers of New York who have always been so welcoming and generous in inviting me to events and making me feel like part of an artistic community.

I am lucky to have been taught by teachers and professors who fanned the flames of my love for literature and creative writing, even when such a career path felt unrealistic. To Esther Diskin and David Kidd at Norfolk Academy; to Eula Biss, Brian Bouldrey, John Bresland, Megan Stielstra, and Seth Swanner at Northwestern University; to Dr. Charlotte Lee-Potter, Dr. Rachel Robinson, and David Tolley at the University of Oxford; to Diksha Basu, James Cañón, Anelise Chen, Brigid Hughes, Heidi Julavits, Emily Skillings, Lynn Steger Strong, and Wendy Walters at Columbia University's School of the Arts. Thank you as well to my colleagues at Blue Flower Arts, whose work serves as a testament to the force and power of literature.

Finally, to my parents, Eric Zhao Yang and Iris Hong Wang. Czeslaw Milosz once wrote, "When a writer is born into a family, the family is finished." Not so in our case. Being your daughter has been the greatest honor of my life. Thank you for always supporting my writing in every way you can—whether through interviews or sourcing archival material—and passing down the stories of your lives, without which the book would not have been completed. I will always be a writer second and a daughter first.